Margaret's
Print Shop

A Novel of the Anabaptist Reformation

Elwood E. Yoder

Herald
Press

Scottdale, Pennsylvania
Waterloo, Ontario

Library of Congress Cataloging-in-Publication Data

Yoder, Elwood, 1956-
  Margaret's print shop / Elwood E. Yoder.
     p. cm.
  ISBN 0-8361-9303-2 (pbk. : alk. paper)
  1. Strasbourg (France)—Fiction. 2. Women printers—Fiction.
  3. Anabaptists—Fiction. 4. Printing—Fiction. I. Title.
  PS3625.O335M37 2005
  813'.6—dc22
                                          2005009383

MARGARET'S PRINT SHOP
Copyright © 2005 by Herald Press, Scottdale, Pa. 15683
  Published simultaneously in Canada by Herald Press,
  Waterloo, Ont. N2L 6H7. All rights reserved
Library of Congress Catalog Card Number: 2005009383
International Standard Book Number: 0-8361-9303-2
Printed in the United States of America
Cover design by Sans Serif
Front cover illustration by Allan Baruch
Book design by Sandra Johnson
Maps by Kerry Handel

12 11 10 09 08 07 06 05   10 9 8 7 6 5 4 3 2 1

To order or request information, please call
1-800-759-4447 (individuals); 1-800-245-7894 (trade).
Web site: www.heraldpress.com

To Joy

Contents

Author's Preface

This book is a historical novel about a few Strasbourg printers caught up in the Anabaptist movement in 1525.

Among the many characters in the book, only five are fictitious: the two Knobloch daughters, Agnes and Catherine, and the three printers who work in Margaret's print shop, Peter, Heinrich and Leopold.

All the pamphlets and books mentioned in the story are authentic documents printed in the early sixteenth century.

While Strasbourg today is a French city, in 1525 it was a German city. The interpretation of that year's events is the author's alone, as is the depiction of the historic figures of the era.

The author has used the term *Anabaptist* for clarity, even though the word would have been spoken in a derogatory way in 1525. Likewise, the term *Reformation* is used to help the reader with the context and perspective, but people in 1525 probably would not have used the word.

The author wishes to thank students in his Church history classes at Eastern Mennonite High School in Harrisonburg, Virginia, who read, reviewed, and helped to edit the manuscript. Principals J. David Yoder and Paul Leaman supported this writing project and provided some funding for research through the school's professional-development sabbatical fund.

The author also thanks Michael J. Yoder and Timothy L. Kennel for their very helpful reviews of the manuscript. Most importantly, this book could not have been written without the steady support and encouragement of the author's wife, Joy.

—*Elwood E. Yoder*

Principal Characters

Margaret: second-generation printer, Anabaptist organizer, native of Strasbourg

Heinrich, Peter, and Leopold: workers in Margaret's print shop

Balthasar Beck: Strasbourg immigrant, Anabaptist, printer

Conrad Grebel: Anabaptist leader from Switzerland

Lucas Hackfurt: relief worker, preacher, Anabaptist

Christman Kenlin: a leader of the radical Reformation in Strasbourg

Agnes Knobloch: youngest daughter of Johann and Magdalene

Catherine "Katie" Knobloch: oldest Knobloch daughter; Catholic

Johann Knobloch: owner of a large printing business in Strasbourg; Catholic

Johann Knobloch Jr.: son of Johann

Magdalene Knobloch: wife of Johann; Catholic

Jacob Sturm: City council chairman in Strasbourg; Catholic

Anna Weiler: accused of being a witch; on the run

Matthew Zell: Lutheran preacher in cathedral of Strasbourg

Katherine (Schütz) Zell: gracious host and wife of Matthew; Lutheran

Clement Ziegler: preacher and elderly farmer, encouragers of Anabaptists and others

Gertrude Ziegler: wife of Clement

Jörg Ziegler: cousin of Clement, Anabaptist sympathizer

Other Characters

Hieronymus Balbus: Hungarian humanist, diplomat, and Catholic Bishop

George Blaurock: Anabaptist from Switzerland

Martin Bucer: Lutheran preacher and organizer in Strasbourg

Christopher Froschauer: publisher of the Zurich Reformation

Matthias Grünewald: German painter of altarpieces

Philip Hagen: wealthy citizen of Strasbourg

Hans Hut: self-styled end-times Anabaptist preacher and leader

Nicholas Kniebs: host of emerging Anabaptist house church in Strasbourg

Jacques Lefèvre: Protestant French professor of theology

Sebastian "Lotz" Lotzer: radical German involved in peasants' uprising

Jacob Meyer: member of Strasbourg City Council; Catholic

Hans Müller: Swiss leader of peasants' revolt

Wilhelm Reublin: Anabaptist organizer from Switzerland

Michael Sattler: former monk, emerging leader of Anabaptists

Uli Seiler: one-handed Anabaptist sympathizer from Switzerland

Menno Simons: Catholic priest from Netherlands

Walther Ryff: elderly writer and Anabaptist sympathizer

John Wolff: radical reformer from Benfeld, near Strasbourg

Ulrich Zwingli: leader of the Reformed Church of Zurich, Switzerland

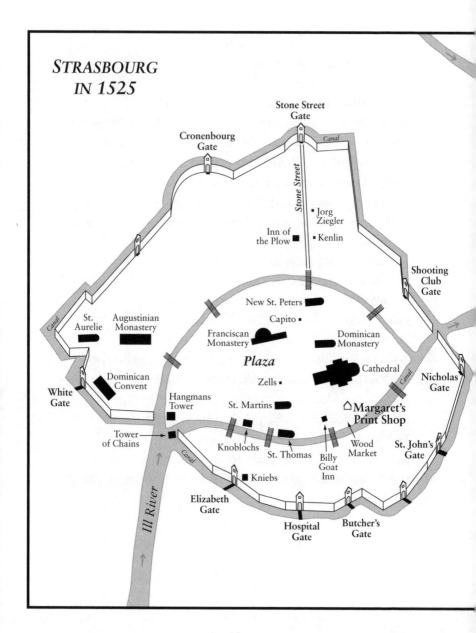

STRASBOURG IN 1525

Stone Street Gate

Cronenbourg Gate

Canal

Stone Street

Jorg Ziegler

Inn of the Plow

Kenlin

Shooting Club Gate

New St. Peters

Capito

Canal

St. Aurelie

Augustinian Monastery

Franciscan Monastery

Dominican Monastery

Plaza

Zells

Cathedral

Nicholas Gate

White Gate

Dominican Convent

Hangmans Tower

St. Martins

Margaret's Print Shop

Canal

Tower of Chains

Knoblochs

St. Thomas

Billy Goat Inn

Wood Market

St. John's Gate

Canal

Kniebs

Ill River

Elizabeth Gate

Hospital Gate

Butcher's Gate

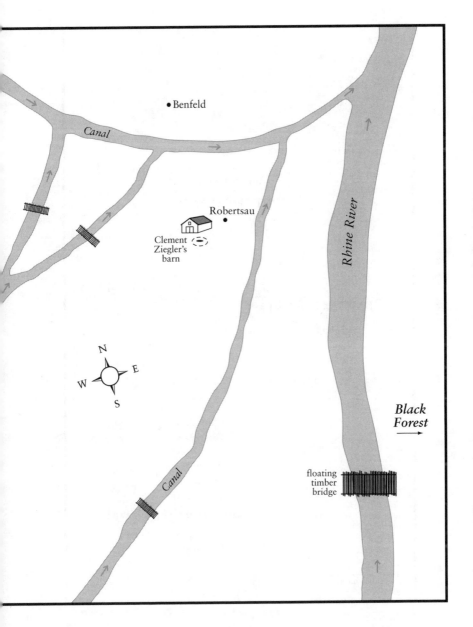

• Benfeld

Canal

Robertsau

Clement
Ziegler's
barn

Rhine River

N
W · E
S

Black
Forest

Canal

floating
timber
bridge

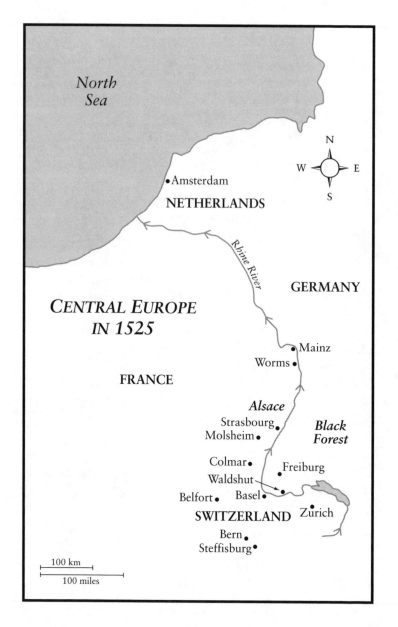

North
Sea

•Amsterdam

NETHERLANDS

Rhine River

GERMANY

***CENTRAL EUROPE
IN 1525***

FRANCE

•Mainz
Worms •

Alsace
Strasbourg•
Molsheim•

***Black
Forest***

Colmar•
Waldshut
Belfort •   Basel•

•Freiburg

SWITZERLAND   Zürich

Bern•
Steffisburg•

100 km

100 miles

Part I

April-May 1525

1

Meeting at the Bridge

The old barn had long held a secret. For several years during the early 1520s, religious and political refugees who had to run for their lives in south Germany could find safety in Clement Ziegler's grain bin behind the haymow. All who fled judges, nobles, city councils, and bishops found shelter in the old farmer's sagging and weathered barn. So far, the bin had remained hidden from the inspectors. It was clean, though dusty, with a hard mat to sleep on, a stool, and a crude little table.

Weapons, illegal books, and religious pamphlets lined the walls of the adjoining bin. In the spring of 1525 the granary was as full of arms as it had ever been. From the determined intent of the peasants, who stored their primitive armaments there, it appeared to many observers in and around the city of Strasbourg that the great biblical tribulation was about to erupt.

Outside the weather-beaten barn on a brisk Monday evening in late April, two men took a leap of faith at Clement's crackling bonfire. A red-bearded Anabaptist preacher from Switzerland reached into a bucket of water, filled a dipper, and poured half of it on one man's head, then poured the rest on the other man.

"Your public declaration of faith declares your intent to live for Christ," Conrad Grebel said. He winced as he helped the two men stand up. "Whatever the cost."

Water dripped onto each man's collar, but they were confident in their new confession of faith. Though the cool air made his joints ache and feet hurt, the preacher shook their hands and embraced them. "You've entered into a new life," he said to the men.

Turning to the small group of onlookers seated on bales of straw and logs at the fire, Grebel said, "In the days we live in, it takes courage to get baptized again. It may bring persecution. Does anyone else wish to be baptized?"

No one accepted the invitation. Margaret and the others soon disappeared into the darkness of the night, back to their farms or to the city. They had witnessed a radical action by Grebel and the two faith seekers, now Anabaptists. Their treasonous baptisms would eventually bring them trouble from the civil and religious authorities.

Some preachers and self-styled prophets believed this new movement of rebaptizers signaled the end of the age. The signs of it seemed clear. Thousands of poor peasants had risen up in a violent revolution against the rich nobles. The age-old Catholic Church was breaking apart, and a new group of religious radicals had moved into the city.

In the shadow of the great Gothic cathedral in Strasbourg, huddled down in her print shop beside the canal, Margaret disagreed that this was the end times. A printer by trade and family tradition, Margaret believed her pamphlets and books would help turn back the powers of darkness that blackened this unusual year.

Optimistic by nature and impulsive in action, Margaret agreed with the peasants' demands. Further, she had joined the evangelical Reformation, and now she had become attracted to the message of the more radical Anabaptists. She liked to go out and listen to old man Clement preach beside his fire, or to find out more from visiting preachers like the fiery Grebel. At twenty-eight years of age and unmarried,

Margaret figured she lived on the edge of accepted patterns of conduct for women anyway.

Recently, when a handsome and eligible bachelor showed up in Strasbourg from south Germany, Margaret wasted no time getting to know him. Unfortunately, Christman Kenlin had noticed her flirting with Balthasar Beck, and her tall suitor grew more jealous by the day. The attention she received from two men at once made her uncomfortable. Margaret sensed she'd soon have to decide between them.

Even more important, her new interest in Anabaptist beliefs could bring down judgment from the city council, the bishop, and the emperor. Settling into her daydream in earnest now, she could almost see dancing flames on the horizon. Perhaps everyone was right; perhaps it *is* the time of the Great Tribulation.

On this bright Tuesday afternoon the old barn stored away one more secret. Jacob Sturm, the round but jovial city council chairman, had sent his nephew out to visit Clement's barn, to check for anything suspicious and to keep the old farmer on his guard. Sturm had no evidence of anything illegal being hidden there, but as he did about every six months, he sent someone to investigate anyway.

At first startled and then angered at the interruption of his activities, Christman watched Sturm's nephew come into the barn through a side door. From a comfortable little perch high in the haymow, Christman's embarrassed companion quickly dressed, gathered her belongings, and headed for the ladder that led to the main floor.

Before the unsuspecting city inspector knew he was there, the muscular six-foot-five Christman slammed him to the floor, threw him against the wall, and knocked him unconscious with a heavy wooden beam. On an angry impulse, Christman hit the man again.

Christman's heart pounded. If he'd get caught, he'd pay with his life. Without hesitating for very long, he quickly grabbed a rope hanging on a nearby wooden peg, tied up the dead man's legs, and dragged him outside toward a grove of trees nearby, out of sight of the elderly Zieglers' farm house.

Cowering in the shadows, Anna Weiler had seen it all happen—from the cruel attack to the cowardly cover-up. An accused witch who was running for her life, Anna had watched Christman drag the body out of the barn through slits in the granary walls. In a horrified daze, she wished this had only been a hellish nightmare.

While Christman quickly dug a shallow grave, Anna sparked back to reality and decided she had to move on, immediately. She had just witnessed a crime, and she didn't want to talk again to the man who had already taken advantage of her in the haymow. "What if he tries to pin this crime on me?" Anna wondered. Men had used her before for their own purposes, and it could easily happen again.

In one long, blurred moment Anna collected her meager belongings, tied her small, cloth bag shut, pulled up her hooded shawl, and headed out through the creaking barn door.

Gertrude, Clement's congenial wife, noticed Anna coming down the lane, and she wrapped a loaf of bread to offer the worried traveler. Stuffing the bread in her bag, Anna thanked Gertrude for letting her hide in the barn and pleaded, "Can you give me money to buy boat fare?"

"My, my, in such a hurry to leave, and in the middle of the day?"

"I must go now."

"If you insist," Gertrude responded, as she reached for several guilders.

"Oh, thank you, Gertrude, and please tell Margaret where I've gone," Anna whispered as she hurried down the lane. "Tell her I'm in the city of Worms."

The men who worked for Margaret had gone home for the day. A sharp knock on the door jolted her back to reality from a late-afternoon nap. She had expected Beck to come by soon, but this didn't sound like his knock.

It was Christman, frazzled and anxious. "There'll be a meeting tonight on the other side of the bridge," he quickly explained in his deep voice. "We want you to come. It's a strategy meeting for the peasants' revolt, and we need you to print a pamphlet that outlines our demands."

Trying to look awake and alert, Margaret asked, "When will you meet?"

"As soon as it gets dark, in the pine forest just across the bridge. And bring your new friend along," Christman scowled. "He's needed too."

"We'll be there," Margaret replied.

With a glance over his shoulder to see if anyone had noticed him, the lanky Christman hurried away.

These were trying times for anyone in business, especially a woman running a print shop that employed three men. Yes, her father had faced difficulties when he established the shop forty-five years earlier, but today revolution smoldered in the countryside all around Strasbourg, and it had destroyed large areas of Germany. With crude swords, primitive weapons, farm implements, and a few unreliable guns that they had stolen or captured in battle, peasant farmers clamored for change.

With curls dancing on her forehead, Margaret inspected the pamphlet she was printing. A citizen in Strasbourg had written a short essay in defense of Matthew Zell, a well-known and liked pastor, who preached in support of the Lutheran Reformation. The two-page pamphlet, printed in German so it could be read by common people, warned of Matthew's removal by the Catholic bishop and encouraged the faithful in Strasbourg to defend his powerful preaching.

In the kitchen at the back of the print shop, Margaret finished eating her supper of a small bowl of soup and a hard roll. Her bedroom, the only other room in the house, was small but adequate. She had shared it with her first husband. Before they had been married two years, he, along with many others in Europe, had died suddenly and helplessly of the dreaded plague. This too, many believed, was a sign of God's wrath and of the beginning of the Great Tribulation.

Margaret's mind quickly turned toward pleasant thoughts about Beck. She could almost feel his strong, gentle arms. He'd hold her tonight, she was sure, and their love would grow, as it had since he had come to town a month ago. Whether Beck saw Margaret first or the other way around, neither really cared. Their hearts now reached toward each other, like the fragile but persistent flowers that had burst through the hard ground along the canal, stretching toward the warm April sun.

Beck had explained some of the radical ideas he had about faith to Margaret, though he wasn't pushy about them. She listened carefully to his thoughts, which were similar to those Grebel taught at the church-around-the-fire services. Margaret liked the new ideas Beck had picked up among the Brethren in Switzerland. And beyond his beliefs, she thought he was strikingly handsome. She wanted to marry him, but so did the powerful Magdalene Knobloch's beautiful daughter, Agnes.

This time Margaret knew the sharp rap on the door was Beck's. She smiled, brushed back her coal-black curls, and hurried to open the latch.

Beck ducked to enter the low doorway, greeted Margaret, and invited her out for a walk. "It's a beautiful evening, wouldn't you agree?"

"I'm ready to go. Let's go by the canal."

Beck wrapped Margaret up in his arms. "I'm ready for an

evening alone with you, but tonight, my printer friend, we're headed for the bridge. There's going to be a meeting of leaders in the peasants' revolt."

"I figured you'd know about it already. I'll go if you can keep business out of our conversation on the way."

Beck gently squeezed her hands. "Agreed. And besides, if we focus on each other, nobody will guess where we're headed."

The brisk April evening hinted of warmer days soon to come. Margaret and Beck took jackets along because neither expected to return until early the next morning. They zigzagged through the stacks of logs and rough lumber in the Wood Market outside Margaret's shop. The best way out of the city led across the canal and through the Butcher's Gate.

On the bridge over the canal, they stopped to watch the water of the Ill River flow around the city toward the powerful Rhine River. In each other's arms—she trim and petite, he tall and thin—it was a wonderful spring evening. Some early flowers bloomed in the beds the city fathers had planted along the banks.

"Beck, I'm so glad you moved here from Freiburg. You'll be able to use your printing skills here—there's plenty of work."

"I'm sure you're right, Margaret, but you know as well as I do that these are hard times to be starting a new enterprise. I'll just keep working for Knoblochs' shop for the first few months that I'm here."

"You'll succeed, Beck. I know you will." Printing, Margaret knew from experience, was a good business to be in if you could handle the risks. Scholars wanted ancient literature printed, others wanted science books published, a few wanted technical manuals. For the general market, there were religious books and pamphlets to print, both Catholic and Lutheran.

"Will the gathering at the bridge be safe?"

"I think so," replied Beck, silently hoping he was right. "The farmers in the countryside are demanding a lot of changes; I'm sure there's trouble ahead."

The Knobloch daughter may have noticed that she and Beck were growing closer, but Margaret didn't care. This man was hers, at least for now. In a moment, they headed for the gate that led through the wall and out of the city.

About twenty thousand people lived inside Strasbourg during the 1520s. They were reasonably safe from the violence that wracked the countryside. Outside the walls, no one was safe. The farmers had attacked convents and monasteries, nobles had been chased out of their castles, and the fighting between the farmers and the nobles had destroyed villages.

Margaret and Beck saw signs of the peasants' revolt at the Butcher's Gate. A dozen farmers and their families were headed toward the city for safety from the destruction. The Strasbourg City Council had set up the Franciscan monastery as a refuge for battered peasants who lived in the nearby regions of Strasbourg.

Beck grabbed Margaret's hand as they hurried past the pitiful and dejected peasants. They would take the longer and less-traveled route to the bridge that stretched over the Rhine, about three miles from Margaret's shop.

Behind them rose the great Strasbourg Cathedral. Its massive pink limestone walls were interlaced with stained-glass windows and flying buttresses that took the weight of the pointed roof out beyond the main walls to the ground below. To Margaret, the cathedral symbolized the power and authority of the Catholic Church. Anyone who challenged its surly stare risked being thrown out of the Church, or worse, burned as a heretic. She hoped the meeting that night wouldn't catch them in the long reach of its powerful grip.

They crossed two more canals, and ahead of them lay the creaking timber bridge. The mighty Rhine had established Strasbourg's wealth years ago. In the 1520s it was the primary artery for trade in central Europe, a main street from the Swiss Alps in the south to Holland in the north. There'd be the toll to pay and the guard to pass by, but a citizen of Strasbourg shouldn't have trouble crossing the bridge, even though the revolt threatened every structure in society right then.

The old bridge was really nothing more than a flexible, floating, wooden walkway that stretched from one bank to the other. The city council of Strasbourg maintained it because it was the last bridge across the Rhine before it emptied into the North Sea hundreds of miles downstream. That night there would be an unofficial gathering of a few farmers, rebel leaders, and a couple of printers to assess the progress of the revolt. By the time they crossed the bridge, it was dark.

Christman met them on the other side. "Follow me," he grunted, as he turned toward the woods. Margaret and Beck could easily follow him because of the bright moon that lit their way deep into the forest. Shadows danced across the path in front of them as they walked. Margaret clutched Beck's arm as they followed their guide.

Suddenly Christman lurched to the left and led them between two huge fir trees, directing them into a clearing where a small group of men waited for them. Hearing only the sounds of the forest, an owl, and the rustling of leaves, Margaret counted nine in the secret company, including their guide.

"We need your help," Christman said to Margaret. "It's urgent that you print our demands and help us distribute them in Strasbourg and the surrounding countryside. And—"

Beck interrupted. "Let's start at the beginning. I'd like to know who I'm dealing with here." Even in the moonlight Margaret could see Beck squint, as he always did when concerned.

"That's reasonable," Christman responded. "Three of these men are from Switzerland and the rest are from Germany. Hans, you do the introductions."

One of the men on a log rose and shook hands with Beck and Margaret. Margaret nearly gasped aloud at the enormous size of the man's hand and his powerful grip. "I'm Hans Müller, this is Wilhelm Reublin, and next to him is Uli Seiler."

When the two men rose to shake hands, Seiler stuck out his left arm because his right hand had been hacked off, leaving only a stump. "My other companions here are Germans," Müller continued with a sweep of his hand around the circle. Four men rose in turn to shake hands with Beck.

Then Müller got down to business. "In the last six weeks we've written out our protests, and we've summarized them in twelve demands that the nobles must agree to or we'll keep fighting." He became more agitated as he spoke, but he remembered to keep his gravelly voice low to avoid being overheard by spies in the woods.

"A printer in Waldshut agreed to produce them last week for circulation in Switzerland. Margaret, we need you to print our articles for distribution in south Germany." When Müller gestured toward her with his burly arms and giant hands, she instinctively pulled closer to Beck.

"This isn't a very good time to announce your demands," Beck replied. "Sturm's watchdogs on the city council will destroy any pamphlets that might stir up the peasants to arm themselves and revolt."

"Jacob Sturm is a tolerant man," growled Müller. "Even if he catches you printing the pamphlet, he'll look the other way, I'm sure."

One of the Germans jumped to his feet, loosened a chunk deep in his sinuses and spit hard. "We're sick of having no say in choosing our own priests," declared Sebastian Lotzer, known to all simply as "Lotz." With clenched fists, he continued. "And the old system of keeping us tied down like serfs of long ago has to be abolished. We must be given the same rights to fish and hunt in the streams and forests as the nobles. And we must be paid for our work! Why do the nobles treat us like animals?"

As Lotz paced, Müller continued. "We are ready to submit all our articles to the test of Scripture, and if they are contrary to the Word of God, we will withdraw them."

"We'll need a week to print them," Margaret said to no one in particular. "I'm finishing a small pamphlet tomorrow, and then there's another job that must be done, and by the end of this week I'll set up the press to print your demands."

"We'd be grateful," Müller replied. "I'll come by in a week to pick them up. And we'll pay all your expenses."

"They'll be stored at Ziegler's barn, but come by my shop to pay me."

Lotz thrust his manuscript toward Margaret, which she put into a pocket inside her loose-fitting, gray wool jacket.

Because the guard closed the gates to the bridge at midnight, Margaret and Beck hurried back through the forest toward the Rhine. Christman strode out ahead of them, guiding and watching for trouble. At a temperature almost as cold as the river, Christman offered a quick "have a good evening."

The ten-foot-wide floating bridge rode higher in the water that spring than it had during the winter. The river would be at its highest from June through September as the snow thawed high in the mountains of Switzerland. Not many people traveled over the bridge late at night, but during the day it was a bustling business route carrying Alsatian wheat, rye, prized wines, gray cloth, and wool all over Germany.

Margaret was happy to step off the bridge on the Strasbourg side of the river. After the long walk across, it took a number of steps on solid ground before she no longer felt the swaying.

Back inside the security of the Butcher's Gate, Beck stopped Margaret on the bridge over the canal. They watched the water flow by and held each other comfortably. Beck broke the silence. "I love you Margaret, and I want to get to know you a lot better."

Being careful not to allow any change in her smile or embrace, Margaret wondered if this would be the moment she'd been waiting for.

"But I'm really not sure about a lot of things right now, Margaret." He was squinting again, Margaret noticed. "Clement believes we're living in the very last days before Christ's return and the judgment day."

"Lot's of people have said that before, and they've always been wrong."

"And the war with the peasants, Margaret. It's vicious and out of control. It sure seems like the Great Tribulation the Bible talks about."

"Are you scared, Beck?"

"What do you mean?"

"You have me, don't you? Doesn't that count for anything?"

"Oh, you sure know how to destroy a man's worries about the future."

"But am I right?"

"Yes, you are, Margaret. Holding you here in the moonlight does help to balance out the crazy things going on these days."

Margaret figured that if an embrace could ease his fears a little, a kiss might erase them, so she reached for him on tiptoes.

If they had been looking from the bridge over the canal, they could have seen a trace of the soaring fire at the Ziegler

27

barn in the countryside beyond the city walls. Clement was probably preaching again tonight about the end of the world. But Margaret and Beck didn't notice.

Or had they looked up into the night sky, they might have seen a bright lantern burning in the cathedral tower that hovered high above them, only a few hundred feet away. But that flame didn't get their attention either. They were making their own little blaze just then.

Two lights competed in the Strasbourg night. The one from the Catholic Church had dominated the area for centuries. The other light, much more recent in origin, burned from among those who dared to gather at the barn outside the walls to discuss new understandings of faith that they claimed came out of the Bible.

Margaret turned long enough from easing Beck's worries to notice the outline of a tall man walking quickly through the street near her print shop. Christman was checking on her, Margaret judged, and if he had seen the two of them on the bridge, which he probably had, he would be angrier than he already was. She wished Beck would just ask her to marry him so this duel could be settled. Until then, well, she'd just have to wait and see.

2

Clash in the Black Forest

At dawn the next morning, bells in the cathedral tower chimed out a call to the first prayer service of the day. Margaret awakened out of a sound sleep. After a quick cup of hot tea and a slice of bread, she opened the shop for business.

That day she would finish the Bullheym pamphlet, a small order of only five hundred copies. Her three workers arrived at seven and put the printing press into action. After she had carefully inspected the first two pages they produced, they knew how to finish the job.

Shortly after seven-thirty, Jacob Meyer, a city council member, banged on Margaret's print shop door. Meyer, who was disliked by most folks in the city, presumed to act as the unofficial inspector for the council, and Margaret didn't know what to expect from him.

"A man's missing," he said sternly. "If anyone knows the whereabouts of Sturm's nephew, we need to know about it."

"What happened?" Margaret asked.

"We have no idea. He simply disappeared. That's why council members are making their rounds this morning. Speak up if you or your employees hear anything about his disappearance." After a glance around the shop, the self-appointed examiner dashed down the street.

At eight o'clock, Margaret left to visit her longtime friend Katherine Zell. Married to the well-known Lutheran pastor Matthew Zell, Katherine lived in a modest house in the center of the city because friction with Catholic leaders prevented them from living in the cathedral parsonage.

At twenty-seven, the lively Katherine was only a year younger than Margaret and was known for her gracious hospitality. They had been friends in grade school, catechism class, and only two years ago Margaret had served as a witness at Katherine's grand wedding.

"Good morning, Katherine!"

"And a warm welcome to you, my friend Margaret! It's so good to see you again."

"I thought I'd come to check on the pastor's pregnant wife," Margaret said with a chuckle. "You're starting to show quite well."

"Come in, Margaret, we've got a lot to do today."

"How's your work with the refugees proceeding, Katherine?"

"Not very well, quite honestly. They're coming into the city by the dozens, faster than we can care for them. The old Franciscan monastery is full and we don't know where to send the overflow."

"Will the bishop send funds to help the women and the children?"

"Hardly," Katherine said sharply. "He's in with the nobles and doesn't care what happens to the families of the men they kill."

"What's your next idea? If I know you, you have something in mind."

"Well, are you busy today? Do you want to go with Matthew and me to the forest on the other side of the river? We're headed to the battlefield where the farmers are gathering to fight the nobles. Matthew and I want to talk them out of fighting and ask them to go home to their families."

"Seems like a pretty grand scheme to me, Katherine. I think I can go. The shop will run just fine today. We have plenty of work."

"How are things with you and Beck?" Katherine asked with a flourish and a telling smile.

"You know I love him, Katherine, but he hasn't asked me to marry him yet. He's worried about the war and the events swirling around us. But I think I'll soon convince him that we should marry."

"It took three years before Matthew asked me. Men have to think it's their idea before they'll ask a woman to marry them, I guess."

"Speaking of men, Katherine, give me about an hour to go visit Beck over at the Knoblochs'."

"Sure. Meet us in front of the cathedral at ten o'clock. Get ready for a long day and possibly an overnight stay. And watch out for those Knobloch women. They can be downright nasty when they're mad at you."

The route to the Knoblochs' printing business led past both St. Martin's Church and the St. Thomas parish. Facing the canal, the business was located in a mammoth building that had been passed down to Johann Knobloch by his father, also a printer.

With a frown on his face, as always, the owner of one of the largest printing enterprises in Strasbourg met Margaret at the door. "Are you here to see me or one of my men?" he asked.

"If you don't mind, I'd like to talk to Beck for a few minutes."

"All right, but don't take long."

Just outside the door where they could easily be seen, Margaret explained to Beck that she'd be going with Katherine and Matthew to the forest on the other side of the bridge for the day.

Then the confrontation Margaret hoped to avoid came into view. Up the street marched the domineering Magdalene

Knobloch, with Agnes in tow. Margaret braced herself. She knew that Beck had noticed Agnes, as all the men had, but she was also quite confident that nothing would happen between them without Magdalene's permission.

"Good morning, Mrs. Knobloch," Margaret offered.

"Yes, it is a good morning for business and being productive," the matriarch of the Knobloch press coldly replied. "And the sooner Beck returns to his duties inside, the better."

Agnes usually looked down when her mother was near. She did manage a glance at Beck, however, and a slight smile in his direction didn't go unnoticed.

"You'll finish your conversation quickly," Magdalene demanded, "and Beck will get back to work." With that they brushed inside, though Agnes glanced up at Beck again on the way in the door. Margaret was sure she noticed another smile directed at the man she had come to see.

"I hope to get back home before dark," Margaret said.

"I'll come by your shop late tonight to see if you made it back," Beck answered. With a quick squeeze of his hand, Margaret turned and headed toward Katherine's house.

The preacher and his optimistic wife rode an open carriage with Margaret aboard to the bridge over the Rhine. The steady and experienced horses wouldn't bolt or panic while crossing the long and swaying wooden perch. They and their driver had made the trip many times before.

Deep in the Black Forest, to the east of the river, the peasants gathered. With their hoes, spears, and swords, they lined up against Count Rudolf of Sulz, whose three thousand foot soldiers and two thousand horsemen overwhelmed the unorganized and ill-equipped peasants. Many of them grasped weapons that Christman had moved out of Clement's arsenal, deep in the bowels of the sturdy barn, in the dead of the night.

Matthew was intending to reason with the peasants in order to get them to go home to their farms and families. After an hour-and-a-half ride, he reined in the horses at an unusually large clearing in the dense Black Forest. They were at the battlefield.

Word quickly reached Müller and Lotz that the Lutheran cleric from Strasbourg wanted to talk with them. Through a series of messages sent back and forth, they agreed to meet the Zells at a location behind their determined but poorly equipped soldiers.

Müller and the single-minded Lotz may have been surprised to see Margaret in the carriage with the Zells. On the other hand, very little could arouse the emotions of these battle-hardened men. They stood for a list of twelve economic demands. A woman on the battlefield, even one they knew, wouldn't change their determination to fight for those changes.

"My dear brother Müller," Matthew began, "I come to you and ask that you and your men stop fighting and return to your wives and little children. How can your fields be planted this spring without you there?"

With no emotion, Müller waved off Matthew's weak opening argument. Gesturing at no one in particular, he said, "Listen, preacher. Our wives will handle the spring planting just fine without us."

"My wife and children have everything to lose if I go home today without fighting the duke," Lotz snorted. He spit violently, just as he had the night before. Deep within this battle-hardened German revolutionary, Margaret heard the angry voice of the peasant revolt erupt. "Strasbourg's merchants get rich in the city, but we only get poorer in the countryside. I'll not have my sons grow up with the bondage of serfdom and abuse that I've experienced."

Matthew's response seemed feeble in comparison. He hadn't

shaved for about four days, as usual. His stubbled face looked smooth, however, compared to the surly beards of these desperate warriors. "My dear brothers, I have preached Luther's message of faith and freedom in Strasbourg for four years. I want change just as badly as you do. But I find no Scripture which, to the honor of God and the common good, justifies the murder of nobles, however you may have been treated."

Flags on both sides of the battlefield fluttered behind them in the warm spring breeze of the Black Forest. Men grasped their weapons, primitive wooden tools or iron guns, and anxiously waited. A few had only sticks gathered from the nearby woods. The Zells' driver had taken the horses to a nearby stream for water while Katherine and Margaret stood and anxiously hoped for the best.

Margaret noticed her business competitor astride a dark-brown, prancing stallion in the distance. He too had taken the day off from work. Patiently waiting for the slaughter, Johann struck an intimidating profile. Margaret made a note in her mind to tell Beck that she would save him from a life of torment by keeping him away from the pretty Agnes Knobloch.

"We seek divine justice and godly law," Lotz grumbled. He reached for inspiration from the great Reformer himself as he continued to speak. "Martin Luther preaches the equality of all men, regardless of social class. He preaches well. It follows that we must be able to choose our own pastors; we must be released from serfdom; fields and forests must be available for anyone to hunt in; and the death tax must be abolished. Widows and children are left with no livelihood when they pay that tax." Margaret knew that peasants by the thousands all across Germany agreed with him.

"If our demands are contrary to the Word of God," Müller insisted with a gravelly voice, "they will be withdrawn."

"May I speak, Matthew?"

"If you wish, Katherine."

"I call on you, brothers, in God's name to stop the killing. The Franciscan monastery in Strasbourg is full of mothers and children who have fled from this terrible slaughter. The Relief Committee is doing all it can to help those who suffer, but the suffering will stop only when you lay down your weapons."

"Will you take our demands to Count Rudolf," Müller barked, "who waits across the clearing, ready to butcher us all?"

"If we can circulate our demands to more people," Lotz said, "we can raise enough foot soldiers, with or without weapons, to overwhelm Rudolf and his savage nobles." Lotz spit so hard his whole body shook in rage. "We're wasting our energy, Hans. It's time to fight."

Matthew lurched forward with one more thing he wanted to say. "Brothers, when you are ready to dissolve your Christian Union of the peasant armies scattered throughout southwest Germany, I will bring all the necessary parties together for talks in Strasbourg. I can assure you of safety if you take my offer. Send word at any time to the cathedral."

Margaret, Katherine, and Matthew returned to their carriage while Müller's men began their desperate attack against Count Rudolf and his armed soldiers. Fighting erupted across the field as the Zells' carriage headed back toward the river.

In the slaughter that afternoon, more than seven hundred peasants were killed before darkness set in. Many more lay on the ground wounded and unattended to, moaning in the midst of their slow, painful deaths.

Only twenty-six armed soldiers of the count died. At dusk the nobles' shields glittered in the last glow of the setting sun, triumphant in battle and streaked with blood across their holy crosses.

Johann, a Catholic noble fighting to defend his rights,

decided it was time to crush the preaching of Matthew Zell. If the stubble-faced preacher sided with the peasants, Johann reasoned, then that made Luther's heresy a disease that must be cut out with a very sharp blade.

To those who believed they lived in the time of the Great Tribulation, the littered battlefield with dying peasants confirmed it. Luther led a movement to change the church, economic upheaval threatened the lives of thousands of peasants, and radical reformers tenaciously acted on ideas that challenged faith on all sides. In an age of ruin, warfare, and monumental change, apocalyptic expectations that the end of the age was close swept across Europe like fire through a dry forest.

It was already growing dark by the time Matthew, Katherine, and Margaret, in a silent, reflective mood, arrived back at the bridge over the Rhine. Matthew's warm and friendly personality reemerged as he spoke with the guard at the bridge. "The fighting's bad, but you know the old farmer Clement Ziegler predicted it would happen."

"Ah, yes, Clement Ziegler, of the gardener's guild," Matthew replied.

"You know, Pastor Zell, after God saved him from drowning in the great flood last year, Clement has had special revelations about future events."

"Has he encouraged the peasants in their revolt?"

"I'd say he has."

"Katherine and Margaret, I'd like to stop by Clement's farm tonight and pay him a visit. It's a part of my duties as pastor, you know. Driver, head this carriage around the northern route and stop in the village of Robertsau."

Matthew hadn't actually asked Margaret whether she was willing to ride to Zieglers' farm. She wanted to go home to her print shop, find Beck, walk with him to the canal, and hold him in her arms. That didn't appear to be an option.

A recently butchered pig roasted over an open fire outside Zieglers' barn. Clement started a roaring fire about every other night. Only two days ago, Margaret had witnessed the baptism of the two men by Grebel.

About eight townsmen and women gathered around, talking with Clement and listening to his biblical interpretations of the end times. The social activist and self-appointed interpreter of biblical prophecy was surprised but pleased to see the distinguished Zells arrive.

After he gave slices of meat and a mysterious soup mixture from the big kettle to all who wanted it, Clement talked about the dreadful fighting between peasants and nobles in recent weeks. "In February of last year, Matthew, when the planets met in the sign of Pisces, many predicted that a terrible evil lay ahead. The battle today in the Black Forest is the first part of that fearful tribulation. Many of the men who died on that battlefield today believed they were doing God's will."

"Times have changed, Clement. Your gardeners' guild and the other nineteen guilds in the city, including Margaret's printing group, hold more economic power these days than do the tired feudal farms of the countryside. This fighting is about livelihoods."

"Oh, but Matthew," Clement replied, "many of the men fighting today believe they are fighting the great antichrist, Pope Clement VII himself, who lives far off in Rome. Martin Luther started the attack on the Catholic Church a few years ago. The peasants are answering Luther's call."

"No!" Matthew boomed with all the force he could muster. "This revolt has nothing to do with Luther's reform movement. I've made it clear in my sermons from the cathedral pulpit that Luther wants spiritual changes, not political changes. Luther does not approve of this fighting—the nobles must be respected."

"You know, Matthew, I'm opposed to violence, but I believe the farmers in the countryside need justice. Perhaps there's no other way to bring about the changes they want. Whose side do you think our Lord Jesus Christ would be on, if he would have been in the Black Forest today?"

Clement's appearance in the darkening evening, illuminated by the hot, hissing, and soaring fire, was strange and scary. His long, stringy hair, his protruding belly, his missing teeth, and his wrinkled old clothes made him appear like one of the prophets, Margaret thought, as she chewed on the roast pork. Perhaps Jeremiah or Amos or Ezekiel.

"The Catholic Church needs change, Matthew. What does infant baptism mean except citizenship in a city or noble's territory? Why do the priests and bishops worship Mary? Where is the true preaching of the Word?" Clement bellowed.

"A prophet like John the Baptist," Margaret thought.

"You must come to hear Matthew preach," Katherine interrupted. "He preaches reformation from the clear Word of God. You need to come to the cathedral and listen to him, Clement."

"I am suspicious of religion in the great cathedral, Katherine. Though I hear there have been some changes, I'm still skeptical."

"Come with me to the house," Gertrude Ziegler whispered in Margaret's ear. Always wearing a cooking apron and missing an important front tooth, Gertrude told Margaret about Anna's hasty departure from the barn. "She was in an awful hurry to leave, Margaret. In the middle of the day!"

"Where did she go?"

"She asked for money to buy passage to Worms. Poor thing, she headed down the river by herself. I felt so sorry for her."

"You did your best, Gertrude. Thank you for keeping her

and taking such risks. I thank God for you and your husband." One of God's special angels, Margaret later explained to Beck, helping poor souls along their way to heaven.

"It's late, Clement," Matthew said as a way of bringing his pastoral visit to a close. "We'll be going now."

"It's about time," Margaret thought, "but it's probably too late to catch Beck."

"Come to the cathedral on Sunday when I preach. Right now I'm preaching a series of sermons from Paul's letter to the Romans."

"These are the last days, Matthew," Clement replied. "Remember, as the Israelites carried a sword in one hand when they rebuilt the wall in the days of Nehemiah, so must we use the sword of the Spirit, which is a proper understanding of Scripture, to build the New Jerusalem in our day. May His kingdom come!"

Margaret remembered the baptism of the two Anabaptists earlier that week, beside this same bonfire. "Christ's kingdom is coming," she thought to herself. "With brave preachers like Clement and Grebel, and peasants ready to die for what they believe in, the church and the social structures of the day will have to change, and sooner rather than later."

Just before midnight, after Margaret inspected the work her crew had accomplished that day, she heard a quiet knock on her door. With a small candle she welcomed Seiler, one of the Swiss men she had met in the forest the night before. She could easily see the outline of the cathedral in the night sky behind him.

He gestured toward the Black Forest with his one hand. "A lot of our men were killed today. The nobles have overwhelmed us. Müller sends me with instructions that we need *Twelve Articles* printed immediately so more people can learn about our demands for change, before it's too late. He wants at least a thousand copies, and we'll pay your full wages for the work."

"Stop back in three days," Margaret answered. "I'll start on it right away."

With that, Seiler hurried off into the moonlit April night. He and other tired and hungry men worked all night, shuttling the weapons of their fallen comrades back to the clearing by the bridge. Another night, when the guard could be bribed to look the other way, they would move them back to Zieglers' barn until they were needed again.

Margaret wondered if Seiler would find his way back safely to the forest. Count Rudolf and Johann would be on the move tonight, she was sure, looking for the likes of Seiler and others who fought against them in the forest. If he or any of his partners were caught, they'd be strung up on the gallows the next morning before the sun came up.

3

Set to Print

Margaret's men went right to work Thursday morning. They set up the press to print Müller's declaration of independence for the peasants, *Twelve Articles*.

Heinrich and Peter worked as compositors. First, they carefully read the handwritten articles and determined the length of the finished pamphlet. Heinrich judged that they could do the job in a small, eight-page pamphlet. They'd print four pages on each side of a large sheet of paper, then fold it twice to arrange the eight pages in order. *Twelve Articles* was long, but if they used their smallest letter size, they'd be able to get the job done in time for delivery on Friday.

Heinrich and Peter first arranged to print pages one, four, five, and eight. On the other side of the large sheet, they would print pages two, three, six, and seven. It was hard to line up the letters from left to right and upside-down so they would print properly. Further, Heinrich liked to line up the right edge of his work, so he juggled the letters and blank spaces to make the right margins even.

Margaret's shop had dozens of carefully crafted lead letters. The letters had to be exactly the same height, or some letters would be faint while others would be dark. They also had to be the same thickness so the lines of type would be straight across the sheet all the way down the page.

On that morning both men had their sleeves rolled up to their elbows. By ten o'clock the sun peaked over the cathedral and streamed down through the shop's open window.

Heinrich, who was twenty-four, accepted his work gladly. It challenged his mind, and the books and pamphlets he printed were changing south Germany. He and the other printers of his time believed that Johannes Gutenberg's invention of the printing press in Strasbourg a few years earlier had helped to ignite the powerful changes taking place in Europe. Margaret called them faith fires. He figured she was probably right.

At break time Margaret, Peter, Heinrich, and Leopold, her third hired hand, discussed *Twelve Articles*. Müller and Lotz, determined and hardened by the injustices of their day, wanted both religious and economic changes. They demanded the right to choose their own pastor and called for the removal of the tax on cattle, because it was not commanded in Scripture. Further, the peasants wanted to abolish serfdom, a system that kept them obligated to the nobles.

"This is a sign," Heinrich speculated aloud, "of the new times we live in."

"The end times, according to the old preacher Clement Ziegler," Margaret added.

In other articles, the leaders of the peasants' revolt demanded fishing and hunting rights, firewood from the forests, payment for work performed for nobles, and the freedom to use the nobles' meadows to graze their cattle. Article twelve asserted that the peasants would withdraw their demands if they were found to be unscriptural. Margaret recalled Clement's interpretation of the revolt from the evening before.

"I think Clement's right," she said.

She adjusted her heavy work shawl and the men sprang back into action. She thought aloud as they got back to work, "They really do see themselves carrying out Luther's religious reforms."

Jacob Sturm's huge brown beard shook as he rapped on the shop door. It sounded important. "We're making our rounds to the guilds again this morning, Margaret, warning members not to assist the peasants in their unlawful revolt." Sturm's warning carried weight; he was the most important official in Strasbourg's city government. All the big buttons he wore on his work coat added to the appearance of authority.

"We have a business to carry on here, Jacob. We'll carry through on the decisions of our guild leaders."

"I appreciate your cooperation, Margaret. Your father always remained loyal to the Strasbourg council. He established a fine print shop here. I trust you'll follow in his footsteps."

"I'm doing my best," Margaret replied with a gesture toward her men, "with their help. Have you met Balthasar Beck yet? He moved here from Freiburg last month."

"Met him this morning at the Knobloch shop, on my rounds. I believe you and he have been seeing each other?"

"Yes," she admitted with a smile, "it's true."

"If he likes Strasbourg and wants to become a citizen, he'll need to pay a fee, register with a guild, and swear an oath of loyalty to the constitution. He'll pay taxes, serve in our military when needed, and occasionally perform guard duty on the city walls."

"Thanks for the information and your visit, Jacob. For now I want to make this print shop prosper."

"A fine goal indeed," Sturm said with a wink. "You'd probably do even better with a man like Beck around."

Changing topics, Margaret asked, "Has your nephew turned up yet?"

"Not yet, but we're leaving no stone unturned in our search for him. It's got to be foul play, Margaret. My nephew had no enemies at all. I have no idea who would have wanted to get rid of him."

"Could he have taken off to another city without telling anyone?"

"I don't think so," Sturm answered, and without hesitating added, "Oh, there'll be a hanging outside the Stone Street Gate at noon today. A man who goes by the name of Lotz, one of the peasant leaders in the battle yesterday, was captured. The council agrees with Count Rudolf and Johann Knobloch that we need to set an example for the citizens who've supported the peasants' revolt. Have a good day."

"So that's why he really came by," Margaret said to Heinrich after the door was closed. "They're going to hang Lotz to set an example. At noon, so lots of people can be there. Guess he's almost done spitting." She glowered in disgust.

To get to the hanging during their lunch break, Beck and Margaret had to cross a small island, the main part of the city being situated inside the two prongs of a canal that circled the city. Centuries earlier, when the Romans had established Strasbourg, they wisely placed the center of town a long way from the surging summer floods that occasionally rose from the Rhine. The canals directed the Ill River around the city, provided a stable place for docks and warehouses to store goods, and connected the city to the Rhine.

Around the front of the cathedral Beck and Margaret turned right and then left, past the Dominican monastery and through the horse market. A crowd of people, headed in the same direction, slowed them as they waited to cross the bridge that led to the gate.

It was impossible to get close to the gallows, and the condemned Lotz never saw Margaret or Beck. Showing no fear, the angry voice of the peasants' revolt spat once more in disgust when the hangman threw the rope around his neck. The onlookers didn't have to wait long before the executioner yanked the platform from underneath the seething German rebel, leaving him to dangle and twitch until he turned blue and hung limp.

The white clouds above Strasbourg floated lazily by, as usual in April, though Margaret noticed one small, dark cloud in the distance. It would probably bring an afternoon shower with it. Like the sky with a single rain cloud, the noon crowd of curious onlookers only had one older woman who wept openly for the executed man. Margaret tried to console Lotz's aunt, the one member of the dead man's family who had heard about the hanging in time to come. Beck stood uncomfortably by while Margaret talked to the woman and tried to help dry her tears.

Soon the woman turned to leave. "His poor wife doesn't even know he's dead," she said. Margaret and Beck looked once more at the grizzly scene of death after they watched the downcast woman scurry away to deliver bad news. Beck held Margaret in his arms, wiped a tear from her cheek, and led her slowly away from the gallows.

Back inside the gate, they walked slowly down Stone Street, through a neighborhood where members of the gardeners' guild lived—a rough lot, independent-minded and sympathetic to the demands in *Twelve Articles*. Clement had lived in this area before he took up farming in the countryside. Jörg Ziegler, a fierce and striking younger cousin of Clement and a friend of Margaret, made his home there.

"They certainly made a statement today by that hanging, wouldn't you agree, Margaret?" Jörg had invited them to gather around his small table by a door that faced Stone Street. "They're trying to set an example that will scare the rest of us," Jörg said with anger.

"It's a puzzle to me," Margaret replied. "Luther's been preaching reform for five or six years. Matthew Zell preaches at the Catholic clergy to reform their ways and calls on the common folk to lead good, moral lives. So when the peasant farmer rises up to seek changes in the practical things of life," Margaret slammed her hand on the table, "he gets slaughtered."

"That's the way things have always been," Beck said.

"What I feel the worst about now is Lotz's poor wife and children. Who will care for them?"

Margaret's curls glistened and bounced in the sun as she walked back to the other side of town with Beck. Her tanned, olive face danced when she finally laughed again. With hands and fingers in motion as she talked, she led Beck to the food market to pick up a few supplies. He was learning that Margaret could be persuasive, even forceful at times. That day he had seen her full range of emotions.

They talked about everyday things and Beck's difficult work situation at the Knobloch press. They both agreed that he'd need to get out of there soon. Right now, though, with the push to get *Twelve Articles* printed and the turmoil of the peasants' revolt, the details of where he'd work in the future were put on hold.

Peter and Leopold had the press set up to produce *Twelve Articles* by seven-thirty Friday morning. In the printers' guild, Leopold was a pressman. Peter helped him when needed. Their job was to take the letters, lines and pages from Heinrich, apply ink to the type, and press the paper to make pages for the pamphlets, books, or broadsheets the shop printed.

The printing press was a simple concept but it took skill to complete a job accurately and precisely. They used a large wooden tray that held letters and lines for four pages. It had to be located squarely under the press. In the Alsace Valley, where Strasbourg was located, there were dozens of wine presses that operated in the same way. A man pulled a lever attached to a big wooden screw in the middle of a large wooden structure. When he pulled the lever, it forced the platen—a heavy, square piece of wood attached to the screw—down onto the paper and type.

Because paper was so expensive, the first sheet through the press on any job needed to be inspected in order to eliminate costly mistakes. It was the first time anyone could read the pages as they would appear in the pamphlet to make sure everything was spelled accurately.

In the early days, Margaret's father had printed a number of books on high-quality parchment made from calfskin. Paper was new during the days of Gutenberg and Margaret's father, a few decades ago. The paper used in Strasbourg's print shops was produced locally, but it wasn't consistent in thickness and it came to the shop ragged around the edges.

Margaret inspected the first sheet that Peter and Leopold pressed. She read the introduction and the first several articles. Heinrich and Peter had done a good job the day before and the printing could proceed.

First, they placed the paper in a frame covered with a much heavier sheet of paper that had four large openings. The frame, or tympan, was then closed and laid over the letters and pages. Peter pushed the tray in under the center of the press while Leopold pulled the lever to apply just the right pressure on the paper. Too much pressure and the letters would smear, not enough and the words would be faint and hard to read.

When Peter opened the tympan to pull the paper out, he had to hang the large pieces of paper on strings that hung from the ceiling of the print shop. The ink, a mixture of lamp black and linseed oil, needed to dry before they could print the other side of the paper. While Leopold inked the letters with his leather ink ball, Peter hung the pages to dry and put a new sheet in the tympan. If everything went as usual, they would print about twelve hundred pages in a day. While Peter and Leopold operated the press, Heinrich set the letters and type for the four pages that would be printed on the back side of the paper.

Margaret directed the work, inspected the pages, and helped out where needed to keep the process moving smoothly. She also worked at a small desk in the print shop, managing the finances and business arrangements for the shop.

The next week, on Tuesday afternoon, two men arrived at the shop. Margaret and Beck had already met Reublin in the forest on Monday of the previous week; she recognized his big, silver belt buckle and stubby black mustache. Reublin brought another man with him, but they hadn't come to pick up *Twelve Articles* nor did they mention them.

"Margaret, I'd like you to meet George Blaurock," Reublin said, "a leader among the Brethren of Switzerland."

Blaurock was known for getting right to the point with his actions and words. "For several years Reublin and I have studied the Scriptures with Ulrich Zwingli, pastor of the cathedral parish in Zurich. We discovered that faith in Jesus Christ needs to be a voluntary decision, a believer's own choice. Further, Margaret, we find no command to baptize infants in the Scriptures."

"Have you baptized your children?" Margaret asked.

"Several couples in our group have chosen not to do so, including my wife and me. In January we baptized ourselves again as adult believers. We believe it's the biblical method of baptism. Believe me, we've been studying the Bible."

"How has Zwingli responded?"

"He has asked the town council of Zurich to ban us from the city," Reublin replied, "and if we refuse to stay away, we will be imprisoned."

"We don't believe baptism saves a person," Blaurock added. "Zwingli led us to the fountain of Scripture, helped us interpret it, and now he has pulled away from carrying out what we've discovered."

Leopold noticed Blaurock patting his bald spot and instantly liked the husky Swiss visitor.

"What else have you found?" wondered Margaret.

"How much time do you have? I came here on business, based on Reublin's recommendation, but I'm happy to tell you more about our beliefs if you really want to know."

"Let's take it from another perspective," Margaret answered. "How do the Brethren fit into the war the peasants are fighting in the countryside?"

"We're committed to the way of peace, Margaret, though some from our communities are involved in the fighting. We find no support in the New Testament for fighting or killing our enemies."

Margaret glanced at Reublin and wondered how he fit in with the Brethren.

"The reason we've come here today," Wilhelm continued, "is to ask for your services in printing a statement about our beliefs on baptism." Blaurock pulled a long, handwritten manuscript from under his jacket and handed it to Margaret. It appeared to be about fifty pages long.

"We need a printer who will produce our writings, Margaret. Reublin here says Strasbourg has an open, tolerant attitude toward the Lutheran reform movement right now. Your cathedral preacher Zell is calling for many changes. We need you," Blaurock said with a forceful gesture toward Margaret and a glance at her men, "to help us state why we believe in baptism only for those who are old enough to confess Jesus Christ as their Lord and Savior."

"Well, there have been changes in Strasbourg, but they only go so far," Margaret replied as she looked up from the document to her visitors.

"We saw a man hanged last week," Heinrich said without

much feeling. "Seems the city fathers and Count Rudolf of Sulz wanted to send a message to the peasants." Reublin squirmed and wrinkled his face in anger.

"We're not afraid of what will happen to us," Blaurock said. "We're ready to die for our beliefs."

There was a sharp rap at the door, and Margaret had a hunch it was Müller. She was right. At the door stood he and Seiler, ready to pay for the *Twelve Articles* pamphlets and begin distributing them to peasant farmers in the Black Forest.

"Isn't it risky for you to come here?" Margaret asked after she closed the door.

"The times are urgent," Müller replied, "but we're prepared to take risks and even die for the sake of our cause."

"Your articles are ready, but Leopold already delivered them to Zieglers' barn last night. They'll be safe there until you pick them up. We printed your dozen demands onto eight pages."

"Good, how much do we owe you?"

"Five gulden would cover all our expenses and pay the workers."

Müller reached into his leather pouch and found the silver coins to pay his bill.

"Christman Kenlin will probably be there to show you where to find them. If he's not, ask Clement," Margaret instructed.

Before the peasant leaders left, Margaret introduced Müller and Seiler to Blaurock and explained why he was visiting. "He brought us a job explaining why the Anabaptists believe in rebaptism. Blaurock is a leader among the Brethren from Zurich."

Müller and Seiler weren't in any mood to sit and debate the theology of baptism. "Seems to me," Müller said sternly, while he glared at Reublin, "there may be a little conflict here with your involvement in our peasant revolt. We'll attack Freiburg next week." Müller glanced around the circle and swung his big hands around the room to include everyone as he said, "Join us at Offenburg if you're with us."

Seiler shoved the door open and the two men hurried out the door to get their pamphlets. They were ready to announce twelve basic demands to the people of south Germany, and if the pamphlets didn't change the social system in their favor, they were prepared to keep on fighting. They had little time for the likes of Blaurock's peace-loving Anabaptists.

Margaret couldn't immediately resolve the conflict in her mind between Müller's radical actions and Blaurock's new ideas. What she wanted was a bit of strong-arm theology from Beck. Just the thought of the pretty Agnes hanging around his workplace drove her mad. She needed to act, and soon.

That night, when Müller and Seiler came to get their pamphlets, the barn concealed another secret. The sagging roofline rose like a sentinel from the countryside around it, long having kept watch over Robertsau and the surrounding fields. The Zieglers had farmed for a living, but in recent years Clement was far more interested in preaching about the end times than in raising crops.

An Anabaptist refugee had come from Switzerland that day, and Christman, on duty as a lookout, had given her the room in the hidden grain bin. On the run and exhausted, she slept soundly with her infant child on the hard mat. The nobles in the revolt had slaughtered her husband, and because she and her husband hadn't baptized their daughter, the young mother felt she had few options but to flee north. How much further north she'd have to run remained uncertain.

She did wake up long enough to hear Christman open the door of the bin beside her, shuffle around with a small candle and a few other people, and then walk them to the giant barn doors, back out into the dark night. Whether they had picked up or stored weapons or printed materials, she couldn't tell. Finally, after all was quiet, except for the noise of the rats running around in search of food, she easily slipped off to sleep again.

Clement and guards like Christman didn't talk to anyone about the refugees who stayed in the grain bin. Christman had been the first to call the protective barn an arsenal. How much longer could they keep the authorities from discovering the sermons preached at the outdoor fire, the second baptisms that occasionally took place there, and the weapons stored in the grain bin?

4

Spread of Reform

In church on the first Sunday in May, Matthew preached from Romans. "We are justified by faith," he cried out from his perch in front of the congregation.

For the past several years, the Catholic leaders in Strasbourg had locked Matthew out of the cathedral's finely crafted stone pulpit. So, a few citizens, assured by a sympathetic city council that nothing would be done to stop them, had built a big wooden podium from which Matthew could preach. It would only be a matter of time, most reformers believed, until he could use the more impressive stone pulpit. But the standoff symbolized the tension between supporters of Luther's Reformation and the Catholic city officials.

"The pure Word of God has led me to reject many of the doctrines of the Catholic Church," Matthew boomed. "There is a gap in the old church between the words of God and ways of man, and Scripture must be the only standard against which our new church is measured." Matthew was contagiously funny and personal, but when he preached his words rang out and reached to the far corners of the huge cathedral.

"For fifteen hundred years," he proclaimed with authority, "the holy, immortal gospel has been crushed and human doctrines have been substituted." His words echoed throughout the huge cathedral. "But now, in our own time, a great era of change, the Word has been released from bondage by our dear brother Martin Luther from Wittenberg, and the laws of God can be taught instead of the laws of the pope and the bishop."

After the sermon, in the great open plaza in front of the cathedral, Margaret and Beck met Katherine and Magdalene. In tow behind Magdalene followed her obedient husband, Johann. The Knoblochs had heard Mass separately in a side chapel of the cathedral.

"Good morning, Magdalene," Katherine said. "A beautiful spring day, isn't it?"

"You're beginning to show quite visibly," Magdalene responded coolly.

"Oh, yes, I am, Magdalene. And Matthew and I couldn't be more excited about having this baby in our home."

"You should make sure you give the child a proper Catholic baptism. A Christian baptism."

"Matthew will baptize the child in the cathedral in our own service, Magdalene, and it will certainly be a Christian service."

"Officials in the Vatican and the bishop at Molsheim will not approve of your false baptism," Johann chimed in with a frown.

"Johann," Margaret asked in order to redirect the conversation, "how is Beck doing for you?"

"His work is quite adequate," Johann quickly answered.

"He'll need a woman to find his way in the business world," Magdalene added, glancing at both Beck and Margaret. On the outside Magdalene worked at appearing friendly, but inside she churned with envy that Beck had resisted the advances of her daughter.

"The ice-woman is freezing over again," Margaret thought with a grimace.

"Margaret and I have enjoyed each other's company since I came to Strasbourg a few weeks ago," Beck responded. "She, like you, Mrs. Knobloch, will succeed in the printing business."

Turning toward her husband, Magdalene said, "When Johann married me I brought him resources and good connections." Looking at Beck, she added, "These are dangerous times, you know, what with the peasants' riots and the Lutheran heresy. If you get in on the wrong side of Sturm and the council, you'll have to leave our city, or worse."

"I take work from paying customers," Margaret answered, knowing Magdalene's comments were directed at her, "Lutheran or Catholic."

"What about those heretics who baptize themselves twice?" Magdalene scowled. "Do you print for them as well?"

"The emperor and the pope in Rome have both condemned them and their writings," Johann said.

"Of course you know that Luther has survived, and his ideas have spread rapidly around Germany," Margaret replied.

"And the Anabaptists are starting a new church based on what they believe the Bible says," Beck added with his concerned squint.

"We will not allow those heretics to survive in this city," Magdalene declared.

"And the so-called Reformation led by your Dr. Luther, Katherine, will be crushed," Johann added.

Though the spring morning was growing warmer by the minute, the conversation had turned frigid. The Knoblochs were intent on stopping the split that had torn the Catholic Church in two. They were also, like others in the Strasbourg establishment, determined to root out the unbridled radicals with their false beliefs.

Katherine speculated after the Knoblochs left, "When Luther burned the pope's letter of excommunication on a bonfire in Wittenberg, he lit up a blazing Reformation of the church all over his beloved Germany."

"And for him to now deny the Anabaptists the right to

interpret Scripture the way they see fit is a contradiction, I believe," Beck declared.

Seeing Matthew making his way toward them, Katherine invited Margaret and Beck to visit the Franciscan monastery with them the next day.

"Mrs. Knobloch won't like me taking off work," Beck responded. "But I'll be there if Margaret's going."

On Monday morning, Matthew and Katherine knocked on the door of the print shop where Beck and Margaret were ready to walk with them to the Franciscan monastery. Beck had asked the Knoblochs for a full week off of work. Reluctantly, Johann had agreed. Beck wanted to visit the refugee center with Margaret and go to Freiburg for the peasants' battle. Heading across the city, Beck felt like a free man.

The monastery was a big building with a tall, square tower. For two hundred years it had served as a center for friars in the order of St. Francis of Assisi, a godly man of the people who lived in Italy during the 1200s. It had recently been closed and the friars were forced to go elsewhere; now it was in use as a center for refugees fleeing the peasants' revolt.

The volunteers in the building carried on the work of St. Francis, housing the widows of dead peasant fighters and their little fatherless children who huddled around them. Hundreds had streamed to Strasbourg from all over southern Germany. It was a city of refuge for the poor and the suffering, and for those whose faith differed from the Catholic Church, especially Anabaptists.

The hospitable Katherine and gracious Lucas Hackfurt administered the food, clothes, and medical supplies that the city gave to the refugees. Lucas worked full-time for the city in relief work, while Katherine volunteered her time. The two of them had worked out a manageable division of labor during the crisis that had been created by the revolt.

"Katherine tells me you've been seeing Margaret," Matthew said to Beck as they waited outside in the large open plaza. Shopkeepers all around the plaza had already opened their doors and windows for business. Later in the day, children would play across the plaza, musicians would prop up their hats and play to make a few pfennig, and a person could buy just about any kind of food desired.

"Yes, we've been visiting each other for several weeks now," Beck responded.

"It's a good thing for a man and woman to be together," Matthew said. "Love is a gift of God."

The women joined the men as Matthew launched into a little sermon about marriage right there in the square. "Marriage is one of the great ordinances of God. For too many centuries the Church required its priests to remain single. In the past two years several former Catholic priests, including of course, myself, have married." With a gleam in his eyes and a smile on his face, he exclaimed, "It's scriptural for a man, even a preacher and pastor, to be married!"

"What got this speech started?" Katherine wondered aloud.

"Oh, seeing these two together reminds me of the gift we've found in each other," Matthew answered with a twinkle. "And I hope others can find the same thing."

"There's no need to rush things, Matthew," Katherine responded. "They'll find their own way without any little lectures from you."

"True enough," the preacher answered. "Sermon ended."

At their lunch table in the square Beck announced his intention to go to Freiburg with Reublin and Müller for the next peasants' battle. He explained to his trio of lunch partners that he had studied and lived in Freiburg for several years and wanted to help negotiate a peace there, if at all possible.

"The city leaders in Freiburg will not give up easily, even with thousands of peasants in revolt," Beck explained to Margaret and the Zells. "I'm going to go and see if I can help resolve the differences. You'll keep your print shop going very well while I'm gone, Margaret."

"Beck, I've been managing the print shop for two years now by myself. You go do what you want and when you get back I'll be doing very well, thank you." Beck realized that Margaret had just established herself as the manager of her own enterprise; the shop was her business, but her quick smile signaled that he hadn't been rejected.

Beck chuckled. "You're a strong woman, Margaret. Sometimes I wonder what I'm getting myself into falling in love with you."

"Don't wonder about it" Katherine beamed. "Just accept it."

"A man thinks rationally; women think with their hearts," Matthew joked, grinning at Beck.

"Yes, and if women ran things there probably wouldn't be a peasants' war going on right now," Margaret shot back.

"Just thinking with your heart doesn't stop conflicts," Matthew said.

Katherine broke in. "This is going nowhere."

"And I've got to be going," Beck said. "Anybody want to join me for the journey? I should be back by Saturday."

Seeing no takers, Beck rose to leave, gave Margaret a hug, shook the Zells' hands, and left to get his leather travel bag in the small room he rented. It was a tiny place, with barely enough space to turn around, but he had a narrow bed, a chair, and a tiny table. Because it was near the plaza, Beck could swing by his room and head out the Butcher's Gate in just a few minutes.

This was a good week for Beck to travel, because his turn to watch Zieglers' barn came the following week. A few of the men took a week at a time sleeping in the barn or handling the needs of the refugees who lived in the granary. The handsome and eligible bachelor Jörg Ziegler was on for this week, so Christman could go back to sleeping in his own house.

Victory over the city of Freiburg, about fifty miles from Strasbourg, proved to be a high point in the war for the peasants. Müller's ragged army of more than eight thousand farmers had surrounded the city and laid siege to it for eight days. They cut off the water supply for the residents, who expected reinforcements but were disappointed when they never arrived.

Peasants in the countryside around Freiburg seethed at the unjust taxes imposed on them by the Catholic Church of southern Germany. The peasants to the east of Freiburg, around the Benedictine monastery of St. Peters, welcomed Müller's liberators. Most of the rebel fighters around St. Peters had heard *Twelve Articles* read to them because very few of them could decipher the words in the pamphlet for themselves.

The town clerk acted as messenger between the Freiburg city leaders and Müller's invaders. Beck had run into the clerk a few times when he had studied at the University in Freiburg. On the sixth day of the siege, he created an opportunity to talk with him.

"How long can the city hold out?" Beck asked.

"Perhaps a week, maybe ten days if we're lucky."

"Do you know where my friend Michael is these days?"

"Michael Wüst?" the clerk asked.

"No, Michael Sattler," Beck replied.

"Yes, I know Michael Sattler. He's a prior, second in charge under the abbot, over at St. Peter's monastery."

"Thanks for the information," Beck said to the clerk as

the messenger hurried out of the camp headquarters, back to his embattled city, about a mile and a half away.

That same day, Beck ran into Sattler in a tiny village on the road between Freiburg and the monastery. Beck learned that the peasants had "liberated" the monastery and "released" the priests the day before. In a plundering frolic, the poor farmers ate the food, drank the wine, took the money, destroyed the library, and burned the abbot's house.

"I'm not sure where I'm headed, Beck. With the siege of Freiburg and the capture of the monastery, our options are limited. Perhaps south," the gentle Sattler said, "to Zurich."

"To join the Anabaptists?"

Sattler glanced at his female friend and traveling companion. The two had known each other for years, and now both were leaving the Catholic Church, he a former monk and she a helper in a convent. He had already asked her to marry him, though neither knew where they could find a priest willing to marry them. She was fleeing from the frenzied peasants' attacks along with Sattler, even though she had served the poor in the area for years with acts of charity.

"I doubt it, Beck. We want to find a place where we can live safely and figure out what we believe. What do you know about the Anabaptists?"

"Two of them visited my friend Margaret's print shop last week," Beck answered. "One of their main beliefs is rebaptism, or baptism received after a public confession of faith in Christ. They also teach the way of peace, as they claim it is taught in the New Testament."

"You and I barely opened the Scriptures at the University of Freiburg," Sattler said as he stared toward the fighting in the west. "Why didn't we read it more?" At the university, where the two men had studied, the professors waited to see what the peasants would do to their buildings and Catholic books.

"We only had the Bible in Latin, Michael. Today, though, I'm learning more about the Scriptures."

"Luther's New Testament, ah, what a gift to our Germany," Sattler thoughtfully responded.

"Margaret, my friend with the print shop, is printing a statement on baptism right now, and she hopes to print Luther's German translation of the New Testament this fall."

Two farmers marched through the village, headed west, probably to the siege of Freiburg. Sattler and Beck concluded that they had better each head their own way to avoid trouble.

"Come to Strasbourg sometime and visit me, Michael. I believe you also know, from your university days, Wolfgang Capito, preacher at the church of St. Thomas in Strasbourg. He'd love to see you as well."

"Thanks for the invitation, Beck. For now, I—that is, we—want to find out more about the Brethren in Zurich. Maybe we can take you up on your offer and visit you in Strasbourg when things settle down. We'll see you again sometime."

Sturm and a Strasbourg council member came up the Rhine to negotiate the surrender at Freiburg. The two sat around a table in the cathedral, along with Müller, Seiler, and the mayor of Freiburg and his clerk, to write and sign the treaty of surrender. Sturm wore his official big-button coat.

The mayor of Freiburg was forced to join the Christian Union of the Black Forest region, a peasant organization, to supply artillery, troops, and supplies, to pay three thousand florins as a tribute for the costs of the siege, and to decide with the Union how to dissolve the convents and monasteries in the region.

While Sturm settled the surrender inside Freiburg, Beck found passage on a small boat headed down the Dreisam

River to the Rhine and Strasbourg. Sattler and his traveling companion, seekers on a common journey, walked south through the dense Black Forest toward Zurich. The turbulent religious and political conflicts of the decade were about to dramatically affect all of them.

Late Saturday morning Beck told Margaret, Leopold, Heinrich, and Peter about the siege and capture of Freiburg. Though their cleanup was just about finished, and the men were eager to leave for the day, Heinrich explained the beliefs about baptism he had found in the small pamphlet they were printing for Blaurock and Reublin.

"The Anabaptists believe baptism is only for those who choose to accept it, which doesn't include infants," Heinrich said.

"Radical beliefs," Margaret said.

"But are they based on Scripture?" Beck asked.

Heinrich jumped in. "It's hard for the average person to judge whether this pamphlet or any of the things we print are based on Scripture. So few copies of the Bible exist for us to examine." He buttoned his shirt and reached for his cap to leave.

"Sometime this summer or fall we must print a German translation of the New Testament so the people can read the Gospels for themselves," Margaret said.

"Or have it read to them," Leopold added. "Not many of us can read, Margaret, but we're eager to have others read for us."

"You're right, Leopold, which makes the character and teaching of our leaders that much more important. We can print pamphlets and even the four Gospels, but they must be interpreted for the people of Strasbourg and the Alsace region around us who can't read."

That evening Margaret and Beck walked along the canal with no particular destination in mind. In the midst of the many changes taking place around them—a Lutheran Reformation in the Catholic Church and a peasants' uprising that threatened Strasbourg itself—Margaret and Beck laughed, talked, and enjoyed their time together.

As Beck told her about his chance meeting with Sattler, the priest from St. Peter's monastery, Margaret wondered again what took men so long to decide about women. She was ready to plan for marriage, but in her day it was unheard of for a woman to ask a man to marry her, even though she might run her own business and manage every other part of her daily existence. She felt happy near Beck, though, and the strength of her optimism while wrapped in his arms matched the strength of the city walls as the gates closed for the night.

5

Butchering of the Peasants

Duke Antoine of Lorraine set out to crush the peasants' revolt. The duke and his noble friends didn't completely destroy the peasants, but they did manage to kill more than eighteen thousand. After the massacre at Saverne, north of Strasbourg, any hope for victory over the nobles vanished.

On Tuesday evening during the second week of May, Müller worked on sewing together a banner for his troops. Intense and focused, he was determined to bring the nobles to their knees. For several generations in south Germany, the badge of the rebel movement had been a heavy peasant boot. It was their primary stamp, sewn on their flags and banners alongside a Catholic religious symbol, such as a picture of Mary or a crucifix.

On a quick stopover in Strasbourg between battles, Müller met just inside the Elizabeth Gate with those who were interested in the peasants' war. The house stirred with the bustle of conversation, laughter, and opinions about the peasants' chances in the coming clash with Duke Antoine. "Hans, do you really think you can defeat the nobles?" Margaret asked the husky Swiss leader.

"We have so many angry farmers on our side, the duke will be forced to give in to our demands. He'll have to agree to every one of the twelve articles."

"But you'll have to fight him to get that."

"We're ready, determined, and unafraid."

They met in the home of Nicholas Kniebs, a man who

lived with his family on the narrow strip of land on the south-west side of the city between the two canals that circled Strasbourg. He stood within the circle of the Lutheran Reformation, but sympathized with the newcomers, the Anabaptists. Kniebs was a quiet man, but his home was frequently used for discussions and gatherings about the changing religious and social events of the mid-1520s. It took only about ten minutes to walk to Kniebs' house from Margaret's print shop.

"All we really want is what belongs to us," Müller began. "The nobles have stolen our grain and produce for so long, we don't know what it's like to earn an adequate living."

"What's your level of command?" Beck asked.

"Several of us will lead the next attack. I'll be in charge of the Altorf Band." Müller stretched the flag in his hands. "This flag, sewn right here in Strasbourg under the shadow of the Great Cathedral, will inspire my men to fight with courage and strength. We're tired of serving the count and men like him. They'll have to agree to the twelve articles when we're done with them!"

"Are you aware that Luther has condemned your violence?" Kniebs asked gently.

"I'd say Luther waffles in his beliefs, then," Müller shot back. "Four years ago he courageously stood up and confronted the emperor at the Diet of Worms. We'll soon take our stand against the nobles at Saverne and crush them."

Margaret grabbed the fabric and jabbed a needle through the banner with her left hand, stitching the finishing touches. She noticed Leopold, one of her pressmen, out in the kitchen discussing with two of Müller's men the upcoming fight. His balding head was unmistakable even as it became darker and harder to see clearly inside the house. Two lanterns vigorously fought the darkness, symbolic of the battle soon to come between the peasants and the overwhelming nobles.

Raising the banner that Margaret had just held, Müller

rejoiced. "Great! It's done. Who'll join me in the fight at Saverne? It's only a day's journey."

"On Friday we start the job for Anabaptist George Blaurock," Margaret replied. "Seems the Anabaptists in Switzerland want the world to know why they reject infant baptism. They also don't believe in fighting. What do you say to them?"

"There comes a time when men of faith must defend what's right, regardless of the cost. All I can figure is that the Anabaptists must want to keep the rich and powerful in control of their towns and farms."

"It seems the more we read from Luther's pamphlets and the sections of the Scripture that are available to us, peace makes sense," Beck responded to Müller. "Put the demands of your *Twelve Articles* together on the table with Blaurock's faith and I believe you'd have something powerful."

Müller wasn't listening anymore. He was in the kitchen talking to Leopold and the other men about plans for the next day.

Early the next morning Sturm and city council members fanned out to visit the merchants of Strasbourg. "Keep your men and business away from the revolt," Sturm warned Margaret. "Any Strasbourg citizen caught among them will be charged with treason. We're selling flour from the city's supplies to all citizens at a very reasonable price. Taxes on food are being lifted as long as the revolt lasts." It wasn't hard for anyone to figure out that the city council wanted to keep its citizens from leaving to join the rebels.

"Any news about your nephew?" Margaret asked.

"Not a thing, Margaret. Two weeks ago he vanished. We'll get to the bottom of it eventually."

Müller wouldn't be buying cheap food from the city council anytime soon. Neither would Leopold, Margaret's pressman. From their small houses near the Stone Street Gate, they left on a determined mission to join the Lower Alsatian peasant army. Jörg watched the men walk past his house on the way out of the city. "I hope you can defeat the duke," he thought to himself.

Nearly forty thousand peasants occupied the territory in and around the town of Saverne, which was a full day's walk northwest of Strasbourg. When Duke Antoine marched on the town and the peasants, Müller hastily wrote an appeal for help addressed to the citizens of Strasbourg. He reminded them of the many residents of Strasbourg in his army.

The leaders in Strasbourg, however, were in no mood to help the rebels. The peasants had stolen food from monasteries and robbed homes in the countryside. According to the religious establishment, Müller's troops had broken God's law.

The dreadful day of battle arrived on the fifteenth of May. The grizzled Müller fought alongside the optimistic Leopold. Farmers bravely held up their banners, waved them in the wind, and used whatever weapons they had, but the battle ended in a crushing defeat for the peasants. The duke's mounted cavalry cut down eighteen thousand of its enemy in a single afternoon. Their glittering swords sparkled in the sun, cutting, slicing, and dripping with blood.

A taunting noble charged Leopold on his horse, stabbed him, ran over him, trampled his flag, and left him to die on the battlefield. The duke cornered Müller but kept him to deal with later.

Another twenty thousand rebels, with nowhere to go, surrendered in humiliation. For most of them, going back to little farms situated on noble estates simply wasn't an option. If they returned to their homes, they'd be imprisoned, or worse.

It didn't take long for news of the pitiful results to reach the cathedral and Margaret's shop. Sturm hired the Knobloch press to print very important banners announcing the bishop's appearance in the city during the last week of May. As Beck lifted the announcements, allowed them to dry, then read one of them, he wondered how drastic the Catholic bishop's retaliation would be. Beck guessed the bishop would strike out hard.

From Wittenberg, several hundred miles to the northeast of Strasbourg, Luther followed the peasant uprising with growing alarm. At first he had cautiously supported the peasants, as Clement had explained to Matthew around the fire about two weeks earlier. But as the fighting grew worse, Luther supported the nobles and spoke out strongly against the peasants.

The Knobloch press had run copies of Luther's statement, which attacked the robbing and murdering hordes of peasants. Suddenly, the character of Luther's Reformation had changed. Or at least Margaret believed it had.

Reading *Christian Baptism* challenged Margaret's thinking. This was more than an ordinary print job. She eagerly read the ideas of an Anabaptist writer she didn't know, ideas that kept her attention and sparked her curiosity about the most radical elements of the Reformation.

In the introduction, the writer stated that he would have preferred to keep quiet about his beliefs, but he wrote the pamphlet in response to an attack on believers baptism by Ulrich Zwingli of Zurich. This writer didn't fear the light, and Margaret knew that a growing number of people in Strasbourg agreed with his beliefs.

Margaret, Heinrich, and Peter worked hard on the baptism pamphlet, though their progress was slow because they had to fill in for Leopold, whose body still lay exposed to the vultures somewhere north of Strasbourg. Occasionally, Margaret discussed the contents of the pamphlet with her plodding, floppy-capped compositor, Heinrich. A steady presence in the shop, Heinrich was always more than happy to discuss theology with Margaret.

In another print shop, not far away, the beautiful and available Agnes made a bold pass at Beck. She had stopped at the press he was managing, and he had to pause, look up, and listen. Usually shy and reserved, she looked directly at him and asked if he'd go on a short journey with her after work. "I have a letter to deliver to my uncle, near the White Gate," she said.

Beck had certainly noticed the Knobloch daughter. Her dark complexion, slender form, and conquering smile could melt any strong man's will to resist. Under the layers of clothing she wore around the print shop, Beck easily noticed her perfect figure. "I have other plans for this evening," he replied.

"It's very important that I make this journey, and I'd rather not travel alone."

Beck paused, glanced down at the ink that was drying on the paper he had just pressed, and wondered if one of her parents had put her up to this.

Though his hunch was accurate, she seemed to read his mind. "I've come to you on my own."

"As I've already said, I have other plans for this evening."

"Oh, please, Beck. Please go with me, just this one time. I'll make it worth your while." Most of the men in the shop would have said Beck was mad for turning down this gorgeous woman's advances. He thought he had been rescued when his partner walked up to the press to resume operations.

"I'll meet you right after quitting time, and my uncle will give us a good dinner, I'm sure," she said. With a quick smile that destroyed his will to resist, she brushed against him, turned, and hurried upstairs.

Beck figured he had about an hour to figure out an escape plan, then Magdalene approached his press and stopped. "The letter Agnes spoke to you about must be delivered this evening. I'd be most pleased if you'd escort her and bring her safely home. These are dangerous times for single young women to walk alone at night." Before Beck could respond, she was gone.

Just outside the door after work, Agnes was waiting for him. Without raising his voice, Beck said again, "I already have other plans for this evening."

"But I want to get to know you," she quickly answered.

"Perhaps another time," was the best Beck could offer as he hurried past her, away from the Knobloch press, and away from temptation.

"Beck, I need to hear you and some other people talk about these radical ideas on baptism," Margaret said.

Beck had just settled into a wooden chair and, slumped down to rest in her little print shop. "Sometimes you think too much, Margaret. Just print the document. Blaurock's guilders are as good as anyone else's."

"There are different beliefs around us, Beck. For centuries the Church has baptized infants. Several years ago, Luther almost dropped the practice, but now he's decided to keep it. The Anabaptists want to baptize only when there's a public confession of faith."

"Like I just said, sometimes you think too much."

Alone in her shop with the man she loved, Margaret soon diagnosed his frazzled mood and adjusted the room's settings to levels that helped him relax. Beck welcomed her simple remedies.

On Friday night, Kniebs joined Margaret and Beck on their journey to talk with the Zieglers at the barn.

"I wonder if Johann Knobloch ran his sword through Leopold yesterday," Margaret said as they crossed the two canals on the way to Jörg's house. "The Knoblochs upset me just about every time I think about them."

"A rivalry with the Knobloch daughter?" Kneibs asked.

"You've named it."

"They're also your business competition. Right, Margaret?"

"That's right. But they're so snobbish to me, I just can't stand it."

Jörg was happy to join the walkers on their way to his cousin's barn. "I'll bet the buzzards and the forest scavengers had a feast up there around Saverne today," he stated dryly. "Our world's about the same tonight, Margaret. Thousands die trying, but the powerful are still in control."

Robertsau lay just ahead of them. A few fires were burning here and there to push back the shadows and cook the evening meals. There weren't very many people on the road.

The Anabaptist woman from Switzerland and her child had found shelter by now in the converted Franciscan monastery, and during late May, no one else stayed in the barn. On the other side of the granary, no one had shuttled weapons in or out because the peasants had been so soundly beaten at Saverne. Most people sensed that the peasants' revolt had been dealt a fatal blow.

The men who volunteered to stay in the loft above the grain bin overnight still came on a regular basis, but they usually stayed away during the day unless they knew of unusual circumstances.

"Hello, brother Ziegler," Beck called out as they walked in the old couple's lane.

"Well, well, who do we have coming here tonight?" Clement cried out. "Are you here to find out if I helped the peasants at Saverne yesterday? Shall we talk about the Church, or do you just want some good food?"

"Your food's great, Clement," Margaret replied with a laugh, "and we'll eat some if you have any left, but I brought these stragglers along here to listen to us discuss the beliefs in a document I'm printing right now."

"Where's the writer from, Margaret?"

"I've never met him, but he's an Anabaptist from near Switzerland."

Clement looked up from the soup he had created over the fire. "I know of the ideas that went into *Twelve Articles*, my dear Margaret. Does that make the writer partly responsible for the slaughter of those farmers yesterday?"

"How much do you know about the Anabaptists, Clement?" Beck asked.

"Several have visited me here, and I hold many of their beliefs, but I'm no expert," he said as he patted his belly. His missing teeth were obvious when he smiled. "Anabaptists are different from the Catholic Church and Luther's new Reformation church. When they read something in the Bible, they want to act, make changes, and live according to what they've discovered."

"But why is rebaptism crucial to them?" Margaret asked.

"Oh, you're mistaken, Margaret. They don't want to rebaptize; they want to baptize those who make a genuine confession of Christ for the first time, as youths or adults. Of course, everyone they baptize these days has already been baptized as an infant."

The wind shifted, picked up speed, and turned cooler. In the distant sky, the little party at Clement's house could see storm clouds moving their way. They knew rain would soon follow.

"Weren't some Anabaptists involved in the peasants' war, Clement?" Margaret asked.

"Sure," Clement responded. "As with any new movement—theirs is only a few months old—you have a variety of beliefs and practices. Most, however, believe in peace and nonresistance. The author of your little pamphlet about believers baptism probably helped generate ideas for the *Twelve Articles* you printed. Both pamphlets were written for the average person, or for that matter, anyone who will accept the ideas."

"We'd better soon get back to the city," Kniebs said to his travelers. "It's going to rain."

"One more question, please, Clement," Margaret said quickly.

"Go right ahead."

"How will these Anabaptists survive if no one protects them? The Bishop of Strasbourg protects his own, Luther has the nobles to defend him, but who will support the Anabaptists?"

"Margaret, we have to go," Beck said as the men started to walk away. They could hear the thunder rolling toward them.

"Read that document you're printing carefully, Margaret," Ziegler shouted as they walked out the lane. "You'll probably find your answers in there."

"Thanks for your time, Clement," Margaret shouted, as the four city residents hurried for the Stone Street Gate. Inside the city walls a soaking rain drenched them. Margaret tightly clutched the leather pouch in which she carried the statement on believers baptism. With her other hand she held on tightly to Beck as they made a dash for the print shop.

Much later, Beck tried to avoid the mud puddles as he walked back to the barn for his night watch. It was his week to be on duty.

The demanding Catholic Bishop of Strasbourg hadn't come to town during the last week of May on a friendly pastoral visit. It had been two weeks since the nobles had slaughtered the peasants at Saverne. With his executioner behind him, the bishop was on tour to render justice to captured peasants.

Just outside the Cronenbourg Gate, on the north side of the city, heads would roll. Beck spotted Müller among the prisoners. His enormous fists were clenched and his burly arms tense. There was no way out. The bishop's measures were swift and sure; his executioner would chop off six heads early the next morning as a demonstration that little had changed as a result of the peasants' uprising. Economically, of course, he was right: The peasants wouldn't experience significant improvements on their farms and fields for another two hundred years.

But the Roman Catholic Church had split wide open. Men like Matthew Zell had challenged beliefs and practices that had been in place for more than a thousand years. The Lutheran Reformation had worked up storm clouds for the Catholic Church.

Had either the Bishop of Molsheim or Luther talked to Margaret, however, they might have noticed lightning in the distance. A radical reformation was about to ignite flames more threatening to the old order than even Luther's shower of sparks.

About two hours after midnight, while the city slept, a tall, shadowy figure crept up the side of the bank outside the Cronenbourg Gate. Soaking wet from his swim across the canal, he scaled the steep incline leading to the bank where the bishop's prisoners waited through their last night on earth.

Müller saw the sneaking form coming and realized that maybe there'd be one more chance to escape the blade set to whack his head off in the morning. Christman pulled himself on his stomach to Müller's side and with a sharp knife began quietly cutting the ropes that bound his wrists and ankles. The wretched guard snored.

When Müller was free, he turned to the other men and began working on their ropes. Christman quickly slid away, down the incline, back into the water, and across the canal. The water was cold and the air made him colder yet, but he waited for the men on the other side of the canal. Five men slipped across, but the sixth man apparently didn't know how to swim, so he stayed behind.

Without waiting, Christman gave the order, "Follow me." In about fifteen minutes, they had skirted the northeast side of the city and soon spotted the outline of the old barn on the dark horizon.

"Everybody take a different route," Christman demanded, "and I'll meet you there." The men fanned out and arrived at the barn from five directions.

The brisk May night had chilled the escapees, but there were no dry clothes to put on. Awake now, Beck jumped down from the loft and met Christman. He recognized Müller, but none of the others.

"We've got to get out of here, fast," Müller grunted.

"You can stay here and get warm in the hay," Beck replied.

"Not me," the toughened peasants' war leader answered. "I'm headed to the Black Forest. Who's with me?"

Four cold men nodded agreement, but before they could go, Christman offered to get them some food. Rapping softly on the Zieglers' door, he awakened the generous preacher's wife. When Christman explained what he needed, Gertrude emptied out her bread bin and offered it to him.

"Much obliged," the night visitor replied.

Müller lunged at the food, and he and the other men devoured it on the spot. In a moment after Christman pointed them toward the bridge, they were gone. Before Beck could respond, Christman turned and headed back out the lane.

At the bridge, the fugitives knocked the guard unconscious, opened the gate, and hurried across into the dense and dark Black Forest.

For now, the men had escaped, but Beck knew that if they were ever captured and tortured, they could identify both him and Christman. Then the old barn's secret would be out and he'd be sent to the Hangman's Tower himself.

The next morning, the embarrassed bishop was enraged that his guard had allowed five men to escape in the middle of the night. After the one remaining prisoner was executed, two guards paid for the mistake with their own heads.

Part II

June-July 1525

6

Frolic at the Summer Fair

A thunderstorm dumped a welcome rain shower on the merchants assembled for Strasbourg's annual summer fair. Nobody seemed to mind the rain; it drove the sweltering heat away, washed the brick cobblestone roads, and refreshed the crops growing just outside the city walls.

For at least a hundred years, and maybe more, Strasbourg's merchants had held an annual business fair to show off their products and wares. People from the western mountains and the eastern forests up and down the Rhine valley gathered there for an exchange of ideas and goods, and to see the products of other merchants. Bigger cities in France, Germany, Italy, and Russia held larger and more well-known fairs, but Strasbourg's grand summer market helped the local economy and brought buyers and sellers from far and wide.

The fresh air after the storm lifted everyone's spirits. From St. Martin's Church near the cathedral to the Franciscan monastery, dealers lined up to show off their merchandise. Wandering visitors looked at ribbons and silks from Paris or Florence, textiles from England, and furs from Switzerland. Local merchants sold white or gray cloth, a heavy-duty, black linen and wool mixture, or practical, essential fabrics for sturdy, warm garments.

Margaret carefully examined material for a dress she wanted to make. Though she had one less worker at the shop, Heinrich and Peter had made progress with the Anabaptist document on baptism, so today she and Beck were able to take a break and enjoy each other's company at the fair.

"What color do I look best in?" Margaret asked.

"It doesn't matter much to me," Beck answered.

"Isn't this gray cloth just beautiful?"

"It sure is, Margaret. How much do you need to make a dress?"

"Oh, let's look around some more for just the right texture and fabric."

In the mix of the people who reappeared after the storm, two men made their way through the crowd looking for Margaret and Beck. When they had asked at the print shop, Heinrich had told them to look for the couple in the market area.

With good food for sale at inexpensive prices, Blaurock and Seiler stopped by a small window, ordered two dinners, and sat down at a little table to wait. They scanned the crowd in the plaza.

"This place hasn't changed much, even with the peasants' revolt," Seiler observed.

"Yes. The rich still rule and the Church stays the same," Blaurock added. He tapped his fingers on his stomach—he was hungry. They had left Zurich three days earlier and this was their first real meal.

While the Swiss men ate, Christman spied Seiler sitting at the table. They had fought together in the Black Forest against Count Rudolf and had met with Margaret and Beck at the bridge about six weeks earlier. He went to the table and asked, "How are you, Seiler?"

"Well," he responded. He wiped his left hand and stuck it out to shake Christman's left hand. "Join us, will you?"

"I'd be pleased to, Seiler. Who's your partner?"

"This is George Blaurock, from Zurich. We're here to pick up a pamphlet from Margaret."

"What's it about?"

"Baptism," Blaurock answered through a mouthful of food.

"Are you an Anabaptist?"

Blaurock nodded once in the affirmative while he chewed on a tough piece of beef.

Christman clenched his fists and flexed his biceps as he said, "I wish we had some leaders in Strasbourg with the courage of the Anabaptists. What's the latest in Zurich?"

"Hey, there's the couple we're looking for," Seiler interrupted. "I'll be right back."

He headed into the plaza and invited them to join the trio. Blaurock added two more chairs to the table.

It was an odd assortment. Seiler attacked his food while the heavily bearded and balding Blaurock ate his dinner like someone who'd had lots of practice; his stout belly proved that he liked to eat. Christman, formerly from southern Germany and now a member of the cloth makers' guild in Strasbourg, towered over the others.

"I assume the three of you know each other," Seiler asked Margaret, Beck, and Christman.

"That's right," Margaret answered. If only he knew the details, she thought to herself.

"And you remember George Blaurock?" Seiler asked.

"Yes," Margaret replied.

"George was ready to inform us on happenings in Zurich," Christman stated. "Among the Anabaptists."

Blaurock scowled as he wiped his mouth and began the update. "A growing number of families have refused to baptize their babies. The cathedral pastor, Ulrich Zwingli, has us on the run, wants us out of his territory. It seems Zwingli led us to the water, then didn't let us drink. Don't get me wrong; he did a lot of good things for us, like getting rid of icons and images in the cathedral and abolishing the Mass. But then he tried to restrain us when the Zurich Council wouldn't support him anymore."

"I assume you're here to pick up your pamphlet on believers baptism?" Beck asked.

"We are," Seiler answered. "Is it ready?"

"By tomorrow or the next day," Margaret replied. "I have one bundle ready to go, and the second is almost finished."

"Good," Blaurock said as he finished his third piece of bread. "Great food here in Strasbourg."

"Yes," Christman answered. "Our food's quite good, and we put on a nice fair. But our Church reforms are going slowly." He flexed his biceps again. "We need change, here, now, in the Church. Where did you start in Zurich?" Christman asked.

"Zwingli helped us last year to tear down the icons, images, and ornaments in the cathedral," Blaurock answered.

"A great place to begin," Christman responded. He turned to look at the cathedral steeple rising above the houses and buildings in the plaza. "Several of us have been talking about that very thing in recent days. It's time to get rid of the icons and statues in that cathedral."

Holding the package of fabric in her lap, Margaret turned toward Christman with a serious look. "What good will that do?"

"You've got to start somewhere." Christman glanced around him see who might be listening, then continued. "We failed in the peasants' revolt. Now it's time to start in the city, right in the cathedral. They did it in Luther's Wittenberg and they've done it in Zurich."

"What's the goal?" Margaret asked him.

"The old has to go. Let's bring in the new."

"Do you have any idea what the new is?"

Blaurock noticed Margaret's sharp comeback and proposed an idea. "Zwingli wrote a pamphlet last year about icons in the house of God. He made a forceful statement for change. Maybe you ought to print that document here in Strasbourg, Margaret."

"I'll print for paying customers like you, George," Margaret said. "And I'm for the Reformation, but I'm not a revolutionary. Listen, there's a house church meeting tonight over at Nicholas Kniebs's. All three of you are welcome. We'll leave when the bells chime for the evening service. Join us if you'd like."

At a wooden bench along the footpath by the canal, Margaret turned to Beck and said, "I've known you for nearly three months, but I don't know much about your parents."

"I'd love to take you up the Rhine to Waldshut," Beck replied. "It's a beautiful little town along the river between Switzerland and Germany. I hope we can visit my home before too long."

"I'd like to meet your mother. With my parents not living any longer, I'd love to meet your whole family."

With an arm around her, Beck agreed. "You're right, Margaret. You don't know much about me. I have two sisters living near Waldshut too. My brother lives in northern Germany."

Margaret smiled and glanced into Beck's eyes. "A trip this fall would really be beautiful," she suggested, "with the leaves in the Black Forest changing into fall colors." She rested her head on his shoulder. The shadows along the canal grew longer as the day moved toward evening.

"Let's get something to eat before we head over to Kniebs's house," Margaret offered. "Your place or mine?"

They laughed as they stood to go. It was always Margaret's place. Beck couldn't even stand up all the way in his tiny room. He slept there but he couldn't entertain guests.

"We're off to Margaret's little print shop."

"Again," Margaret teased.

When the bells chimed for Vespers, the evening prayer service, the action began. Luther's foot soldiers spread out across the city to three of the Catholic parishes and the great cathedral itself. Christman and three other fearless men led the raid to remove all icons from the church buildings.

"The second commandment forbids the use of idols," Christman told his men. "You shall not make for yourself an idol. The Bible supports us in our plan to destroy these godless images that are evil before the Lord. Luther himself has removed them in Wittenberg."

Christman led the unlawful attack on the images at the cathedral. They destroyed paintings, scooped up relics, and smashed the baptismal font used for baptizing babies. Though Christman's men didn't oppose the baptism of babies, they saw the highly decorative and expensive basin as an idol and they believed that God wanted them to pitch it out. Only a few faithful gathered for the service that evening, and they soon scattered, as did the priest who was there to read the Latin ritual.

At one end of the merchant booths near the fair, one of Christman's partners led the strike in St. Martin's parish, a church much smaller than the cathedral. They attacked the paintings, statues, relics, and main altar. In fifteen minutes they created a lot of damage. They either smashed the images where they found them or pitched them out into the streets.

Another man took a group and invaded the Church of St. Thomas. They wrecked the silver images, threw out the paintings of the saints and martyrs, and broke the case that held a piece of wood, supposedly from the cross on which the apostle Thomas had been crucified.

"God was angry with Israel for setting up idols in their temple," their leader told the six men who were helping him to cleanse the church. "Eventually God tore down Israel's temple."

On the west side of the city, by the White Gate, St. Aurelie's third collaborator broke into the parish of St. Aurelie and ruined whatever he could get his hands on. The big, glimmering cross was ripped down. "Idolatry!" his men shouted. They smashed the altar and cut up the paintings. When they came to the grave of St. Aurelia, which lay in a side chamber of the church, their leader gave an unusual order. "Open the tomb and see if that old woman's really in there. Find out if we've been lied to all these years."

With a couple of tools they pried the lid off the tomb. When the men looked in they saw only a few decaying remains.

"Pitch them into the street" were the orders. The clatter of bones scooting across the cobblestone road signaled the end of their destruction. It hadn't lasted more than twenty minutes. Christman had given instructions to meet along the canal by St. Thomas Church when they were finished.

"Don't give them anybody's name if they question you," Christman warned. "The city council will need to act like they're upset, but the truth is that they agree with the Reformation movement. They like Luther and the changes he stands for. We'll be safe if we can keep out of sight for a while. Return to your homes, men. May God bless Martin Luther and the new faith he's brought to the church."

"How can you justify the use of violence to change the church, Christman?" Margaret asked angrily. The meeting at Kniebs's house had already started when Christman arrived.

"King Josiah cleaned the temple and threw out the idols," he growled in his deep, distinctive voice. "You know that when King Solomon allowed the idols of his foreign wives to be set up in the temple of God, it led to his downfall."

"Yes, and Christ himself cleansed the temple of the merchants before his own crucifixion," Blaurock added. "There is a time for action and holy anger, but we're discovering in Zurich that Christ set up a church that doesn't need brick and stone buildings to meet in."

"We want to remove the Catholic priests and establish Lutheran preachers in their place," Christman responded.

"Then we can protect the true church of Christ."

"Did Christ have protection when he was crucified?" Margaret asked.

The Thursday-evening meeting at Kniebs's house gave those who attended the freedom to ask whatever questions they wanted to ask. Fast, thorough, and long-reaching changes had erupted in 1525. Kniebs's safe-haven living-room gathering gave Anabaptists and other dissenters a chance to talk about their fears, hopes, and dreams.

"The city council will protect us, even though they may need to make an example of someone to show that they're in charge," Chrisman predicted.

"And to keep the bishop happy," Beck added.

"In Zurich, we don't need a bishop or a cathedral," Blaurock told the group. "We meet in homes, as the early church did. We have no altars, no images, no paintings, and no relics. Only God, our faith, and each other."

"Soon we may not have our heads left," Seiler answered sharply. "We're going to need protection or our little communities may crumble."

"If good Christians were in charge of the city council in Strasbourg," Chrisman interjected, "we could bring about radical changes."

The force of his declaration startled Margaret. "Christians *are* in charge," she said. "But it seems that Luther's Reformation is forcing us to choose which type of Christian we want to associate with. Catholics in the parishes, Lutheran preachers here and there, like Matthew Zell, and Anabaptists, like Blaurock and Seiler."

"You need to know that Anabaptists believe in the way of nonresistance," Blaurock said to everyone, but to Chrisman in particular. "Christ died on the cross to save us from our sins, but also to show us a new way to live."

"What will you do when they start to execute all of you

peaceful Anabaptists?" Christman asked skeptically, eyeing Blaurock.

"Give up our lives like Christ did, I suppose," he answered. "Jesus told Peter to put his sword away. I believe that we must put ours away as well."

"I'm not convinced regarding nonresistance," Seiler said. "I guess that's why I joined the peasants' revolt. I need to learn more before I can accept the way of peace."

Margaret sensed that Seiler was prepared to defend himself whenever needed. He'd go down fighting before they chopped off his other hand.

By the time the sun had risen over the cathedral Friday morning to shine in Margaret's print shop, city guards had grabbed Christman. He stood erect and confident, ready for questioning before the Strasbourg City Council.

"Were you the instigator of the violence last night?" Sturm asked sternly.

"I participated," Christman answered.

"You will need to swear a new oath to the city in order to stay, obligating you to obey all rules and not carry out any more violence against sacred objects. And you will pay a five-guilder fine. Otherwise you must leave the city at once."

After a break to allow the head of the cloth makers' guild to reason with Christman, he flexed his muscles, clenched his teeth, and decided that paying the fine and swearing the city oath again were better than leaving Strasbourg for good.

"We won't be so easy on you the next time, Kenlin," Sturm warned.

By evening Christman was back in his home near the Stone Street Gate, angry and wondering what he would do next. Thinking about how the bearded button-man had tried to frighten him, however, made Christman laugh out loud.

Christman and the men who had joined him in ransacking

the churches the night before wanted change. Now. As the shadows lengthened and the bells chimed for Vespers, he leaned back on his three-legged stool and schemed up a trip to visit Zurich. He wanted to meet with Seiler, Blaurock, and other Anabaptists. Their reformation seemed to be going better than the one in Strasbourg. He needed answers and ideas before he would act again.

"Could I get Margaret to go along?" he wondered.

7

Defense of Marriage

Wolfgang Capito wanted to get married. Problem was, he had spent all of his life serving the Catholic Church as a scholar, teacher, and a priest, which meant that when he was ordained, he had given up the possibility of getting married, ever.

Only a few months earlier, at age thirty-two, Wolfgang had moved to Strasbourg to become the pastor of the Church of St. Thomas, not far from Margaret's print shop. St. Thomas was one of the Catholic parishes that Christman's men had sacked.

Soon after arriving in Strasbourg, though, Wolfgang had been listening to—and agreeing with—the convincing sermons of Matthew Zell. And it wasn't long before he had joined the Lutheran Reformation.

Preachers like Matthew and Wolfgang were Protestants, a term that would come into use in the 1530s. They *protested* many of the teachings and practices of the Catholic Church, which had controlled Europe for more than a thousand years.

In about the ninth century, for reasons hardly anyone could remember or explain, the pope had decreed that priests and others who worked in the Church could no longer get married. Priests who were married at that time had to choose between their wives and the Church; some left the church altogether and others separated from their wives. Church leaders had taken a few of the writings of the apostle Paul on remaining single and applied them to those who wanted to be priests, monks, and nuns.

When the clear-eyed and wheezing asthmatic Wolfgang announced to the city of Strasbourg that he wanted to get married, the Catholic authorities immediately challenged him. Strasbourg in 1525 had both Catholic and Lutheran church services. A few but growing number of Anabaptists lived in the city as well, meeting secretly in homes. The Bishop of Molsheim decided that when a man of Wolfgang's status decided to break with the tradition and teaching of the Church he had pledged to uphold, he must be questioned and confronted.

The truly surprising factor in Wolfgang's announcement was that the woman he wanted to marry was none other than the lovely Agnes Knobloch, daughter of one of the most powerful Catholic families in the city. The news puzzled Beck. He was relieved that she would not be chasing him anymore, but he couldn't figure out how Wolfgang and Agnes could have even known each other, much less courted and gotten engaged. Johann and Magdalene, Agnes's protective, domineering, and staunchly Catholic parents, would no doubt have shielded her from the Lutheran pastor.

Margaret learned about the Capito-Knobloch engagement from Beck, who heard about it from the men at work. From a business perspective, the news made her anxious. With more than twenty print shops operating in Strasbourg, the Knoblochs ran one of the largest. Margaret worried that if Agnes married a Lutheran, against her parents' wishes, it might make life more difficult for small print shops like hers that were printing books and pamphlets in support of the Reformation.

Margaret went to talk with Katherine about this turn of events. "Your husband will be key to Wolfgang's success in getting married and not imprisoned or run out of the city, Katherine."

"That's true," Katherine answered, "but I'm not worried, and you shouldn't be either."

"Too many times I've watched the Knoblochs push other people around. They're powerful people. Johann's mother tried to ruin my father's business years ago."

"We're dealing here with a couple getting married, Margaret. Matthew will be able to convince the city council to support the marriage."

Matthew walked into the kitchen to join the women.

"The bishop has decided to make an example out of Wolfgang," he said. "Wolfgang has written many articles and books for the Catholic Church. He's an intellectual, and he'll be a powerful spokesman for the Lutheran Reformation. But his marriage is where the bishop will try to draw the line."

"What's the bishop's plan of action?" Margaret asked.

"He's ordered five clergymen in Strasbourg to appear before him at Molsheim within five days."

"Who are they?" Katherine asked.

"Wolfgang, of course, plus relief worker Lucas Hackfurt, and two others," Matthew said.

"Who's the fifth, Matthew—is it you?" Katherine asked anxiously.

"Yes," Matthew said, tapping his fingers on the table. "We need a plan of action, and we need it soon."

"What are we going to do?" Katherine asked.

"First, Margaret," Matthew said to his guest, "can you print copies of Luther's book that defends marriage for priests?"

"I believe we could work it in very soon."

"Second, Wolfgang and I should preach sermons this Sunday on God's plan for men and women in marriage. Third, the five of us need to appeal to the city council for protection."

By the next morning, Saturday, the Bishop of Molsheim had excommunicated the five ministers. An agent of the bishop posted their names and the reason for their excommunication on the doors of the cathedral and of the nine parish churches located throughout the city. Underneath the powerful bishop's signature appeared the signature of the Archbishop of Mainz, the next level of Catholic Church authority.

Meanwhile, Matthew and Wolfgang prepared their sermons for Sunday and went to visit Jacob Sturm.

"We need the city council to plead our case before the bishop," Matthew began.

"The people of our churches and many of the citizens of Strasbourg will stand behind you," Wolfgang wheezed. He wore a funny little, round, black cap and always had his collar turned up.

"You realize, of course, that the bishop's power carries the full weight of the Catholic Church," Sturm lectured. "Beyond that, the emperor is at the pope's mercy."

"Yes," Matthew responded, "but Strasbourg is an imperial free city. Emperor Charles won't challenge Strasbourg unless the people support the pope's actions. And most of the people in this city are in favor of priests getting married."

"Don't let the bishop intimidate you, Jacob," Wolfgang added. "The city council must establish its own identity and power if the Lutheran Reformation is ever to take hold here."

Sturm was a thoughtful and balanced man. "I'll take it up with the council on Monday morning," he replied.

While the Strasbourg City Council chairman met with the two preachers and talked about the marriage of former Catholic priests, Beck put in his last Saturday-morning hours for the week at the Knobloch print shop. He wasn't sure if he wanted to talk to Agnes or not, but he did want to find out how she and Wolfgang had become acquainted. When she walked through the shop on her way to the stairs that led up to the Knobloch residence on the second floor, he summoned the courage to intercept her.

"Agnes, may I speak with you?" She stopped and looked at him, but didn't say a word. "I hear you're engaged to Wolfgang."

Nodding ever so slowly, she confirmed the news. "It's true."

"I wasn't even aware you knew him."

"He didn't turn me down, Beck, like you did. I'm so eager to get out of this house. You had your chance."

Their eyes met for a moment, and then she quickly turned to leave. Not knowing what else to say, Beck blurted out, "Let me know if I can help."

Word spread through the Stone Street Gate area and out into the countryside to Clement's farm that Matthew Zell and Wolfgang Capito would preach on marriage. People who rarely attended church planned to attend.

The Church of St. Thomas had a "chapter" governing its religious affairs. The chapter of St. Thomas included members of the nobility, merchant families like the Knoblochs, priests, religious experts, and scholars. They planned to stop Wolfgang from preaching on Sunday. But Matthew's popularity secured his position in the cathedral enough to ensure that there would be no trouble there.

"Marriage is established by God," Matthew boomed from his wooden pulpit on Sunday. "Peter and the other apostles married, and leaders in the early church took wives for hundreds of years before the Catholic Church required celibacy of its priests. Living as a single person is a high calling of God, but requiring this of all clergy is a human tradition.

"Further, the bishop should clean up his own house before condemning priests who want to marry. We all know that some priests break their vows and father children, though they are not married. How much better in the eyes of God if the priests and nuns who claim to live devoutly would simply get married. I call on the Bishop of Molsheim to put right the churches, monasteries, and convents here in Strasbourg. Eradicate them of the immorality inside, before condemning Christian priests who have honored God with holy matrimony."

Sturm squirmed in his seat. "Matthew is right," he thought, "but the city council still has to face the power of the bishop, the pope, and the emperor. How can we resolve this dilemma?"

Meanwhile, at St. Thomas, the powerful Church authorities literally stood in the way of Wolfgang, blocking him from entering the pulpit. The people of the parish, however, had other ideas. They came with their hoes, rakes, and sticks to give Wolfgang the chance to speak. They moved into the aisles and side wings of the church and stood shoulder-to-shoulder around the church, waiting for him to climb into the pulpit. When the Catholic officials saw the citizens of the city supporting their preacher, they backed down and let him speak. The large crowd included Clement.

"Our text today is from the book of Genesis," Wolfgang began. "God established marriage in the Garden of Eden when he created Eve and presented her to Adam. A vow not to get married violates God's wishes.

"Refraining from marriage leads to sexual sins and disorder in the Church. Marriage is God's way of allowing us to express our sexual desires in the proper way. The Bible doesn't say that those who remain single live on a higher spiritual level than those who get married. True, those who remain single can serve God in a more focused way, but even the apostle Paul did not condemn married men and women to a lower level before God.

"There comes a time when traditions must change," Wolfgang nearly shouted. He wanted everyone in the church to hear what he was saying, so he had to speak as loud as he could. "Luther is right. Marriage is not a sacrament; rather it's a living and honorable ceremony of a man and a woman before God, uniting themselves to raise children in a Christian home. Luther himself has married. It is time for the priests of Strasbourg to have the same privilege."

Action proceeded on two fronts on Monday morning. Christman, Jörg Ziegler, and others ransacked the Dominican convent near the White Gate. The nuns left quickly or moved to other convents.

Just a short time later, Christman and Jörg broke into the Augustinian monastery nearby and drove the scurrying monks away. They removed the paintings, images, and icons, and smashed the altar in the chapel. When the Bishop of Molsheim got word later in the day of these actions, he realized that his grip on the Church in Strasbourg had been seriously weakened.

On the second front, the city council took up the question of priests who had married. "If we enforce the bishop's ban on the priests, we anger the people," Sturm told the council as he fingered his buttons. "But if we ignore the ban, we risk having the entire citizenry of Strasbourg excommunicated. The emperor would be forced to act on the ban, and we'd have to fight to defend ourselves."

"We must make an example of these priests." Johann Knobloch frowned as he spoke to the council. "Who are they to violate the traditions of the Roman Catholic Church?"

"This letter from Emperor Charles V was sent to all the lands under his control," said Jacob Meyer, the self-appointed city inspector who served on the council as a representative of the mason's guild. "It demands that we follow the decisions of the Diet of Worms. As you all know, four years ago at that diet, the emperor and the pope declared their opposition to marriage for priests. The emperor now reminds us that we are obligated to carry out this edict."

"I have an idea," Sturm offered. "The next diet is to be held at Speyer, in January of next year. The emperor's representatives will gather with Church officials and representatives from the imperial cities, including Strasbourg. Let's ask the bishop to postpone any decision on banning marriage for priests in Strasbourg until there's a ruling on the matter in January. If we call for the Church to deal with priests who live in sin, we may have more leverage to protect Zell, Capito, and the others. I say we ask the bishop for more time."

With reluctance, the Bishop of Molsheim accepted the city council's request and agreed to wait on disciplining priests who married until the diet could rule on the matter. He had few options, however, as so many of the citizens and residents of Strasbourg defended the marriage of priests. Wolfgang would be able to marry Agnes as long as he could get her Catholic parents to cooperate.

Johann and Magdalene, however, were anything but cooperative. Aghast at their daughter's secret romance with the non-Catholic preacher, they were embarrassed among their friends in the cathedral. True, their daughter had found a man who, apparently, could afford marriage and would give her a financially stable home, but their future son-in-law was Lutheran, of all things!

For the moment, the relationship between daughter and parents appeared to be a draw. She had found an eligible and responsible man who could provide her with a decent life, the marriage had been publicly announced, and the Knoblochs were not willing to block the marriage just yet. They had an older daughter who was still looking for a man. Though the younger sister was much more beautiful and could find a man easily, they didn't like the thought of two daughters in their house long term. For now the situation was tolerable, though less than ideal.

Wolfgang had arranged a meeting with the Knobloch parents, but their relationship would remain very formal. Perhaps they could get to know each other better later on. Meanwhile, Agnes continued to find ways of disappearing every once in a while to visit the local preacher. And they weren't discussing theology.

Margaret put her print shop into high gear to carry out Matthew's first suggestion, a Strasbourg edition of Luther's defense of marriage for priests. Luther had written at least four documents on Christian marriage in which he instructed priests, monks, and nuns to get married. His longest statement on marriage had been printed only three years earlier. In the same month, Luther himself had married a former nun. When he left the monastery, he too gave up his "man-made vow" to never marry.

Margaret decided to summarize Luther's main ideas about marriage in a small pamphlet that could be printed quickly and easily distributed. After conversations with the ever-positive Matthew, she was confident that the citizens of Strasbourg would pay at least half a gulden to buy and read Luther's ideas about marriage. Though only about twenty percent of the citizens in Strasbourg could read, Margaret supposed they would buy the pamphlet and read it aloud to those who couldn't.

"What a great way for you and Beck to review the basics of Christian marriage," Matthew said to Margaret as they worked at summarizing Luther's main points. "Your print shop stands at the crossroads of a new era, Margaret. Beliefs about marriage are bound to change as more priests marry and as more people learn what the Bible says on the subject."

Stunned, Margaret stopped her work and flashed a stare at her friend. "We're not engaged yet, Matthew. Don't rush things."

"Sorry. I stepped over the line on that one."

To get the conversation moving in a different direction,

Margaret announced a bold plan. Resuming a more relaxed stance, she said, "We must print a German language Bible in this shop. It would be a huge investment of time, energy, and money, but I believe people would buy copies of the Bible, and it would pay off."

"You're always thinking about business, aren't you, Margaret?"

"You have to think about whether the product will pay for itself."

"Oh, that's true, Margaret, but there are times when you have to do what's right and best, even though it may not pay off. Wouldn't you agree?"

"Yes, like your sermon this past Sunday on Christian marriage. And what about the one hundred thousand peasants who died trying to change the old way of serfdom, working their whole lives for rich nobles? Did they do the right thing, or were they just foolish?"

"I don't believe they did the right thing at all. Their revolution was not what Luther had in mind."

"You talk so much about Luther. Is Luther always right?"

"I suppose he's human, but for now he's our leader in the Reformation of the church."

"What about the baptism of infants, Matthew?" Heinrich the printer broke in. "Do you think the Bible supports this practice?"

"You probably know that Luther almost adopted the practice of believers baptism," Matthew responded, "but he finally decided to keep infant baptism as one of the ceremonies of his new church."

"Why?" Margaret asked.

"How can you have a church if not everyone in the territory is registered as an infant?"

"The church depends on registering infants in a given territory?"

"I'm not sure what you're asking. How would you know who your members were otherwise?"

"Why not allow the people to choose whether they want to be a part of the church?" Heinrich asked. "The Brethren in Zurich operate that way."

"You mean those Anabaptists," Matthew said in a harsh tone. "They're radicals, rejecting virtually everything the church stands for and holds to be true. Luther has no time for them. Let's get this summary pamphlet printed and to the people. Long live the Reformation!"

Margaret didn't want to continue arguing with Matthew. She sensed that the greatest difference in belief among the Catholics, Lutherans, and Anabaptists was their understanding of the church.

Tonight it actually was Beck's place. Because it was his week to watch the barn at night, Margaret decided to walk him to the Zieglers' farm.

They climbed the old wooden ladder up to the haymow, then scrambled further up through the hay to his little loft. There he showed her a mat, a thin blanket, a chunk of wood that served as a chair, and his small bag of clothes. No frills there.

The most interesting part of the tour, however, was the grain bin down below. Though the peasants' war was almost over, a collection of weapons stood watch, propped up in a line like a picket fence along the west wall in the first bin. The arsenal had served a generation of peasant rebels, and if the authorities didn't discover the room, it would likely remain as a storage room for the next skirmish.

Far too dusty for an actual printing press, the second bin stored finished pamphlets and books, hidden away from the powers that might destroy them. "If Blaurock doesn't show up soon to pick up his pamphlets on believers baptism," Margaret thought, "I'll store them here."

In one side of the small chamber, Beck and Margaret examined a big bundle of books. A printer from nearby Worms had shipped a bundle of the new English translation of the New Testament to the barn for safekeeping. In a sudden turn of events, the printer learned that his books would be allowed in London, and he began shipping them downstream to Amsterdam, then to England. The heavy bundle was wrapped tightly, but the two printers did manage to pry one copy loose. Not being able to read a word of English, though, all they could do was admire the quality of the printing and binding.

"We have to print one of these in German," Margaret declared.

"Why do you say 'we'?"

"Are you going to work for the Knoblochs forever, Balt?" She had never called him that before, though she sort of liked the shortened version of his first name, Balthasar. Everyone referred to him by his last name, Beck.

"No, but it makes me the money I need to rent a real room somewhere."

By the time they had tucked the English Bible back into its package, it had grown dark outside, and inside the barn it was almost pitch black.

With little else to do there, they headed back toward the print shop, taking the route along the canal. In the midst of small talk, they reflected on the rapid-fire changes taking place around them and the variety of beliefs and practices. Three main religious groups competed in the marketplace of ideas: there were Brethren, ridiculed as "Anabaptists," and Lutherans and Catholics.

For now, about the only thing they were sure of was their growing love for each other. It would survive, Margaret believed, whatever came their way. Soon they reached the little bridge over the canal.

"Well, here's *our* bridge," Beck said with a laugh.

"Don't get lost on the way back, Beck. And don't you dare swing by to see that pretty Knobloch girl," Margaret kidded. "I like you just the way you are, and I don't want anyone else to change that."

"And I like your kisses," Beck responded. After bending down for another one, he walked south to the Butcher's Gate, pushed out of the city, then quickly turned east toward the barn in Robertsau. "Alone again," he thought to himself.

8

Abolishing the Mass

In the midst of Strasbourg's fast-moving Reformation, Margaret's love for Beck grew and blossomed. A powerful undercurrent of change threatened to split the Catholic Church, but Margaret believed that her love for the new printer in town would make her strong enough to stand against the surging waves that crashed in all around. The tide was coming in, threatening Strasbourg and southern Germany with breakers that could rearrange everything they swept over.

Regardless of the constant motion, though, the early days of summer brightened Margaret's outlook on life. Flowers bloomed in boxes and beds by the canal, vineyards blossomed in the countryside, and the warm sun nurtured her growing attraction to Beck. She wanted to be with him whenever possible—a walk during their lunch break, a stroll to the fair during its last days in town, a trip to the forest on the other side of the Rhine bridge.

Risks lay ahead, however. If she could ever get him to marry her, he'd be expected to buy his citizenship, which would probably mean military service in one of the emperor's many wars. The two of them would certainly print for a business, but their attraction to the more radical reformers in the church might jeopardize their economic and social standing in Strasbourg. And the dreaded plague still hung around. All too often, it claimed young people in their prime, who were unconcerned about status, age, or religion. No one was safe from its fatal effects.

Once, during a visit to the merchant booths at the fair, Margaret and Beck ran into Wolfgang and his new fiancée. They visited briefly, with Margaret moving on as soon as they could politely maneuver away. She couldn't explain why she felt so badly toward the Knobloch women, but then neither could she entirely explain her newfound love for Beck, so she stopped trying to analyze everything.

They liked to get away from the crowd to go sit on a bench by the canal. The base of a bridge blocked the view of their hideaway from one side. And a slight bend in the path protected the view from the other direction. They talked and laughed on their little seat. When the shadows grew longer, they held each other closely to keep the darkness away.

Once before, Beck had loved a woman, but in the end, it hadn't worked out. Margaret had been married before, though it seemed like a long time ago. Her attraction to Beck grew daily and felt brand-new. Love, when the real thing comes along, blossoms like a flower in all its glory, and this love affair was in full bloom, fragrant, tender, and alive.

For years, as a child, teenager, and now as a young woman, Margaret had attended Mass every Sunday in the cathedral. Latin, the age-old language of the Roman Catholic Church, was always used. Margaret knew the pattern of the ritual, but not the meaning of the words. She had been told that the heart of the ritual lay in the Eucharist, or communion. Every Sunday the priest read from the official reading for the day, prayed—all in Latin—and then administered the sacred bread and wine. All the while he kept his back toward the people—so he would be facing toward the east, the Church authorities said. Margaret had been taught that the elements became the very body and blood of Christ and that they were the means for gaining salvation from sins.

Not everyone agreed, however. A few years before, Luther

had challenged the Roman Catholic doctrine of the Eucharist. He preached that Christ's presence coexisted with the bread and wine in communion. In response, King Henry VIII of England condemned Luther for his heretical views. This condemnation pleased Pope Leo X so much that he crowned King Henry "Defender of the Faith." Luther's view really wasn't all that different from the pope's, but it was different enough to get him kicked out of the church.

That was in Wittenberg, far to the north of Strasbourg, where Luther lived. In Zurich, to the south, Zwingli held a third point of view. Overlooking a beautiful lake and a grand view of the Alps, Zwingli used his platform in the cathedral to preach that the Lord's Supper was only a ceremony that helped people remember the broken body and shed blood of Jesus. He didn't believe the bread and wine actually became the body and blood of Christ. The Anabaptists, having been taught by Zwingli, held similar views.

On Tuesday, Blaurock and Seiler came to pick up their bundles. Had there been any delay in the arrival of the two men, Margaret would have sent the bundles to the barn. Peter and Heinrich had packaged up the octavo pamphlets, *Christian Baptism,* and prepared them for shipping to Switzerland. Blaurock paid Margaret for her work, thanked her, and left immediately for the dock by the canal.

Seiler and Blaurock intended to move their packages as far as possible upstream by river, then to take them to Zurich and the surrounding regions by horseback. They grabbed the ropes tied around the pamphlets, muscled them down to the canal, and bargained for passage on a boat headed out to the Rhine and then north.

After morning Mass at the cathedral chapel, Magdalene Knobloch noticed two men moving their two big packages toward the canal. She went home immediately to inform her obedient husband, who promptly asked for an inspection of the packages.

About a year earlier, in order to try to slow down the Reformation, the Strasbourg City Council had passed an action that required all printers to submit their documents to a special committee. Very few pamphlets or books printed in the city were actually read by the committee, however. But when the influential Knoblochs asked for a reading, the bundles were seized, and several copies of the Anabaptist document were distributed to official readers.

"How long before we can have our packages?" Blaurock asked.

"Probably three to four days," the guard responded. "Who printed these pamphlets for you?"

"What difference does it make who printed them?" Seiler asked.

"Just a routine matter—for the forms I need to fill in," the guard said.

"We had them printed at the press near the Wood Market," Blaurock said.

"Come back Friday to see if you can have your bundles."

Blaurock and Seiler stayed around for a while, hoping there'd be a change in their favor. The Brethren in Switzerland needed those pamphlets to help explain Anabaptist beliefs, as soon as possible. Apparently, they were going to have to wait a few more days. The two men began looking for something to do in Strasbourg for a while.

When Beck sat outside during lunchtime with the men at the Knobloch press, the talk ranged far and wide. On warm days, they perched themselves on a tiny strip of grass growing along the edge of the canal.

Some days the men discussed the emperor's distant wars and whether they would have to fight in them. Other days their talk turned toward the local brothel, the women who worked there, and the city council's occasional attempts to regulate the place. Beck also kept up on the latest comings and goings of Agnes and Wolfgang's romance. He never quite knew how much of what he heard was true.

Today the men debated whether anyone had ever swum across the Rhine near Strasbourg. Most thought it had never been done, but a few believed that it had. None of them knew anyone who had tried it, and so there was no way they could prove any of their arguments. "That was the way these silly debates always end," Beck often thought. At the end of his lunch break, he was usually ready to get back to work.

Right after lunch, three men stopped by Margaret's print shop. She recognized one of the men. "Name's Hans Hut," he said. Margaret remembered his voice and huge blond mustache from the meeting by the bridge during the peasants' revolt. "Friends here are John Wolff and Christman Kenlin. I believe you know Christman."

Margaret glanced at Hut for a second, and then answered, "Yes, Christman and I know each other."

"We've got a printing job for you, Margaret," Hut told her.

"Come inside and let's talk." Margaret glanced toward the cathedral as she pulled the door shut. Blaurock had stopped by the shop to tell Margaret about the mess the Knoblochs had created for them earlier that day. Margaret thought, "I'll have to be a little more careful about who is seen coming in my door."

"Hut's from south Germany," Christman said, and then added, "a book salesman." Hut's bobbing mustache flared under his cropped hair and gray hat.

"I sell books wherever I can," Hut told Margaret. "Printers like you and Beck are essential in helping to reform the church. Books and pamphlets are God's way of striking out at evil in these last days."

"I wouldn't doubt we're living in the end times," Margaret sarcastically responded. "With so much change around us, the end's got to be near." Hardened by the very political and religious changes Margaret joked about, the men smiled politely.

"Sure is, Margaret, and that's the reason we're here today," Christman said. "We've written a petition asking the Strasbourg city council to abolish the Latin Mass."

The bells chimed from the spire in the cathedral. "Hear those gongs?" Hut asked. "They're calling people to idolatry, old traditions, worthless forms, and empty Latin words."

"I don't disagree with your evaluation about the Mass, Hans," Margaret said. "But what good do you think your petition will do?"

"Time's right in Strasbourg to get rid of the Mass and conduct our worship services in the German language."

Christman picked up where Hut left off. "When we threw out the statues from the cathedral two weeks ago, the city council slapped me on the hand. Nothing serious. And they defended the right of the preachers to get married. We think the council is ready to abolish the Mass, as Luther has preached for several years."

In the short pamphlet they wanted Margaret to print, the men stated their opposition to the Latin language because only a few understood it. They were opposed to the priest remaining so distant from the people, standing with his back to them. But mainly, their petition challenged the ancient Roman Catholic belief that the bread and wine actually became the body and blood of Jesus.

"This statement is powerful and could get all of us in trouble," Margaret said to the men. "You may be right about the council's openness to change, but powerful nobles may decide to draw the line with this document and make examples of you—and me."

"Zurich and Wittenberg have already abolished the Mass." Hut said fervently. "Time's right for Strasbourg now. Once the Mass is abolished, more seekers will choose the second baptism and accept the water of renewal that declares their faith in Christ."

Beck walked in the door of the print shop before Margaret could ask Hut what he meant by that last statement. "What in the world are you doing here?" she asked.

"I'm a delivery man this afternoon, and I have just a second to stop by and say hello. Looks like you have a full house."

"Should I print a petition to abolish the Mass?" Margaret asked. Beck examined the document, looked the men over, and soon agreed with Margaret that she should take the job.

"We're doing a small print job right now that outlines Luther's beliefs about marriage. Then we'll be ready for yours," Margaret said.

"I'll stop by later, Margaret," Beck said. "I have work to do."

Seeing Christman in Margaret's shop made Beck jealous, but he had to keep moving and get back to the Knobloch press for another errand.

The next day Wolff and Hut decided to attend Mass in the St. Lawrence chapel, in one of the side wings of the cathedral. A third-century Roman emperor had killed St. Lawrence for his Christian beliefs. The two men were convinced that the early-church martyr certainly wouldn't have liked the ritual that the Catholic priest would lead that day in the chapel named in his honor.

The Mass began with the priest making the sign of the cross and chanting a psalm in Latin. Then the priest lined out an ancient formula, the Kyrie, which offered a plea for God's mercy. The priest then followed with a hymn of praise, sung in Latin. Very few people had come today.

After a spoken prayer, the priest read from one of Paul's epistles, chanting the verses from the Latin Bible. Then he recited the assigned Gospel passage. A small choir followed with music set to the words of the Nicene Creed, an early-church confession of faith.

The next part of the Mass is what Wolff and Hut were waiting for. An offertory prayer, again in Latin, accompanied the preparation and presentation of the bread and wine. After a series of prayers and readings, all in Latin, the people were ready to receive the Eucharist, one of the seven sacraments. Crossing themselves, they filed forward, and the priest placed the morsel on their tongues.

In the Middle Ages the Church had begun the practice of withholding the wine from the people so that the "sacrifice of Christ's blood" wouldn't accidentally be spilled. When the priest raised his wine cup in order to drink, the leathery-faced and fearless Wolff jumped to his feet and shouted, "Why aren't the people allowed to drink the wine? Didn't Christ share the cup with his disciples at the Last Supper? It's time to abolish this service of the antichrist. Rome sets the rules for what happens here and we can't even understand the words."

All eyes were on Wolff, including the priest's, who turned to face his heckler. "Sit down and honor this sacred moment of worship in God's temple," he sternly warned.

"No, you sit down, and allow the Holy Spirit to be truly heard in this service."

Wolff knew he needed to speak and act quickly. The priest was getting upset and the people were obviously restless. "The Lord's Supper is only a ceremony to help us remember the suffering and sacrifice of Christ for us," Wolff said to the priest and the people. "We don't need this ritual of Latin, candles, and meaningless chants. Let us hear the Scriptures in German, in a language we can understand. These are the last days, and this is a service of the antichrist, which will soon come to an end. I will preach today from the assigned Gospel reading."

As Wolff moved to the front of the chapel, a cathedral guard arrived to remove him. One of the choir members had slipped out to get help as soon as Wolff had interrupted the service. After the guard grabbed him and led him out, the priest quickly drank the wine and offered a few short words to close the service. "Go, it is over," he concluded, and the shaken people rose to leave. Hut left too. In a moment, the priest disappeared out a side door.

Late that afternoon, Wolff stood before a magistrate, unafraid, waiting for his penalty to be announced. After the priest described Wolff's interruption, the judge ordered him out of the city immediately. He should not return upon pain of imprisonment for ninety days.

"God will be the judge," yelled Wolff as they yanked him out of the room. "The antichrist will be destroyed soon."

Many of the merchants who had come to Strasbourg for the three-week fair had packed up and moved on to fairs in other cities. The locals remained, of course, and outside a favorite eating-place that evening, Blaurock and Seiler met with Hut and Christman.

"This city is ripe for a radical message," Hut declared. "I believe people will join us if we can act on a number of different fronts at once."

"And get thrown out of the city, like Wolff?" Blaurock asked.

"Whatever it takes to get our message through," Hut replied. "You're not afraid are you, George?"

"If Zwingli doesn't scare me anymore, than neither does Sturm."

The soup Blaurock ate didn't have much meat in it, but the beans and bread made up for it. The men enjoyed the good meal and conversation. A blueberry pie topped off the evening.

"Is Margaret the printer with us?" Seiler asked. "Will she join the Anabaptist movement?"

"I'd say she's on a journey, like all of us are," Blaurock answered. "Give her and Beck some time, and I believe they'll help start a Brethren congregation here in Strasbourg."

"She printed our *Twelve Articles*," Hut said.

"And the pamphlet about baptism," Blaurock added.

"And she has agreed to print our petition to abolish the Mass," Christman said. "She'll come along eventually."

"Christman, you've had eyes for Margaret, if I'm not mistaken," Blaurock boldly said.

Christman glared at Blaurock for a moment, but then figured he might as well admit what Blaurock had deduced. "She's a strong woman," he answered, flexing his biceps as he usually did when he was agitated. "And I do wish she'd marry me."

"We need to get her to come to Switzerland and see our Reformation," Seiler said. "With her print shop and position in this city, we need her among us."

"Seiler, you can't force anyone to be a Christian," Blaurock said. "This is not another state church with judges and soldiers to enforce its rules."

Seiler stood and said, "I'm ready to go." Blaurock and Seiler traveled light and had set up camp in the forest near the bridge. They had a few days to wait until the city council's committee had inspected their pamphlets.

"We'll see you later," Blaurock said.

"There's a meeting Friday evening at Clement Ziegler's

farm," Christman said. "You're welcome to come." Ziegler's cooking fire and preaching times varied from week to week. No set pattern for Anabaptist meetings had yet emerged in the city.

"I'd guess we'll be there," Seiler responded. "We don't have much else going on."

Christman invited Hut to stay with him at his house near the Stone Street Gate and paid the bill for the food.

The young Wolff, kicked out of Strasbourg for ninety days, headed for his home in the nearby village of Benfeld. The stars lit up the warm June night. Their mystical appearance convinced him that the end of the age was at hand. He believed Gutenberg's invention of the printing press was God's final instrument to help spread the message of reform in a church that was desperately sick. "The Mass must be eliminated," he thought, "before the end of the age arrives. The Church must be cleansed before the return of Christ."

A shooting star that disappeared in the distance appeared to be a sign to Wolff that the pope's office, the papacy, would soon fall as well. He might stay out of Strasbourg for ninety days, but then again, he might not. "I must help get ready for the coming end."

With that Wolff stepped into his little house and greeted his wife. He checked in on his sleeping child then sat down next to a flickering lantern to read Revelation again. The books of Daniel and Revelation never ceased to inspire him. Now that a judge had run him out of Strasbourg, he wanted to read about the day of the antichrist again before going to sleep. Perhaps tomorrow he would find a new way to hasten the return of Christ.

The only eyewitness to the murder of Sturm's nephew at the barn lived on the streets and alleyways in Worms, north of Strasbourg. Anna Weiler didn't know anyone to whom she could turn, so she moved from place to place, finding cover at night wherever she could. Accused witches, she had learned, weren't welcome anywhere.

Anna thought about going back to Strasbourg and staying in Zieglers' barn, but there was no way she could face Christman. She thought her quick departure from the barn that day must have tipped him off to the fact that she had witnessed the attack and burial.

Sturm continued an intense search for his nephew. He quizzed people in Strasbourg but picked up no leads. Christman avoided the city council chairman like the plague. So far, Sturm had not caught up with him for questioning.

Soon Zieglers' granary hid a desperate man. One of the five who had escaped the bishop's executioner had returned to the barn. In his home area he'd be recognized and caught, he explained to Christman, and immediately executed. So when he got hungry enough, he decided to go back to Strasbourg and try Gertrude Ziegler's good will.

Christman instructed the haggard, heavily bearded, and dejected former prisoner that he could only stay three days. To risk staying longer was asking too much from the Zieglers.

On the third night, Christman planned a daring escape route for the worn-down runaway. In the bottom of a large bundle of cloth due to be heading to the Netherlands, Christman created a compartment big enough for a man to crawl inside. With three loaves of bread from Gertrude's kitchen and a corked keg of water, the man stuffed himself into the compartment, made sure there was an opening to breath, and waited for the boat to leave the next morning.

"Amsterdam," Christman wrote on the package.

By nine o'clock, with the sun already high in the sky, the canal boat slowly made its way to the great, wide Rhine, turned north, and carried its cargo to another city far away. With a little luck, the man would start his life over in the Netherlands and never return to the Alsace valley. With bad luck, other packages would be stacked around his, he would suffocate, and he would be dead for a week before the ship's crew figured out what was stinking so badly.

9

Judgment on Baptism

When he checked the records the next morning, the priest noticed that Wolff had failed to baptize his new daughter in the Catholic Church. In order to keep tax records accurate, the judicial system in Strasbourg kept a careful list of babies who had been baptized.

Around noon on Friday, two guards knocked on Wolff's unpainted wooden door in Benfeld, not far from where the Zieglers lived.

"We have orders to inquire about whether your child has been baptized," a guard announced.

"Who sent you?" Wolff asked.

"The Chief Judge of Strasbourg," barked the guard. "Have you presented your newborn to the priest for baptism at the cathedral?"

"No. The pope's baptism is a mark of the antichrist."

"You have five days, then, John Wolff, to take your child to the cathedral for holy baptism and have her listed in the magistrate's official book of Strasbourg residents. If you fail to do so, you will be banished from the area."

As abruptly as they had arrived, the guards turned and marched away, stomping their boots on the hard clay path.

After talking about it, the first person Wolff and his young wife turned to for advice was Clement. In the middle of the afternoon, they walked down Zieglers' lane, met him in the garden, and the three of them sat under a shade tree to talk.

The Wolff couple's infant daughter, not yet baptized and asleep, lay nearby in a big, woven basket.

"You and I are both against infant baptism," Zeigler told the couple. "But you'll be the ones to discover what punishments come from choosing to act on your belief." Ziegler tried to encourage them, but he knew from long experience that the power of the Church carried the authority of the state behind it. "You'll have to decide whether you baptize your daughter as you've been ordered, or move elsewhere."

After they'd talked for a while, the old preacher concluded, "Come back tomorrow night. We're having a meeting and several of the Anabaptists will be present. You can find out what your options are and where you might be able to move to."

In the print shop, Margaret, Heinrich, and Peter worked on the pamphlet that summarized Luther's beliefs on marriage. The Wittenberg preacher encouraged priests to marry, and he celebrated the holiness of the marriage bond. But Margaret noticed that Luther also, at least in his most recent statements on marriage, had required that parents baptize their newborn children in the church.

The few Anabaptists she knew, such as Blaurock, Seiler, and now Hut, were opposed to infant baptism. She had heard that in Switzerland they rebaptized each other and were nicknamed "Anabaptists," or rebaptizers. Margaret had read that Luther corrupted the ceremony of baptism by insisting that parents baptize their children. The thought crossed her mind that in the next year or two, if she could get Beck to ask her to marry him, she could easily be expecting a child. Would she and Beck baptize their baby?

As usual, when Margaret wanted to discuss something with a woman who would understand her, she turned to the ever-gracious and optimistic Katherine Zell. After Katherine welcomed Margaret into her kitchen, they enjoyed each other's company and talked about Margaret's relationship to Beck and the business in the print shop. Eventually, their conversation turned to changes in the church.

"I'm sure glad Sturm was able to make the Catholic bishop stop his ban of priests who took wives," Margaret said. "Getting married shouldn't be a crime!"

"Yes, but we're not finished with the bishop yet," Katherine replied. "Matthew's certain that the diet that meets at Speyer next year will vote to take drastic measures against married priests."

"Does this mean that followers of Luther will have to break with the Catholic Church completely?" Margaret asked. "Will the break in the church here be as strong as in Wittenberg, where Luther preaches? You'll baptize your baby when its born, won't you, Katherine? That is, when he or she is born," Margaret said with a laugh.

"Of course. I'm surprised that you'd even ask, Margaret."

"Are there no other options than to baptize our newborn children?" Margaret asked.

Matthew walked into the kitchen and greeted the women.

"Why don't you take Margaret into the cathedral, Matthew, and show her the baptistery," Katherine asked. "Her mind's on child-related subjects these days."

"Would you like to take a look, Margaret?" Matthew asked. With a nod she agreed.

In a great cathedral, the baptistery was usually very elaborate, though Strasbourg's was an exception. In a side chapel, Matthew showed her a large, simple basin, which priests used to baptize the babies of the city and surrounding countryside.

"This little tub gets used a lot, you know, Margaret. It seems that when God told Adam and Eve to be fruitful and multiply, the parents of Strasbourg took him seriously!"

In another room, Matthew showed Margaret the records that listed all the infant baptisms in the Strasbourg area. "These are what we base our taxation policy on," he said. Margaret paused to look at a column on each page of the record book for deaths.

"It's true," Matthew said. "Many children die before they become adults."

"Do you believe infant baptism is a sacrament established by God, Matthew?"

"Of course. Luther says the Church couldn't have been wrong for all these hundreds of years. And besides, it keeps order in the church and in society when church leaders know exactly who lives in an area. We can easily keep up with people that way."

For reasons Margaret couldn't explain, Matthew's arguments didn't seem very convincing. She wondered what the Bible said, she wondered what the practice of the early church had been, and she wondered about the Anabaptists. The eight-page pamphlet about baptism had influenced her thinking. "Thanks for the tour, Matthew. Next time I'll have to bring Beck along."

"Do that. I need to get to know him better."

After a gentle hug with the very pregnant preacher's wife, Margaret returned to the print shop. It was quitting time and Heinrich and Peter were putting their tools away. Heinrich wrapped the ink-ball tightly in leather to keep it pliable. Drying paper hung on string all around. The big lever was fastened in place and the press was raised until the morning.

"How's the Zell job going?" Margaret asked.

"Good progress," Peter responded, "though we need to replace Leopold sometime. We could use another pressman. I'm back and forth and we're able to fill in, but three men working in here would be ideal."

"Well, if we can turn out nearly the same amount of pamphlets and books with one less man, why replace him?"

"To save the backs and sanity of the other men working in here. You're always thinking about making money, Margaret."

"You have to in business. See you tomorrow morning."

On the Feast of St. John, the bells tolled at daybreak for the usual morning prayer service, followed by Mass. The most devoted went to the nearest parish church or the cathedral to start their day. With the coming of the Reformation, however, fewer and fewer residents of Strasbourg did anything special on the numerous Catholic feast days throughout the year. Of course, everyone followed the church-year traditions from Advent through Christmas, from Lent to Easter, and on Pentecost. But Luther said that many of the feast days were contrary to Scripture, so in areas where his ideas were strong, Catholic traditions were quickly being dropped. Only a few would celebrate and fly banners from their houses or porches.

Time moved on rapidly in its regular rhythmic cycles for Margaret and other citizens of Strasbourg. The feasts throughout the year, the annual fair, the ebb and flow of Advent, Lent, and Easter, the regular ringing of the bells for Mass—all of these kept things stable and orderly.

On the other hand, the educated in 1525 knew that the calendar was off by ten days from when it had been established centuries earlier. Someone needed to fix it. And increasingly, many believed they lived in the end times, the day of the antichrist. Luther wrote and preached about the Catholic Church and believed that the papacy was the antichrist. Disease, famine, and the invasion of Europe by the Turks led many to feel they lived near to the return of Christ and the day of judgment.

On a warm Friday in late June, Margaret worked on putting the finishing touches on the pamphlet of Luther's beliefs about marriage for priests. She could hear the bells toll for regular Masses, offering an invitation to prayer and the Eucharist. At lunchtime she met Beck, and they hiked to the wooden bench along the canal, where they made small talk and ate cheese, bread, and grapes.

The wiry Wolff worked hard on his small farm to the north of Strasbourg, his wife by his side. Under the hot sun they cleaned rocks out of their small fields and wondered whether they'd have to leave their land. Was it really worth giving up their plot and house because of a disagreement over the baptism of their daughter?

Hut worked alongside Christman in a cloth maker's shop. They wove fabric throughout the day, as did other workers in shops clustered in the cloth makers' guild near the Stone Street Gate. They shipped their fabrics all over Europe on the canal, the Ill River, up and down the Rhine, and across the roads that crisscrossed northern Europe. At lunch break Hut read and studied a copy of Luther's German translation of the book of Revelation.

Blaurock and Seiler found work at the Butcher's Gate, loading boats with all sorts of merchandise headed for various parts of Europe. They sweated in the sun, lifting wares from the dock to the boats and then unloading shipments from other boats to the dock. They made enough money to buy food and to rent a room in the city rather than sleep hungry under the stars near the bridge.

"When I ran errands for the Knoblochs yesterday," Beck began, "I noticed some things about Strasbourg."

"Tell me," Margaret said.

"First thing is that we spend a lot of time talking about faith, but most people in this city just want to make money."

"What makes you say that?"

"I went in and out of other print shops, made deliveries, picked up supplies, and the city is alive with business activity."

"True enough, Beck. What else?"

"Well, I don't think people are as worried about the end times as I've been led to believe."

"They're more focused on this life and making money?"

"Yes, the real world seems to be about business."

"Maybe now you understand why making an income is important to me?"

"There's more," Beck continued. "I found a new restaurant yesterday, called Fish Mongers. I know we're headed out to Clement's barn tonight, but he always has the same stew going. Let's try the place out tonight."

"Sure, lead me to it."

"Another thing I saw yesterday, Margaret, was an apartment for rent."

"Are you ready to move and find more comfortable quarters, Balt?"

"I sure am," Beck quickly answered. "But I also need to save my money so I can start my own business soon."

"Sounds like your mind's on finances and making money too," Margaret said with a telling smile. "What kind of a business do you want?"

"I don't know, maybe a print shop, like yours, Margaret."

For a moment Margaret wondered if she could pop the question, but then she backed off. It just wasn't a woman's place to ask a man to marry her.

"Printing's a good business, Beck, if you work hard and make good decisions."

"Hey, we'd better get out of here and head out to my place. How about food and entertainment at the old farm tonight after all, instead of Fish Mongers? Interested?"

"I'm in," Margaret responded. "But I want you to take me to that restaurant soon."

"I will," Beck said.

On their walk across the canal to the little village east of town, Margaret asked what Beck knew about the Agnes's engagement to Wolfgang. "I hear what the men at work say," Beck said, "but I don't know if it's reliable. We see her coming and going during the day, but nobody's sure where she's headed. Possibly to the preacher's house."

"What's the word on the street about how her parents feel about the engagement by now?"

"They're not very happy about it, I'm told. But when you can marry your daughter off to a man with some money, you'd better do it. She's absolutely gorgeous. Why she chose to marry a preacher I'll never understand."

"Women don't only go after good-looking men, you know, Balt. Sometimes they see other qualities in them that they like too."

"Sure, Margaret. Like the rusty coins stored up in their banks and under their mattresses. It's all about money, I'm beginning to believe."

Margaret grabbed Beck and jerked him to the side of road. "You're about more than money to me, Balt. I have money. Right now it's you that I want, not your silver."

"Forgive me for opening my big mouth, Margaret. I guess when I'm around you, I feel free and easy."

"You're forgiven," Margaret said, with a gentle hug. She promised him, through only a look, that more would come later.

It seemed that when Clement built a roaring fire and cooked up his pork stew, it was a signal to people for miles around that there'd be good food for the body and the soul. With Hut in town from southern Germany, word spread through the community that he and Clement would preach on the end times. Blaurock and Seiler came for the food after working on the docks. Margaret and Beck left their print shops after a workday of printing. The tanned and rough Wolff, his wife, and their newborn daughter sat on a heap of straw and wondered if this would be their last visit to a Ziegler "church service." A total of about forty came from the city and countryside, including Christman and Kniebs.

"Followers of Christ must expect abuse and torture," Hut declared to the group. Clement had invited him to start off the preaching and discussion. "Paul says in second Timothy that everyone who wants to live a godly life in Christ Jesus will be persecuted." He looked thin next to Clements's protruding belly.

"There will be terrible times in the last days," Hut continued, again referring to Timothy. "People will be lovers of all sorts of evil, and pretend to be godly, but without any real spiritual power. Paul tells us to have nothing to do with them. Evil men and impostors will go from bad to worse, deceiving and being deceived."

Hut's voice rose. "My brother and sisters, the antichrist is loose in the world today. Evidences of these last days are the plague that cuts down the strong and weak alike, famine, and the invasion of the Turks from the east. But most of all, the peasants' war marks the beginning of the final three and one half years before Christ returns to rule with his saints. Based on the books of Revelation and Daniel, we are now in the time of tribulation. I believe the end will come in May of 1528, three and one half years from the time the peasants' war began."

Margaret shifted on the bale of hay, newly cut from Ziegler's field. "How could Hut be so sure of himself?" Margaret thought. "Are we really in the last days?"

"God is gathering the elect together from far and wide," Hut preached. "The Bible says in the book of Revelation that

God will gather 144,000 together, and then the end will come."

The shadows lengthened, the fire burned hot, and flames leaped from the wood. By now everyone had their fill of Clement's pork and cabbage stew, though no one knew exactly what all went into it.

"Who will be among the elect of God, in that 144,000?" Wolff asked.

Hut turned toward Wolff and thought for a moment. All 461 feet of the cathedral spire, the tallest in Europe, rose behind him. Margaret sensed that he was about to move out from underneath its shadow of power and control.

"It is baptism, my friends," Hut stated slowly. "The elect will be those who keep themselves from the abominations around them. For centuries, the Church, represented by that cathedral over there, has required infant baptism." He turned for a moment and gazed in the direction of the city walls and the imposing spire on the cathedral. On the very pinnacle stood a cross, reaching toward the sky. "Our Lord Jesus instructed his followers to go out into all the world and preach the good news. The Gospel of Mark states that whoever believes the preaching and is baptized will be saved. How can your little daughter that you hold in your arms believe my preaching when she's so young? You see, baptism should follow belief in the Lord Jesus Christ."

Clement took over for a moment. "Hans Hut comes to us from southern Germany. In his territory and in parts of Switzerland, there are Anabaptists who refuse to baptize their children and who have rebaptized each other."

"What happens to them?" Christman asked.

"So far," Hut said, "only exile from their homelands. No martyrs yet. Some have been locked up in prison, though, like our brother here from Zurich, George Blaurock."

The group's attention shifted to Blaurock, one of the leaders of the Brethren. "My friends," he said as he rose to speak, "Conrad Grebel did baptize me a second time about six months ago, a glorious day that I shall never forget. Since then, the city council of Zurich has made life very difficult for my wife and me. But we believe that baptism which emerges from the confession of our faith is the most biblical means of baptism."

"Didn't God instruct the Israelites to circumcise their children in the Old Testament?" Kniebs asked. "Isn't infant baptism similar to that?"

"The Brethren in Zurich have scholars among them. We have learned that for hundreds of years in the early church, baptism was reserved for those who confessed Jesus as Lord of their lives. As you can see if you look at this woman's baby, that is impossible for children to do!" The group smiled and some nodded in agreement. "We believe the church has corrupted the sacred ceremony of baptism."

Hut continued. "The Bible speaks clearly to three witnesses in baptism. In the first letter of John, we read that the elect of God give witness to the baptism of the Spirit, or their inner commitment to follow Jesus, the witness of water baptism, and the witness of blood. This last witness marks our time, the age of the antichrist, the time of pestilence. Those who are faithful will be persecuted, and some may die a martyr's death. We fear that will happen soon in Switzerland."

Margaret remarked to the group, "We should be thankful to have such a tolerant city council here in Strasbourg and such open-minded preachers. We can only hope that Strasbourg continues to offer its citizens peace and refuge from the persecution facing believers elsewhere."

Clement rose, walked to where the Wolffs sat, and took the child in his arms. She slept soundly in the night, and the group could easily see her in the dancing shadows. "John and his wife have a difficult decision to make," Clement said.

"They need to baptize this child by Monday or leave the area. We can all see that the elect of God have started to face tribulation even here in Strasbourg. John and his wife may face their third baptism."

"But we haven't yet received our second baptism in water," Wolff cried out. "A baptism that we choose, of our own free will!"

Blaurock rose and invited the parents to accept water baptism on the spot. The Wolffs didn't hesitate and Blaurock soon poured a pitcher of water on their heads, "in the name of the Father, the Son, and the Holy Spirit."

Blaurock then went to Clement, took the baby from his arms, and stood near her parents. "We pray that you guide these parents, O Lord, and lead them to make decisions that are pleasing to you. May you protect them and help them to raise this child up to have faith in your saving grace and love. In Christ's name we pray. Amen."

Several of those nearest Blaurock chimed in with a chorus of amens.

Three things happened on Monday. First, Hut and Christman picked up and paid for the petition from Margaret's press that called for an immediate end to the Latin Mass.

Second, Blaurock and Seiler loaded their two bundles of pamphlets on a boat that was headed up the Rhine. The censorship committee noted the topic of the pamphlets—baptism—and where they had been printed. The record book said "the print shop near the Wood Market."

Third, Wolff and his wife took their baby, loaded up their worldly goods on two mules, and headed south. Blaurock had given them the name of someone in Waldshut who would give them a place to stay and provide John with a job.

125

As a young girl, Margaret often heard her father use a phrase from the Old Testament book of Genesis: "Let there be light," God said, "and there was light." Her father had believed that the printing press brought light to the issues of his day. "Thank God for Johannes Gutenberg," he had told her, "and print all sorts of documents, because in the midst of them, light will shine through."

Never before had Margaret believed that light was needed so much as right then. She must print an inexpensive German copy of the New Testament for the citizens of Strasbourg. Illumination would only come through the written Word of God—a beacon, she believed, that led the seeker to the living Light, Christ himself.

"Beck, you and I need to talk," Margaret stated. "Do you know how many books there are in the New Testament?"

After Margaret's tall, squinting, student paused and scratched his scruffy chin, Margaret concluded, "Well, you should know. I intend to teach you about the New Testament." With that she reached for her copy of Luther's German translation of the New Testament, sat down near him, opened it, and began to examine the elegant printed pages. "The Gospel of John," she instructed. "Start reading."

10

Charges of Witchcraft

About a hundred miles northeast of Strasbourg, in the city of Worms, Anna paced the floor in a prison cell near the cathedral. After she had been captured on the street as a drifter and then identified by an official report from Strasbourg, the judge in Worms had agreed that she was a witch. Now she faced the prospect of spending her life in jail.

Years earlier, while learning to read at a summer school in the city of Speyer, Anna had studied with Katherine Schütz of Strasbourg, now Katherine Zell. Katherine and Anna had lost track of each other, but just recently Katherine had learned of Anna's miserable circumstance.

There were all sorts of ways of accusing someone of being a witch, but when a woman was charged, it was almost impossible for her to go free. Thousands had been falsely charged, most of them women, and many of them had been put to death.

Anna was charged with killing children and other creatures. One day, her accusers claimed that, in the shape of a cat, she had tried to kill a neighbor's child, but the toddler's father had wounded the cat with a knife and driven it off. Later, the claim continued, Anna had been found with a wound in the corresponding part of her body.

"I'd like to visit Anna in Worms," Katherine explained to Matthew during their Monday-morning break.

"There's very little you or I can do for her once she's

accused of being a witch," Matthew responded.

"True, but we can encourage her, read Scripture, and pray with her. Anna's not a witch—she's been falsely charged!"

"You're probably right," Matthew answered, "but we'll need another reason to travel to Worms, Katherine. How about if we deliver copies of the pamphlet Margaret is printing for us to booksellers in Worms and Speyer. While we're there, you can drop by and see Anna."

"Can Margaret go with us?"

"Sure," Matthew answered. "I'll talk to her this afternoon when I stop by the print shop to pick up my packages."

A handful of scattered white clouds lazily graced the deep-blue summer sky as Matthew left his small house to walk down the cobblestone streets toward the Wood Market. There merchants sold kindling wood and sawn lumber to customers in the plaza near the cathedral. Margaret's shop door stood open and the wooden shutters on the windows were hooked back to allow air to circulate inside.

"Are you keeping your men busy these days?" Matthew asked.

"I sure am. Right now we're printing copies of Martin Waldseemüller's *Four Voyages of Amerigo* for a bookseller in Barcelona. When we finish, Beck has expressed some interest in delivering them. What do you think of this new land explorers claim to have discovered, called America?"

"I think the native people, whoever they are, will need the gospel preached to them," Matthew replied. "The reason I've come, Margaret, is to invite you to go with Katherine and me to Worms tomorrow to deliver the pamphlets you've printed for us. Would you like to go along?"

The main reason Margaret traveled anywhere was to find more printing work for her business. Thinking it over for a moment, she believed she could probably find in Worms some pamphlets or books to print. "Yes, I'd love to go along!"

"Good. We'll leave first thing in the morning."

The gentle Lucas Hackfurt had earlier expressed interest in going to Worms in order to examine the relief operations in that city. Since the peasants' war ended in May, the former Franciscan monastery had been bursting at the seams with refugees from the Alsace region. Lucas's mission gave the Zells another good reason to make the trip.

Elegant old castles lined the Rhine from Strasbourg to Worms, monuments to an earlier era in which nobles ruled and peasants were enslaved in the feudal system. Though the nobles had won their battle with the peasants, many noble families sensed they were losing their grip on power and prestige. Looking carefully, one could notice cracks in the foundations of those massive castles.

The four travelers floated rapidly downstream in an old wooden cargo boat. They arrived at the dock in Worms by Vespers on Tuesday evening. The bells in Worms sounded similar to those in Strasbourg. Here in Worms, though, a little farther north in Germany, the Reformation had firmly taken over. So it seemed odd that Anna cowered in a dank, musty prison cell, accused of witchcraft. Accusations of witchcraft in the 1520s had declined from earlier decades, but women still suffered under the misguided fears of those who used the weak and lonely to explain away the unknown.

The Zells, Margaret, and Lucas found lodging at an inn next to the great Imperial Parliament building. Four years earlier Martin Luther had stood in that building and defended himself before Holy Roman Emperor Charles V. Luther courageously refused to deny his writings or the teachings in them and was condemned by the emperor and the pope.

Margaret's room reminded her of Beck's tiny apartment.

The hard pallet that served as a bed took up most of the room. "Beck would laugh if he could see me now," she thought.

The Strasbourg travelers went four different directions the next morning. Matthew visited the preacher in the cathedral and contacted several booksellers who would sell the pamphlets produced by Margaret's press. Lucas found the relief administrator in Worms and examined his operations. They were using a converted monastery, having chased the monks out a few years earlier.

Margaret visited the university in Worms to discover if anyone needed their books or pamphlets published. Professors often paid a little better for their books or pamphlets than other writers, especially if they were scientific or geographical materials.

Katherine found the jail and asked to see Anna. After the guard carefully wrote down Katherine's name, where she was from, and several other details, he led her to the cell. She hardly recognized Anna's thin, drawn face. Anna was given almost nothing to eat in prison and had little to look forward to except an occasional visitor. The visits were rare, though, because anyone who came to see her might eventually be hauled in front of the judge for questioning. The judge might want to know why anyone, family members included, would want to visit a witch in jail.

"I guess I made some enemies," Anna told Katherine. "If someone wants to get you out of the way, just accuse them of being a witch and blame a bad situation on them. The judge will believe the accuser. He even said he'd give me life in jail rather than burn me, because Luther's Reformation had made the city a little more tolerant than before."

Katherine's mind drifted to the burning of an old woman that she and Anna had witnessed, when they were studying as girls there in Worms. The woman had been accused of being a witch, and the authorities thought they were being generous when they tied gunpowder around her neck to help her die more quickly. Katherine snapped back to the present. "Is there anything I can do for you, Anna?"

"You should be taking it easy, Katherine, as pregnant as you are," Anna said with a slight smile. The wrinkles on her forehead and cheeks made her look like a very old woman. Her blonde hair hinted of an earlier time when she had been beautiful and her eyes had sparkled.

"Bring your child up in the ways of God," Anna murmured in despair. "Help the poor and needy, but there's no use trying to do anything for me."

"Didn't you grow up in Molsheim?" Katherine asked. "That's just a few hours walk from Strasbourg."

"You have a good memory, Katherine. My childhood memories of Molsheim are pleasant, but they're fading with each day I rot in this prison. Maybe you could ask the bishop himself to free me."

"You know, Anna, that's actually not a bad idea. Perhaps Matthew and I could stop by the bishop's palace in Molsheim on the way home and talk to him."

"Don't waste your time. I'm Lutheran now. And so, I believe, are you."

"True enough, but it never hurts to try. Here's some food I brought you. May it strengthen you in the name of our Lord Jesus Christ." Katherine's pregnant belly had provided all sorts of hiding places under her dress to slip food in past the guard's nose. If the prison hadn't stunk so badly, he might have smelled the food. Then again, his nose was full of hair and he reeked of alcohol.

At the university, Margaret struck up a conversation with an elderly man who was reading in the library. She recognized him because he had visited Strasbourg in the past, looking for someone to publish his pamphlets on home-style medicine. Walther Ryff didn't have medical training, but his pamphlets sold well.

Upon introducing herself, Margaret talked with Ryff for about an hour. She learned that his pamphlets were selling in cities like Worms, Speyer, and Colmar and that he wanted to publish a book on medicine for home use. He had started to write his book, he said, for the common person who couldn't request a doctor's help because of the cost, or who couldn't get to a doctor. In his sixties—and with a strikingly full head of white hair—he was an old man for that time. When he talked to Margaret, his unsteady hands trembled just a bit.

"My book will sell if I can get it finished and published," Ryff declared.

"What makes you think people will buy your book?" Margaret asked.

"Because people come to me all the time with their questions, and I'm not a doctor, so I can't charge them. Many times they have come back to me with stories of how I helped them. My remedies can be made in the average person's home to help with headaches and the croup."

Margaret did some quick thinking while she chatted with this self-styled, self-educated writer of remedies for everyday ailments. It was common in the 1520s for printers to invite writers to stay with them for a time while they wrote their books. The publisher, then, had first rights to publish their materials. "Have you considered living with a printer to finish your book?" she asked.

"Indeed," Ryff answered. "Do you have someone or somewhere in mind?"

"Possibly. I run a print shop in Strasbourg and might be interested in publishing your book. How long would it take you to finish writing it?"

"I'd guess three or four months. It will sell, I'm sure."

"Why don't you come to Strasbourg and visit my shop? I

think I could find a room for you to live in. You can write in the shop, and this fall, I'll publish your book."

"I'll work for room and board, and we'll split the profits of the book."

"Fifty-fifty on the first five hundred copies, then I take seventy percent of the profit after that. Agreed?"

"That's pretty steep, but I like Strasbourg. Does Clement Ziegler still live around there?"

"Yes," Margaret said, and after describing her relationships to him, she asked, "How do you know him?"

"When we were young men, we entered training together for the priesthood. After a trial year, we left and went our separate ways. I'll be eager to see him."

Margaret stood to leave, shook Ryff's unsteady and gnarled hands, and invited him to meet her at her print shop by the Wood Market the next Monday.

At the inn that evening, the four Strasbourg travelers compared notes on their day.

"You're always looking for a business deal, aren't you, Margaret," Matthew said, laughing. "Can you make money with him?"

"I think so," she replied. "Did you make money off your pamphlets, Matthew? I made money off of you, and I hope you made some money too!" Katherine and Lucas laughed out loud.

After Lucas reviewed some ideas for improving the refugee center in the former Franciscan monastery in Strasbourg, Katherine blasted the church-and-state system that had imprisoned Anna. After she had reviewed the details of Anna's fate, Matthew asked, "What do you want us to do about it, overpower the guards and free her?"

"Buy one of those new guns and shoot the judge?" offered Lucas.

"Or," Margaret mused with a wicked grin, "we could tunnel underneath the prison and get her out in the middle of the night. Or do those guards actually stay awake at night?"

After they all laughed about the situation, because they didn't know what else to do, Katherine offered another outrageous suggestion. But she stated it seriously, and the laughing stopped. "Let's visit the bishop himself on the way home. Anna grew up in Molsheim, where he lives. Maybe he'd have sympathy for the woman and help us get her released."

"Oh, sure," Matthew answered. "The wise old bishop would just love to see me. He wants to put me under the ban, just as soon as the emperor arrives from fighting the French this December. He'd help us like the Duke of Lorraine helped the peasants at Saverne. Kill 'em all."

Katherine stood her ground and argued with all three of them at once. Other guests at the inn noticed the animated discussion and wondered what the point of difference was.

"You want to march up to the bishop's palace, knock on the door, and ask him to help release Anna Weiler?" Matthew asked.

"That and allow him to get to know you so the next time he wants to excommunicate you, there's a face behind the name," Katherine replied.

"That may be the best reason for going, Matthew," Margaret said. "Meeting the bishop and letting him actually see you might help you out in the long run."

"So you think that if I meet him and ask him to release Anna, I may reap dividends later when he tries to put pressure on the married priests of Strasbourg?" Matthew asked.

"Sounds like a pretty good business deal to me. Invest now, profits later," Margaret replied with a smile.

After a pause, Matthew said, "All right. I'm convinced. Will you go, Lucas?"

"Sure, I'd like to meet the old boy myself."

Thursday turned into more of a sightseeing adventure in Worms than a business trip. In the morning, Matthew led the foursome to the very spot where Martin Luther had taken his stand against the emperor. He recalled that someone had said that when Luther stood his ground and defended his beliefs, he stepped across the threshold into a new and more modern age. Or as Hans Hut, the flaming Anabaptist, might have put it, "the end of the age."

After lunch, Margaret slipped away from the others and went to the jail. After patiently answering every question the guard asked, she walked down the hallway to Anna's prison cell. The smell made her nauseated.

"Anna, I can't stay very long, but I want to ask you a question," Margaret began after they greeted each other. "Why did you leave Clement's barn so quickly three months ago?"

"You talked to Gertrude, didn't you?"

"I did, and she thought it unusual that you left in such a hurry. What happened?"

Anna took her time responding, staring at the floor, and then looking up at Margaret from underneath her hooded shawl. "It was that tall man Christman Kenlin," she said. "He took advantage of me."

"As a woman, you mean?"

"Yes," the dejected prisoner continued, "and I just couldn't take any more, so I ran away when he wasn't looking."

Startled with this information, Margaret hesitated and looked away in thought. Slowly, she offered, "If you ever get out of here, come and stay with me. We need more time to talk."

"Watch out for Kenlin," Anna warned. "He'll use you."

A rattling of keys from the warden alerted Margaret that he was coming and that it was time for her to go.

"I'll do what I can," Margaret said.

"Just pray," Anna sighed. "It's all that's left for anyone to do now."

Traveling up the Rhine was slow and hard. Shippers used a variety of methods to get their boats back upstream, all very slow. So the Zells, Margaret, and Lucas had arranged an overland route by horse carriage to Molsheim on Friday.

The carriage moved fast, and along the way at least four different sets of horses were used. The bumps jolted and jostled the riders mercilessly. Katherine's extra rider went for free, but the weight of that extra passenger made her feel like she'd been through a war zone by the time they arrived, late in the evening. After paying the fee for the carriage, they checked into an inn in Molsheim. A visit with the bishop would have to wait until the next morning.

Word of their arrival had reached the bishop before they called on him. After the monk at the front gate received their request for a visit, they waited for at least an hour before they got a response.

"The bishop is busy today," the monk stated coldly. "What is the purpose of your visit?"

"The pastor of the cathedral in Strasbourg would like to meet his Excellency," Katherine replied. "We are also seeking help for a woman who grew up in Molsheim."

By ten o'clock Margaret noticed that most of the monks had returned to their workplaces after the morning services. Soon the little monk returned and informed them that the bishop would receive them, but only for a very short visit, as he was busy.

The bishop was tall and thin, with neatly trimmed white hair and a sharp, long nose. His clear blue eyes provided a window to the mind of an intelligent man.

Before the bishop, Matthew said, "Your Excellency, we bring you greetings from Strasbourg. I'm glad we are able to meet."

"What is the purpose of your visit today?" the bishop demanded.

"My husband, Matthew, has been eager to meet you, Excellency" Katherine said. "He works side by side with your priests in the cathedral."

"He has married and broken the vows of a priest," the bishop said without any show of emotion.

"Excellency, we believe that marriage is of God," Katherine replied. "May you find it in your heart to accept Matthew as a true preacher of the Word."

"We have no power to change the traditions of the church," came the piercing reply. "The apostle Paul wrote that a man can best commit himself to the church as a single man. Now tell, me, how are things in Strasbourg?"

"The fair was a success this year, Your Excellency," Margaret volunteered. "The printing business thrives, printing both Catholic and Lutheran documents."

"And Anabaptist documents?" the bishop asked.

"Yes," Margaret replied. "Anabaptist documents are being produced for the Swiss Anabaptists and those living in south Germany."

"We hope they stay there. They are the scourge of the earth," the bishop said with scorn.

"They care for people," Lucas interjected, "as we do in helping the refugees of the peasants' war."

"God will provide for those who have needs," the bishop smugly responded.

"There is a lady of Molsheim who has a very great need, Your Excellency," Katherine said. "She lived in this village many years ago and studied writing and reading with me in Worms."

"That's not so long ago," the bishop replied. "You're still a young woman, and soon to be a mother I see."

"In September, with God's help, Your Excellency," Katherine replied. "The woman I refer to is Anna Weiler, who has been accused of being a witch. She sits in prison in Worms."

"God will judge his own and separate the wheat from the tares," the bishop declared.

"Had this woman lived a godly life she would not be sitting in prison now. The Holy Scriptures, in the book of Exodus, says that we should not allow a witch to live. Is this the main reason you have come to see me today?"

"Won't you please help her, Your Excellency?" Katherine begged. "She will die in the prison cell. In your mercy, please find it within yourself to speak to the Bishop of Worms and seek her release. Find out who her family is in Molsheim and you will discover that she is a good woman. In God's name, please help."

"We will look into the matter when the opportunity arises." With that the clear-eyed bishop wished the group a good day and sent them on their way.

On the road between Molsheim and Strasbourg, the four travelers discovered about thirty men walking in the direction of Strasbourg. Matthew asked what they were doing and where they were going. They told him that the parish minister in the nearby village of Kensingen—a man Matthew knew and a Lutheran—had been forced to leave that morning. To show their support for the minister, more than one hundred men walked with him for several miles. The men had returned to the village, but the Catholic officials had stationed troops at the gates and barred them from reentering until they repented of their false allegiance. About a third of them had refused to do so and were now retreating to Strasbourg, seeking refuge.

Lucas and Katherine promised the exhausted men shelter and something to eat at the former Franciscan monastery in Strasbourg.

Margaret arrived back at the print shop late Saturday night. Heinrich and Peter had made good progress that week printing *Four Voyages of Amerigo*. She was tired from her journeys, but satisfied. In one week, she had stood where Luther had made his stand against the emperor, had met the Bishop of Strasbourg, and had hired a writer to publish a medical manual that she would sell to people who wanted to live longer and become healthier.

Back in her little bedroom Margaret was glad to be home, but she missed Beck. "He probably had no idea what to do with himself in my absence," she speculated. With that pleasant thought, she blew out her candle and fell asleep.

11

Conducting an Inquisition

While Margaret traveled with the Zells, Beck became fascinated with ideas about the New World. He had carefully read the book Heinrich and Peter were printing that described Amerigo Vespucci's travels to foreign lands. The book had been written when Beck was a boy, and in the preface the author had used the name "America," a name that had become widely used.

Four Voyages of Amerigo was ready for distribution and sale in Strasbourg and cities nearby. The bookseller in Spain had hired Margaret to print and distribute the books in south Germany, rather than pay expensive costs to ship the books from Barcelona. Margaret had worked on the book for several months, fitting other pamphlets and print jobs in that were more urgent.

On Saturday mornings Margaret organized her work, planned ahead, and cleaned the shop alone. Heinrich and Peter usually got Saturday off.

A week after her return from Worms, Margaret asked Beck if he would like to deliver sample copies to the bookseller in Barcelona. "I'm ready," Beck responded. "I'll take off work and leave on Monday."

"You seem in a big hurry to go," Margaret said. "Will Knobloch give you another week off?"

"I really don't care if he doesn't, Margaret. I'm ready to leave their employ."

"Well then, Beck. You deliver two copies of the book and

make a final agreement on how much he gets from the profits when the books sell. I'll start shipping the books to Speyer, Colmar, Worms, and Basel immediately. Who will you take along?"

"I'd like to take Wolfgang and his friend Jacques Lefèvre," Beck answered.

"Who's this friend of Wolfgang?"

"Lefèvre is a radical professor from Paris—or at least he was until some other professors ran him out for his unacceptable beliefs. He's come to Strasbourg to live with Wolfgang for a while until it's safe to go back."

"When will that be?"

"It's pretty strange right now in France. The French king was captured two months ago in a war with Charles V. So the emperor has him locked up in a prison in Spain. In the meantime, the pope issued a statement encouraging the Catholic parliament in Paris to attack heretics in France. Reformers like Lefèvre are on the run until the king is released from prison, which might be this month or next year—who knows?"

"So how did you get to know him?

"I met him at the Thursday evening discussion group at Kniebs's house. He talked to Hans Hut and they made the connection that Conrad Grebel, one of the leaders of the Anabaptists in Zurich, had studied with Lefèvre in Paris. Lefèvre has translated the New Testament from Greek to French, and his commentaries have emphasized salvation by faith alone, against Catholic tradition, a lot like Luther."

"But why are you taking these two men with you?"

"When I told Wolfgang I might travel to Barcelona next week, his eyes lit up and he asked if he could go along. He's never visited Spain, and with all the new exploration going on in America, he's eager to see the country that sends out explorers. He'll pay his own way, of course."

"And since Lefèvre's staying with Wolfgang, he'll go along too, right?"

"Yes, and he's got money to pay his own way."

And so it was decided. Beck would go to Spain to conduct Margaret's business; the Lutheran preacher of St. Thomas Church, soon to be married to the Knobloch woman, wanted to see a new land and travel; and the brilliant French professor, exiled from Paris, would travel with them to the city of explorers, Barcelona.

Their luggage was light and their route easily mapped out. Each man had a small bag with a couple of books and a change of clothes. Beck took along two copies of *Four Voyages of Amerigo*, Wolfgang carried a German New Testament and a copy of Luther's recent commentary on the peasants' war, and Lefèvre brought his French New Testament and a book entitled *In Praise of Folly* by Desiderius Erasmus.

On Monday morning they struck out on horses over the canals, through the Butcher's Gate, and south through the Alsace valley toward Belfort. From Belfort it wasn't far to the Saône River that flowed to the Rhone River and south to the Mediterranean Sea. For a small fee, a man who ran a stable by the river, serving travelers, promised to feed and water their horses until they returned. On the return trip they'd load their horses on a boat and float downstream on the Ill to Strasbourg.

Lefèvre guessed that if anyone in southern France figured out who he was, he might be forced back to Paris, but he wasn't worried. He was growing a beard to accent his distinguished and handsome face, and as his whiskers grew, he looked less and less like a professor of theology from Paris.

Christman helped operate the arsenal of weapons, pamphlets, and books that went in and out of Zieglers' barn.

When he learned from Clement that Beck would be gone for a week or more, he took over as the arsenal's lookout. At lunchtime on Monday, he stopped by Margaret's shop.

"Good day, Margaret. How are you?"

"I'm fine, and you?"—"What is he doing here?" she asked herself.

"I wondered if there were any pamphlets or books you wanted delivered to the barn? I'm watchman this week."

"Not right now," Margaret answered. "I'm trying hard to stay out of trouble," she added with a forced smile, trying to ease a tense situation.

"Nobody would suspect you of being a troublemaker," he politely responded. "I've really come to invite you to an open house at the Stone Street area cloth makers' guild. We run an annual event to bring people in and show them what we do. Would you be interested?"

"I'm pretty busy this week, Christman. I'll have to pass on your invitation."

"Then how about a meal together and we go afterward to Nicholas Kniebs's house for Thursday-evening discussion?"

Margaret wanted Christman to move on quickly, and she figured the easiest way to do that was to agree to go with him Thursday evening. She'd be going to the Kniebs's house anyway. "Okay, I'll be ready after quitting time."

"Good, Margaret. I know of a great little place to eat. Do you like fish?"

"Sure."

"I'll be here soon after quitting time on Thursday. See you then."

The three traveling partners sailed quickly downstream through southern France on their way to Spain. This region had been aflame with the Inquisition, a terrible time of persecution carried out by the Catholic Church during the previous several hundred years. Anyone who held different views from the Church, such as minority groups of believers like the Cathars or Waldensians, had come under severe judgment. If the condemned didn't immediately respond, he or she would be tortured into confessing to being a heretic. Then they'd be handed over to the state for punishment, often burning at the stake. Brutal inquisitors used words of Jesus from Luke's Gospel, "make them come in," to justify their actions.

According to the twisted, callous, and faulty interpretation of the fifteenth- and sixteenth-century Inquisition, Christ himself in the Gospel of John had ordered that heretics were to be burned: "If a man abide not in me, he is cast forth as a branch, and is withered; and men gather them, and cast them into the fire, and they are burned."

As the three men traveled by ship around the southern coast of France and entered Spanish waters, Lefèvre told Wolfgang and Beck about Torquemada, the first Grand Inquisitor in Spain—and perhaps the worst inquisitors of all time. For fifteen years Torquemada had terrorized Jews, Muslims, and any minority Christians who didn't hold the official views of the Church. Estimates were that he burned about two thousand at the stake. As their boat sailed along the east coast and the region of Aragon, Lefèvre said, "Here Torquemada burned more than 430 people. After his death edict of 1492, most of the Jews fled Spain."

Beck remarked to Lefèvre as they watched the Spanish coast in the distance from their ship, "You're saying that, when I was two years old, Christopher Columbus sailed to the West Indies and in that same year the Jews were run out of Spain?"

"Exactly," he sharply replied. "We live in an age of intolerance."

"You're on the run from a Catholic parliament in Paris,"

Wolfgang said, "and I'm under fire from the Bishop of Strasbourg for wanting to get married. Beck, are you in any kind of trouble with the Church?"

"Not that I know of, but as Margaret and I read the pamphlets she prints, we're more and more attracted to the radical ideas of the Anabaptists. I'm fascinated by the beliefs of Clement Ziegler, Hans Hut, George Blaurock, and others like them. Margaret printed a pamphlet on believers baptism recently for the Anabaptists in Switzerland. It made a lot of sense."

"You watch out for the Anabaptists," Lefèvre warned. "If they're not yet accused by the emperor, they will be soon. They're bound to end up like the hundreds of people here in Spain who choose to believe differently than the establishment. Let's just hope we can get in and out of Barcelona without being plunked down in prison ourselves. If the Grand Inquisitor finds out about our beliefs, he'll have three more burnings to amuse the faithful and frighten the heretics.

"Here, stick your hand in this little iron box." Lefèvre grabbed his backpack and shoved it toward Wolfgang and Beck with one end open. "The hot coals will burn the flesh off your bones. If you confess your heresy, they'll burn the rest of your flesh and bones at the stake. If you didn't confess, they'll burn the other hand to make you think about it and stick you in prison for a very long time. The swelling will probably kill you if the gruel they feed you doesn't."

Beck hadn't expected the hustle and bustle of the people in Barcelona. A Spanish explorer had discovered new lands, and now others followed, from Spain and neighboring Portugal. Gold and silver had already started to trickle back into the Spanish economy, raising expectations for an even better standard of living for the rich families of Barcelona.

On the other hand, some of the merchants of Barcelona

realized that cities on the western side of the Spanish and Portuguese Peninsula, such as Lisbon, Cadiz, and La Coruña, stood to profit most from the new exploration in the Atlantic Ocean. Barcelona opened east into the Mediterranean Sea. These days Turkish pirates prowled those waters, robbing, pillaging, and drowning the weak.

Wealthy kings and queens funded mariners and adventurers who sailed west and south with little fear and high hopes of profit. Not too many years earlier, when the three travelers were boys, Vasco da Gama had sailed all the way to India around the Cape of Good Hope at the southern tip of Africa. The dangerous, difficult, and expensive overland routes to Asia through Islamic territory weren't as popular anymore. Times were changing for Barcelona merchants.

Almost four days after he had left Margaret's shop in Strasbourg, Beck met the bookseller who had contracted work to Margaret. The Spaniard knew a little German, and Beck understood even less Spanish, but they patiently conducted their business. The bookseller complimented Beck on the quality of the two books. After establishing the cost, the bookseller and Beck agreed on a fifty-fifty split of the profits. Based on the number of books they had printed and the intended markup, Beck could pay the bookseller his profit. Margaret then would collect the balance from the sale of the books.

At the university in Barcelona, Lefèvre and Wolfgang studied the map of the New World in the library. The Spanish proudly displayed their accomplishments. Columbus and Vespucci had died years ago, but their discoveries had changed the world. These days, in the 1520s, the most daring and adventurous sailed for America, searching for land and gold. Catholic monks boarded those same ships for far-flung lands and went along to Christianize the natives and baptize their babies.

That evening Beck posed a question for Lefèvre and Wolfgang. "Should Margaret print a book that describes how to conduct a witch trial? The book encourages judges to pursue suspected witches and concludes that just about all witches are women. Its title is *The Hammer of Female Witches*. The bookseller thinks it would sell well in Europe; he thinks Margaret could make a handsome profit."

"What do you think Margaret would say?" Wolfgang asked. The Strasbourg preacher with the little black hat answered his own question: "If I know Margaret, she'd turn this job down. Authorities everywhere would buy it, but the book would be used on real people as a weapon of intolerance and abuse."

"You're right," Beck said. "I turned the bookseller down because I figured Margaret would object. You've confirmed my hunches."

"When will people be able to stand up for what's right and not be cut down like hay before a sickle?" Lefèvre wondered aloud. "When will differences of belief be tolerated?"

"When a hundred thousand peasants get mowed down like a spring cutting of hay, and witches are burned by the hundreds, I'd say we still have a long way to go," Wolfgang replied.

Relaxing just a little, the Strasbourg travelers began to talk about less weighty subjects. The preacher checked to see that his collar was turned up; Lefèvre struggled to comb his unruly hair; and Beck stretched out his gangly legs.

Hundreds of miles northeast of Barcelona, in Germany, Anna endured another lonely day in her tiny prison cell. The only visitor that day would be the grubby warden bringing her some reeking food and a dry piece of bread. The Inquisition wasn't theory to her—she cowered under its crushing demands day and night.

Several years earlier Anna's husband had been killed fighting for the Catholic emperor against non-Catholics in northern Germany. Yes, she had allowed herself to be taken advantage of by two or three men, but only because she was lonely. When she had threatened to expose her latest abusive lover, he had accused her of being a witch in the disguise of a cat. In the courtroom the judge had undressed her down to the waist to confirm the mark the man claimed would prove his charge. Though it was clearly only a birthmark, the judge was eager to please Anna's accuser and play up to the gawking of the men who gathered like hungry vultures in his courtroom.

Once he had pronounced her a witch, Anna was as good as dead. Since then she had been on the run, with Clement's so-called arsenal outside Strasbourg being one stop along her lonely journey to nowhere. Anna realized that this dark and damp prison in Worms might be her final destination.

Beck picked up the theological conversation. "From what I can gather from the Anabaptists, they believe in a free church, unguarded or controlled by any government. That makes a lot of sense to me, but we haven't seen a free church for so many years in Europe, I'm not sure we'd know what one looks like." Margaret would have noticed the squint on his face.

In a plaza near the center of Barcelona, not much different from the one in Strasbourg, the three men were eating and watching the bustling economic activity around them. Despite the liveliness, the sense of oppression was palpable.

"I believe the early church stood clear of the Roman government," Lefèvre said. "Not until the time of Constantine in the early fourth century did Christians join with the government." He spoke with the authority his profession gave him.

"So, how do you evaluate Emperor Constantine's conversion in the year 312?" Wolfgang asked. "Was it good for the church, or bad?"

"I'd say it was bad," Beck answered.

"But it made Europe Christian for the past thirteen centuries," Wolfgang shot back, breathing heavily.

"What does Martin Luther say about the peasants' war?" Lefèvre asked.

"Luther condemns the peasants and says they were being disobedient," Wolfgang answered. "He doesn't believe the peasants had any right to try to change the government. That must happen naturally over time."

Beck sneered. "Governments just naturally change over time to help out the poor peasants. Sure they do. All three of us know governments are based on keeping power, and as long as possible."

"So who supports Luther and his Reformation?" Lefèvre asked.

"The rich nobles of Saxony," Beck angrily replied.

Wolfgang's breathing grew almost silent, his jaws slowly churning. "You've got to have a state government to protect your church," he finally said. "Luther would be dead without his protectors. And then where would the Reformation be today?"

"Perhaps Luther would be dead, like other heretics, " Beck responded. "But I'd guess his church would be free, like the Anabaptists are."

Wolfgang pushed his plate and cup back, rose, and strolled into the plaza. On the other side of it, four guards pushed a bent-over prisoner along, shackled and beaten, either on the way to be sentenced or back to prison for a longer stay, or worse, to be burned at the stake. Wolfgang assumed he was a man; he couldn't quite tell. The Spanish Inquisition was merciless. Anyone who stood in its way was brushed aside and trampled.

"You've touched on a raw nerve, Beck," Lefèvre told his

printer friend. "Leave Wolfgang alone and don't bring up Luther and his Saxon noble protectors again unless you want a quarrel. Or a fight."

Christman arrived right on time Thursday evening. Margaret had wondered all week about how to get out of her agreement with him. She had given in just to get him out of her shop, and now it was time to honor her agreement or disappear for the evening.

"This is too much," Margaret said to herself as Christman opened the door to Fish Mongers. "What will Beck say when he finds out?" she wondered. She kept the conversation on small talk, deflecting anything he asked that would bring up faith, her work, or the man she loved. This was just a social evening out, Margaret assured herself, plus she got a good meal out of the deal. But Remembering Anna's accusation of him, and she became more on edge and wary.

But Christman seemed animated and happy to be with her. Even at the Kniebs's house, he was open and contributed to the discussion. He had left the rough side of his character at the door.

Margaret hoped he wouldn't want to walk her back to her print shop afterward, but he did, and she quickly told him "thanks, and good-bye," and reached for the door latch.

"Thanks for a wonderful evening," Christman said. "I'd sure be glad to see you again. You know, Margaret, I've lived here most of my life, I know this city, and I know your family. We'd make a great business team."

Margaret didn't have to wonder what he meant. He was probably right about the local connection being good for business, but from what Anna had told her, there was a side of him that he kept well hidden.

"Thanks for the dinner and conversation, Christman. I'll see you later."

The trip home from Barcelona took longer than the trip to get there, primarily because the boat ride up the Rhone and Saône rivers was slow and tedious. Unless the wind blew favorably, in which case sails could be used, oxen and mules pulled the boats upstream to where the horses had been stabled. From there they galloped to Belfort, found a boat headed for Strasbourg, led the horses aboard, and floated down the Ill River.

Two bulky towers met them at the entrance to the city. Between them, over the canals that separated the water around the city, stood bridges that spanned the canals. The roofs of the bridges were covered and slanted to protect the city from unfriendly invaders, like the Turks who were advancing on Europe right then. The hangman of Strasbourg occupied one of the towers. On the third floor he kept the condemned waiting, with little else for them to do except scrawl their names and messages on the walls.

Even in the friendly city of Strasbourg—the Anabaptists increasingly saw it as a city of refuge—those who stepped outside the accepted lines of official belief or who violated the laws of the city council could end up in the Hangman's Tower and face a dreadful day with the executioner.

Margaret agreed with Beck's judgment; she would not have printed *The Hammer of Female Witches*, the inquisitors' guide to burning witches. She told Beck that during his week-and-a-half absence more Anabaptists had arrived in Strasbourg. And the discussions at Kniebs's house had been vigorous, with baptism of infants the topic of debate.

It took a little time to get the energy flowing in their love affair again. In Beck's absence Margaret had worked hard managing and directing the work in the shop, doing a man's work as needed. At dinner that evening, Beck described the geography of their trip to Barcelona. Margaret never brought up her time with Christman.

"I have an idea for a trip," Beck said. "Colmar would make a great place for us to visit and spend a few days looking around."

Margaret smiled at the suggestion and was reminded of why she wanted to marry Beck. Though he had strong opinions, he didn't pressure her into decisions, but gave her a lot of room to be herself. And he loved her for exactly who she was. While he talked about the trip to Barcelona, she also was reminded that he had ideas. Usually, they were good ones too.

Beck's description of the Spanish Inquisition brought Margaret back to reality and made her sick. Behind him she noticed the Hangman's Tower in the distance and was aware of the cathedral tower behind her. "These symbols of power are always present, reminding us, warning us, threatening us," she thought.

"My little press is helping to change Strasbourg and south Germany," Margaret said to Beck. "On the other hand, powerful forces have tightened their grip on little people to keep them in line."

"I'm with you," Beck replied, squeezing her hand. They looked at each other for a moment and wondered about the future.

To celebrate their reunion, they walked together along the canal, connecting the bonds of their love, arm in arm, determined to take a stand for what they believed to be true and right. In those days of turmoil, they wondered just where to turn for the interpretation that seemed best and sure.

At least their love had remained firm. For that they were grateful, and after a kiss and a strong embrace, Beck headed to his cramped little room and Margaret returned to her little bedroom in the back of the print shop by the Wood Market.

On the way in the door Margaret noticed the long, moonlit shadow of the cathedral spire resting directly on her sturdy little house. If Christman watched from somewhere out there in the shadows, he'd have to soon accept the fact that she wanted the newcomer, not him.

12

Confronting the Jews

Near the end of July 1525, Johanan Loria, the local rabbi, sparked a vigorous debate. Backed by city council, Sturm had ordered the Jews living in Strasbourg to wear their little yellow identification badges at all times. Actually, no Jews lived inside the city walls of Strasbourg—they had been expelled 150 years earlier and lived to the west of the city, just outside the White Gate. The Bishop of Strasbourg also decided to crack down on the Jews, the one group he figured he could still easily control. So the bishop summoned the rabbi and ordered him and the other Jews in the region to wear yellow badges, in the shape of the Star of David, whenever they left their houses. It was a heated encounter. Rabbi Loria stood his ground and challenged the bishop's orders like no rabbi had done for two centuries.

The Jews in many parts of Europe had been technically required to wear the yellow badges for generations. But enforcing the edict was a local matter and often occurred at opportunistic moments.

After the meeting with the rabbi ended, the determined bishop demanded that Sturm and the city council crack down on the Jews.

At about the same time that the bishop was trying to intimidate the city's Jews, the end-times-obsessed Hut arrived in Strasbourg from travels in Switzerland. He wanted to print a pamphlet he had translated from Latin, which claimed to all who read it that the true Messiah had come and called on

Jews to convert to Christianity. It detailed reasons from the Old Testament why the Jews should convert to Christianity.

But Hut wasn't the only one trying to convert Jews. Luther had also written a pamphlet that urged the Jews to join the Reformation movement.

Hut went to Margaret's shop early one day to seek her printing services. When he informed her that the writer of the pamphlet was actually a Jew from Aragon, Spain, who had converted to Christianity, she guessed Beck wouldn't like it. "I have a good friend who just returned from Spain, where the Inquisition condemns and executes Jews," she said. "What you want from me is to print a pamphlet seeking the conversion of the Jews to Christianity and explaining their errors?"

"You've heard of the *Star of David* pamphlet, I assume?" Hut asked.

"I saw a copy in Worms. Why should I print this pamphlet for you?"

"All around us we see signs of the end of the age. Biblical prophecy tells us that many Jews will come to Christ in the last days. I believe that Luther's Reformation has opened the door for many Jews to believe in the true Messiah."

Hut realized he wasn't convincing Margaret to print his pamphlet, but he thought perhaps she might do the job in order to make a profit. "I'm visiting friends in Strasbourg and I'll stop back in a few days to find out your decision." With that the tall German handed the pamphlet to her and left.

Margaret had given Ryff, her self-educated doctor of home remedies, a desk in the corner of the shop. From his little table, Ryff was organizing and writing a medical book. He couldn't help but hear the conversation she'd just had with Hut. "That pamphlet would probably sell," he told her. "Do you know anything about what has happened to Jews in Strasbourg in the past?"

"I know they've been persecuted and pushed outside the city walls, but beyond that, not much," Margaret told him. "What do you know?"

Being remarkably informed on a wide variety of subjects, he replied, "In the middle of the 1300s, the plague struck hard in Strasbourg, and many people died. Then an earthquake destroyed homes and killed even more people. The desperate residents decided that the Jews were to blame. And so, as in other cities of Europe at the time, more than two thousand Jewish men, women, and children were burned to death. Only a few children and some of the beautiful women were spared from the fire. Of course, Catholic Church leaders repented shortly afterward, but the damage had already been done. By 1390, all Jews had been expelled from Strasbourg."

"So that's why they live outside the city walls today?" Heinrich asked.

"That's right," Ryff replied. "I've learned from Clement that Sturm and the city council need to decide how hard to crack down on the Jews. Seems our overbearing bishop is putting pressure on the council to act."

"How do you know so much about the Jews?" Heinrich asked.

Ryff responded slowly. "Good question. When the truth is told, my grandfather was Jewish."

"So how did your family get separated from the Jewish community?" Margaret asked.

"Seems the city fathers in Strasbourg didn't mind if Jewish men occasionally visited the official city brothel. When my grandmother, who worked there and wasn't Jewish, became pregnant and gave birth to my father, he was adopted and raised by a non-Jewish family who lived inside the city walls. After my father married and had children of his own, we moved around a lot."

"Have you ever been married?" Margaret asked.

"No. It's much easier to keep on the move by yourself than with a family."

Katherine's warm kitchen in the center of the city often operated as a counseling center for people who found themselves in difficult situations. Working through her husband, who communicated with Wolfgang, she had invited Agnes to come and visit.

"Tell me about your family," Katherine asked.

"My mother and father have four children," Agnes began. "My older sister lives at home, like I do, one of my brothers is fighting for the emperor in France, and an older brother runs his own business."

"How has it felt for you to be the youngest?" Katherine asked.

"Smothered. My parents have been very protective. They love me, of course, but I'm old enough to be making my own decisions."

"Like marrying Wolfgang?"

"Exactly. They're not going to stop me this time."

"Marriage is a great thing. It's also a lifetime commitment. Are you ready for that?"

"Yes, and I'm ready to get out from under my parents' roof. They've been so restrictive of my freedom to get out and do what I want to do."

"What do you want to do?"

"Well, I'm going to marry Wolfgang, and then we'll see."

Katherine changed the subject toward more shallow matters, and the two women talked for a while.

"Well," Katherine said as it came time for her to prepare lunch for Matthew, "you come back here to talk anytime you want to."

"Thanks. I'll probably do that."

The most well-known Lutheran organizer in Strasbourg was thirty-four-year-old preacher Martin Bucer. Once a Dominican friar, now married to a former nun, the stocky and powerfully built man had written about the Jews. Bucer believed the Jews should get rid of the Talmud, a religious book they used alongside the Old Testament. They should not be allowed to build a new synagogue, Bucer wrote, guessing that eventually the Jews would want a bigger meeting place because the shed where they worshipped only had room for about ten men.

Bucer also believed that Jews should engage in work that is wearisome, unprofitable, and below the occupations of good Christians in Strasbourg. Jobs that Jews could hold were ditch digging, masonry, chimney sweeping, sewer cleaning, laundry work, and the carting of ashes.

Bucer and other reformers taught that, according to the book of Deuteronomy, the Jews of Europe were condemned for being unfaithful. Jews must take an oath, Bucer wrote, not to do any harm to Christ and his true religion. He also said they shouldn't argue about religious beliefs, and they must go to regular Christian preaching to teach them of their errors. Further, they needed to pay the city council a tax for their protection.

Bucer had convinced Sturm that action was needed against the Jews; it would keep the bishop satisfied that the city council was doing something and it would relax his criticisms of the Reformation movement. It may have only been coincidence, Margaret thought, but it was strange that the morning after Hut presented his "conversion" pamphlet to her, Sturm showed up at her shop like he did whenever something important was about to happen.

"Good morning, Margaret," Sturm began. "The city council will enforce the requirement that Jews wear their badges at all times. If you see any of them not wearing badges, notify us immediately. Further, we've decided to round up all Jewish writings and destroy them."

In answer to Margaret's question about news of his nephew, Sturm said, "Nothing. Three months of absolute silence." Margaret noticed a tired and angry look emerging in his face. In an instant, he turned and left.

Margaret debated in her mind what to do next. She knew that certain groups in her day would always be persecuted: Jews, accused witches, minority Christian groups like the Anabaptists, and anyone who didn't hold the correct "Christian" views. She wondered if Kniebs would be courageous enough to invite Rabbi Loria to a Thursday-evening discussion group.

When Margaret asked Kniebs, he agreed, much to her surprise. The word quickly went out to gather that evening for discussion on the place of Jews in Christian Strasbourg.

Rabbi Loria made a reasoned and impassioned plea for toleration. "We are descendants of God's ancient people, the Israelites. We have been forced out of Palestine, the Promised Land, only for a while. Someday the land of Israel will be ours again.

"Today the Turks control our holy land and we live in many small communities through Europe, North Africa, and the Middle East. We want to be faithful to God's call in our lives, even though we don't live in the land God gave our ancestors."

Hut asked the rabbi, "But do you believe in the true Messiah, Christ of Nazareth?"

"Certainly, he was a great prophet and wise teacher," Loria responded. "But there were many who claimed to be the true Messiah during Roman times, though none was able to establish a Jewish nation because of the power of the Roman armies. At our Passover feasts we celebrate the

Exodus out of Egypt, when Moses led our people to the Promised Land. The true Messiah will help us regain the sacred land of Judah and Galilee."

"Who do you believe the Messiah is or will be, if not Jesus Christ of Nazareth?" Margaret asked.

"In the very last chapter of the Old Testament we read that in the day of the Lord, God will send the prophet Elijah to announce the Messiah's arrival. We set a plate at our Passover meal in case the prophet comes to begin his work."

"Elijah already came—his name was John the Baptist," Hut insisted.

"According to your interpretation," Loria shot back. "But why have Christians been so hard on the Jews?"

Hut reviewed for the group the way in which the Gentile Pilate tried to release Jesus, a Jew, and not execute him. In response, the Jews had answered Pilate that Christ's blood would be on them and their children. "It's in Matthew," Hut said. "Look it up."

"We don't use your New Testament," Loria replied.

"That's why you must read my pamphlet outlining how Christ is the true Messiah from the pages of the Old Testament. If I had a copy, I'd give you one."

"I've read similar documents before."

Ryff asked the rabbi the next question. "Is there any hope of receiving better treatment at the hands of the city council here in Strasbourg?"

"Your Reformation movement has the city council crossed up with the Catholic bishop. Both groups want to punish my people."

"Will you wear the yellow badge?"

"I don't have a choice. The yellow badge identifies me so I can be taken advantage of in every possible way."

The next day the bishop's imperial guard swept through the tiny Jewish community on the outskirts of the city. They found no more than ten houses where Jews lived. In each home they found the book they were looking for, the Talmud.

To the Jews, the most important book of religious law besides the Torah, or the five books of Moses, was the Talmud. The first copies of the book had just recently arrived from Venice. The Jews loved the new books, but the imperial guard rounded up copies of the Talmud and other religious volumes they discovered, especially in the rabbi's home, and planned to burn them.

The bishop's office had organized the book burning well. To publicize the event, the bishop's guard printed a woodcut image of the suspected ritual murder of a baptized Catholic boy. According to the charge, a generation earlier the boy had been slain by the Jews of Trent in northern Italy. The woodcut, printed at the Knobloch press, showed nine Jews holding the boy on a table while they bled him to death, catching his blood in a bowl. The accusation stated that the Jews murdered the boy and collected his blood for their Passover. This alleged execution symbolized for Christian Europe the evils of Judaism. Jews were being regularly accused and executed in Europe for the ritual murder of Christian children. The guard posted notices around the city and announced a book burning for Saturday, the Jewish Sabbath.

On Friday, Hut stopped back at the print shop to find out if Margaret would print his pamphlet, which he claimed demonstrated from the Old Testament that Jesus of Nazareth was the true Messiah. The pamphlet was needed to convince the Jews to join the Christian Reformation. In spite of her sympathies toward the plight of the Jews and others in her day who experienced persecution, Margaret agreed to take the job. "Hut will pay for it," she reasoned.

After Vespers on Saturday, when the shadows began to

lengthen, the burning began. The guards piled the books together and used hot coals to get the blaze ignited. Margaret winced at the burning of the fine volumes, not because she agreed with what the Talmud said, but because she recognized the quality and value of the works themselves.

"This will be a losing battle," Margaret thought as she and Beck watched the fire burn. "There are too many printers and too many presses." She knew that using fear and book burning as a way of controlling unacceptable ideas would fail, even though the Catholic Church would continue to try to keep people in line through various means of intimidation.

But Gutenberg's printing press had ushered in a new era. Though the authorities tried to stop the printers, new ideas spread quickly. As with the persecution of the early Christians, attempts to suppress new beliefs only fanned the flames of faith. Just about anybody—Anabaptists, home-styled doctors, Jews, scholars—could get their thoughts and perspectives printed. The Church and council might crack down on some groups or individuals, but that couldn't stop the spread of printed materials that challenged traditions.

On their way back to the cathedral area that evening, Margaret and Beck talked about the book burning. "They'll never be able to stop the printers from producing pamphlets that don't agree with the Catholic Church," Margaret began.

"True, Margaret," Beck said. "The printing press changes things for those with new ideas. I believe the city council needs to stop persecuting people with different beliefs."

"It will take time, but new points of view will eventually overwhelm the power of the imperial guard."

"I'm glad you're on my side," Beck said with a grin. He squeezed her hand and then wrapped his arm around her as they walked along the canal.

"I'm ready for the trip you promised me to Colmar, Balt. Let's set a time to go."

They stopped in the plaza by the cathedral to look at the printed announcement of the book burning. "The Knobloch press," Margaret read.

"I didn't even know we did that one," Beck said.

"Guess it's a pretty big shop. The printing press can be used in whatever way people want it to be used, for good or for bad."

They studied the horrifying execution sketch. "We have to use our press to promote reason and tolerance, printing ideas that build up and help people to live better lives," Margaret said.

"Our press?"

"Sorry, just a slip of the tongue," Margaret replied. "But it's not a bad idea," she quickly added.

"A wish I have right now is that you kiss me," Beck responded. "Follow me."

At their wooden bench by the canal, the two embraced and held each other close.

"Beck, did I do the right thing by agreeing to print Hut's pamphlet? He's such a brash fireball about his beliefs."

Beck raised his finger to say "no business talk now." There'd be time enough to shape the world of ideas later. For now, two printers sent messages of love to each other. The words, neither written nor spoken, were easy to understand. It was a warm July evening, and the temperature on the little perch by the canal was rising.

Christman organized a group from Stone Street on Sunday evening. Around his kitchen table, they agreed to resist the bishop's demand to turn in Jews who weren't wearing the yellow badge. "We just won't do it," Christman told the independents from the north side of the city.

On the other side of the city, Agnes had the shutters of her second-story bedroom window pushed all the way out to try to get a nighttime breeze going in the stuffy house. An hour after the informal resistance meeting on Stone Street broke up, she noticed the outline of a tall man, stationed in the shadows on the street corner below, just outside her window.

Within minutes, Agnes crept down the stairs, slipped out the front door unnoticed, and disappeared into the humid night. The dark silhouette on the street corner had also vanished.

Part III

August-September 1525

13

Invasion of the Turks

On the first Wednesday in August, the citizens of Strasbourg learned that the "scourge of God" was threatening Christian Europe. Informed residents of Strasbourg had known for some years that the Ottoman Turks were marching into Greece, Serbia, Bosnia, and Hungary, so it was hardly a surprise when the emperor's ambassador, a Hungarian named Hieronymus Balbus, came to town seeking money, soldiers, and support for the war against the infidels.

The short, stocky, dark-haired Hungarian stood to speak at an assembly of the city council. The public had been invited to attend, so Margaret, Beck, Matthew, and Katherine went.

"Citizens of the most Holy Roman Empire awaken," the husky-voiced patriot bellowed. "I beg of you. Do not allow the heretics from Constantinople to destroy Hungary with their hairy warriors on horseback."

Margaret shifted in her seat. This would not be like one of Matthew's Sunday sermons.

"Today the engineers of Süleyman are building a bridge over the Sava River near Belgrade," Balbus continued. "You remember that when Martin Luther took his stand for the Reformation in Worms, four years ago, Emperor Charles V was young and new to his position. So was Süleyman, sultan of the Ottoman Muslims. But while Charles fought the French in Europe, Süleyman conquered Belgrade and then the island of Rhodes in the Mediterranean Sea. I warned the emperor and the Diet at Worms to send money and troops to defend Hungary, but no one listened. Now the situation is much worse."

Katherine's baby kicked while she listened. She wondered for a moment if her child was a boy and if he would be entangled in fighting the emperor's battles against Süleyman's troops in the east. The two leaders, each eager for more power and wealth, would probably battle for decades.

"Today," Balbus thundered, "the Ottoman sultan has one thousand men building a bridge over the Sava. Next month he'll build a bridge over the Drava River. Then the infidel intends to march up the west bank of the Danube River with one hundred thousand men and conquer Vienna. After that all of Europe lies before him."

Balbus jabbed his fist into the air. "The emperor has sent me to Strasbourg today. Each of the sixty-five free imperial cities is required to supply two hundred soldiers for the emperor's battle in the east."

Matthew whispered to Beck, "He already has three hundred men from Strasbourg fighting in France. The emperor has two battles going at once. No one wants to fight the Turks. What are they going to do, force us to fight?"

"In the name of almighty God," Balbus shouted, "the esteemed emperor, the blessed Virgin, and the most holy pope, join the battle and save Christian Europe. Otherwise you may find Muslim infidels roaming the streets of Strasbourg, raping your women, robbing your homes, and burning your beautiful cathedral."

Beck thought, "There'd be some folks here in Strasbourg who wouldn't exactly mind if the cathedral burned." He was thinking of Hut, Christman, and Jörg. Seiler would hardly shed a tear either.

"Here's another reason for helping to defend the Empire in the east," Balbus continued. "Your good Bishop of Strasbourg has called for a new crusade against the infidel. These men are the scourge of God, they violate the holy land of the Bible, they've destroyed the great cathedrals in Constantinople, they sin against the Holy Scriptures, and they are without God and the blessings of the Virgin Mary. Take up your arms, men of Strasbourg, and defend your land, your heritage, and your faith."

It was a hot evening in Strasbourg. The sweat ran down the Hungarian's forehead and the front of his shirt was soaked. A good rain shower earlier in the day had broken the humidity, but the stifling air had quickly returned.

"How will the emperor get the two hundred soldiers he wants?" Beck asked Matthew on the way out of the cathedral. "Will he get any volunteers?"

"A few, perhaps, but not many," Matthew answered. "Only about twenty percent of the residents of Strasbourg are citizens, mostly men. That's the pool Sturm has to draw from to raise his share of the soldiers who are needed in Hungary."

"Or supposedly needed," Margaret said. "Who knows what the truth is?"

"It is true that the infidels have conquered just about everything east of Italy," Matthew answered. "They must be stopped or the Hungarian's prophecy about invading Strasbourg may come true."

"Will you go, Matthew?" Margaret asked.

"As a citizen I may need to join the emperor's forces, but as a new husband and soon-to-be father, I want to stay here."

"In one piece, I might add," Katherine said. They laughed, though they also realized the situation was serious. Europe was under siege from the east, soldiers were needed, and Matthew might be assigned to go. Beck, on the other hand, could volunteer in the bishop's crusade, but he wouldn't be forced to fight because he wasn't a citizen of Strasbourg. He was a resident of the Holy Roman Empire, however, and that placed him ultimately under the authority of the emperor's army.

The Hungarian wasn't the only visitor to Strasbourg during the first week of August. Religious refugees from all over south-central Europe flocked to Strasbourg because of its tolerance and openness to different points of view. No one powerful religious reformer presided at Strasbourg, so a variety of religious beliefs flowered in the city.

The Anabaptist migration to Strasbourg had begun as a trickle earlier in the year, but by August it ran like a small but steady stream, mostly following the Rhine itself. Zurich and the Swiss regions where the Anabaptists lived was only about eighty or a hundred miles to the southeast of Strasbourg. The Ottoman Turks hadn't bothered Swiss cities yet because the mountains perched them so high in the sky that Süleyman left them alone. At least until now, that is.

Part of the reason the old barn had kept its secret for so long was because refugees who stayed in the granary came at intervals that lasted weeks or sometimes even months. Beck watched the barn in early August, but nobody hid there then. A few weapons remained, left over from the disastrous peasants' revolt. For now there wasn't much to monitor at the barn. Most exiles from other places who fled to Strasbourg could find someone to keep them in the city.

The escaped prisoner whom Christman had shipped north in the bottom of a bundle of cloth had survived, beating all the odds. He was working on a dock in Amsterdam, trying to learn Dutch.

Had the Emperor Charles V and the Sultan of the Ottomans—Süleyman the Magnificent they called him—sat down with Michael Sattler, they would have found some things in common. The three of them were close in age. Each also had received a distinctive education—the first to rule the Holy Roman Empire, the second to govern an Islamic empire that stretched from India to Spain, and the third to run a monastery.

Sattler met Beck Thursday evening at Kniebs's discussion group. "You invited me to Strasbourg nearly four months ago, and so I thought I'd take you up on the invitation," Sattler told Beck.

"It's great to see you again," Beck responded. "This is like the university days at Freiburg." Beck and Sattler both stood tall, though Sattler's dark hair and chiseled face contrasted with Beck's light-brown hair and fair complexion. "Welcome to Strasbourg!"

"Thanks. I'm here to catch up with friends like you and Wolfgang."

"Did you know that Matthew Zell preaches here in Strasbourg also?"

"Matthew Zell, from the university, preaching in Strasbourg?"

"And he's married. His wife's expecting a child next month. Where are you staying?"

"At Wolfgang's house. He's got lots of room to keep guests. Do you know Jacques Lefèvre?" One side of Sattler's mouth rose slightly higher than the other when he talked. His tone was steady and deep.

"Yes, Lefèvre and I traveled together with Wolfgang to Barcelona last month. Are there other motives that bring you to Strasbourg, perhaps connected to the Anabaptists you went to visit in Zurich?"

"You guessed correctly, Beck. The Brethren in Zurich and the outlying areas are under heavy fire these days. The Reformation pastor at the cathedral, Ulrich Zwingli, he has them on the run."

"You haven't joined them yet, Michael?"

"No, my wife and I know many of them, and their leaders. But we haven't been rebaptized yet."

"Does 'yet' mean that you may eventually?"

"Probably. Learning from and getting to know the Anabaptists has been a journey for us in the last several months. My new bride couldn't come along to Strasbourg with me. Right now we're happy newlyweds, enjoying life and figuring out God's next steps for us."

"Do you miss the monastery and the security you had at St. Peters?"

"I miss the long hours I could devote to study and reading, but not the rest of what goes with being a monk. But now, of course, I have to work for a living," Sattler said with a laugh.

"I have to work for a living too," Beck said. "Ever heard of the Knobloch press?"

"I remember you telling me about a printer you were seeing. Is that still going?"

"Sure is, Michael. Margaret and I spend a lot of time together, but we're not engaged yet."

"Marriage is a pretty good thing. I'll see if Wolfgang can invite you two over for a meal, so I can meet her and so we can catch up in more detail. Sort of a reunion from university days."

Sturm led the city council in a very important discussion the next morning of how to respond to the Hungarian's request for troops to fight the Turks. Balbus did come with the power of the emperor behind him, but Strasbourg kept its independence from the empire as an imperial free city. Sturm explained to the council that the emperor was battling for control in France right then. "He has the king of France caged up in Spain while he defeats his armies. There's no way the emperor can force us to supply two hundred men. So the question is, Should we?"

With all the confidence he could muster, Johann Knobloch rose to solemnly declare his position. "We should honor the most holy emperor's request and supply the army in Hungary with the requested troops. It's our honorable Christian duty. The infidels must be stopped dead in their tracks. The bishop calls for a new crusade to stop the barbarians: Soldiers of Christ arise!"

After a civil debate, the council members agreed to several steps. They would seek volunteers to fight in the east but also make a list of male citizens aged twenty to forty, then prioritize the names on the list based on marriage status and number of children. Finally, they would take a wait-and-see attitude. They agreed that building a bridge across the Sava River didn't pose an immediate threat to Strasbourg. But if Vienna fell to the Turks, the security of their city would be very much at risk.

On Friday night a fight broke out in the plaza near the Franciscan monastery. Johann Knobloch Jr., son of the Strasbourg printer, had just returned from serving in the emperor's army in France. He and some other soldiers were determined to have a good time.

Christman, veteran of the peasants' war, got into a tangle with the younger Johann Jr. when he challenged the wisdom of fighting for the emperor. Drinking a little too heavily, Christman declared that no infidel Turks or Catholic Frenchmen were worth fighting against. "Let's bring change in Germany first," he shouted.

Johann Jr. took offense at those remarks and landed a punch on Christman's right jaw that brought an immediate response from his massive fists. Friends cleared the area, gathered around to watch, and yelled support for one man or the other. Christman fought like a mad bull and Johann Jr. was equally enraged. Fists flew and insults erupted until onlookers came close to blows as well.

Margaret and Rabbi Loria watched from a distance. Finally, unafraid of conflict because he had been through years of harassment and ridicule, the rabbi stepped between the two men, motioning them to stop.

"Get out of the way, yellow star," Johann Jr. mumbled in contempt.

By then, however, both men were looking for a way out of the bloodied fight. Christman hesitated and then turned to his friends and sat down at a nearby table, glaring at his opponent. The soldier wiped the blood from his mouth and boasted to his friends how he'd handled his challenger; he too sat down. The rabbi disappeared into the darkness and walked toward his home outside the city walls.

Wolfgang knocked on the print shop door the next morning. Margaret had run through her usual Saturday-morning routine of bookkeeping, cleanup, and maintenance. "Could you come to my house this evening for dinner and conversation?" he asked. "My sermon's ready for tomorrow and my wonderful fiancée has agreed to help me cook the food. Can you bring Beck along too?"

"We'd be happy to join you," Margaret replied. "Can I bring anything along?"

"Your appetites and your opinions. I've invited Martin Bucer and my future father-in-law. And you know that Sattler and Lefèvre are staying with me, so they'll be there as well."

"Sounds like two women and six men," Margaret responded with a laugh.

"You and Agnes will bring a nice balance to the discussion, Margaret. See you just after Vespers."

The first floor alone of Wolfgang's expansive house could have easily swallowed up Margaret's print shop and Beck's little apartment. He had inherited money from his father and liked his big house, and to his credit he freely shared it with others.

As they passed beef, vegetables, and plenty of bread around the table, Wolfgang's guests engaged in amiable conversation. The preacher at St. Thomas was wealthy enough to have on his table both salt and pepper, which had to be imported from the east.

At age thirty-two, Wolfgang presented himself confidently. Margaret noticed that his clear eyes, full eyebrows, and distinct chin made him handsome. After the meal, the maid cleared the table, and Wolfgang shifted the conversation to an evaluation of the Hungarian's plea for soldiers to fight the Turks. "First, do we think the Turks are a menace to the empire, and second, should Strasbourg supply soldiers?"

Johann Sr., sitting just to Wolfgang's right, started off. "Yes, they're a threat. Reports from Constantinople are that Süleyman plans to march up the Danube and capture Vienna in just a few months. You heard the Hungarian this week: the little beasts are building a bridge across the Sava River as we sit here."

"Isn't the king of France eager to see Süleyman attack the eastern flank of the empire?" Sattler asked. "It seems to me that the French would stand to gain from a distracted emperor fighting on two fronts at once."

"Charles will simply have to raise a large enough army to fight both enemies at once," Bucer said. "The emperor's brother, Archduke of Austria, can fight the Turks while Charles fights in France."

"I hope the French forces can free their king from that lousy prison in Spain," Lefèvre declared. Johann glared at the Frenchman.

So far the women hadn't contributed to the discussion.

Margaret chimed in first. "I hope the emperor's armies continue to be only voluntary forces. Too many men have died fighting questionable wars in far-off places. My father fought for Emperor Maximilian once. He never did understand exactly why he had to fight."

"And I'd like to keep the preacher at St. Thomas close at hand," Agnes added. "Preaching is more important than marching off to fight some godless Turk."

"There won't be any more preaching to do, my dear daughter, if we don't defend the blessed cities of Christ's kingdom." Father and daughter avoided looking at each other.

"Sattler," Wolfgang said, "I understand one of your privileges in the monastery was not having to fight in the empire's battles. Is that true?" The clear-eyed preacher knew the answer to his own question, but wanted to get the soft-spoken pilgrim from south Germany involved in the discussion.

"When I left the monastery," Sattler said, "I left the protection the Benedictine cloister offered me from the wars of this world." Sattler paused, then decided to risk his beliefs with his hosts and their guests. "I still believe in nonresistance. I find Christ's teachings don't allow me to fight for the emperor anywhere, anytime."

Wolfgang and Bucer shifted and sat up in their chairs to listen. Wrinkles of a frown crossed Johann's forehead.

"The Brethren I've come to know and worship with believe in the way of peace," Sattler continued.

"But some of the Anabaptists fought in the peasants' war," Johann retorted. "They don't seem very consistent in their beliefs, if you ask me."

"You're right," Sattler answered slowly. "The Brethren in Zurich, though, under an able preacher like those you have here in Strasbourg, have discovered a different teaching on war and violence in the New Testament. Because we've started to study and read the Scripture for ourselves, we find something quite different from what the church has taught us for centuries." Realizing he was dominating the discussion, Sattler paused.

"Can you trust the common people with their own Bibles?" Margaret asked. She hoped Sattler or someone would say yes to her question.

"Absolutely not," Johann answered. "Latin's been good enough for the Church for centuries, and there's no need to change now. The traditions established by popes and church leaders are all we need."

Jumping in, Wolfgang said, "There's got to be a balance here. Luther has given us the New Testament in German and he's working on translating the Old Testament. Certainly it's good for average people to read the Bible for themselves?"

"But it must be interpreted by those with proper understanding and a good education," added Bucer, the organizer of systems.

"By scholars of the Bible," the doctor of theology Lefèvre added. "The common person simply doesn't have the tools to interpret Scripture properly."

"Why not?" Sattler asked. "The Brethren, or as they're sometimes ridiculed, the Anabaptists, believe that the Scriptures can best be interpreted when believers gather together and read it in community. We've concluded, from our study of Scripture, that we will not go to war against our enemy."

"But certainly," Wolfgang said, "you understand that there are times when every able man must fight to defend his homeland. If the Turks invade Zurich, or Strasbourg, you will defend the city, won't you?"

"I suppose if I have to fight," Sattler answered, "based on what I find in the teachings of Jesus, I would rather fight on the side of the so-called godless Turks than on the side of the so-called Christian armies of the emperor. At least the Sultan's men don't claim to fight in the name of God."

Bucer pushed his glass toward the middle of the table and Johann sat back with arms crossed. They couldn't believe their ears. Sattler's statements startled even Wolfgang, the moderate who tried to bring everyone along with him.

"These are radical beliefs," Beck said. "Are your communities growing? Are they being persecuted?"

"Yes," Sattler answered. "Both growing and persecuted."

"And rightly so," Johann said. "Men who won't fight for their homeland don't deserve to live there."

Sattler replied, "We believe what Christ said we live in another kingdom, not of this world. Our citizenship is in heaven."

"Sounds like theology you brought with you from the monastery," Wolfgang said. He tried to make it into a joke, but no one laughed. "Have you joined the Anabaptists yet?"

"No, my wife and I are still on a journey to find our place, but for now we like to worship with the Brethren."

Margaret found Sattler's confidence attractive. He had the courage to leave the security of a safe monastery and follow his beliefs. That took guts. She began to realize that she liked the beliefs of the Brethren, their boldness, their willingness to stand on what they believed, their refusal to use political power to defend themselves. Like Sattler, she and Beck were on a journey, and she wanted to find the settled faith that he had discovered.

In a setting like this, in front of two Lutheran preachers and the owner of the largest Catholic print shop in town and his daughter, Margaret would keep most of her beliefs to herself. It was a woman's place, of course.

Fortunately, the conversation headed in a different direction for the rest of the evening. For now, she could relax.

"But very soon," Margaret thought, "Beck and I need to travel up the Rhine to visit the Anabaptists." Anabaptists were still coming to Strasbourg for refuge because Bucer,

Wolfgang, and Matthew appeared to tolerate them. And the Catholic bishop didn't live in the city, so he hardly knew the strength of their growing numbers.

"All sorts of Anabaptists have come to Strasbourg," she said to Beck on the way home that evening. "It's time for us to visit them."

"My thoughts exactly," Beck replied.

That night both of them were deep in thought, so after a gentle embrace they went their separate ways. Both realized they had changed since leaving for dinner earlier that evening.

14

Assembly in the Forest

After listening to Matthew preach in the cathedral on Sunday, Margaret and Beck went to Christman's house to plan a trip to Waldshut and Zurich. When Christman had first invited them to join him, Margaret resisted. But Beck convinced her to go along, arguing that he would be the best person to take with them on their trip to Zurich. He wasn't afraid of anybody, he was a leader among the independents in Strasbourg, and he appeared to be a seeker among the Anabaptists.

Christman's face showed signs of the brawl that had erupted in the plaza Friday night. After a simple but satisfying meal near the Stone Street Gate, the three leaned back on wooden chairs and talked.

"Before we go," Christman said, "I'd recommend a meeting of Anabaptist leaders in Strasbourg, together in one place."

"That would be risky," Beck responded.

"I think it's a great idea," Margaret countered. "Sattler's in town right now, as well as Hut, and I'm sure we can get Clement and his wife to come as well."

"Kniebs will show," Christman added. "He supports the radicals, whoever they are. My neighbor Jörg Ziegler would come too."

"Hut's a fireball, and even though he's got it in for the Jews, he'd come," said Beck. "And Lucas should be invited."

"Where's this meeting going to take place, and what are our goals?" Christman asked.

"How about the forest clearing near the bridge, where we

met with leaders of the peasants' revolt?" Margaret asked. "We met there with Müller before he escaped and with Lotz before he got tied up in the hangman's noose."

"You know," Christman said, "I think it would be better to get stuck in the Tower of Chains, beside the Hangman's Tower, and be shipped to a far-off place to row on some ship as a galley slave than to be hung. At least you'd be alive."

"But is life worth living if it's so hard that you can't act on or carry out what you believe?" Margaret asked.

"You're avoiding the second part of Christman's question," Beck said. "What would be the goal of our Anabaptist meeting?"

"Solidarity," Margaret answered.

"Definition please, my dear educated printer woman," Beck said. "What does that word mean?"

"It means we get together and encourage each other, share ideas, and organize the Anabaptist house churches in Strasbourg."

"I'm impressed. Where'd you learn that word?"

"I pay attention to the pamphlets and books that I print and try to learn from them. You can learn a lot that way, Beck."

Christman laughed. "Let's meet Thursday evening. It'd be natural because we often talk about the Reformation and Anabaptist ideas at Kniebs's house anyway. I'll pass the word around on my side of town and you tell the people on your side."

"Can you stay out of trouble until then?" Margaret quipped. "You get in another fight or knock any more icons around, and you'll never make it to Zurich. On the other hand, you could see the world through the hole in the bottom of your slave ship where your oar sticks out. Have you ever seen real live Turks up close? They like to sell tall and healthy German prisoners in the markets of Constantinople."

"I'll be at the bridge Thursday night, Margaret. But let your warning to me go for you as well. Watch what you print, or Sturm and his friends will dismantle that press of yours and sell the wood in the market."

"There's only one friend of Jacob Sturm who really wants Margaret done in. Any idea who it is, Christman?" Beck asked.

"Not a clue."

"It took me a while to notice, but Margaret and the Knoblochs don't exactly have a love affair going. Actually, they make each other mad."

Christman asked, in a way that allowed Margaret the option of not answering, "What did the Knoblochs ever do to you?"

"Well," she began, "this thing actually goes back two generations. My grandfather worked with Gutenberg here in Strasbourg, learned printing from him, and then got started in his own print shop. Not being much of a businessman, Gutenberg made very little money with his new press. Some big boys in Mainz did, though, and they tried to run my grandfather and anybody connected to the Gutenberg name in Strasbourg out of business.

"Knobloch is a grandson of one of the businessmen in Mainz who ruined my grandfather. Knobloch's father tried to run my family out of business too, but he never succeeded."

"So it's mainly bad business blood then?" Christman asked.

"Well, about thirty years ago, before I was born, the Knoblochs actually shut down the family print shop for a month while the almighty city council decided whether my father had printed too many radical documents—unwholesome sermons that weren't on the approved list, things like that. When there are personality differences and business rivalries, nasty things can happen. And they did."

"Perhaps we can keep this rivalry from going on to the next generation," Beck said.

"Don't be so sure," Margaret answered. "Johann and Magdalene have a son who's getting his own print shop started here in Strasbourg these days. Did you ever meet him?"

"Yes. I met him a couple of times at work," Beck said, "but he's kept his distance from me, and for that matter, from his parents."

"I probably would too if I were their son," Margaret said. "You've got to realize, Beck, that there are folks in this city who want to shut me down. Maybe you'd better think about that for a while."

"Don't let Johann or Magdalene scare you," Christman growled. "I can take care of them if you want me to."

"This is depressing," Beck said. "Let's go for a walk and get some fresh air, Margaret. Thanks for the dinner, Christman. We'll see you on Thursday."

"Guess we'll have to plan our Switzerland trip later," Christman answered.

In the heat of the middle of August in central Germany, life slowed. Farmers sat beside their carts and sold vegetables. Shade trees along the canals were popular spots to cool off and relax. Families entertained themselves, couples took long walks, children played with the simplest of toys. Occasionally, there'd be music in the plaza outside the cathedral. Margaret could always hear it from her shop, just a stone's throw away.

Nearly three hundred men from Strasbourg fought for the emperor in France, but less than a dozen had volunteered to fight the Turks in Hungary. Most fought for money, not for the cause.

In the midst of distant and unpopular wars, news continued to trickle in about America. A sailor came through town, sightseeing in the north, he said, before heading out again on one of the many Spanish galleons headed across the Atlantic Ocean.

One of the guilds sponsored an evening of storytelling by the sailor in the plaza outside the cathedral. People eagerly came to hear tales of the newly discovered land. He talked about the strange native peoples, their odd habits, their pagan religions, and the gold that had to be there, if only they could find it.

Beck listened with fascination to the man's stories. They reminded him of the book Margaret had published about these new lands. Christopher Columbus had died about twenty years earlier, but other brave explorers had taken his place, seeking fame and fortune.

Margaret guessed that a few of the young men in the crowd would soon head to Lisbon or Madrid, seeking work on one of the king's ships headed to America. Charles V could fight wars in Europe and conquer natives a world away, all at the same time.

Müller, fugitive leader of the foiled peasants' war, decided to try his luck on one of those Spanish ships headed to the New World. He had heard about good jobs on ships that sailed from Spain's great cities west. In the middle of August, in his house on a tiny homestead high in the Swiss Alps near the village of Steffisburg, southeast of Bern, he explained to his patient but tired wife how he had escaped the execution-er's axe in Strasbourg.

With huge arms propped on his small, wooden table, he detailed his latest campaign. Having little to lose, he had or-ganized a rag-tag band of leftover ruffians and attacked Count Rudolf of Sulz, the nobleman who had killed so many peasants at the battle in the Black Forest. They had been mer-ciless in their offensive, pillaging, killing, destroying, and burning everything on the count's manor. "Rudolf deserved it," Müller told his wife.

His spouse of ten years had worked like a man for the past three, planting and harvesting and managing their animals, while he traveled throughout south Germany, fighting nobles. She was ready for him to come home and stay put, but he explained that, after murdering Count Rudolf just a hundred miles east of Strasbourg, he'd have to keep on the move, at least for another year or two. Then maybe he could settle down.

For now, his thin and pale wife and their two young sons would have to continue to rely on their neighbors. "Fredli," Müller said to the Joder farmer who lived down the road, "I need you to keep looking out for my wife and boys on the farm."

"We'll do what we can, Hans. But when will you come home and work your own fields? It's too much for your wife to handle by herself."

"It's going to be a year or two. I have to disappear for a while. You might as well know I'm a wanted man."

"Tell me something. Have you run across any Anabaptists in your travels?"

"Yes. They're springing up in towns and villages all over the place."

"I just wondered. We've had a few come through here— seems they've been chased out of Zurich."

"Well, I have to go," Müller said. "Much obliged for your help on the farm. I'll pay you back someday."

Within twenty-four hours after Müller had crossed the threshold of his little Swiss cottage, he left for Belfort, Germany. From there he followed the same route to Barcelona that Beck had followed a month earlier.

Meantime, his discouraged wife took a broken basket and went to pick a few newly ripened tomatoes in the garden.

Sliced on a piece of bread, they'd have to do for supper that evening for her and the boys.

In her print shop, Margaret directed the work on Hut's pamphlet, which was intended to convert Jews to Christianity. "It will pay the bills," Margaret reminded herself.

Peter, Heinrich, and Margaret shared the jobs among themselves. Heinrich, the compositor, did most of the arranging of letters and lines of print. Peter ran the press. He inked the letters, shoved the tray in, and pulled the big lever that lowered the letters onto the paper. Then he raised the letters, lifted off the paper, hung it to dry, and started the process all over again.

Margaret proofread the manuscript as the pages were printed and made sure supplies were on hand to do the job. Occasionally, she had to replace letters that broke. By now, with over twenty printers in Strasbourg, there were several craftsmen who made letters that she could buy. That saved her from making her own, as Margaret's father had done.

Margaret spread the word on her side of the city about the Thursday-evening meeting. "Travel by yourself or in pairs," she told those she invited. And she assured them that Beck would lead them to the meeting area in the forest once they had crossed the Rhine.

During a conversation at the printer's guild meeting, Margaret learned that a disagreement had emerged between the Lutheran preachers Bucer and Wolfgang. Both men wrote books and read the scholarly materials of their day, in Latin or German. Wolfgang had just published a commentary on the Old Testament book of Habakkuk.

Bible commentaries in the 1520s enabled scholars and preachers to state their beliefs. Readers could probably learn something about the book of the Bible he commented on as well. Habakkuk's "the righteous will live by his faith" became a much-used Old Testament verse for the Lutheran leaders and others who reformed the church. The apostle Paul also had used it several times in his writings. And Luther had scrawled in the margin of his Latin Bible that the just shall live by faith "alone."

Wolfgang echoed Luther's theme about salvation by faith alone, but then went on to speak against infant baptism. He didn't think anyone should be rebaptized, as the Anabaptists claimed, but he couldn't find infant baptism taught in the Scriptures. Still, Wolfgang wrote, newborn children should be baptized, as he himself did regularly in the St. Thomas baptistery.

That's where Bucer went after Wolfgang. It sounded to Bucer like Wolfgang leaned toward the Anabaptists in their understanding of believers baptism. In some respects this was true. Wolfgang gave lodging to several visiting Anabaptists in his home. His hospitality, and the openness of others in Strasbourg to Reformation ideas, led the Anabaptists to call Strasbourg "the city of hope."

Margaret knew that it was a pretty amazing turn of events when one of the established Lutheran preachers in the city moved, to his own peril, no doubt, in the direction of the Anabaptists. When Wolfgang showed up at her print shop door on Wednesday to inquire about printing his next commentary, on Hosea, Margaret inquired further. "Why are you coming to me?"

"I'm ready for a change in publishers," he answered.

"Your other printer didn't do a good enough job?"

"The quality was fine, but I don't appreciate having my books reviewed by the censorship committee. I'm a Lutheran scholar, not an Anabaptist radical."

Wolfgang showed Margaret a copy of the Habakkuk commentary. "This is the format I'd like you to follow."

Margaret noticed the Knobloch insignia at the end of the book. Printers didn't always put their names on their works, but Knoblochs usually did. "So Johann and Magdalene turned him in," Margaret thought. "They should encourage their future son-in-law, not push him away."

"Yes, we can do it," Margaret told Wolfgang. "We'll go right to work on it. I'll read your commentary, obviously, but we've never turned anyone in to be censored."

"That's why I came here, Margaret. I'm sure you'll do a good job."

During her walk to the bridge with Beck, Margaret speculated that the meeting would be a lot like the one that had taken place in the forest four months earlier. On the other hand, Beck pointed out, only four of those at the first would be at the second: Hut, Margaret, Christman, and himself. It was another strategy meeting, but there wouldn't be any plans for armed resistance. Strategizing for what, though, Margaret couldn't exactly say.

Margaret went ahead to the clearing in the forest. She remembered the two huge fir trees that framed a sort of doorway into the thick forest, a doorway to a convenient meeting area about half the size of the plaza outside the cathedral. The logs that Müller and his men had moved in to sit on still lay there. She hoped the leaders of this meeting wouldn't have the same fate as Müller and Lotz.

By nightfall, eleven travelers had gathered under the fir trees. Gertrude came with Clement, bringing the number of women in the circle to two.

Margaret invited Lucas, the gentle relief worker and preacher, to start with a prayer. Then she told the group, whose faces were almost impossible to see, about the last time four of them had met in that clearing. They had planned a revolt, she explained. She and Beck had agreed to print

Twelve Articles. Their courage had been strengthened. Unfortunately, the peasants' uprising had failed, though not for a lack of leaders and planning.

Hut interrupted. "The peasants' revolt is not finished yet. In Waldshut, at least one congregation of Anabaptists has taken a stand against the authorities. They still speak for the rights of the peasants."

"What you say is true, Hans," Sattler said. "But the Anabaptist leaders in Zurich don't agree with those methods. We reject the power of the state to protect the church. And though the Anabaptists in Waldshut agree with us on believers baptism, we disagree with them on the use of force to reach our goals."

Clement spoke up. "Margaret is right. Here in Strasbourg, the peasants' revolt has been defeated. But the radical church that seems to have emerged out of the revolt lives on." He gestured across the river. "Every day more Anabaptists come here because of our tolerant pastors—Zell, Capito, and Bucer."

"Still, " Jörg retorted, "they would about as soon drown us in the canal or hang us like they hanged Lotz as have the Anabaptist movement take root here. Zell's in the same league as Luther: 'Slay, stab, and smite them all,' he told the nobles."

Night sounds began to break the stillness of the forest, an owl, flittering bats, and a breeze rustling the branches. The guard at the bridge may have alerted his superior about a larger-than-usual number of travelers across the bridge, but probably not. No sign of any unfriendly visitors so far.

Beck stood and reminded the secret assembly that only two or three Anabaptist groups met regularly in Strasbourg. "You can hardly even call them Anabaptist," he said. "A couple dozen people searching for the truth in small groups."

"I don't think we have to fear any of the powers in Strasbourg," Christman declared. "You've got to understand that the bishop can't suppress the Reformation here because the city council has men on it who like Luther's ideas. We can make radical changes with little fear of persecution."

"Are you aware of the way Wolfgang Capito leans in the direction of the Anabaptists?" Margaret asked. "He wrote against infant baptism, which upset Bucer."

"Has he taken the next step of supporting rebaptism for those who believe?" Sattler asked.

Margaret explained that Wolfgang only denied the biblical basis for infant baptism, though he still baptized babies and that he clearly disliked the Anabaptist idea of rebaptizing believers.

"Sounds like Zwingli," Sattler responded.

"What will it take to encourage the Anabaptist movement in Strasbourg?" Gertrude Ziegler asked. Like her husband, the self-styled preacher's wife had spent a lifetime encouraging others. "Our little farm in Robertsau is always available for meetings."

"As is my house," Kniebs nodded in agreement.

"Help me out, please," Jörg insisted. "I'm struggling to distinguish the Anabaptists from the Lutheran reformers. What are some of the differences?"

Margaret asked one of the guests from south Germany to speak, either Sattler or Hut, saying, "You've lived among them and know how to answer better than those of us who live here."

Hut yielded to the university-trained Sattler. "I'm living with Wolfgang right now while I'm visiting Strasbourg. As I learn from him—and he's a fine scholar, by the way—I can outline several ways Anabaptists interpret their faith differently from Luther. Whether it's Capito or Zell, Luther stands behind them. In fact, I read Luther's writings in the monastery over the last several years. They are one of the reasons I left to seek the truth."

"What's on your list?" Jörg asked.

"On the basics of faith and the Christian life, we agree," Sattler said. "But the Anabaptists will baptize only believers, not newborn children. They believe we should separate ourselves from the world, and they hold a very different understanding of the church."

"And they believe in the way of peace and love for their enemies," Hut added.

After a discussion of these beliefs, the group settled on an informal plan for the weeks ahead. First, Margaret, Beck, and Christman would head to south Germany and Switzerland to visit with Anabaptists and discover more about their beliefs. Second, Clement and Kniebs agreed to continue hosting regular meetings where Anabaptist ideas could be discussed. Third, the group encouraged Margaret to print more pamphlets and books that supported the Anabaptist movement.

"You understand, of course," Margaret reminded the group, "that my print shop is a business. We print all sorts of documents—Catholic, Lutheran, and nonreligious. Our goal is to make a profit."

"That's fine," Gertrude said, "but make your business serve Christ in the midst of all the decisions you make. We can't separate the business world from the religious world."

"Your press is needed among the Anabaptists," Sattler said. "I'm sure when you visit Waldshut and Zurich you'll be able to pick up printing jobs."

"So you can count the money you'll spend traveling to Switzerland as a business expense," Clement joked.

"I'll cover the expenses to Waldshut," Beck said. "That's where my mother lives."

"Perhaps she's already joined the Anabaptist congregation," Sattler said.

"If so, she hasn't written to me about it."

"That's not the kind of thing you want to put in the mail,"

Hut reminded the group. "We're living in the last days, you know. The antichrist seeks to stop the advancement of the kingdom of God."

Margaret interrupted. "I believe this is a good place to end our meeting." Everyone laughed in agreement. If they allowed Hut to get started, he'd talk all night about the end times. "This place is spooky enough," she said, "without reviewing everything the Bible says about the great tribulation, Hans. We'll go back one or two at a time. Beck will lead the way to make sure you all find your way to the bridge, and I'll come last."

Inspired and invigorated, Margaret and Beck steadied each other as they walked across the bridge. The pontoon passage floated easily above the surging river. It took a while, as usual, for their land-based equilibrium to return after they stepped onto the western bank. From there it was a three-mile hike to the city.

"A warm August night," Margaret mused, "with a quarter moon in the sky, the shape of the cathedral visible in the distance as a beacon for our journey, and a man I love to walk with. What more could I hope for?"

On second thought, she added, "Enough German Bibles to go around, a church that wasn't run by powerful lords and nobles, freedom to worship as one pleases."

One of their favorite spots in Strasbourg was just inside the Butcher's Gate, on the bridge across the canal.

"You know, Margaret, the two main canals around the city join up again on the east side."

"That's brilliant, Balt," Margaret said with a chuckle.

"What I mean," he responded, pretending to be irritated, "is that if we join the Anabaptists, it'll be like these two canals joining into one. Our lives and their radical beliefs. That's exciting and frightening at the same time."

"Why is it frightening?"

Beck was silent for a minute. Then he spoke. "We've both been downstream on the Rhine. We know where the water takes us when we travel on it. But after a certain point, we no longer know the twists and turns in the river. The terrain is unfamiliar. It's the same with joining the Anabaptists. We can't predict the direction this journey will take. If we tie in with these radicals, it's hard to see where it will lead us."

"What's all this talk about 'us' and 'we,' Beck?"

"Just thinking about the future, Margaret. That's a hard thing for me to do, as you know."

"I do know. But let's not worry about the future right now. Just enjoy this special moment with me.

"By the way," she added. "Is this your canal, or do you own the one on the other side of the city?"

"This one has to be yours," Beck answered. "It runs by the print shop."

They laughed and turned to each other, leaving more weighty concerns to float away downstream.

Two people walked into Margaret's shop on Friday morning with news to deliver. The first was Agnes, who had ventured over to the Wood Market to warn Margaret about Christman. "I know him well," she said. "He'll put on a good front and treat you well, then betray you when it serves his interests."

"How do you know Christman so well?"

"We had something going once, then he dropped me like a stone when he was finished with me."

"He seems to have a mind of his own."

"He does, and when Wolfgang told me about your upcoming trip to Switzerland with him, I just thought I'd give you some friendly advice from a woman who knows. Watch him and don't get tied up with him emotionally. He'll take advantage of you in any way he can."

Before Margaret could steer the conversation in another direction, Agnes walked out the door and up the cobblestone street.

Beck walked into the shop later in the morning with the news that when he had asked off work for two weeks in September, Johann had said that he needed employees who didn't always want time off, so he'd just have to look for other work when he got back.

"He didn't seem mean about it," Beck said, "he just said that he would find someone else who wasn't traveling so much."

"Did he pay you all of the wages you have coming?" Margaret asked.

"Sure did. So I'm ready to take you on a trip."

"Okay, world traveler, help me get some work done this afternoon and tomorrow, then we can go."

"Maybe we could open up a shop in Zurich."

"Is that a proposal or a business venture?"

"Neither. Just kidding."

"Well, printer man," Margaret shot back, "if you're working for me now, get busy and make me some money."

"Heinrich, can you make room for Beck this afternoon? Seems he's unemployed."

"We'll take him." Heinrich winked. "I think I've seen him around before."

15

Journey to Switzerland

By Monday of the first week in September, when Margaret, Beck, and Christman left for Waldshut and Zurich, the strong currents in the Rhine had weakened as a hint of fall lay in the warm Alsatian air. Heinrich and Peter had enough work in the print shop, making copies of Wolfgang's commentary on Hosea, to keep them busy for at least two weeks, and Ryff plodded away on his writing table in the corner of the print shop.

The travelers headed first to Waldshut, a tiny village on the northern bank of the Rhine in southern Germany. As a crow flies, the village was seventy miles from Strasbourg. On their route, through the hills, valleys, and mountains of the Black Forest, they would have to go twice as far.

The three stayed at Freiburg the first night, though they saw little evidence of the changes for which the peasants had fought earlier that year. The Catholic Church and city council governed in a way that allowed for few changes, either religiously or politically.

They arrived in Waldshut by the afternoon of the second day. While Christman paid for a room at a small inn, Beck and Margaret visited Beck's mother. Aging and feeble, she welcomed Margaret into her home, and they visited over supper and through the evening. Beck told his mother about his life and the changes taking place in Strasbourg. When he got to the part about losing his job, he said to his mother, "I'll be working for Margaret now, and she owns a print shop."

Beck's mother didn't waste many words. "Are you two engaged?"

"No mother, we're not. Just good friends."

After a glance at Beck, Margaret added, "I'd be glad to have you come and visit me in Strasbourg."

"Oh, no," she replied, "that journey through the mountains is rough on old bones. I've gone that way before, when I was younger."

The tiny size of Waldshut surprised Margaret. She guessed that several dozen families lived in the little farming village. The nearest bridge across the narrow Rhine lay in the next village downstream. Behind her the mighty Black Forest rose up with its huge fir trees. "Travelers don't just stop by Waldshut on their way to somewhere else," Margaret thought. "You have to make this your destination."

On Wednesday morning they met the pastor of the Anabaptist congregation in the village. He was one of the leaders of the peasants' revolt in south Germany and the author of the pamphlet on believers baptism.

"Thank you for printing my pamphlet," pastor Balthasar Hubmaier said to Margaret. "We have a church meeting tonight and you're welcome to attend." That night Wilhelm Reublin, whom Margaret had met twice—in the forest meeting during the peasants' war and in her print shop—would be there to baptize more Anabaptist converts.

Margaret learned from Mrs. Beck that most of the people in the village had joined the Anabaptist congregation. The rulers and councils that could have stopped them lived so far away from the settlement that the people, at least for now, could worship as they pleased.

After tending to the small garden behind the house and feeding the chickens, Margaret and Beck walked down the main street and greeted people Beck knew. Seventeen years earlier Beck had left Waldshut to begin his studies at the University of Freiburg. Very few friends his age still lived in the village, but many of the older people recognized and welcomed him.

In the afternoon they took a walk down to the river and waded in the water to cool off. A few small boats floated by on their way to Basel, a larger city downstream where the Rhine turned north toward Strasbourg. The travelers planned to follow that route on their return trip.

Beck considered this town home, even though he had studied and lived elsewhere for many years. He learned from a neighbor, an old man who had watched Beck grow up, that Reublin and the village pastor would baptize at least a dozen people that evening at the church.

Beck's neighbor friend hadn't joined the movement yet. "Young people are more radical than we old fossils," he joked. "I'll have to wait and see what happens before I join."

Christman joined Margaret, Beck, and Mrs. Beck on a bench near the back of the small church. He had kept an eye on Margaret's every move, she noticed, but so far he'd done nothing out of line. She hoped it would stay that way.

The pastor greeted the visitors, read from Scripture, and then turned the preaching over to Reublin. To Margaret, the message sounded like the pamphlet she had printed on believers baptism.

"Baptism should be received by those who make a new confession in Christ," Reublin insisted, "as a second witness to the Holy Spirit's work in one's life."

"That sounds like Hut's idea of the three witnesses in baptism," Margaret thought. "Spirit, water, and blood."

When he had finished speaking, Reublin invited those who wanted to join the Anabaptist movement to step forward. He took a metal dipper, scooped water out of a bucket, and poured it on each believer's head. "In the name of the Father, Son, and Holy Spirit."

In Waldshut, no icons or images remained in the church, the services had been changed to German so people could understand them, and the Catholic priest said Mass only once a week, on Sunday afternoon. It seemed to Christman that the Anabaptists had taken over the village.

The next morning Margaret and Beck joined Christman and Reublin outside the small church. They sat on rough boards that had been situated on stumps near the church doors.

"The Anabaptists govern this village," Reublin said, almost proudly. "Though the peasants' revolt failed elsewhere, we've accomplished the goals of the fight here."

"How are you connected with the Anabaptist movement in Zurich?" Margaret asked.

"Leaders from Zurich, like George Blaurock, come here to give us spiritual direction. But we run our own church, without the threat of government persecution like the Anabaptists in Zurich."

"Blaurock sits in the prison tower in Zurich right now," Reublin added. "Zwingli, the city council's preacher, is clamping down on the radical Anabaptists. I've been on the move in recent weeks to avoid his guards."

"It feels like the Anabaptists have gained the upper hand in Waldshut," Christman said. "That's different from what I've learned about other Anabaptist communities. In Strasbourg, *Anabaptist* is a bad word to Catholic and Lutheran authorities alike."

"True," Reublin said, "the folks in this little village have established an Anabaptist commonwealth like no other place that I'm aware of. That makes us unique—the power of the government will protect the growing Anabaptist movement."

From what Margaret had learned in recent months, pastor

Balthasar Hubmaier's beliefs on the use of force to protect the church were out of step with other Anabaptist leaders, at least the ones she knew. They'd have to find out in Zurich.

After lunch on Thursday, Margaret, Beck, and Christman left Waldshut, crossed a bridge into Switzerland, and paid for a carriage ride to their destination about twenty miles away. The driver followed a rough, winding road through a rolling plateau that rose toward the south. Beautiful, well-tended vineyards, heavy with grapes, dotted the countryside.

The trio took two rooms at a comfortable inn overlooking Lake Zurich. The spires of the cathedral dominated the sky-line as Margaret and Beck enjoyed the view of the soaring snow-capped mountains in the distance.

Reublin had been banished from Zurich, along with other nonresident Anabaptists, so he didn't travel with the other three. Yet he told the driver of the carriage, a man he knew, to inform Conrad Grebel about the arrival of three guests from Strasbourg. It took the driver until Friday morning, however, to catch up with Grebel, in a little village to the east of Zurich.

Grebel, a twenty-seven-year-old scholar and clearly the leader of the Brethren from Switzerland, met the Strasbourg travelers at their inn just before lunchtime on Friday morning. His unruly, red, curly hair didn't obey any attempt to comb it; his neatly trimmed beard was a much darker shade of auburn. Margaret noticed that he moved a little slower than most men his age. It appeared he had very sore joints.

"I'm sorry we can't meet under more favorable circumstances," Grebel began. "Margaret, we've met before, in Strasbourg, I believe."

"Yes," she said. "You baptized two men at Clement Ziegler's barn. We've been talking about baptism and Anabaptist beliefs ever since, around his little fire."

"You are probably aware that the Zurich City Council has banned all meetings of Anabaptists there. Most of the leaders are preaching and baptizing in other places, like Reublin and me, or they're perched in Zwingli's prison over there," he said with a gesture toward the guard house. "George Blaurock and Felix Manz are locked up right now."

"Why has Zwingli turned against you so violently?" Christman asked.

"We studied with him, learned from him, followed his teaching for several years. But a number of us finally decided we could no longer wait for him, so we moved ahead."

"Is your city council kept in check by the Catholic bishop, as in Strasbourg?" Margaret asked.

"No," Grebel replied, "Zwingli holds almost full control over the pace and pattern of the Reformation. Further, he's paid by the city council, so he's obliged to honor their decisions. The Catholic presence is practically nonexistent.

"Let me tell you about the growth of the movement," Grebel continued, glancing around to see who might be listening. Margaret sensed that he had come to meet them only because Reublin had asked him to, and that he didn't want to stay any longer in Zurich than absolutely necessary. "Anabaptist congregations are springing up in many places in the mountain villages around Zurich. Many are asking to be rebaptized. I have baptized dozens myself, though our church only got started in January, here in Zurich."

Beck noticed that Grebel spoke and presented himself like an educated man. He remembered from his trip to Barcelona that Grebel had studied in Paris where Lefèvre taught.

"We've met several Anabaptists from this area in my print shop in Strasbourg," Margaret said.

"You're a printer?" Grebel asked with interest. "And have you printed documents for some of the Anabaptists?"

"We printed a pamphlet on baptism, a petition to abolish

the Mass in Strasbourg, and Hut's pamphlet to convert the Jews"

"Margaret's press also printed copies of the peasants' demands, *Twelve Articles*," Christman added. "Of course, the peasants were butchered." He flexed the biceps. "Will your movement in Switzerland survive?"

"We pray to God that it will," Grebel answered. "We have good, educated leaders, many from wealthy families, like myself. But these are not days for the weak of heart. Though I'm not afraid of prison, my friends, I am a prudent man, and I must leave the city before I'm noticed."

Margaret spoke for the three of them and said, "Thank you for meeting with us, Conrad. We want to meet with you again and learn more."

"It just so happens that you've arrived in Switzerland at a very important moment," Grebel said as he slowly rose to leave. "An Anabaptist pastor viewed as treasonous by the government will be burned at the stake tomorrow. Travel to the other end of this beautiful lake that you see out the front door, and you can witness his third baptism in blood tomorrow at noon. I warn you, though, if you watch this execution, you'll end up either applauding the executioner or joining the Anabaptists. There's very little middle ground."

Even though his pain was obvious, Grebel walked away from them with the stature of a man born into a noble family. He wore peasant clothing, however, to avoid being noticed. He pressed a big, brown, broad-brimmed hat down on his head and strode out the door.

Margaret, Beck, and Christman agreed on a plan. Margaret knew of a well-established printer who worked in Zurich. She and Beck would visit him that afternoon. Christman would scout out the city and reserve passage on a boat across the lake to where the doomed preacher would be burned. He might then head out to the village east of town where Grebel was preaching and teaching. They'd leave on the first boat the next morning.

Two days earlier, in Strasbourg, Magdalene had come to the print shop near the Wood Market to speak to Heinrich and invite him to her house for dinner that evening. "My husband and I would be most happy for you to meet our oldest daughter, Catherine."

Heinrich looked to the floor to avoid answering. He didn't want to go, because he feared the Knobloch family. He tried to think of a reason to say no, but nothing came to mind. As he thought, he saw a fly run into a spider's web in the dark corner behind the front door.

When Heinrich looked up and agreed to come, Magdalene smiled. "We'll see you this evening."

Heinrich closed the door behind her, then stopped to examine the fly caught in the web. The spider was slowly advancing on its prey.

It was a bold proposal, but not unusual for the early sixteenth century. The Knoblochs were trying to find a suitable husband for their daughter, and they had invited this eligible bachelor to dinner to assess his compatibility with the family.

Their urgency in finding a mate for their oldest daughter, now twenty-five, came in response to a visit by Giovanna Veronese, a nun from Venice. She had traveled into southern Germany, seeking women to join her ministry to the starving women and children who wandered the streets of Venice. Any volunteers would have to bring a financial endowment with them.

Heinrich soon learned that Catherine, known by most as Katie, had become attracted to Mother Giovanna's ministry. He also picked up in the conversation that the Knobloch parents, though not totally against the idea, were going to do everything they could to find a husband for their daughter before she made such a drastic decision to renounce marriage, move to Venice, join a convent, and feed the poor.

In Zurich, Margaret sought directions from the innkeeper to Christopher Froschauer's print shop. "Follow the Limmat past three bridges, then look for his sign facing the river. You can't miss it."

Froschauer welcomed the printers from Strasbourg into his business. It was much larger than Margaret's shop, and she admired the efficiency of two presses running at the same time. There were seven workers besides him, lots of paper hung up to dry, and a full-time bookkeeper working on a desk near the door.

"I hear you print Bibles," Margaret said.

"Yes, mainly New Testaments though, and a few books of the Old Testament, as Luther translates them into the German. But we arrange the word order and vocabulary to match the Swiss vocalization, so our readers in Switzerland get Luther's fine translation work in a form they can easily read. I can hardly keep up with the demand."

"How many books of the Old Testament has Luther translated?" Margaret asked.

"Only about six or seven so far, but I've added other books of the Old Testament that have been translated by Zurich scholars. Is this your husband?"

"No, I'm sorry I didn't introduce you." Beck figured he'd even the score with Margaret later.

"Beck's a printer friend from Strasbourg," Margaret said. "He works for me in my father's print shop, located near the cathedral."

"Ah, Strasbourg!" Froschauer exclaimed. "Birthplace of the printing press, home of Johannes Gutenberg. It must be a joy to print there. What kinds of manuscripts do you print?"

"All sorts of materials, Mr. Froschauer, from technical Latin medical documents to pamphlets that support the

Reformation. But we've never printed a New Testament in German, though that's my dream for the future."

"A worthy dream indeed. My Testaments are snapped up as soon as they leave the print shop, with orders for many more. This Reformation of the church is not only good for men's souls," Froschauer said with a twinkle in his eye, "but it's good for the printing business as well. Do you know the Knobloch printers?"

"We know them," Beck said. "They're Margaret's competition, one of the largest print shops in Strasbourg. I worked for them for a few months."

"They taught me a few tricks when I visited Strasbourg years ago. Give them my regards if you see them."

"I'll do that." Beck noticed that Margaret hadn't agreed; her attention had shifted elsewhere.

After a visit of about thirty minutes, Margaret thanked Froschauer for his time and assured him this was just the inspiration she needed to get started printing her own German translation of the Bible in Strasbourg.

Wearing a black leather hat atop his lanky frame, Christman went to Zollikon, south of Zurich, to inquire about the whereabouts of Grebel. The directions he was given led him to Grüningen, to the southeast.

Upon further inquiry, a young man told him, "If you're looking for Grebel, follow me. There'll be a meeting tonight east of here." Apparently, a guard from Zurich had come looking for Grebel, so he had fled, leaving only a message that he'd preach that night at the cave. "For now it's a secret Anabaptist meeting place, but how long we can keep it that way is anybody's guess."

Christman immediately decided to follow his new acquaintance to the cave, to check out the meeting and hear Grebel preach.

"We may believe in nonresistance," his traveling partner told him, "but we do take reasonable precautions. You'll have to identify yourself along the pass in order to go further. Otherwise, when you arrive at the cave, no one will be there."

When the woodsman who just "happened" to be near the path seemed confident that Christman wasn't a spy from Zurich, he allowed the travelers to pass. Christman identified Grebel immediately by his brown, broad-brimmed hat. Grebel saw him as well and welcomed him to the meeting.

"Someone in Zurich noticed me and came looking for me in Grüningen," Grebel told him. "I sure hope you're on our side," he added with a laugh.

"I'd say I'm moving in that direction, but I've got to know how in the world this little rag-tag group would ever defend itself."

"I'll talk about that in my sermon this evening. Your printer friends, will they be around for a few days?"

"We're heading across the lake to the execution that you told us about tomorrow morning."

"Good, I want to talk to them about a small printing job we need for the Anabaptists in Switzerland. It's hard to get our pamphlets printed around here anymore."

Grebel's lonesome wife cared for their three little children in Zurich. They had decided not to baptize their newborn daughter in the Zurich cathedral. In doing so, Grebel had turned his back on a large family fortune and the financial security that he could have had for his family.

His voice boomed in the ancient cave. Christman guessed that about fifty people were there, including a few children. A small fire tried to turn back the chilly mountain air that moved in when the sun went down.

Grebel soaked up the warmth as best he could while he spoke. "Tomorrow our pastor friend will give witness to the third baptism of blood. More of us may need to give this witness in the future.

"But we may not fight back with the sword!" he stated as he looked at Christman, seated on a rock in the back. "Christ's kingdom is based on love and nonresistance. Our Lord himself, on the eve of his own death, refused to allow either his disciples or the angels in heaven to protect him from the powers of his day. 'My kingdom is not of this world,' Christ told his captors. We believe in the way of peace because of the example of Jesus and his teachings, which tell us to 'love our enemies.'"

Christman shifted uncomfortably. He'd seen hundreds of peasants mowed down by the power of the nobles' swords and guns. "Like sheep being led to the slaughter," he thought. "These huddled Anabaptists, singing so freely and courageously in this cave, out of the hearing of any cathedral or city council, must expect the same. Blaurock and others like him, like that preacher who waits to be burned tomorrow, have only themselves to blame."

Margaret and Beck searched out Blaurock in the Zurich prison. Though bruised and beaten, his courage was undaunted. He appeared thinner than when he had sat in Margaret's print shop five months earlier, asking them to print the pamphlet about believers baptism. Margaret noticed that his beard needed a trim. She could see that Zwingli's guards didn't give the prisoners any frills, just the daily gruel and water.

"How's your church in Strasbourg?" Blaurock asked. He usually got right to the point.

"Do you mean the Anabaptists?" Margaret replied. After Blaurock nodded, she told him that they hadn't joined the movement yet.

"Oh, you need to soon," Blaurock said. "We need people

like you with education, training, and skills to help lead the way. Have you talked to Conrad Grebel?"

"We met him this morning," Beck answered.

"In the city?" Blaurock said in dismay. "They'll nail him!"

"We talked to him at the inn where we're staying," Margaret said.

"Well, if you see him again, ask him about the small pamphlet that he's written, outlining some of our beliefs. We need someone to print it."

"We're headed to the execution tomorrow morning. Will he be there?"

"Probably, but he'd better stay in the back where the authorities don't see him. He's a marked man."

"That's long enough," the guard growled as he rattled the bars and opened the door. "You must leave now."

Margaret and Beck wound down the long staircase inside the guard tower. Once outside, they walked along the river and noticed a festival of some kind taking place on a high lookout over the city. They climbed the steep stairs and followed their ears to the music and celebration.

Magdalene's invitation had stunned Heinrich. Now the family was reclined to the living room and, at their invitation, he sank into the softest chair in the room. The eldest Knobloch daughter sat across the room, said little, and tried to look interested in him. By now Heinrich understood why no man had yet proposed marriage to her.

Her father talked on and on about the business, about his desire to bring a son-in-law into the family who could eventually take over, and about his great wealth. It all made Heinrich's head spin. If he would agree, he could have money, switch jobs immediately, and marry one of the most eligible women in Strasbourg.

"I know that you are experienced in the printing business," Johann said. "And we have a job opening right now. In fact, you can start here in the morning."

"And our house is large enough," Magdalene added, "that once you marry, you could live with us until we can find a house suitable for a young couple."

Heinrich was almost exactly the same age as the Knobloch daughter. He was an eligible bachelor, and he did know about printing. But he wanted time to consider the proposal. "I think I understand what's being offered," Heinrich managed to blurt out. "But you'll have to give me a few days before I can give you an answer."

"Of course," Magdalene replied. "I'll come to ask your response in two days. If you're not interested, we can certainly find another man."

The two printers from Strasbourg never did exactly figure out what the festival was all about, because they found a little corner to themselves with a grand view of Lake Zurich and the mountains beyond. The moment was spectacular. The view was nice too. Margaret wondered if Christman had gotten passage on a boat to the other end of the lake for the next morning.

"Now who's worrying," Beck kidded her. "We'll find a way over there. For now let's relax. We're far from home, nobody knows us here, we have rooms at the inn, and we have each other. What more could we ask for?"

"To get Christman back safely," Margaret answered. "I bet he got mixed up in something bad. He's such a hot-head, I'm afraid he'll get in trouble."

"Worrying again, Margaret? He can take care of himself." Margaret sensed a small dose of jealousy in Beck's voice.

"Did you see what they did to Blaurock in that dingy prison cell?" Margaret asked.

"No. I was just there to inspect the jail cells so I can help improve the Hangman's Tower in Strasbourg."

"Stop it. Why won't you take what we've seen this week more seriously?"

"I'm very serious about what we've seen. Perhaps I'm just cutting up a little to give us a chance to restore our sanity. It seems we're moving closer and closer to joining the Anabaptists. And that is a scary thought, when you think about it for a while."

"You think too much," Margaret said as she put her arm around him.

"But you just told me to get serious!"

"Forget the world out there for now and focus on us for a bit."

"That's what I was trying to do," Beck replied as he lost his ability to speak. It was a moment worth remembering. Behind them lay the tranquil and calm Lake Zurich. About twenty miles away, near the other end of the lake, an Anabaptist preacher prayed on his knees, ankles shackled to the guardhouse floor. It would be his last night on earth to pray to God.

Several hours after midnight, long after Beck and Margaret had fallen asleep in their rooms, Christman slipped into the inn. The dozing innkeeper heard the tall man come in and cocked his head. "With the Anabaptists," the innkeeper guessed. He'd inform the authorities and pick up a small reward for his services. With the sure prospect of a few more guilders in his pocket, he fell back asleep at his little lookout behind the check-in counter.

16

Witness in Baptism

Aboard the boat Saturday morning, Christman wondered why they were traveling twenty miles to watch a preacher burn to death for his beliefs. Margaret explained that, like any other sensational event, people are drawn to the spectacular and the unusual. They'd seen hangings in Strasbourg, Beck reminded the trio, but never someone burned alive. Margaret pointed out the stark contrast between the magnificent snow-capped mountains towering over a peaceful blue lake and the gruesome reality of what lay just ahead.

They arrived in the village of Lachen shortly before noon. Vineyards on the slopes above the lake hung full with big clusters of grapes. Small farms dotted the countryside. Some families were working around the lake, making their living by catching and selling fish to customers in the village markets.

The unrepentant Anabaptist preacher would burn at the stake in a village controlled by the Catholic Church, unlike Zurich with its city council that had broken with Rome. Not officially ordained, yet gifted, he had preached far and wide in other areas after receiving his second water baptism in St. Gallen, a village about thirty-five miles away. He preached forcefully, baptized many, and irked the authorities in Lachen. Upon returning home from preaching in St. Gallen, he was arrested and sentenced to death as a heretic.

It wasn't hard to locate the action in the village square. People had already gathered to get the best places to see the blaze. Two hooded executioners set up the tall wooden stake, arranged a pile of kindling at the base, and tied the victim with his hands behind the pole. His mouth was gagged with a tight cord to keep him from preaching to the gathered crowd.

Within fifteen minutes, the Catholic priest arrived and asked the preacher one more time if he would give up his heretical beliefs and rejoin the Church. The preacher's wife and young son stood next to the kindling, resigned to their husband and father's fate. Their attempts to reason with him and get him to recant had failed.

From his bucket, the executioner dumped hot coals on the kindling. It sparked and roared into action. The Anabaptist leader soon lost consciousness and fell limp, still tied to the stake. An hour later, all that would be left was a few charred remains of his mangled and scorched corpse. Lachen officials allowed the family to bury him in a local cemetery, but only because the family was well known and had lived there for generations. He had received the sacraments all his life and had been confirmed as a teenager, but he had chosen the route of a heretic when he received his second baptism of water.

Margaret remembered that Hut had warned of the tribulation believers would face in the end times. "This man received his third baptism, in blood," he would have said had he stood beside her in the plaza that day.

Before the three had time to think about where they would go next, Christman felt someone grab the back of his arm. He spun around, ready to defend himself, and then recognized the auburn beard under the brown hat. "You're a little on edge, aren't you Christman," Grebel chuckled. "Did the burning get to you?"

"I say he should have joined the peasants' revolt four months ago and fought back," Christman retorted. "He's partly to blame for being led like a sheep to the slaughter."

"Those who draw the sword will die by the sword," Grebel said.

"What kind of theory is that?"

"From the teachings of Jesus."

"Sorry, I just don't think it's a practical way to live or start a new church. You Anabaptists are going to be chewed up and spit out like worthless shells."

"From the shells will come a kernel of life," Grebel answered. "In his death, our friend, now in the hands of God, will spark the conversion and baptism of others. When the church of Christ is persecuted, that's when it starts to grow. I've got to keep moving so they don't roast me next. We're having a baptism service tomorrow evening at the Rhine Falls, about forty miles north of here. You are welcome to come. In fact, the reason I tracked you down here in Lachen is to see if you'd print my pamphlet of Anabaptist beliefs. But right now the boat that I need to catch is leaving—you can catch the next one on your way to the falls. I'd like to discuss business after the service tomorrow night. If I stick around here much longer, someone will notice me. Spies are everywhere."

"Yes, like that innkeeper last night," Christman answered. "He's the one who ran you off to the cave yesterday."

"Thanks for the tip. It's just not safe for me in Zurich anymore." He turned and headed toward the dock.

Margaret had no appetite to eat lunch anytime soon. "Let's buy our tickets for the next boat out of here and find food elsewhere," she instructed the men. They weren't in any mood to debate her.

"We should hear Zwingli preach tomorrow morning," Beck said to Margaret and Christman aboard the boat headed north. Their boat fare allowed them to get off at two smaller villages along the lake or return all the way to Zurich.

"He'd probably sound a great deal like Matthew," Margaret reflected, "quoting Luther a lot and promoting the Reformation movement. I'll bet he uses Froschauer's Bible."

"We've got to decide when we're going home," Christman said. "We've attended an Anabaptist service in Waldshut, visited with Grebel, and I've even heard him preach."

"But we missed that service in the cave," Margaret reminded him. "I'm ready to head up to the Rhine Falls tomorrow night after we hear Zwingli preach."

"Why do you want to go to that baptism service?" Christman asked. "To watch the next crop of peasants who will get torched, or thrown in the prison tower like Blaurock?"

"Or to get that business deal that Grebel talked about?" Beck asked. "Margaret never forgets about her little print shop back in Strasbourg."

"Do you want a job when we get back, Beck?" Margaret asked sarcastically. "If we can hear Grebel preach and pick up a business contract in one evening, then it's worth our time and money to go."

"I like you, Margaret," Christman said. "You think in down-to-earth categories. I wish you had helped us fight the peasants' war. We could have used your practical skills."

"I'm a woman, remember. I'm expected to know my place and stay in it. Had I fought with you in the Black Forest against Count Rudolf, they would have treated me like just another one of their peasant slaves. I'd have been violated and used for their pleasure and amusement. As long as I'm in a profitable business, I'm accepted, in spite of the fact that I'm a woman."

Glancing at the two men, Margaret added, "It makes life a lot easier for a woman like me to have a man around."

"I'm available, Margaret, whenever you're ready," Christman stiffly offered.

Before anyone could respond, the boat's captain announced, "Prepare to land!"

Margaret grabbed Beck's hand when they walked down the plank onto dry land. "I'm yours," she said with a smile and a quick embrace.

Back at Zurich, they grabbed bread and fruit on the run and found rooms at a different inn. Christman informed Margaret and Beck that he'd meet them outside the cathedral, one way or the other, at noon on Sunday. He said he probably wouldn't be back for the night.

Margaret and Beck followed the music back to where they had been the evening before. Young men and women danced, musicians livened the air with their instruments, and families gathered on blankets around well-filled food baskets. This lookout over the city had once been a Roman fortress, an outpost of the Empire. The fortress was long gone, though Margaret learned that the festival celebrated Zurich's independence from foreign powers.

The couple joined in one dance that was easy to learn and then sat back most of the evening to watch and relax. This all seemed so far removed from the execution they had witnessed that morning. They'd been gone from home for nearly a week; even Strasbourg seemed a long way off.

Before Heinrich could leave for some time off Saturday afternoon, Magdalene came back to Margaret's shop to find out what he had decided.

"I'm interested," was all Heinrich could offer.

"There's a traveling stringed quartet giving a concert in the cathedral chapel this evening," she said. "You two can go and enjoy the music."

It actually turned out to be a pleasant evening for Heinrich and Katie. They had enough in common to occasionally keep a conversation going. They both had grown up in Strasbourg and had attended the same school.

During their walk back to the Knobloch house afterward, Heinrich felt the pressure when his partner for the evening announced in a stiff and formal way, "If I can't find a man to marry soon, I'm going to join Mother Giovanna's convent in Venice."

Heinrich thanked her for a pleasant evening and hurried into the dark streets of Strasbourg. At one corner, he broke out of his absent-minded wondering, looked right and then left, and tried to decide which way to turn. "That's my life right now," he thought with a chuckle.

On Sunday morning, Margaret and Beck found their way to the great cathedral that dominated the Zurich skyline. At the proper time, Zwingli strode in and stood in his pulpit to preach. "He does sound a lot like Matthew," Margaret thought, though Zwingli held a much more prestigious position in Zurich than Matthew did in Strasbourg. By the end of the sermon, Margaret detected an attitude in Zwingli she didn't like, though she couldn't have explained it to anyone.

Zwingli led the Reformation movement in Switzerland by himself, except for the Anabaptist movement, of course, while Luther led the Reformation in Germany. Reformation beliefs and practices in Strasbourg lay somewhere between what the two great reformers preached. "No wonder so many religious refugees stream to Strasbourg," Margaret thought while Zwingli lectured the congregation on his version of the Reformation. "They can slip into the city, unnoticed, without fear of an overbearing leader."

Two guards along the main street in Zurich, on the other hand, had noticed Christman the night before. Margaret and Beck found this out when a short man with a walking stick approached them in the plaza outside the church. Christman had gotten into a scuffle with the guards, the man said, and he had ended up in Grüningen overnight, sleeping in his barn.

"I'll lead you to your traveling partner," the farmer told Beck. "Follow me."

When they got to Christman, Beck thanked him and asked, "Do you know the way to the Rhine Falls near Schaffhausen?"

"Yes, I've been there several times. Why do you want to go?"

"We've never seen the falls. Nothing like them near Strasbourg."

"We're going to an Anabaptist meeting there this evening," Margaret added.

"Good!" the farmer exclaimed. After he glanced around, he added, "Can I show you the way? It's only about twenty miles from here. My old horse is slow, but we can easily make it there in time for the service if we stop a couple of times to water the poor girl."

They headed out immediately, with the four of them sharing bread, cheese, and grapes on the journey.

"You'll love the falls," the farmer promised. "My wife and I traveled there on our honeymoon years ago. She's dead now; the doctors couldn't help her. And my only son was hired to fight in one of the emperor's wars, I think in the east against the Turks."

As the farmer had predicted, they plodded into a clearing beside the Rhine just before the service began. The falls could be heard but not easily seen from where they stopped. Margaret, Beck, and Christman hiked up to a lookout for a better view. Margaret wished they had more time to sit and enjoy the crashing water and roaring. After Christman headed back to the clearing, she sneaked a kiss and a hug.

"Let's come back here sometime when we're a little more relaxed, Beck," she pleaded.

"Sounds like a great idea. You know, Margaret, whenever I'm with you I'm having a grand time." With that Beck scooped her up and whirled her around toward the falls.

"Put me down! That's dangerous!"

"Any more than coming here?"

When Margaret didn't answer, they tried to figure out just why they were at a falls in northeast Switzerland on a Sunday evening in September. Before they could arrive at much of an answer, Beck stole a quick kiss, and then they hiked back down to join the Anabaptist gathering.

The farmer from Grüningen joined Christman on one of the logs placed around the clearing. They made an odd couple, the short farmer next to the tall guildsman.

"You know the peasants' war started here about a year and a half ago," the farmer said. "A countess in a castle nearby, tried to send her peasants off to the river to gather snails while they needed to gather hay from their own farms. They rioted and that triggered the revolt all across south Germany."

"I hope they stuffed some snails down her throat and strangled her," Christman snarled. "That would have been justice for the old lady."

Grebel worked his way through the crowd, shook hands, winced when someone gripped hard, and welcomed the newcomers. "Remember," he said to Margaret, "I want to ask you about that printing job when the meeting's over. Here, at the risk of losing your attention during my preaching, look this short manuscript over," he said with a smile.

Margaret believed she understood why Grebel stood out as the leader of the Swiss Anabaptists. Educated, handsome, and self-confident, he came from a noble family. And, she leaned over and said to Beck, "he's younger than you are."

"I hear he lived a wild life while he was a student in Paris," Beck retorted. "He blames his sore joints on early years of sin."

216

"He's still got you by eight years."

"Just read your manuscript while he preaches if he's a distraction to you, Margaret. I'll be sure to join your little business meeting with him afterward—to make sure you don't try anything."

"He's married, Beck, so back off."

Out of the corner of his eye, Beck noticed a familiar face in the crowd. "Incredible. Look who's here."

"Michael, the last time we saw you we were making plans under the firs by the bridge. What brings you here?" Beck asked.

"I come every Sunday night that I can," Sattler responded. Christman came over and shook hands as well. The two of them towered over the others.

"I'm a seeker," Sattler said. "Haven't been baptized, but I come to learn what these Anabaptists are all about. My wife and I live nearby, though she doesn't always come to these meetings."

"My topic tonight is the character of the church," Grebel began. "On a field trip during my school days in Zurich, our teacher showed us the beginning point for two mighty rivers, the Rhine and the Rhone."

Beck perked up. He had traveled down the Rhone on his way to Barcelona a few weeks earlier.

"The snow-capped mountains and a huge glacier provide the two rivers with their first trickle of water. Each flows for hundreds of miles, after which the Rhine empties into the North Sea while the Rhone empties its waters into the Mediterranean. They start within twelve miles of each other, high in the Alps, but they flow in opposite directions.

"The Brethren come out of the same Church as the Reformed Church of Zwingli, but we head in radically different directions. Zwingli uses the Zurich city government to

217

enforce his religious ideas, so that everyone has to agree—or get out. How many of you had to get out of the city?" At least a dozen hands went up.

"Our idea of the church is one that includes those who freely join, without force. That's where our river of thought flows the opposite direction from Ulrich Zwingli's river, or Martin Luther's, for that matter."

"Or Wolfgang's, Bucer's, and Matthew's," Margaret thought.

"Let me tell you a story I learned in a history class in Zurich. On the Lindenhof, that wonderful lookout above the main street in Zurich, are remains of a Roman fortress. During the time of Emperor Decius, in the middle of the third century, Christians came under a time of severe persecution. All citizens in the Empire, including those in far-flung outposts like Zurich, had to offer sacrifice and obtain a commissioner's certificate witnessing to the act. Just a quick little sacrifice to the emperor, pledging one's highest loyalty. No harm done, right?"

Margaret wondered where this story was going. Her image of the Lindenhof was of dancing and a spectacular view of Lake Zurich.

"There were two Christians in Zurich," Grebel said as he shifted uncomfortably, "who refused to bow their knees to the power and authority of the emperor. Felix and Regula claimed that God's authority was higher than the state's power, and they lost their heads because of it. Literally, they were decapitated because they claimed that Jesus Christ was their Lord, not Emperor Decius.

"Today, we need the faith of Felix and Regula. Christ's church is not governed by the edge of the sword, a city council, or the control of a single, strong preacher."

"Yes, and that church will be mowed down like the peasants in the Black Forest who tried to fight Count Rudolf,"

Kenlin thought. Grebel's view of the church was too idealistic, in his opinion.

"The church must be voluntary, like this assembly," Grebel said, sweeping his hand over the gathering. "All of us were baptized with water when we were babies. When you receive your second water baptism, you give witness to the Spirit's work in your life. From a genuine commitment to follow our Lord and Savior, Jesus Christ, comes a desire to unite ourselves with the true church, one that is voluntary and free from the powers of this world.

"Some of us witnessed the burning of one of our preachers yesterday. Christ and the apostles give us the example that, when we give up all and choose to follow Jesus, we will face hard times, even death, as did Christ himself."

"He's getting to the punch line, for sure," Christman thought to himself. "He'll ask for volunteers who want to join the movement and get baptized."

"There has always been a free church since the time of Christ. And they've been persecuted, killed, and slaughtered because they believed so differently. The idea of a free church almost died out when the emperors of the fourth century made Christianity the official religion of the state. Under the support and protection of princes and nobles, the Church lost its most vital quality, the voluntary, free decision of believers who choose to give up their own lives to follow Christ.

"Join me by the water for baptism."

Though a debate waged in Margaret's mind, arguing the reasons for and against it, she believed that this was the time for her to give witness to the Spirit's work in her life. She glanced at Beck. "Will he go with me to the water?" she wondered.

When Beck followed, Grebel scooped up water and poured it on their heads while they waded ankle-deep in the river. They could hear the crash of the falls in the distance.

Nothing out of the ordinary took place, just the refreshing confidence that their new confession of faith had joined them to a movement that rejected political power for its strength. Christman and Sattler watched from the banks of the river. Grebel hurried to get out of the cold water, though not before six seekers received baptism.

Grebel explained to Margaret that he had written a pamphlet outlining a few of the main beliefs of the Brethren. He wanted her to print it and then ship copies to him in Grüningen for distribution. The character of the church, the life of discipleship, baptism, separation from the world—these were the main topics.

Margaret agreed to do the work. She didn't know when it would be finished, but she thought they could work his job in by the end of October.

"Try not to give Zwingli any hint this pamphlet is being published," Grebel instructed Margaret. "He'll be furious when he sees it, and he'll come after me with a vengeance."

The farmer from Grüningen told Christman about a barn near the falls that they could use for lodging that night. He said he always used it before heading south on Monday morning. The owner of the barn offered a standing invitation to anyone at the Sunday-night meeting to sleep overnight. Christman figured the offer was the best they had. "Sort of like old man Ziegler's arsenal outside Strasbourg," he told Margaret. So the three of them slept in the barn with several other travelers, six cows, a restless bull, two horses, and a rooster who woke them up earlier than anyone wanted.

At nearby Schaffhausen, Beck located a guide to take them to Basel on the Rhine. Taking well-worn footpaths around the rapids, they had passed Waldshut in a small boat by midafternoon on Monday.

The next morning, at Basel, they boarded a larger boat and sailed all the way to Strasbourg, arriving at the bridge by evening. Margaret looked forward to the three-mile walk to the print shop, through familiar territory, and then home.

When she arrived at the print shop, Margaret noticed an official-looking document on her desk, placed there by Heinrich or Peter. It was from the Strasbourg censorship committee, delivered with their unmistakable stamp. She needed to appear before them, was all it said. "Welcome home," she thought. "I'd better put Grebel's manuscript away and out of sight for a while. Until this storm cloud passes over."

17

Troubles in Strasbourg

Johann and Magdalene marched furiously toward the church of St. Thomas. They intended to find the wheezing pastor and condemn him for an absolutely unforgivable sin. Their daughter Agnes had just informed them that she was pregnant.

"It could only have been the preacher," Agnes had explained. That made the powerful Knoblochs fighting mad.

Johann kicked open the door of Wolfgang's study at the church. "How dare you have sex with our daughter before you get married," he bellowed in a rage.

"You're an illegitimate, godless, whoremonger," Magdalene shouted. "You're no different from any other priest. Or man, for that matter." She spat in disgust.

"Just you wait until the Knoblochs get finished with you, preacher." Johann shook his fist at Wolfgang. "You'll be sorry you ever came to Strasbourg."

Wolfgang stood with his back to the wall, shocked at the dreadful news, and frightened by the ferocity of the Knoblochs' rage. With a trembling voice barely above a whisper he asked, "Are you sure your daughter is pregnant?"

"You should know about these things," Magdalene screeched. "She hasn't been seeing anyone else these days, and she's engaged to you, you evil man."

Wolfgang realized he was in an awful predicament. One of the most powerful families in Strasbourg threatened to destroy his ministry and reputation as a Reformation preacher. Further, they might not even allow him to marry their daughter.

"If what you say is true," Wolfgang said, "we'll have to get married right away."

"Don't be so sure about that," Magdalene blasted back. "We don't think you're the right man for our daughter anymore."

As soon as Johann nodded in agreement, they turned and stomped down the cobblestone walkway as quickly as they had arrived.

Two days later, when Wolfgang had mustered up the nerve to visit the Knobloch home and talk to the irate parents, he discovered that his fiancée had already been sent to live with an aunt in Mainz, about a hundred miles away. The wedding appeared to be off, indefinitely. He had created this situation for himself, they told him.

A piece of bad news also awaited Margaret when she returned from Switzerland. The Zells' baby had been born prematurely, was sick from the beginning, and died before the parents could have it baptized. Margaret was stunned. She went to visit Katherine but found the distraught mother inconsolable. Katherine blamed herself for the baby's death, while others, especially those opposed to the Reformation movement that Matthew led in Strasbourg, assumed that God had passed judgment on the Zells.

In the midst of these tragedies, news from the censorship committee was not good either. They wanted Margaret to answer a series of questions about her printing activities. From talking to others, she discovered she wasn't the only printer facing the powerful committee. Controlled by the Catholic minority in Strasbourg, it was able to block printers who turned out Lutheran and Anabaptist documents.

To further aggravate the unsettled state of affairs in Strasbourg, a clattering preacher from the German city of Ulm had arrived preaching in favor of the Lutheran Reformation. He condemned the pope with harsh language and had produced a wandering list of forty-three traditional church teachings that were based, he said, on fables, spiritless laws, and imperial mandates. The former monk and mystic stirred up feelings and opinions, both for and against the Reformation movement.

This self-appointed spokesman preached two points of view that Margaret disagreed with. First, he urged German knights to take up arms in defense of the Reformation and to fight those who stood in the way of Luther's gospel. Margaret held a growing conviction that fighting was wrong, especially in defense of the church.

Second, Margaret believed that putting the Scriptures and pamphlets into the hands of the average layperson would advance the gospel and promote the Reformation. This meandering preaching parade, on the other hand, insisted that only trained preachers, like himself or Luther, could adequately interpret or understand the proper direction for the Reformation. Margaret printed pamphlets for the laity, for those who had little or no other means to learn about faith, the gospel, and the church. The visitor's critical pamphlet and condemning sermons turned her off.

Hut wasn't afraid to take on the preacher's pompous beliefs in public. He asked the holy man why Frederick the Wise, the knight who defended Luther, still had the largest collection of relics in northern Europe. Right in Wittenberg, where Luther preached, Frederick claimed to have a piece of the burning bush before which Moses stood, an entire skeleton of one of the children massacred by King Herod, a bucket of soot from the fiery furnace through which Shadrach, Meshach, and Abednego walked, milk from the Virgin Mary, and straw from the manger of Jesus. "An incredible collection," Hut pointed out as he chuckled to the speechless cleric. "Maybe Martin Luther needs to clean up his own back yard before preaching reform elsewhere."

The petition to abolish the Mass in Strasbourg was what the censorship committee wanted to question Margaret about. Hut, Christman, and Wolff had paid Margaret to print the pamphlet several months earlier. It had upset the Knoblochs and other members of the censorship committee. The outcome was that Margaret was to stop printing "inflammatory materials that might stir up riotous actions or false beliefs."

The whirlwind of activities came so fast that Margaret was left in a daze. Only five days earlier, Grebel had baptized her in the river by the waterfalls in Switzerland. Now Wolfgang was on the run for his preaching position, and maybe worse. Katherine had nearly broken down with depression, and the city council bore down on Margaret's business affairs.

At least Beck, the man she loved, still stood like a rock in her defense. They took a long walk along the canal, as they did whenever Margaret needed to talk through a difficult issue that faced her.

"If we print Conrad Grebel's pamphlet, they'll arrest us for sure," Margaret said to Beck. "His ideas are so radical that we'll be in big trouble if they catch us."

"It's your decision," Beck answered. "We can print the pamphlet and get it out of Strasbourg without anyone knowing, I think. We can store it in Clement's arsenal. On the other hand, if this is something you believe in, then let's go for it, and take whatever consequences come our way."

"I wish I could talk to my father and ask his advice," Margaret said softly. "He would know what to do."

"Didn't he follow his convictions and print sermons that challenged the big boys here in Strasbourg?"

"Yes, but that was a generation ago. Today a printer can lose her business, or worse, if she gets on the wrong side of the city council. We don't have any strong defenders in positions of leadership right now. Wolfgang is hiding out, while Bucer is critical of him and the Anabaptists. Matthew's in no mood to speak out boldly, and the growing number of Anabaptists in Strasbourg will probably bring down a backlash against them by the council."

It didn't take long for Margaret's fears to be confirmed. Sturm gave in to pressure from the bishop, the Knoblochs, and the council. That evening, two guards broke up the Thursday discussion time at Kniebs's house. The guards wrote down the names of those who attended and threw Kniebs in the jailhouse overnight. A "secret and illegal meeting" was the only charge he ever heard. After a lecture from Sturm about underground meetings of religious radicals, Kniebs walked out of the prison three hours after sunrise.

Ryff sized up the situation on Friday at lunchtime. "This Reformation has its own energy, almost a life of its own. Like a pendulum, sometimes the reformed protestors gain the upper hand, other times the Catholics. The Catholics are turning out as many pamphlets as followers of Luther and Zwingli. They see the advantage of the printed page just as much as Bucer or Capito or Zell."

"How long will it be until the emperor tries to control the printing presses?" Beck asked.

"That will probably come eventually," Ryff said, "but for now, it's a battle for the hearts and souls of the people of Germany."

Margaret took most of what Ryff said cautiously, though right now he seemed to make sense. The pendulum, at least temporarily, had swung in favor of the Catholic minority in Strasbourg. "Thanks a lot, Wolfgang," Margaret thought to herself. "When you get the Knoblochs mad at you, they take it out on everybody they don't like."

"So how do we get the pendulum moving back the other way?" Margaret wondered aloud.

"It's probably best for you to print a document or two in Latin, maybe even the writings of a Catholic scholar," Ryff answered. "I'd recommend printing some nonreligious material for a while to give the appearance that you aren't a radical Anabaptist."

"And if I am an Anabaptist, then what?"

"Then you'd better be very careful what you say, do—and print." With unsteady hands Ryff picked up his medical manuscript. "This is the kind of material you need to print. In fact, I'm so close to being finished, you may want to start on the book, and by the time you're ready to print the end of it, I'll be done. I only have one chapter left to write."

Beck ate the last of his roll and walked over to the press in the middle of the print shop. "Congratulations, Gutenberg," he said to the wooden apparatus. "You've unleashed a powerful dragon. No one can control you, and you're going to be around a long time."

"Beck," Ryff said, "have you ever heard where Gutenberg got his ideas for the printing press? From China, where stories of dragons come from. Seems the Chinese developed movable type long before Gutenberg, but they never allowed the average person to use it. Here, today, anyone with a bit of skill and some business sense can put it to work."

"I've heard that a dragon breathes fire," Margaret said. "Those who don't fall in line behind the big dragon on the city council will probably get scorched when it hisses in their direction."

"The printing press dragons are all tame," Ryff said. "They're under the power of people. The people disagree, argue, have differences. They use whatever means they can muster to get at each other. So don't blame the dragon if someone gets burned. Use its power and energy for your own goals. That's what I'd recommend."

By the end of the week, the news had circulated throughout Strasbourg that Wolfgang had made Agnes pregnant. In counseling with Bucer, Wolfgang agreed that he must confess his sin at church on Sunday.

When he went to the Knoblochs to inform them of his plan to confess on Sunday, he took the imposing Christman with him. Even so, Wolfgang was chased away and threatened again with removal from his job.

To be safe, Christman agreed to invite a number of his friends to attend church on Sunday morning. Just to keep the peace, he and Wolfgang agreed, and to prevent the Knoblochs from disrupting the service.

The pulpit of St. Thomas functioned as a Lutheran platform for reform in Strasbourg. This morning Bucer presided. Wolfgang, who normally led the worship service, now sat on a seat in the front row and waited for the moment to make his confession. Those sitting near him could easily hear him breathe.

Christman's friends sat around the edges. A large man who had helped to lead the demolition of images in the church only weeks earlier sat near the main doorway in the back. Christman sat next to Wolfgang.

The ruckus began after the sermon, when Bucer announced that Wolfgang had a confession to make. One of the Knobloch uncles leapt to his feet and launched into a series of criticisms. Christman rose quickly, walked back the middle aisle, and stood next to the man, glowering down at him. One of Christman's men joined him on the other side.

By then, another uncle had risen to continue the chant. "Capito should be thrown out of this church and banned from the city," he began. Two more of Christman's partners quickly moved up next to him and put him back in his seat. By then it was clear that they had won the upper hand.

Wolfgang rose and walked to the pulpit with his collar

turned up, as usual. His normal confident bearing was lost for the moment. With sagging shoulders, he confessed his sin and asked the congregation for forgiveness, which prompted the Knobloch uncles to get up and leave the church. He said he would do whatever it took to make the situation right, and then he sat down.

That evening, at his home on Stone Street, Christman heard a sharp knock on the door. On the other side stood Johann Jr., whom he had fought in the plaza a few weeks earlier, and three other men. Before Christman knew what hit him, the four men jumped him, pounded him to the ground. By the time they left, two minutes after they had come, Christman was bleeding at the mouth, had a cracked rib, and lay bruised and motionless on the floor.

When he regained consciousness, Christman realized he had been paid back. The intruders had even ransacked his little apartment. He slowly reached for a chair, set it upright, and struggled to sit in it. In the dark, pounding with pain, he wondered what to do next.

Settling on the belief that Gertrude Ziegler would help him, he crept stiffly down Stone Street, talked the guard into opening the gate for him, and dragged himself down the long road, across the canals, to Robertsau.

For several days, while resting in the Ziegler's barn, Christman's generous host baked bread for him, cleaned his bandages, and carried steaming bowls of soup from the big kettle with her bunched-up apron to nurse him back to health.

The usual Thursday-evening discussion group at Kniebs's place was off for a few weeks. Nicholas's wife had insisted that the Anabaptist meetings be held elsewhere in order to keep him out of prison. As a result, many people went to Clement's farm Sunday night to see friends and catch up on community news. Even though the meeting was never publicized, some kind of invisible network had passed the word along, and people came.

Margaret chatted with Christman, who was slowly regaining his strength. Hut and Lucas Hackfurt were there as well, and even Ryff had learned of the meeting, though not from Margaret; he was there for the discussion.

As usual, Clement spoke first. "Our brother Christman is healing nicely, though he'd better think twice about staring down a Knobloch in church anytime soon. I'll let each of you decide if he deserved to be beat up, but let's talk about how a follower of Christ should respond to violence. How do we respond when someone knocks us senseless, justly or unjustly?"

"Hit back harder," Hut replied while he cleaned his mustache of food remains. "And hope they don't pull out a sword to run you through."

"What did Christ say to Peter in the garden of Gethsemane?" Clement asked the group.

"Put your sword away," Margaret answered.

"And he told Pilate that his kingdom was not of this world," Lucas added.

"That's right," Clement said. "Responding to force with force will never get us anywhere, especially if we're trying to clean up the church."

"But won't any movement that refuses to use force just wither away and die?" Jörg asked.

"It may wither away and die even if it uses force," Clement answered. "Look at the peasants' revolt."

"There simply weren't enough peasants to defend themselves," Christman said quietly.

"Christ had thousands of angels at his command when He was persecuted," the old farmer reminded his listeners. "But he chose not to call them into service against the Jewish authorities or the Roman soldiers."

"Let's leave the Jews out of this discussion," Hut said. "They have to pay for their sin of nailing Christ to the Cross."

"The Romans nailed Christ to the cross," Clement reminded Hut, "not the Jews. Christ died on the cross for the Jews as well as Gentiles. Look at how he died, as a martyr, giving up his life willingly."

"We saw an outrageous burning in Zurich about three weeks ago," Beck chimed in. "A Swiss preacher stood for what he believed in, and they burned him at the stake."

"That's the character of the church," Clement replied. "Down through the centuries, many have died for their convictions and refused to fight back, because that's just not the kind of church Christ established. Look at the disciples. All of them, except John, died a martyr's death, like your Swiss preacher."

Not everyone accepted Clement's peace teaching that evening. Christman nursed his wounds and his pride. He'd have to think about it more.

On their walk back to the print shop, Margaret asked Beck, how, according to Clement's understanding, Wolfgang should respond.

"Wolfgang is clearly in the wrong," Beck said.

"I know that, but now what should he do, with his bride-to-be living in Mainz, that is?"

"Leave that one alone, Margaret. Wolfgang will have to find his own way through this one. There's nothing you or I can do for him."

"Should we go ahead and finish his commentary on Hosea?"

"You're nearly finished with the job, Margaret! It's business; you've got to follow through."

"Now you're starting to sound like me," she said with a

chuckle. "What if I were to take Katherine and go to Mainz to visit Agnes?"

"You can't be serious, Margaret."

"You're right, Beck. I don't know if I'm serious or not. But it might be one way of turning the other cheek, to quote the preacher tonight."

"You've changed since your baptism, haven't you, Margaret? You're really buying into Anabaptism. That pamphlet from Grebel has turned you into a radical, believing in peace and all that, huh?"

"Well, I do care about Wolfgang and Agnes, and maybe there's a way I can help. Besides, a trip to Mainz might be just what the doctor ordered for Katherine's depression."

"I love you," Beck said as they paused on their little bridge in the cool September evening.

"Don't get all mushy now. I've got a lot of things on my mind."

"But where do I stand with you? Are your ideas and beliefs more important than me, Margaret?"

"Of course not. It's just that I need time to think about my beliefs. Give me a little space and I'll be all right."

"Hey, are you ready to talk about a wedding?"

"You mean Wolfgang and Agnes?"

"No, Beck and Margaret. How does that sound to you?"

"Are you asking me to marry you, Beck?"

"You know me, I'm a little slow making up my mind, but once I decide, it's locked in. Will you marry me?"

"Yes, Beck. I will."

"I'm the happiest man alive right now, Margaret."

"And I'm glad you came to Strasbourg. I'm convinced our lives came together through God's plan."

Beck held Margaret's hands and gazed at the water in the canal. "I hope that divine plan has some heavenly protection and good will in store for us. We're going to need it. We're living on the edge of society now that we've been rebaptized."

"We'll face the future together, Beck. Two are stronger than one."

After a gentle embrace, Margaret looked into his eyes and asked, "Are you afraid?"

"A little. Things could get messy for us when the authorities decide to crack down on the Anabaptists. But I have good news."

A little reluctant to break the mood, Margaret asked, "Is it really something I need to know right now?"

"Well, I think you'll want to know this. I've already talked to Matthew and he's willing to marry us."

Margaret was surprised that he'd already talked to Matthew about their wedding. She slowly asked, "Will he marry us when he finds out we're Anabaptists?"

"There are other preachers besides Matthew. If he backs out, we'll get someone else. My love for you is what I want you to feel tonight."

"Don't you think that just maybe you should have talked to me before asking Matthew to marry us?"

With a laugh that released the tension, their arms and lives came together in the brisk nighttime air, giving them strength, courage, and warmth.

18

Examining the Lord's Supper

Before Margaret could talk to Katherine about going to visit Agnes, Sturm delivered a one-page announcement about an important meeting that would take place in a week. Through his huge beard, Sturm explained why Zwingli planned on coming to Strasbourg: "I'm trying to help settle some differences between Luther and Zwingli. They disagree about what happens to the bread and wine in the Lord's Supper."

"And Zwingli's agreed to travel from Zurich to Strasbourg?" Margaret asked.

"Yes. He's so convinced his views are more biblical than Luther's that he's agreed to come for a discussion. Luther won't come, though he wrote me a letter saying that a meeting between them should take place eventually. And the Catholic position on the Lord's Supper should be presented alongside Luther's and Zwingli's interpretations."

Margaret was impressed with Sturm's courage in presenting the Catholic argument too. Strasbourg was located between Zurich and Wittenberg, so it made sense for him to initiate a discussion between Luther's supporters and Zwingli. But adding the Catholic position in the debate seemed risky. "He's probably been pressured by some powerful members of the city council to include the Catholic view," Margaret reasoned, "but it should be a significant event for Strasbourg and the Reformation in spite of the politics involved in setting the meeting up."

"Have you solved the case of your missing nephew yet?" Margaret asked Sturm.

"No, Margaret, but we're still working on it. There's a one-hundred-guilder reward offered for any information that leads us to his whereabouts."

After Sturm left her print shop, Margaret was eager to visit Katherine. Delivering the happy news about getting engaged to Beck would surely cheer up her depressed friend.

"Good morning, Katherine," Margaret began, "how's the preacher's wife today?"

"As good as can be expected."

"I've got great news."

"We can use some good news around here. Tell me what you know."

"Well, it's Beck and me."

"Did he finally come around and ask you?"

"Finally, Katherine, just last night! He wants to get married the middle of next month."

"Congratulations on being patient. Sometimes you have to wait a long time for a man to make up his mind. And it's important that he thinks it was his decision."

"He already talked to Matthew about marrying us."

"Great, so let's make wedding plans."

"Actually, Katherine, that's not the real reason I came today. I was wondering if you would go with me to Mainz to visit Agnes."

At first, Katherine was reluctant to go, but the more Margaret talked and explained her reasons for going, the more the trip north seemed to be a good idea. Katherine agreed to leave within two days.

Margaret and her print-shop men had almost finished the work on Wolfgang's Hosea commentary. They had printed two hundred copies, which would be sent to most of the universities in northern Europe. Written in Latin, its intended audience was theologians and scholars, not the average lay person.

Margaret and Beck planned for the next printing job. They would take Ryff's suggestion and begin printing his nearly finished medical manuscript. In German, it was filled with Ryff's practical, homespun medical wisdom. They planned for an initial run of five hundred copies, agreeing that if the first printing sold well, they'd produce more.

"This book will sell," Margaret told Beck.

A trip out of town appeared attractive to Margaret right then. Her world had turned upside-down in the past several weeks, and she believed that time away with a good friend would help her face the future with renewed courage. But it dawned on Margaret that on the journey to Mainz and back she'd certainly tell Katherine about her water baptism in the river while visiting Switzerland. "Oh well," Margaret thought to herself, "the truth about my beliefs needs to come out eventually."

Each day since Beck had asked Margaret to marry him, he had renewed that intention. They laughed together, walked together, and talked about plans for marriage, and Margaret felt that her outlook on life had lifted. Still, the swirling changes of the fall, with all that was going on, made life a day-to-day challenge. At least now she had a man to walk with her. Not just any man, though—Balthasar Beck, the one she had wanted all along.

Heading downstream in the fall of the year seemed easy. Katherine and Margaret bought passage to Mainz, boarded a canal boat near the print shop, changed to a larger boat near the creaking wooden bridge that spanned the Rhine, and floated downstream toward Mainz. Though their boat moved with the current downstream, it was headed north, toward the Netherlands and the North Sea.

The scenery along the Rhine riverbanks invigorated them. Beautiful forests, occasional vineyards and wheat fields, villages on the highlands in the distance, and old castles here and there created a splendid view for the two travelers.

Along the way, the women talked about why they were going to visit Agnes. They tried to predict how they'd be received and planned what they'd say to her. Though it seemed awkward for Margaret, she believed that this journey to visit her longtime rival was crucial to the health of her growing faith. If the visit could help her business contacts, then so much the better.

After a night's rest at an inn in Mainz, Katherine and Margaret set out to find Agnes. They asked at the inn, at the cathedral, and in the plaza. Finally, they were given directions to a stately old house along the river. The woman who answered the door stalled. It became clear they had the right house, but it was unclear whether they'd get to see their Strasbourg acquaintance. The Knobloch aunt didn't intend to let them past her.

Suddenly, Agnes appeared at the door, and the aunt invited them in, though not cordially. At the kitchen table, Margaret explained the reason for their visit. "We know you've fled from a difficult situation in Strasbourg, Agnes, and we've come to visit, to show you we care about you."

"This problem is my own fault," Agnes said. "I don't blame anyone but myself. I love Wolfgang with all my heart, but I really don't know what to do next."

"She can live here as long as she needs to," the Knobloch aunt coolly said. "The baby can grow up in our home."

"I think it would be so much better if Agnes's baby could grow up in a home with its own father," Katherine responded.

"You're right," Agnes answered. "But right now I don't see any way that will be possible."

"Agnes," Katherine said, "let me get right to the point and present you with an idea Margaret and I talked about on the way here." Katherine's lost smile seemed to reappear, Margaret noticed, and her cheeks gleamed rosy again. "I'd like to invite you to come back to Strasbourg and live with me."

As Margaret expected, the Knobloch aunt grimaced without saying a word. Agnes showed no emotion at all. She'd been humiliated, criticized, and sent off to a relative in a distant city. The smile that had captured Wolfgang was gone. But she looked straight into Katherine's eyes—a sign, Margaret thought, that she hadn't rejected the idea.

"Matthew and I live in a big house," Katherine said. "We have a nice guest room that you'd be welcome to use, for as long as you'd like."

"Agnes lives here now," her aunt answered. "Your offer is out of the question. In fact, ladies, I see no further reason why you should stay here in my kitchen. The matter's been settled."

"When are you leaving for Strasbourg?" Agnes asked.

"Tomorrow morning," Katherine answered.

"The offer is from both of us," Margaret said. "It's time I begin to build a bridge toward you, and your family. I'll support you and care for you in whatever way I can, even though I don't have a big house like Katherine's."

"From you, Margaret, that's an amazing offer." Slowly, and measuring each word, Agnes continued. "I'll need some time to think this over." She glanced toward her aunt, then said to her two visitors, "I'll be at the loading dock on time to board if I'm going along; otherwise, go ahead without me."

Strasbourg lay about one hundred miles to the south of Mainz, a three-day journey on a boat pulled by mules or horses. Agnes did not come to the dock to travel with Margaret and Katherine. Reluctantly, they left without her, but they took full advantage of the time to relax and to talk.

On the first day, under the warm south German sun, Margaret told Katherine the details of her recent trip to Switzerland. As she told the story, Katherine realized that Margaret had joined the Anabaptists. Without hesitation, Margaret described her water baptism by Grebel. "Has it changed her life?" Katherine wondered. Margaret explained that her baptism had simply declared a new confession of spiritual awakening to Jesus's call to come and follow. That led her to join a church that didn't have any walls, buildings, organizational structure, or protection.

"The Anabaptists don't have much you can call a church," Margaret explained. "Just their small home groups, meeting wherever they can. Around Zurich, Conrad Grebel's church meets more often in a cave than anywhere else."

"We'll make an amazing trio if Agnes decides to move back to my house in Strasbourg," Katherine mused. "You, an Anabaptist; me, the wife of the Lutheran preacher in the cathedral; and a pregnant fiancée of a preacher. Won't that give people something to talk about!"

"I hope she stands her ground and comes back," Margaret said. "It's time she steps out on her own and gets away from her parents' control. My parents are both gone, but I can't imagine them treating me like the Knoblochs have treated Agnes."

By Sunday, their third day on the slow-moving boat, Margaret and Katherine were ready to get home. They walked the last three miles from the pontoon bridge, agreeing that they would remain good friends even though Margaret had joined the Anabaptists.

Sturm had planned for several months to hold the discussion on the Lord's Supper in Strasbourg. It finally began on the last Monday in September. Luther had responded to

Sturm's invitation, stating that Matthew and Bucer could represent his point of view quite well.

Zwingli would come to the discussion to clarify his beliefs and to establish himself as the leading spokesman for the "representative" point of view.

So, while refugees continued to straggle into Strasbourg from the farms destroyed during the peasants' war, while the threat from the Turks in the east continued to grow daily, while the lingering plague took its weekly death toll, church leaders in Strasbourg got ready to debate the finer points of the Lord's Supper. It seemed rather trivial to Margaret, even a little ridiculous.

Margaret didn't care much for the theological hair-splitting that was going on in the cathedral. She knew she didn't agree with what she had learned as a girl, that the bread and wine actually changed into the body and blood of Christ in the Lord's Supper. Luther didn't sound much different to her, though, as he said the presence of Christ is "in, with, and under" the two elements. "What does that mean?" Margaret wondered.

Zwingli was known to argue that the elements of communion represented the body and blood of Christ, as Paul had written in First Corinthians. Margaret knew that the Anabaptists agreed with him, but Grebel's church in Switzerland went further. From a Corinthians passage, Grebel preached that believers should examine their lives within the body of Christ, the fellowship of Christians, before taking communion. Christ was present, he preached, but in the gathered community of believers, in a church pure and holy before God. When believers have examined themselves before God, confessed their sins, and come together for communion, then, yes, Christ's presence is truly in their midst. But it didn't take a priest in a ceremonial gown to dispense the elements to joyous believers. Grebel emphasized the church and Christ's presence among the believers, not hair-splitting over the presence of Christ "in, with, and under" the bread and wine.

Margaret never did learn where the chief spokesman for the Catholic point of view came from. But she knew that there were priests, scholars, and several bishops, from far and wide, in Strasbourg. Inns were full, little eateries did good business, and the plaza outside the cathedral buzzed with activity.

Margaret slipped into the cathedral occasionally to listen to the discussions. Matthew rose to the occasion. He defended Luther's "in, with, and under" point of view as well as Luther himself could have done. Bucer worked alongside Matthew, but the young preacher ably defended solid Lutheran theology.

Zwingli strode into the city with assistants, books, and a determination to defend his point of view. Margaret remembered him from when she and Beck had attended the Sunday-morning Mass in Zurich. He spoke forcefully and confidently. After all, he was the leading Reformation preacher in Switzerland.

Zwingli had come to Strasbourg with a secondary mission, however. He wanted to warn Sturm about the growing number of Anabaptists in Switzerland and south Germany. "They're a menace to the Reformation church. They refuse to accept the legitimate authority of the church in Zurich, claiming their own ministers are ordained of God. Watch them, Sturm; they'll take over your city like they're trying to do in mine. Warn your city council to be tough on them."

On Wednesday, only a few days after Margaret and Katherine had returned from Mainz, Margaret heard a timid knock on her shop door late in the evening. She opened the door to see Agnes standing there, her downcast face peering out through the shawl she wore on her head.

"Come in, Agnes," Margaret said as she reached for a chair. Exhausted from the journey, Agnes slumped into the chair while Margaret quickly got her some bread and cheese and a cup of water.

"I'm so glad you decided to come. That's a long journey by yourself."

"Yes it is. Especially for a pregnant woman." They laughed and Margaret embraced her guest.

"Let's get you over to Katherine's house and give you a room and a bed. She'll look after you and get you back on your feet."

"Do you think Katherine really meant what she said about me staying with her?" Agnes asked. Lines furrowed her tired forehead—worried lines from many sleepless nights.

"I'm sure she did."

It was dark in the streets, and except for coming into the light of the occasional candle or lamp, they could easily walk to Katherine's house unseen. Agnes knew she would need Katherine's friendship and hospitality in order to survive. In the back of her mind, she wondered what Wolfgang would do when he found out she was back in town. Would he reject her like her parents had done? Had he already found someone else?

Margaret was right. Katherine welcomed Agnes into her home with open arms. Even Matthew added his greeting: "When you're ready, we'll invite Wolfgang over to our house for dinner. I'll alert him that we have a special guest staying with us. I'm sure he'll want to come."

"Give our guest a few days to rest and regain her strength," Katherine chided. "You men all think alike. We'll deal with Wolfgang later."

"Forgive me, Katherine," Matthew said. "I just thought this was one situation I could resolve fairly quickly. You know I have the weight of the Reformation bearing down on me right now, with this discussion on the Lord's Supper."

"Maybe you men should pick some other weights to lift for a while—like the needs of people and families that have broken apart," Katherine shot back.

Looking at the women, he said, "You're not impressed with our theological debates, are you?"

"It seems to me that Christ must be weary of our wrangling over the fine points of bread, wine, presence, or representation," Margaret answered. "You and Zwingli act like enemies when you should be treating each other as allies."

"Yes, we'll need each other to fight the Catholics on one side and the Anabaptists on the other side," Matthew joked.

"Why do you need to fight anybody?" Katherine asked.

"We need to stand for the truth."

"Might not our struggle for the 'truth,' as you call it, destroy the very meaning of the Lord's Supper as it was intended by Christ?"

"Which side of this debate are you on?" Matthew asked Agnes.

"Let her out of this," Katherine said firmly. "Debate your theology in the cathedral, but let our guests alone on this issue."

"You're right, Katherine," Matthew said. "But we do need to think about how to communicate with Agnes's parents. It'll only be a matter of time until they discover that she's back in town. Then we'll see some fireworks, and we'd better have a plan."

"Our plan is to keep Agnes right here in this guest room," Katherine said emphatically. "Margaret and I can figure things out from day to day."

"True enough," Matthew answered. "Margaret, that reminds me, Beck said he wanted to get married on the third Sunday of October, is that right?

"That's right, will you still marry us?"

"Well, yes, why would you even ask?"

243

"Would it make any difference to you if Beck and I held more to Zwingli's position on the Lord's Supper than to yours?"

Matthew laughed. "I'm dogmatic on theology, to be sure, but I'm a pastor, and I work with people all the time. So I try to bend the theology to the people involved. Within certain boundaries, of course."

"Would you marry two Anabaptists?" Margaret asked, intentionally not letting Matthew know if she meant Beck and her or just two people in general.

"It would depend, I suppose. On various things."

"That's the most evasive answer I've ever heard out of you," Katherine said. The three women laughed as the Zells sparred with each other. "Of course you'd marry two Anabaptists if they were your friends. You aren't arguing about the sacrament of marriage in your friendly little discussions, are you, Matthew?"

"Just remember that I almost got thrown out of the church and lost my job because I married you," Matthew answered, on the defensive now.

"Will Wolfgang survive in Strasbourg as a pastor if I'm around and we get back together?" Agnes asked timidly. Her blunt question startled them.

"Sure he'll survive. In fact he'll flourish with the woman he loves by his side," Margaret answered. "Sometimes men act as if they don't need us, but they can't live without us. Wouldn't you agree, Katherine?"

Before she could respond, Matthew blurted out, "You're right, Margaret. I left the Catholic Church because I couldn't stand living by myself anymore. I definitely needed a woman—let me say, I mean, I definitely needed Katherine."

"Quit while you're ahead," Katherine said. "You'll marry these two Anabaptists in three weeks, and I'll be in the front row."

Matthew scratched the back of his neck and looked away.

Even in the dancing shadows from the candles, Margaret knew that his discovery of her new commitments had startled him.

"Katherine, Agnes, I'll be back tomorrow. Thanks for your hospitality, Matthew. Good-bye for now." With that, Margaret headed out into the cool September night, wondering how and why her life had gotten so turned around. It just might be that Matthew would have to back out of his plan to marry them, now that he knew they were Anabaptists. The risks to his reputation might be too great. She closed the print shop door behind her, thankful for familiar surroundings and the chance to think things over and pray before getting some sleep.

The Strasbourg discussions ended without anyone changing their minds. Sturm had increased his political image as a negotiator and mediator. But everyone went home more convinced of the theological correctness of their own biblical viewpoint.

During the week, Ryff had gotten to know two priests who had traveled to the meeting from the Netherlands, several hundred miles down the Rhine. They supported the Catholic view, as did others who had come from various parts of the empire. Ryff knew Dutch, so he could easily talk to them, even though they understood German, the language in which the communion discussion had taken place. He conversed with them at length in the evenings, to practice his Dutch and to find out the latest politics in the lowlands up north, having lived there for several years.

At noon on the day after the meetings ended, the two northern visitors knocked on the shop door. In his best German, one of the priests asked for Ryff, who introduced the men to Margaret. "They're headed back to the Netherlands, now that the debate's over," he said.

"Pleased to meet you, ma'am," one of the men said as he reached to shake her hand. "My name is Menno Simons. We've been pleased to visit Strasbourg for the meetings."

After Ryff translated, Margaret smiled and invited the men in. "Come in and take seats. Can you tell us about the discussions?"

"We're in a bit of hurry," Simons responded. "No one changed their mind about the Lord's Supper, if that's what you're asking."

Switching topics, the Dutch priest, who was nearing thirty years of age, asked Margaret about her brochure on baptism. "Mr. Ryff told us you're printing one, and we'd like to read it on our trip down the Rhine."

Ryff found a copy and gave it to Simons. Before the visitor could reach for a coin, Ryff said, "This one's my gift. Just read it, and you'll learn more about what we discussed this week."

"Thank you, and now we must hurry on. Sorry to leave so quickly, but we have a long journey ahead." Turning to Margaret, Simons offered an invitation. "If you ever visit Holland, please come and visit me." He grinned at his new friend. "Walther, you can come along to translate."

"May God bless your journey," Ryff said, beaming as he shook their hands and sent them toward the canal.

After they left, Ryff handed Margaret a coin. "Here's payment for 'something to read' for those two as they float down the Rhine. Maybe the ideas you produce in this little shop can change the world somewhere else."

"Yes, well, the world had better change quickly or we might not be producing the radical ideas your new friends will read on the boat."

"You're worried, aren't you, Margaret?"

"I am," she slowly answered. "Maybe we should take up Simon's invitation for a visit to the Netherlands. I've never been there."

That evening, Margaret wanted Beck's arms to wrap her up and give her reassurance. "Matthew's not sure he can marry us," she began, "Agnes is in an awful predicament, Anabaptists are on the run, the censorship committee is watching us. What else can go wrong?"

"Let's look at our canal," Beck suggested. Margaret rolled her eyes at him, but went along with his scheme. He was just trying to be helpful. "Just up ahead, the canal from the other side of the city joins up with this side. Then they flow together out to the Rhine where the river gets deep and wide, flowing stronger all the way to the North Sea."

"We've gone over this before, haven't we, Balt?"

Ignoring the comment, Beck went on. "We'll join our lives together soon. After that, we'll always be together, whatever currents come our way. And we can move on, just like the water in the canal, if we need to."

"No, Beck. My roots are here, in this city." Margaret looked up at the great cathedral spire, the tallest in Europe. "Come what may, we'll stay here, work the print shop, and encourage others who have chosen the second baptism, like us."

On "their" bridge over the canal, they were about as far from the Butcher's Gate as from the great cathedral. There was no distance between the two of them, however. Tonight Margaret accepted Beck's strong but gentle love. "It gives me the courage to face another day," she mused. And once they were married, she'd find the strength to go on to the next day, and the next.

"I'm so glad you came to Strasbourg, Beck," Margaret said romantically.

"Boy, I am too," Beck joked.

"Oh, you sure know how to ruin a perfect moment." With that, she turned to let him walk her back to the print shop.

"There's no one else staying with you at the loft in the barn these days, is there?" Margaret asked as she pulled away with a mischievous grin.

"Only me and the bats, the rats, and a friendly snake now and then," Beck answered. "Listen, I saw Wolfgang confess before the church the other day. I can wait a couple more weeks."

"For what?" Margaret asked, leading him on.

"Oh, I'm going to get you now," Beck declared. Margaret pretended to try to escape, and after he caught her, he kissed her gently.

"In two and a half weeks," Margaret responded, "I'm yours forever."

Part IV

October-December 1525

19

Building a Bridge

Agnes had traveled a long way from Mainz to Strasbourg by herself, but the real distance was between her and her parents. She had crossed the creaking wooden bridge that spanned the river near her home, but now she had to reach out to her hostile parents. The divide made the Rhine look narrow by comparison.

They had been right, of course, in sending her to live with a relative in a distant city. "They have always been right," Agnes thought. But now her situation was different. She'd have to stand on her own and try to get back together with Wolfgang.

Agnes wondered about Katherine and Margaret's offer to help. Without a place to stay, her return to Strasbourg would have been nearly impossible, but could they really offer anything more than a room and food to eat? After all, she was still Catholic, though engaged to a Lutheran pastor, and Katherine and Margaret had left the old faith and joined the Reformation movement. About the only thing she was sure of was her desire to see Wolfgang again and find a way to get married to him.

Margaret had finished Wolfgang's commentary on Hosea, and her printers were busy producing five hundred copies of Ryff's medical manuscript. That freed her to help Katherine figure out a solution to Agnes's dilemma. This was the time, Margaret believed, to build a bridge of understanding to the

Knobloch family and stop the dispute that had festered for generations.

A brisk fall wind stung Margaret's face on her walk to the Zells' house. She wrapped her outer shawl tighter, determined to carry through with her mission. It would take time to heal broken relationships, and now that Agnes had recovered from her trip back to Strasbourg, it was time to go to work.

Within two days after her arrival, Margaret and Katherine had arranged for Agnes to work part-time at the former Franciscan monastery, helping the women and children who lived there as a result of the devastating peasants' war. Lucas welcomed another volunteer and gladly put her to work distributing food, cleaning hallways and rooms, and caring for the sick.

The women knew that it would only be a matter of time until Magdalene and Johann discovered their daughter working at the relief center. As expected, when news reached them on the last Monday of September, they tramped out of their house, marched to the former monastery, and cornered Agnes while she cleaned a small room that housed three families.

"So you've come back to Strasbourg, have you?" Magdalene said.

Johann chimed in, "How dare you leave your aunt's house in Mainz."

"We can have you arrested and thrown in jail," Magdalene threatened, "for disobeying your parents."

"Who are you staying with?"

"Why did you come back?"

"I came back to marry Wolfgang, Mother, and in a month I'll be of age to marry without your permission. You'll not stand in my way of doing what's right."

"We'll tell you what's right," her father responded. "You haven't told us who you're staying with yet. Answer us!"

"I'm living with friends who care about me, unlike what I've found in my own home."

By this time the Knobloch dispute had attracted quite a bit of attention, and when Lucas learned what was happening, he hurried upstairs and stepped into the room.

"This woman has come back to Strasbourg without our permission," Magdalene barked at him. "What gives you the right to employ her?"

"She's a volunteer, Mrs. Knobloch. We accept anyone who's willing to work, because we're short on help."

"You should have asked our permission," Johann said. "We'll have you punished for this."

"This relief center is run by the city council of Strasbourg," Lucas responded forcefully. "Everyone knows that we accept volunteer labor. And it is not our responsibility to ask permission from family members before accepting freely offered help."

The Knobloch parents realized that Agnes wouldn't back down or leave the relief center and that Lucas was within his established guidelines for accepting volunteer help, so they made a quick exit.

"We'll find out where you're staying," Magdalene threatened on her way out the door, "and you'll be sent back to your aunt in Mainz, where you belong."

Agnes believed her parents would watch her leave the Franciscan relief center, but that didn't stop her from heading back to the Zells' home near the cathedral after work that day.

"They've discovered me," she told Katherine and Matthew, "and they're angry. Now what?"

"Let's invite them to our house to talk about it," Matthew said, "with Wolfgang and Margaret here as well. We might as well deal with conflict openly."

Katherine agreed and Agnes didn't object. So Matthew went to the three homes to invite each to come on Friday evening.

"Wolfgang, Agnes is back in town and living with us," Matthew explained at the St. Thomas Church parsonage. "Join us Friday after dinner for conversation."

In the Wood Market, Matthew informed Margaret of what had happened earlier in the day and encouraged her to come to their home later in the week. "I'll be there," Margaret answered.

Johann and Magdalene agreed to come, though they made it clear Agnes had to go back to Mainz. "Wolfgang is not the man she should marry," Magdalene told Matthew.

On Friday evening, when everyone was situated in the living room, Matthew began the discussion. "We think Agnes should marry Wolfgang. We all know that your daughter bears Wolfgang's child, and we believe that child would best be raised in a home with its father."

"He has sinned and violated his pastoral vows," Johann replied.

"I have confessed my sin to the congregation," Wolfgang said. "I am sorry for what I have done, and I very much want to marry Agnes and care for our child."

"We know that Agnes came back to Strasbourg against your will," Katherine said to the Knobloch parents. "And we will give her room and food until it becomes clear where she'll live."

"The shame she has brought on the Knobloch family is intolerable," Magdalene responded. "Let her aunt raise the child in Mainz until Agnes can find a suitable husband."

"Do you mean a Catholic husband?" Margaret asked.

"That would be best," the mother answered.

"Wolfgang will care for your daughter and your grandchild," Margaret said. "Isn't that more important than having the correct religious views? We're all Christians, you know, Catholic, Lutheran, and Anabaptist."

"We do not approve of Luther's new ideas or of the Anabaptist heresy," Magdalene answered. "There's far too much room for individual interpretation of what's right and wrong. The Catholic Church has taught us for centuries, and there's no reason to change that now."

"I have joined the Anabaptists," Margaret said. "It's not a heresy, as you say. True, there are some differences of interpretation, as with baptism, for instance."

"If Agnes marries Wolfgang, where will the child be baptized?" Magdalene asked.

"In the Cathedral baptistery," Matthew said. "As children have been for centuries."

"It would be our luck," Johann chimed in, "as this situation has gone so far, that the child wouldn't be baptized at all because the parents had joined the silly Anabaptists you speak of."

"The New Testament calls for the baptism of believers, of those who confess Jesus as Lord of their life," Margaret said.

"Let's not get caught up in a theological debate right now," Katherine cautioned. "We're here to find a way to help Agnes and Wolfgang get properly married, hopefully with their parents' blessing."

"Allow me to make a suggestion," Margaret said. "Matthew is planning on marrying us in less than three weeks. Could we have a double wedding, with Agnes and Wolfgang getting married at the same time?"

"Not with Anabaptists," Johann stated firmly. "We didn't know you'd become that radical in your beliefs. Ulrich Zwingli warned the leaders in Strasbourg to watch out for these rebaptizers."

"Then give us a private wedding," Wolfgang pleaded, "without all the usual banquet, parties, and celebrations. Matthew can marry us right here in his home, then we can go over to the cathedral to have the Catholic priest bless us, if you'd like."

By the end of the evening, the Knobloch parents had agreed to Wolfgang's suggestion. They would let Agnes marry Wolfgang in a private ceremony in the Zell home, followed by a blessing by a Catholic priest and Mass in a side chapel of the cathedral.

"We can have this arranged to take place next week," Matthew said. "You tell the priest, Johann, to be ready for a blessing during the noon Mass next Wednesday. We'll have the private ceremony here before the Mass, and everyone's invited back here for a meal afterward. Is that okay with you, Katherine?"

"It is," Katherine answered. "Magdalene and Johann, we'd be glad to have you join us for a meal after the wedding."

"No, thank you," Magdalene huffed. "We'll need space to deal with the shock after the Mass."

In short order, the Knoblochs rose to leave. Matthew led them to the door and walked them to the street.

"Matthew," Johann snapped, "you stay away from those Anabaptists. They'll corrupt you. If you marry the printer woman and her worker-man husband-to-be, you'll have trouble to deal with. Big trouble. Think about it. Do not marry those two unless you want the weight of the Catholic Church and emperor bearing down on you."

As the Knoblochs walk away, Matthew stood on his cobblestone sidewalk and glanced up at the spire on the cathedral, wondering about Johann's threat. Could the Knoblochs really make life miserable for him? Do they really know Emperor Charles well enough to make trouble? It was possible, he was sure, but he needed to make up his mind on this one— soon.

The next afternoon, Beck and Margaret left the shop for a walk in the countryside. Heinrich and Peter had plenty to keep them busy until quitting time.

The leaves in the Alsace countryside were already past their prime, though lots of red and yellow remained. In the distance they could see the Vosges Mountains rising out of the plains below like majestic, natural cathedrals, carved over the centuries by ribbons of rivers, streams, and an ancient glacier.

"'The earth is the Lord's,'" Margaret said, "'and the glory thereof.' Any idea where that comes out of the Bible, Beck?"

"Not a clue."

"Try the Psalms. You need to learn your Bible."

In a clearing near the road, she told him about the dilemma Matthew faced. "I think the Knoblochs have put pressure on Matthew not to marry us. He hasn't been very open or willing to talk about our wedding with me recently."

"The Knoblochs were pretty determined not to mix Agnes's marriage up with ours, as I remember you telling me."

"That's right, and I'm afraid we'd better go to Matthew and relieve him of the decision as to whether or not he'll marry us."

"If Matthew doesn't marry us, who will?"

"I've been thinking about that." Margaret paused for a moment. "Wolfgang's out of the question right now. We could get one of the Brethren in Switzerland, like Sattler or Grebel, to marry us."

"But they're too far away, unless we want to get married in Switzerland."

"The other possibility is Clement," Margaret said. "He was ordained years ago as a priest for his small town. He knows us, and he knows the Anabaptists."

"He's one himself."

"True enough, and that's why I think he may be the best person to marry us."

"Let's give Matthew a chance to say he'll marry us, Margaret, in spite of the hot water both he and we are in."

It saddened Margaret to realize that she may not get married at the door of the cathedral like her mother and her grandmothers before her. Nor would there be a banquet with lots of food, music, and dancing. "Who would have paid for it anyway," she wondered, "since my parents are both dead?" Weddings had always been a time for the families of the bride and groom to display their wealth and entertain the community. The Knoblochs could have prepared a royal feast for Agnes, but now their lovely daughter would have only a private ceremony, a lot like hers would be, Margaret realized. For a moment she smiled at the idea of the Knoblochs' big bash being reduced to a private affair, but then she reminded herself that she was trying to build a bridge to them, and gloating over their misfortune wouldn't help.

Margaret snapped out of her daydreaming to see that Beck had arranged the food they had brought along. He had spread out the blanket, gotten water from a nearby stream, and made their simple supper look inviting. While she worried and pondered, Beck had decided to make the best of the situation. "We'll make a good team," Margaret thought.

It got dark earlier and earlier as the fall days set in, and they ate quickly so they could start the long walk back before it was too late, and too cold. When they were finished eating, with the shadows getting longer and the air getting cooler, Beck wrapped Margaret in the blanket with him before she could get away. It was easy to hold the man she loved. He wasn't perfect, she knew, but then neither was she. "Listen to his heart," she thought to herself, "let him know he's loved, and don't let him get away. In these changing times, a good man is worth hanging on to." Too soon, it seemed to Margaret, they had to head for the city walls.

Heinrich had managed to keep his date with Katie concealed from Margaret. Though it was more than two weeks since he had seen Agnes's sister, Magdalene had stopped him once and asked if he was still considering the proposition. He was, and so she didn't push him for an answer—yet.

Wanting to talk things over with someone, Heinrich turned to Christman. The two men knew each other, and Heinrich figured he'd be as good as anyone to talk to. Little did he know that Christman had once courted Agnes.

Christman promptly invited Heinrich and Katie to his house near the Stone Street Gate. He also invited his own date in for the meal. Even though Katie didn't know the other woman, they managed a pleasant evening of small talk and enjoyment over a great roast-beef feast. Christman even pulled out his father's old fiddle and played several tunes for Heinrich and the women.

Though it seemed like a brew for more trouble with the powers, Christman invited Heinrich and Katie back for another visit later on.

Heinrich kept weighing his options and trying to figure out whether he wanted to say yes or no to the Knobloch proposal. A yes would give him instant financial security. A no would keep him in Margaret's print shop indefinitely, and probably put him on Magdalene's hit list. Katie seemed friendly enough toward him, and she appeared to want the relationship to continue. Perhaps she was having second thoughts about joining the convent. For now, though, he'd have to keep thinking about it.

The wedding of the Lutheran preacher Wolfgang Capito to Agnes Knobloch, from a prominent Strasbourg Catholic family, was carried out as planned. Matthew married them in his living room, with Katherine, Margaret, and Beck standing as the only witnesses. That was fine, according to the teachings of the Catholic Church, because marriage was the consent of a man and a woman to live together, sharing all things in common. The Church service and banquet were not essential parts of a wedding.

At the noon Mass, Agnes and Wolfgang went to a side chapel in the cathedral for a blessing from the priest. Agnes's parents were there, in the front row, along with her older brother and her sister. Afterward, the newlyweds headed out one door toward the Zell kitchen, and the family went out another door to their house.

After the meal, Margaret decided her question to Matthew might as well be asked while everyone was there; they all knew Beck and she had joined the Anabaptist movement. What difference would it make if she talked about wedding plans in the open? "Matthew, I appreciate the risk you took in marrying Agnes and Wolfgang. Who knows what'll happen to you as a result of what you've done. But I believe it was the right decision. Thank you."

"Where Margaret is going with her comments," Beck said, "is that it will be even more risky for you to marry us."

"Though we'd still like to have you marry us," Margaret said, "we're ready to ask Clement to perform the ceremony so no further damage comes to your ministry in Strasbourg."

Matthew dropped his head and looked at his hands before answering. "I'm so glad you raised the issue before I needed to. It's true that with Zwingli's warning about Anabaptists and the Knoblochs' threat of trouble if I marry you, it really would be best for someone else to perform your ceremony."

"Unbelievable!" Katherine exclaimed. "We argue and debate the fine points of theology, Luther calls the pope the antichrist, the pope excommunicates Luther and his followers, the Anabaptists can't agree with either side, and peoples' lives are tossed around like leaves in the wind."

"We never quite know which way the wind will blow," Wolfgang said. "Sometimes it refreshes us; other times it's bitter and harsh."

"Seems like the wind of the Spirit has blown around a whole group of people who don't fit in anywhere," Margaret said. "We Anabaptists feel a little like the early disciples who were blown by a mighty wind on the day of Pentecost. Stirred things up all right, and launched a church without walls."

"This is no time for a theological debate, Margaret," Katherine said in reply. "Let me know exactly when and where you two will be married and I'll be there." Margaret noticed no disapproval from Matthew.

A glance their way in the cathedral square that evening, however, did cause trouble. Agnes and Wolfgang hadn't left town for a honeymoon or a wedding trip. Instead they had moved into his home immediately. Her parents had been nice enough to give them a wooden bed, in the way brides' parents had done for centuries. "The bed has a stain, though," her had mother muttered.

It was Johann Jr.'s look toward Beck that brought the trouble. He'd been drinking too much again. That's what had caused his fight with Christman in August. Now he happened to notice Beck and Margaret on a bench in the square, watching people go by and passing the time.

"You're no good for this town, you lousy Anabaptist." Johann sputtered as he swaggered in disgust. "I'll block your request to become a citizen, even if you get married."

Beck and Margaret didn't know whether to get up and leave, to sit quietly, or to respond. Before they could do anything, Johann shoved Beck back against the seat and threatened him. "Troublemaker, no-good printer, messing around with my sister. I'll get you, Beck. You better watch out."

Margaret and Beck got up and headed down the little incline away from the square toward Margaret's house.

"Run away, you coward, but you can't hide forever!"

Beck hoped Johann wouldn't follow through on his threat

to block his citizenship request. He wanted the benefits of citizenship in Strasbourg, and he'd likely get it once he was married to this long-time resident and daughter of an established family of printers.

Beck didn't want to leave Margaret alone that night in her house, nor did he exactly want to walk the streets by himself after being threatened. "Just a few more days and I won't have to leave at bedtime."

"Which do you want more," Margaret jested, "to live with me, or to get out of that tiny apartment?"

Grabbing her, he answered, "Whether it's bullies, church officials, or the emperor himself that threatens us, I want to live with you. Not because I'm scared, but because I love you."

"You can let up a little now, Balt," Margaret said. "It'd be nice to be able to breathe again."

Trembling just a bit, still shaken from the scuffle in the square earlier in the evening, Beck relaxed his grip and headed out into the darkness, wary and fully alert, but confident in Margaret's love for him.

20

Getting Married

In early October an artist arrived in Strasbourg who chal-lenged the Anabaptists to focus more on Christ. He also gave Beck an idea for where to go for a honeymoon. Matthias Grünewald visited Kniebs's Anabaptist house church during the first meeting there in a month. He joined the faith discus-sion and also tried to find work.

A middle-aged man, Grünewald's specialty was painting with colorful oils. He had been commissioned to create major works for two successive archbishops in Mainz. He had been a student of the well-known Renaissance painter Albrecht Dürer, and a few of the art-informed residents of Strasbourg were aware of his work.

More and more seekers were coming to Strasbourg every month, men and women like Grünewald who believed the city council would tolerate their radical beliefs. From all over southern Germany, those who, like the Anabaptists, had been chased out of other cities, found refuge in Strasbourg. The Anabaptist fellowship time at Kniebs's house was one of sev-eral that met in the city, in homes or barns, or out-of-doors in the neighboring countryside, like Clement's little church.

Prompted by reading Luther's writings, Grünewald had begun studying the German New Testament for himself. He was now an evangelist for what he believed was the heart of the gospel message. "The Bible must be read with Christ at the center," he told the group at Kniebs's house. "The Old Testament and all of the New Testament writings must be interpreted around the life and teachings of Jesus Christ."

"Can you give us an example of what you mean?" Margaret asked.

"I'll try. The last archbishop I painted for in Mainz wanted a large oil painting of two theologians discussing church doctrine. I pleased the archbishop by painting his face to represent Erasmus, the Catholic reformer, discussing his beliefs with St. Maurice. The Church today has missed the mark, I tell you. Church leaders are more interested in elevating themselves, building huge cathedrals, and defending tradition than they are in following Christ's teachings."

"Have you painted any works that emphasize Christ's life and work?" Margaret asked.

"Yes, about ten years ago I painted an altarpiece for a monastery in Isenheim, about sixty miles south of here, near Colmar. I worked hard to keep Christ central in the painting. I think it's a great piece of art, and I like what I've done, but you'll notice very little emphasis on correct doctrine or the seven sacraments of the Catholic Church."

"Can visitors see the painting?" Beck asked.

"Yes, the chapel at the monastery is open to travelers. In fact, it's a favorite stopover place for pilgrims from northern Europe on their way to visit Rome. But I say we need to visit Christ instead."

Grünewald helped launch a stimulating exchange with the group that evening. But Beck and Margaret didn't participate much; they agreed with him, but they had marriage on their minds. Beck had planned a trip to Colmar for their honeymoon, so he talked to Grünewald after the meeting about the altarpiece at Isenheim. He learned that it had nine panels, and it seemed inspiring enough to go and see when they were nearby.

Margaret's marriage to Beck was going to be a short and simple service. It would take place on Sunday evening, during a typical worship and discussion service at Clement's farm. None of their family members would be there, only their friends from Strasbourg. Katherine had agreed to stand for Margaret as a witness and Beck's witness would be Jörg.

On that third Sunday of October, fall was beginning to push into early winter. Clement built a strong fire to help keep people warm in the brisk, chilly evening.

"Nothing fancy," Margaret had told him. "We'll say our vows to each other, you can preach a little if you'd like, and then pray a prayer of blessing for us. After that, Beck tells me, we're going on a honeymoon. 'South' is all he'll say."

"I'll do my best to make it nice," Clement responded. "We'll make soup and bread for everybody. My good wife can even make a cake."

It was as nice as a wedding service could be—outside, without a cathedral, without a banquet room for the guests, without musicians to entertain. They sang, listened to Clement preach about love from First Corinthians, and exchanged their vows to each other. Simple, short, and meaningful. That's what Margaret had wanted.

Margaret was surprised and delighted to see Wolfgang and Agnes sitting on a straw bale in the back of the crowd. Even though it was an Anabaptist meeting and the newly married couple risked being caught and interrogated, they had come to see Margaret and Beck get married.

So did some of the town's hoodlums. A half-dozen roughnecks suddenly galloped in on their horses for some fun.

"How's the service tonight, preacher?" one of them shouted.

"Baptized any heretics in the river yet?" another barked.

Clement replied calmly. "You may join us if you want to."

"How's the food tonight, folks? You going to pass that cake around?"

Christman and Jörg got up and began to escort the ruffians back out the lane. "We'll go soon," the leader responded.

"Just checking to see if you have any pretty girls here tonight. Oh yeah, got one there in the back. Like to ride tonight, ma'am?"

"It's time for you to turn those horses around and move on," Christman insisted. "Do you want us to have you arrested?"

Laughing from astride his horse, the leader mocked, "This group have us arrested? We'll have you all locked up for an illegal church meeting, marrying people, baptizing them, pretending to hold a religious service without a proper priest."

"I'm ordained," Clement answered.

"By who?" one of them asked. "The bishop or one of the peasants who got killed at Saverne?"

"By the church of Christ, who called me to preach and lead them."

"No use arguing anymore with a bunch of heretics. Let's go. Last chance for the pretty young lady in the back to ride—want to go? We'll give you a lot better time tonight than that old clinker you're with." When Agnes tucked in closer to Wolfgang, he rose and stared at the smirking intruder.

"Here's some bread for the journey," Gertrude said, offered them a loaf. "Take it in the name of Christ."

The leader looked at her, reached down, scooped up the loaves, and turned to race out the lane. Everyone was relieved to hear the hoof beats fade away as they headed down the road, whooping and laughing.

"Thanks for making this a nice service," Beck told Clement after almost everyone had left.

"You're welcome, Beck." the old preacher answered. "I guess Christman will look after the granary. You've put in your time for a while. A new husband shouldn't have many responsibilities."

"There's really not much in there anymore. Most of the

weapons that are worth anything are gone. But Margaret may have a bundle or two of pamphlets she'll want to store in here this fall. From an Anabaptist in Zurich."

Turning to his new bride, Beck asked, "Well Margaret, will it be your place or mine?"

"Oh, stop it. Let's go start our honeymoon. It's definitely my place tonight."

Margaret lined up a week of work for Heinrich and Peter before the couple left for their honeymoon. When Ryff's medical manual was finished, she would have to decide whether to print Grebel's Anabaptist pamphlet next or begin something else. All Margaret knew about the week ahead was that she'd be with Beck and that he intended to have them visit a castle and see a painting. She could live with that.

The journey was an adventure for Beck and Margaret. They traveled through wine country, dotted with quaint little farms, with wheat fields already harvested, and sheep pastures that produced the wool so famous in the Alsace valley. They took a room at an inn that first night within eyesight of the great castle they'd explore the next day. Nothing fancy at the inn, though. It was just a small room that came with supper and breakfast the next morning. And the privacy they hoped for, to laugh, to love, and to get to know each other in a brand new way.

The massive castle of Haut Koenigsbourg dominated the vineyards and plains of the Rhine for miles around. Built as a fortress and home for wealthy nobles earlier in the Middle Ages, it no longer held political power over the region. During the 1520s, councils in cities like Strasbourg, Colmar, and Basel held the power formerly wielded by kings, nobles, and knights.

The owner of the castle had discovered that by opening it to visitors and tourists, he could earn a small income. After a steep climb up the road, the couple crossed the moat and the drawbridge and entered the old fortress.

Already more than four hundred years old when the newly married Becks climbed the spiral staircase to the top of the tower, the castle had at times been controlled by robber barons, who stole from travelers and peasants in the valley below. Built on an ancient Roman fort that guarded the entrance to the western mountains, the highest point in the tower gave Beck and Margaret a fantastic view of the Rhine Valley. They could see far into the Black Forest on the other side of the river, and in the distance they spotted the faint outline of the cathedral spire in Strasbourg. Margaret even thought she saw the clearing where the peasants had fought Count Rudolf's nobles in April.

"You heard that Hans Müller's men killed the count, didn't you, Beck?"

"Who told you that?"

"Christman. He even heard that Müller was on the run to the New World, to escape the threats of the Swiss authorities."

"He'd better run."

"The knight's hall would have been a nice place for a wedding banquet," Margaret mused. Some princess in another time probably used the room for her wedding-day celebration, but both agreed this was no place for religious dissenters in 1525—it was time to move on.

About forty miles south of Strasbourg along the Ill lay Colmar, a city like Strasbourg, though smaller. Here Margaret and Beck found a nice room to stay in, relaxed, ate well, and explored the streets. They discovered a small print shop one afternoon and struck up a friendly conversation with the owner. This man's shop produced pamphlets and writings for the Catholic Church. "My competition," she commented to Beck later.

"Did you know that Grünewald wants to find work making drawings for printers?" Margaret asked Beck later on that lazy afternoon. "He talked to me on Thursday night after the discussion time at Kniebs's. He's on a journey away from the Catholic Church to the radical Reformation. He reads Luther's stuff, but he likes our pamphlet about baptism."

"All right, Margaret," Beck sighed. "You're starting to think about business again, only four days into our honeymoon. It's time for us to go and see Grünewald's masterpiece. Tomorrow morning we head for the monastery of St. Anthony in Isenheim, about fifteen miles from here."

In Strasbourg, Christman decided to use his newly acquired inside information to help himself. He invited Heinrich to bring his date back to Stone Street for a second visit. "I'll cook a special meal," he said.

Heinrich obediently plodded through the city with Katie at his side, unaware of the man's bold plan to pursue the Knobloch woman.

"You mix up a great meal," Heinrich said.

"I work at it," Christman replied.

"Have you ever been married?" Katie asked.

"Never," Christman quickly answered. "But it's about time, I suppose. I'm not getting any younger."

Christman wasn't sure if she knew that he had secretly dated her younger sister. A wild fling, it had lasted only two weeks.

"Are you ready to settle down?" Heinrich asked.

"I suppose I am," Christman said. "It's about time my wife does the cooking around here."

"You're good at it," Katie responded. "Any woman would like to settle down with a man who can cook like you."

"Really?"

"I mean it. Not all women are great cooks, you know." Loosening up a bit now, Katie seemed a little too friendly with her host, Heinrich judged. "But she's with me," he concluded.

"I think men should do more work around the house," Christman said. "I mean, look at me. I do everything around here, clean, cook, entertain. How about you, Heinrich?"

"I take care of my own place," Heinrich answered defensively.

Later, while Heinrich relaxed in the tiny living room, Christman cleaned up with Katie nearby. "You stop by anytime you'd like," he said. "I'll cook you up something special." It was the biggest, broadest pass any man had ever sent her way, and she liked it.

"Maybe sometime," she said as she smiled back.

Just before Heinrich and his date left for the evening, Christman said, "You know, Heinrich, make sure you don't live for other people without following your own dreams. You've got to stand on your own two feet in this life." Then he quietly counseled Heinrich when his date was out of earshot. "Her parents will punish you all your life. Don't take them up on their offer. You asked for my advice, and that's the best I can give you."

The next evening, Christman opened his door to find, to his amused and pleasant surprise, Katie Knobloch.

"Got that special ready?" she asked.

Caught off-guard for a moment, he replied, "Sure, come on in." After the surprise wore off, he got into high gear. She was there to see him, and he had one chance to impress her. "Okay, let's see what we can do here."

First there was the meal, then he played the violin, then they talked, then it was late, but neither one cared. For Katie, it was either find a man or head off to the convent in Vienna. Either way, she'd be away from her parents. And this one, she judged, was a real man. Tall, strong, handsome.

"I can deal with it," she said to herself. "A very nice evening, indeed."

Well past midnight, with the streets nearly pitch dark, Christman chaperoned her back across the city and into the cobblestone alley that took them to the Knobloch house. With a touch and a final kiss, she crept in the front door and silently slipped upstairs to her room. Her escort backtracked into the night and vanished.

Grünewald had been paid by the monastery at St. Anthony to paint the altarpiece for the chapel. He did his work in the same year that Michelangelo worked on the Sistine Chapel in Rome. Because the monastery operated as a hospital for the sick, Grünewald had been instructed that the painting might serve best if it ministered to them.

When Beck and Margaret visited the chapel, the monks had pulled a sick man in front of Grünewald's painting to help him make sense of his suffering and to prepare him for his certain death. Syphilis was the new and terrible plague that ravaged Europe. Some thought sailors had brought it back from America, but no one really knew where it had come from. But everyone knew that it struck its victim quickly, and not even the monks at St. Anthony's hospital could slow down its deadly effects.

Grünewald's painting focused on Christ, as he had said. It depicted the Lord's crucifixion, death, and resurrection—the primary elements of the Christian faith. In the glorious colors of the paintings, and during an era when few could read, Grünewald had created a work of art that told the story of Christ on the cross and in his resurrection. Margaret noticed the Roman and Latin lettering in the painting and the cursive script as well.

Beck studied the panel on which Grünewald had painted the temptation of St. Anthony in the desert. "Anthony had to deal with his passions alone, in the wilderness," he told Margaret, "and monks during his time believed that to be holy, you shouldn't get married. I'm glad that in our time getting married is legitimate and encouraged, even for holy men."

"Quit while you're ahead, Balt," Margaret answered. "Anthony did what he thought was best, and I'm glad you've done what's best. Come on," she said with an smile and a tug, "let's get out of here and find a place to stay for tonight."

"I'm with you on that one, Margaret. Your place or mine?"

One of the most well-known birds in the Alsace valley is the white stork. Margaret loved to watch these graceful birds fly. Their black wing markings and red beaks made them easy to identify. They built their nests on roofs and chimneys in Strasbourg, Colmar, and the other small towns of the valley. A pair of storks, Margaret knew, would return to the same nest year after year, wintering somewhere in northern Africa, probably along the Nile. In mid-October many of the storks were heading south for warmer weather.

Margaret and Beck headed north, though, toward Strasbourg, with a two-day stopover again in Colmar. "A favorite city of Charlemagne, the great king of the Franks," an older couple told Margaret and Beck on a bench in one of the village squares. "He used to come here all the time, promoting his revival of learning."

It wasn't common to find an elderly couple. Usually one or the other would have died from the plague, disease, war, or another cause. The old man had logged for a living, sliding huge timbers down the mountainside to the valley below. They used sleds, he told the honeymooners, and then they'd drag them back up the steep slope for another load. Heavy, dangerous, and demanding work.

"Printers," Margaret told the couple when they asked what their jobs were.

"A noble calling and a splendid occupation for these times," the white-haired logger said. "Do you print Bibles?"

"Not yet," Margaret answered, "but we intend to."

"When you do, bring some to sell in Colmar. We have three printers in town, but none of them print Bibles, and we find it nearly impossible to buy them here."

"And we're about too old to travel to Strasbourg or Basel to shop," the cheery woman commented. She had spent her life in Colmar and would die there, having rarely traveled beyond to bigger cities. Colmar was what she knew. But both of them understood something about the Reformation that Luther had unleashed, and even at their age, though they couldn't read, they wanted to own a copy of the Bible for themselves.

"Ever feel like you just met a messenger from God?" Margaret asked Beck later.

"I knew you would say something like that."

"This winter we must get busy with a Strasbourg edition of the New Testament, in German, from the Beck press. I like the sound of that name, Balt."

"Sounds good to me too."

"Why do you always go by your last name?"

"It's always been that way, and that was my father's name as well. Guess that was a way to keep us distinguished," Beck said. "It's about time for us to head home. I wish we could fly like those storks."

"I want to keep you just the way you are," Margaret told her new husband. "Wouldn't want to risk losing you in Africa somewhere to another pretty bird."

"I'm all yours, Margaret. Don't worry."

In Strasbourg, the grand hostess, Katherine, had planned a banquet reception to honor the two newlywed couples. Because of their unique circumstances, neither the Capitos nor the Becks could have parties after their weddings. "That doesn't mean we can't throw one for them," she explained to Matthew.

The Zell house was large and Katherine liked to host many guests. She invited friends of the couples, others she knew—lots of people. "Come on the last day of the month, and let's make it something no one will forget!" she exclaimed.

Friends brought gifts and Katherine provided food. All the Anabaptist regulars were there: the quiet Nicholas Kniebs and his timid wife; the strikingly handsome Jörg; the muscular Christman, who came to eat as much as anything; Heinrich and Peter; Clement and Gertrude; Lucas; the bony Hut, who sported a larger-than-ever mustache; and Ryff, who brought books along to sell.

When everyone had arrived, Matthew got their attention. "We dedicate these couples to God," he said to the small crowd. "Preaching and printing, good occupations to serve the church. May you each be blessed with long married lives together."

After a prayer, the festivities went on, long into the evening, dimly lit, but with bright hearts and hopes for the future.

21

Wind of the Spirit

It had only been two months since she had heard him preach, but it seemed much longer since Margaret had heard anyone deliver the gospel message with as much clarity and power as Grebel. Margaret soaked up the preaching and the ideas.

"Which way's the wind blowing?" he asked the Sunday-evening congregation at Clement's farm. The Zurich City Council had chased Grebel and other Anabaptists out of town, so they had moved on to other villages, towns, and cities with their message. "Why didn't Nicodemus understand Jesus? He knew the religious law—he himself was a Pharisee—yet he didn't understand Jesus's simple call to be born again.

"The wind of God's spirit wants to blow into our hearts. Today God is doing a mighty work in the hearts and lives of people all over Europe. Neither Pope Clement nor Emperor Charles can stop the blowing of the Spirit's wind. I invite you to open up your hearts to the Spirit of God and join the Nicodemus band of those who say yes to Jesus."

Sermons at the farm usually unfolded in a dynamic and interactive pattern. Listeners often added stories of their own or probed the speaker for more details.

"Conrad speaks the truth," Grünewald said. "Nicodemus was stuck in the religion of his day, just as many are today. He expected Jesus to give him a series of religious rituals that he could perform in order to become born again. Today, far too many rely on buying indulgences to gain forgiveness from their sins.

"When I painted for Archbishop Albert of Brandenburg, he wanted to be elected as the Archbishop of Mainz. Because he had to spend 24,000 ducats to get elected, the pope issued an indulgence so Albert could get his money back. A third of the money raised went to the pope, a third went to the emperor, and Albert, puffed up in his grand palace, got wealthier yet with the last third. What does buying an indulgence have to do with the wind of God's Spirit, of being born again?"

"Nothing," Grebel answered, "as I'm sure you'd agree, Matthias. The Catholic Church has it right in teaching that we begin with sorrow for our sins. It's called contrition. Then we confess our sins, as the Bible teaches. However, we've learned through our studies in Zurich that confession in the early church happened in the gathered congregation, a gathering like this, not in private, to a priest, as most people do today.

"The Catholic Church teaches that priests administer absolution, which brings forgiveness. Priests and bishops, it is claimed, hold the keys to the kingdom of God. So even though your local priest may claim to clear you of any eternal penalty for sin, you'll still be left with an earthly penalty that must be worked off in this life or while you're in purgatory.

"Salvation is a free gift of God. When we say yes to Jesus in our lives, the wind of God's Spirit then blows in our lives, enabling and instructing us how to follow Christ. We don't need to perform works of satisfaction to achieve salvation. Matthias is right. Nicodemus probably expected Jesus to give him a list of options to perform, like saying a certain number of prayers, fasting, giving alms to the poor, going on a pilgrimage to a shrine, giving money to the church, or going on a crusade. Matthias, why does the Church sell indulgences?"

"It's much easier" Grünewald answered, "to buy a slip of

paper to get rid of your earthly penalties than it is to fast, or give money to the poor, or any of those other things you listed. So when the Church needs to raise money for some reason, it offers an indulgence that people can buy to take care of their sins or to get rid of Uncle John's penalties in purgatory. And we all know Uncle John sinned a lot!" Grünewald's face broke into a laugh.

"But buying indulgences goes further," Grebel continued. "The Catholic Church explains that once your sins are all forgiven through the purchase of an indulgence, you can buy more indulgences to build up treasure—or merit—in heaven. The verse they use is from Matthew." He read from his German New Testament, quoting Jesus: "If you want to be perfect, go sell your possessions and give to the poor, and you will have treasure in heaven."

"It's an elaborate system that raises money for the many activities and projects of the Church," Grünewald added.

"But this text doesn't mean that we can buy indulgences and somehow build up merit in heaven," Grebel explained. "We do need to confess our sins; that's biblical. Even though Nicodemus was a religious man, he allowed the wind of God's Spirit to blow into his life, to change his heart to follow Christ from within. But not through a system of religion.

"Which way is the wind blowing?" Grebel asked in conclusion. "There's a lot we don't understand about the times we live in, but I am sure that God's calling each one of us to follow Christ. As a sign of your intention to live the Jesus life, I invite you to be baptized and make a new confession of faith. I'll baptize those who are willing to take the next step of faith next Sunday evening, at the river's edge. Your password will be the question I've asked this evening."

Snow fell in Strasbourg during the first week of November. It wasn't heavy, but it was enough to cover the streets and make them slippery. That didn't stop Margaret and Beck from looking for a different place to live. They didn't know if they'd rent a house or try to purchase one, but they agreed that the small room in the back of the shop wasn't big enough.

Because Strasbourg didn't have a newspaper and because about eighty percent of the city residents couldn't read, the city council had wisely appointed a broker to inform buyers, sellers, and renters of available housing. The system worked, though people could occasionally find a place to rent that the middleman didn't know about.

On Friday, Margaret and Beck went to a broker to find out what was available and set out on a journey of discovery through the snow. One apartment was too small, another too expensive, another had already been rented, and the houses for sale seemed out of their price range. But they wanted their own place, so they persisted.

For lunch, they ducked into an inn for a bowl of warm soup. That reminded Margaret that Nicholas Kniebs owned an inn near their print shop. "Let's ask Nicholas if he has anything available," Margaret said.

"Sure, sure," Beck answered, "and I'm sure he's got a meetinghouse to sell us so we can establish the first Anabaptist Church of Strasbourg!"

"Don't be so arrogant, Balt. Do you have any better ideas?" He didn't, so off they trudged to Kniebs's house, across the canal but still inside the city walls.

When Kniebs said that he did actually have an apartment for rent, Margaret smiled at Beck in amusement.

"Would it be big enough for an Anabaptist meeting place?" Beck asked sheepishly.

"As a matter of fact," Kniebs responded, "I've been thinking about our Thursday-evening discussion times. My house is hardly large enough anymore, wouldn't you agree, especially after last night?"

"I'd agree, Nicholas, but what do you have in mind?" Margaret asked.

"I own a place near your print shop that might work for our meetings. Have you ever tried the Billy Goat Inn? It's had a reputation that's been hard to improve, but I've tried to upgrade its image. I haven't listed the apartment for rent with the city council because my religious beliefs aren't exactly accepted by the establishment, if you know what I mean."

"Could we see the apartment?" Margaret asked.

"Sure. Do you want to go over there right now?"

"We've run out of good options," Beck answered. "And yes, right now would be great."

Though it had only three rooms, it was in their price range, and when Kniebs told the Becks that he thought the Thursday-evening group should start meeting there, they were even more eager to rent from him. "We can sit in the lobby area, and the overflow could move into your apartment," Kniebs explained.

They agreed on the terms for renting the apartment, and agreed that the couple could move in immediately. Margaret paid the first month's rent and told her new landlord that they'd probably move in on Saturday.

Wolfgang, Agnes, and Katherine helped them take their few belongings to the new apartment on Saturday afternoon. It was close enough to the print shop that they could carry everything by hand, the table and chair being their biggest pieces of furniture.

"Our first home," Margaret said to the women as they inspected the place. "At the Billy Goat Inn, of all places."

"A kitchen, bedroom, and living room," Katherine said. "Enough space to get you started with a family." After a quick glance at Margaret, she added, "Family's something I can talk about again. Matthew and I are expecting another baby."

Margaret hugged Katherine, who said, "Maybe if you hurry up and have one too, we can have fun raising them together."

"Sounds good to me," Margaret answered, "but right now I just want to settle down and make this place a home."

After the moving party left, Beck noticed that it had started to snow again. "That baptism party Grebel is holding down by the river tomorrow night is going to be cold."

"Maybe we should invite everyone here," Margaret suggested. Though it would take a lot of work to let everybody know, the more they thought about it, the more it seemed like a good solution.

Alarmed at the rising movement of religious dissenters in his empire, Charles V, Holy Roman Emperor, had sent out a stern letter to all his domains across Europe. "Enforce the Edict of Worms," the emperor wrote. This meant suppression of all Luther's teachings and destruction of materials containing them.

The emperor had written the letter from Spain, where he was fighting a war against the French while simultaneously battling the Ottoman Turks in Eastern Europe. The city council of Strasbourg knew he still wanted two hundred soldiers from their city, as the sweating little Hungarian ambassador had demanded in August, but hardly anyone had volunteered to fight.

Sturm found a comment in the emperor's letter disturbing. He had singled out Strasbourg as a city that tolerated religious dissenters. Sturm stoked his huge, brown beard and fingered his buttons while he studied the young emperor's official notice.

"Those who claim to reform the One Holy Catholic Church are heretics, to be cast out and burned in the fire," the monarch had written. This was not an official proclamation from a parliament of nobles, Sturm knew, but rather it was a sign that the emperor was getting angry at the reluctance of imperial free cities like Strasbourg to stop religious dissenters. Knobloch would be on his back, Sturm guessed, to act with a firm hand, especially against the Anabaptists but the Lutherans too, if possible.

On the second Sunday morning of November it really started to snow. Margaret and Beck needed to act quickly if they were going to invite Grebel to baptize his converts at their inn.

After listening to Wolfgang preach at the Church of St. Thomas, Beck headed to the Stone Street area to see if he could find Grebel. Exactly as he'd guessed, both Grebel and Hut were staying with Jörg.

"Margaret and I would like to invite you to the inn near the cathedral for the baptism gathering this evening," Beck said.

"It will be cold by the river," Grebel replied. "Are you sure you'll accept the risk though? I could be arrested at any time. You know that Zwingli has sent word out to all the cities and territories around Zurich to be on the lookout for Anabaptists, and my name is on his list."

"We've agreed to invite you," Beck replied. "Just tell people to come to the Billy Goat Inn. They'll know where it is."

"It's agreed then," Grebel responded. "Jörg, why don't you and Hans find Christman and the three of you spread out along the road to the river and direct people back to the inn where the Becks live."

"We can catch most of the people this afternoon, I think," Jörg answered. "But sure, we'll station ourselves along the river road and send them back."

"Make sure they know the password before you tell them where we're meeting," Grebel reminded the men.

The snow had tapered off by Sunday evening, though the short beards of Christman and Jörg, standing and watching a nearly deserted road, were almost white. Occasionally, Hut would knock the snow off his long, flowing mustache.

Noticing Christman, a couple traveling toward the river asked, "Which way's the wind blowing?"

"Back toward Strasbourg, my friends, at Kniebs's inn near the cathedral. Better to meet there than along the river."

By the time it got dark, Jörg figured they had reached everyone who was coming to the meeting. When they arrived at the inn, Grebel had already started. People sat on the floor or on chairs from the Beck apartment. The flickering lanterns allowed everyone to see faces and, up close, they could read from the Scriptures.

While Grebel held onto the back of his chair, he launched into his theme of the wind and the Spirit. "Not only is the wind blowing into our hearts, but it's also blowing in unexpected ways." Water baptism, he explained, was not new to the Christian church, but its practice by the Anabaptists was new for the sixteenth-century Reformation era.

"The apostles and thousands of believers in the early church had been baptized upon the confession of their faith. But when early Christian believers sealed their life with Christ and announced their intent to live a Christian life through baptism, it led many of them to suffer persecution. Our brother Hut would say they received their third baptism of blood."

Five people accepted their second water baptism that evening in the lobby of the inn. But the baptisms that evening were not recorded in any official book, nor did they become the basis for taxation, nor did the Church sanction them. They served as a witness, rather, to the blowing of the Spirit's wind, to the intention of the baptized to follow Christ in life, and as a public declaration to the church without walls in the lobby of Kniebs's inn that these followers too had joined the Anabaptists.

Early the next morning, guards pounded on Jörg's Stone Street door and demanded entrance. They asked for Conrad Grebel, citizen of Zurich.

In an instant, Grebel, who was in a small room at the back of the house, had to decide whether he'd run out the back door, as best he could, and head down the street, or stand and face the guards. The thought of his wife and children in Zurich facing the winter without him drove him to slip out the back, into the snowy streets and toward the city gate.

When Jörg tried to stall for time, the guards brushed by him and searched the inn. They interrogated Hut and asked if he knew where Grebel was. He could honestly say that, at that very moment, he didn't know where Grebel had gone.

"We'll catch him soon," they steamed as they headed out the front door. "If you keep him here again," one yelled at Clement, "we'll throw you in prison with him."

When Jörg stopped by the Beck print shop later that afternoon and told them what had happened, they figured that someone had tipped off the city council. "Somebody on the inside is probably getting paid to tell them where we're meeting and who's with us," Beck speculated. "We'll have to be very careful about where we meet and who knows what's going on."

Elsewhere in the Empire, Charles V released the king of France from prison and allowed him to return to Paris. That prompted Lefèvre to plan for his return trip to Paris and resume his teaching position at the university. The king of France would protect him, Lefèvre was certain.

In the east, the Ottoman Turks had backed off their planned invasion of Europe for the winter, though both sides knew that spring would bring open warfare. From his grand palace in Spain, Charles planned to be ready to fight.

In Italy, Pope Clement was sandwiched between the political bickering of the king of France and the Spanish emperor. That tied his hands and prevented him from going after Luther's reformers, much less the new sect of Anabaptists. The pope enjoyed the wealth of the papacy, organized his administration, and continued the Renaissance-style beautification of Rome that had been launched by previous popes.

Heinrich continued to see Katie on an approved basis, about once a week. Unfortunately for him, though, Magdalene had become suspicious of her eldest daughter's affairs. The soft footsteps in the hallway late at night, the rumpled dresses, and her daughter's changed countenance, all led her to believe something was going on. So she asked Johann Jr. to look into the matter and give her a report on his sister's actions.

On that night, Christman thought the barn at Zieglers' might be the best place for their little fling. Nobody would be there on a Monday evening.

When it was dark, at the agreed upon time, Christman led Katie through the Elizabeth Gate and around the long way to the barn. The loft proved to be chilly, but they managed to stay warm under the straw. Apparently, only the barn critters saw anything.

It was on the return trip that Johann Jr., shivering on the canal bridge, spotted his sister sneaking back into their house. His mother had discovered that she was gone from her bedroom, unapproved, and had perched her son by their house to watch all approaches to the front door. Her tall escort disappeared before the watchman could see him.

"You set me up with a man," Katie pleaded to her demanding mother and stiffly cold brother. "Now you're angry at me for following through."

"You were only allowed to see him on approved dates," Magdalene railed.

"He's done for," Katie's brother muttered. In a flash he was out the door and headed to the Hangman's Tower. The official Strasbourg executioner was asleep on his cot, but Johann Jr. woke him and demanded that he come immediately. Though groggy from his sleep and not very happy about heading into the cold at that time of the night, the hangman obediently followed.

"Bring a rope along," Johann barked.

He pounded on Christman's door at about an hour after midnight. "Where does that printer who works for the Becks live?" he demanded to know.

Noticing the hulk behind him, Christman stalled. "Why do you need that information at this hour of the night?"

"He's been fooling around with my sister, and he's done for. Now lead me to his house. I'm pretty sure he lives nearby."

"Let me get my coat and hat," Christman answered. He could slip out the back window and disappear, he figured, but Johann would eventually catch up to him and demand to know why he had fled. And because he wasn't ready to leave Strasbourg for good, that left him with only one option.

It didn't take long for Christman to lead the two men to the right door. "This one," he stated. When Johann knocked on the door, Christman slipped away into the night.

Heinrich didn't open the door immediately, so the hulking hangman broke the flimsy string latch on the door and the two went in to search for the guilty man.

"It's over, you two-timing, no good, Anabaptist scoundrel," Johann growled when they found him.

Before the sleepy printer could react, the hangman had the rope around his thick neck and his hands tied behind his back. The two intruders shoved their gagged and stumbling victim out the door and down the empty streets. "I know the guard at the Cronenbourg Gate," the hangman muttered. "Let's go there."

"An Anabaptist," the hangman explained to the guard. "We're taking him to the tower to be dealt with later."

Just outside the gate they came to the same grassy bank where the bishop's executioner had planned to cut off Müller's head in May. Before the terrorized Heinrich could find a way out, Johann started the grizzly disembowelment that would be necessary to make his victim's body sink to the bottom of the cold canal. Thrusting his long knife in time and time again, the callous executioner from the Hangman's Tower cleaned out the accused man's insides.

With a heavy rock tied to the rope, the hangman threw his prisoner, still warm, off the grassy lookout and watched the body sink to the bottom. It would stay there, he was sure, until it decomposed. No one would ever know what happened.

To finish the deed, the hangman picked up the body parts and pitched them into the canal, to be swept away and out to the Rhine within the hour.

"What do I owe you?" Johann asked him.

"Money to replace the rope. They aren't cheap."

Handing him a few guilders, Johann warned, "Don't breath a word about this to anyone. You'll be the next one thrown in if anybody finds out."

Ryff's medical manual sold well for the Beck press, earning them some money.

"Now," Margaret told Peter and Beck the morning after the murder, "it's time to print Grebel's pamphlet. We'll keep quiet while we work on it. If there's an informer around somewhere, there's no need to let him know our business in the print shop."

"Are you sure it's a man?" Beck asked. When Margaret stared him down, he added, "Just a theoretical question."

It did seem odd that Heinrich hadn't come to work as usual that morning, but nobody knew where he was, so they moved ahead with printing, doing his jobs as well.

Before Lefèvre left for Paris, Beck tracked down Grebel, who was hiding in Clement's barn, and convinced him to go to the Capitos' house. Margaret and Agnes joined the men there for their late-night reunion and discussion.

"Newlyweds, both of you," Lefèvre observed. He turned to Wolfgang and Beck and said, "Watch out, or the King of England will get your wives. He's got his eye on the young Anne Boleyn right now."

"Do you think the pope will grant Henry a divorce?" Grebel asked.

"Nobody knows the answer, Conrad. But if Pope Clement waits long enough, Henry might just divorce Catherine and marry Anne without the pontiff's official blessing."

"He has a daughter, doesn't he?" Wolfgang asked.

"Yes, Catherine's been pregnant eight times since the king and queen married fifteen years ago, but only one daughter has survived. The king thinks their marriage is cursed."

"Because after his brother died, Henry married his wife," Grebel added.

"And now Henry's using a text in Leviticus to try to prove his marriage to Catherine was illegitimate in the first place. Further, the queen of England is an aunt of Emperor Charles. If the pope gives Henry his divorce, the emperor will likely march his armies into Italy and attack Rome."

"Maybe," Agnes said. "We could send my sister to London to replace the queen. My mother's trying to get her married. You know, exchange one Catherine for another. Then the king wouldn't even need a divorce!"

"The king of England needs to learn a few things about marriage," Grebel said.

"Yes, like losing a little weight so all the women he beds down with aren't suffocated," Lefèvre gibed. "He goes through women like Solomon did."

"Marriage," Grebel began to preach, "is established by God and sealed before the congregation by vows between husband and wife. Even Luther recognizes that marriage is something other than a sacrament."

"Keep your marriages strong," Lefèvre counseled the two couples. "Don't let politics or intrigue or dissatisfaction with your partner lead you to divorce."

"A good word," Grebel said. "I know I ran around and lived an ungodly life when I studied with you in Paris. But now I'm married, and even though my parents don't accept my choice of a marriage partner, we're committed to each other.

"The four of you don't know what life will bring your way, whether you'll have children or not, how many, if they'll live, or whether your beliefs will disrupt your chances of having a normal family life. Speaking of that, I need to disappear soon. Seems the city council knows I'm here and wants to stick me in prison. The less time I spend in one place, the better off I am. Thanks for your hospitality."

"And I'm off for Paris," Lefèvre said. "Long live the Reformation in Zurich, Paris, and Strasbourg.

"I'll toast to that," Wolfgang replied.

On the way back to their home at the Billy Goat Inn, Margaret said, "Beck, if you ever try to divorce me with a silly excuse like the king of England's, I'll strangle you."

"I'm sure you will," Beck said with a chuckle. "But don't worry. I'm going to kiss the queen when we get back to our apartment."

"This will cool you down!" Margaret said as she reached for a snowball.

22

Voices of Reform

By Thursday, the third morning in a row that Heinrich hadn't come to work, Beck had gone looking for him. "His apartment," Beck explained to Margaret and Peter, "looked like he just got up and left to go somewhere, without his coat, without any extra clothes, and without any preparation."

"That's strange," Margaret answered. "He is so dependable. What could have happened to him?"

"The latch string on the door was forced open," Beck added, "but I saw no other evidence of foul play."

"Someone may have broken in after he left," Margaret said.

For now, Margaret and Beck decided not to inform the city officials, thinking it better to wait and see if Heinrich would show up in a day or two. The magistrate would take a wait-and-see attitude anyway, Beck thought.

While the Becks wondered what had happened to Heinrich, the people of Strasbourg settled in for a long, cold winter. It was then that Margaret learned about two men in sunnier, warmer climates who were beginning remarkable careers that would help reform the Catholic Church. She was always happy to hear about priests and nuns who wanted to change the old Church. Most people knew that while the Lutherans, Reformed, and Anabaptists had broken from the Catholic Church, there were many others who worked to reform from within. That week, on one of his regular visits to the inn for a meal, a tall, balding citizen of Strasbourg with massive arms and giant hands told Margaret the first story.

It was amazing to watch Philip Hagen devour food, and between bites he told her about his pilgrimage to Jerusalem. "The little man prayed a lot and criticized our rough conduct on the boat. In Jerusalem he insisted on visiting Bethlehem and the Mount of Olives on his own, even though the infidel Turks made that very dangerous."

"Where's he from?" Margaret asked.

"Spain. He went back to Barcelona to study Latin after our pilgrimage. He'll probably be recognized as a saint someday."

"What does it mean to be a saint?"

"Means you get to go straight to heaven when you die, and you can skip purgatory."

"Are you a saint?"

"No, ma'am. Why do you think I went on a pilgrimage, just to see the sights? The Holy Land's a dangerous place. I went to get absolution for my sins."

"Are you in need of forgiveness for sins you committed?"

"Lord knows that's right," Hagen said while he consumed a piece of pie for dessert. "Killed a couple of dozen peasants during the war last summer, hate to say. Their blood is on my hands." An aristocrat, Hagen belonged to the landed and wealthy Strasbourg nobility. "I wish I had the faith of that little man who went to Jerusalem with me. Got on our boat in Venice and sailed for Cyprus, but the sailors planned to throw him off on an isolated island, because he spoiled our fun. We hung around the women, you know, had a little fun, drank some, and then he quoted Scripture and preached at us."

Beck came through the door and Margaret introduced him to Hagen. "He's telling me about a holy man who's studying Latin in Barcelona."

"I'm ready to go there now," Beck said. "It's cold outside."

"The man wanted to stay in Jerusalem and help people," Hagen said. "But the monks told him to get out because it was too dangerous. They had to threaten him with excommunication to get him to leave."

"Any pirates in the Mediterranean?" Margaret asked.

"There sure are," Hagen answered easily, now pushed back and digging with a toothpick. "Three ships left Cyprus for the return trip to Venice and two didn't make it—one from pirates and one from a storm."

"Did God save you for a purpose?"

"No, God saved the little monk. See, he was a soldier a while back, got injured when a cannonball ripped into his legs, and then while he was healing he had a revelation of the Virgin Mary that changed his life. That's when he decided to go to Jerusalem on a pilgrimage, one of the holiest things a man can do, you know."

Kniebs and his frail wife came early to get the place ready for their regular Thursday discussion. The Kniebs's inn again functioned as an Anabaptist meeting place, even though Mrs. Kniebs had voted against it.

Because Hagen seemed in no hurry to leave, Margaret told him about what would happen that evening at the inn, and she invited him to stay.

"Don't really have anywhere else to go, tonight, ma'am. Believe I will."

The regulars came soon after the evening meal. Among them were Jörg, Christman, Agnes, Lucas, Hut, Ryff, and Grebel, still in town.

"Here's our question for starters tonight," Margaret began. "What makes a person a saint?"

Grebel answered first. "I was always taught that saints are ones who lived such a holy life they didn't have to spend time in purgatory. They went straight to heaven and supposedly now pray to God for the rest of us. Ryff, what do you believe defines a saint?"

"Someone who lives a good life."

"Anybody want to add to that?"

"Those who have faith in Christ," Hut said. "The Pharisees lived good lives, but our Lord called them a brood of vipers. Said they had to get right with God."

"We're saints when we accept Jesus Christ as Lord of our lives," Grebel concluded.

"Doesn't that make it a little too simple?" Hagen asked. "The little fellow from Spain went to the Holy Land to cleanse himself and make himself holier. Are you saying that's not necessary?"

"I guess that's why we're having a Reformation right now," Grebel answered. "Pilgrimages and trips to relics and saying rosaries might do some good, but they don't make you a saint."

"Don't you have to have proof of a couple of miracles to your credit for the Church to make you a saint?" Jörg asked.

"Yes, and the Church usually waits about fifty years after you're dead to make it official," Grebel replied.

For the little monk studying in Barcelona, Ignatius of Loyola, the Catholic Church waited sixty-six years after he died to canonize him. Ignatius was recognized because he established a new order of priests, the Jesuits. They traveled as missionaries to America, India, Japan, and China during the 1500s and 1600s.

The Jesuits reenergized the Catholic Church, brought the gospel message to other lands, and helped reform abuses in the Church. Thousands converted to Christianity in Japan, for instance, before the Japanese government ran the missionaries out and martyred hundreds of new believers.

Beck decided to buy his citizenship. In the city manager's little office, Sturm explained to him that he needed to pay a tax, swear an oath of allegiance to the city's constitution, and register with one of the guilds. When he had completed each of those, Sturm said, military service was an obligation that would likely be required. He also said that those who purchased citizenship most recently were often the first taken to fight in the emperor's wars.

While Beck was at Sturm's office on Friday morning, the Spanish printer with whom the Becks had worked earlier in the year stopped by the shop to propose another joint business venture. The voyages of Amerigo Vespucci and Christopher Columbus, along with many others, had opened up a whole new world of discovery across the Atlantic Ocean. The treatment of the Indians in the New World was what had prompted the printer's trip to Strasbourg.

Many priests and monks sailed along with the discoverers, he explained to Margaret, and they planned to convert the Indians to Christianity. There were differences, however, on how to do that. One Catholic professor argued that the Indians should be treated as slaves, and that if necessary, force should be used to convert them. The Spanish printer had come to Margaret to have her publish another writer's point of view, which defended the humanity of the Indians.

"In far-off Hispaniola, an island in the Caribbean Sea," he explained, "Bartholomew de Las Casas has written a pamphlet urging Catholic missionaries to convert the Indians by persuasion, not force." Las Casas was trying to convince others that the Indians had souls and should be invited to accept Christianity, not forced to join by threat of death or injury, as usually happened in the New World.

Margaret noticed that the pamphlet was written in Latin. Las Casas had joined a monastery in Santo Domingo and this was the monk's first pamphlet. It was not approved by the pope and could get both him and the printer who produced it in trouble.

"Will you print this pamphlet for me?" the Barcelonan printer asked. "We need to get his message out."

Margaret hesitated because she wasn't sure if it would sell well, but he offered her a guaranteed amount of money that would at least cover her expenses. Further, it was written in Latin and by a monk, so it might be a safe document to print, unless the authorities discovered that the pamphlet's message ran counter to Spanish practice among the Indians in the New World. Charles V, she remembered, was not only the emperor of Europe; he was the king of Spain as well. If he saw the pamphlet, it would probably make him angry.

"We'll take the job," Margaret responded, "but we won't be able to start on it right away. We're printing another pamphlet right now for a reformer from Zurich who, like Las Casas, has radical ideas."

"I knew you'd take the job," he replied in broken German. "You've got yourself a spirited little print shop going here, don't you?"

"I guess you're right," Margaret said as she turned to the middle of the shop floor. "I tell Beck that this printing press fans the faith fires that burn all around us."

"Will your husband agree to print this pamphlet?"

"I think he will," she answered with a sparkle in her eye.

Just then Beck burst through the door, recognized the printer, and shook his hand. "It's good to see you again," he said with a shiver, "and welcome to our cold northern city of Strasbourg."

It had been almost three months since Müller had fled from his village in Switzerland to the New World aboard a Spanish ship to escape execution. His ship had put down anchor after a perilous journey across the Atlantic Ocean, at the settlement of Santo Domingo on the island of Hispaniola in the Caribbean Sea, where Las Casas defended the rights of the Indians.

In a supreme irony that characterized the age, on the very day his ship landed and the sailors were wading ashore, an Indian attack on the Europeans left an arrow lodged in Müller's rib cage. Within minutes, he bled to death on the sandy shore. In the New World, Müller had been ordered to defend the European nobility, whom he had been fighting against in the Old World.

Eventually, with reinforcements from the European fort, the battle swung back in favor of the Spanish. After the Indians had retreated to the mountains, Las Casas surveyed the dead soldiers, sailors, and Indians who lay scattered across the beach. He went back to his monastery and took up his quill to again criticize the imperialist motives of the European conquerors. Little did the monk realize that one dead sailor that day would have agreed with his condemnations. If he had been given a chance, Müller, now lying face down and bloodied in the sand with his large hands gripping a sword, would have been on the side of Las Casas.

Back in Strasbourg, four days after Heinrich had been murdered, Grebel came to the Billy Goat Inn after dark. It was Friday evening, but the Zurich citizen found the newly-weds at home. "I need to talk to you," he said, looking intently at Beck when they sat down around their little kitchen table.

"Are you hungry?" Margaret asked.

"Truthfully, Margaret, I'm famished. It's not safe to show my face in restaurants around here."

"Why don't you go back to Zurich?" Margaret asked.

"Because even though the Strasbourg magistrate is looking for me, I'm far better off in this city than anywhere else."

"The movement's growing here," Beck said as Grebel began to eat. "I'm not sure Sturm or the bishop or anybody else is going to be able to slow us down."

"It'll help when you get my pamphlet printed."

"We're working on it now and should have it finished in two or three weeks," Margaret said.

When the visitor had nearly finished gobbling down his bowl of soup, he launched into the real reason he had come. "I'm staying in Clement's barn."

"I know the place well," Beck said. "I pretty well know the rats by name."

"I've got their names down too, Beck. But I want to talk to you about two visitors to the barn this past Monday evening." After Margaret offered him cookies, he went on, looking serious. "A couple came into the barn, and I'm sure they didn't think anyone was around. But I was in my cozy little loft, already asleep, when they awakened me."

"Okay, Conrad, why do we need to know about this couple who came into the barn?" Margaret asked. "A man and woman, I assume?"

"Definitely a man and a woman," Grebel answered, "taking advantage of the privacy in Clement's barn for a little encounter in the straw, if you know what I mean."

"Well, let's get right to the point," Beck said. "Did you recognize either of them?"

"Christman," Grebel answered. "I didn't recognize the woman. I know it was him because he was tall, and I got a pretty good look at them as they left.

"So does any of this matter to anyone?" Beck asked. "Christman's playing the field and chasing the women."

"The only reason I wonder," Grebel answered, "is because if he wants to get baptized and join the Anabaptists; he's going to have to come clean on his night life, that's all. I wanted you to know this. So if, after I'm gone, he wants to join, you'll need to ask him if he's repentant and ready to change directions."

Before Margaret or Beck could discuss the matter more with him, the wary preacher said, "Much obliged for the meal, Margaret. I just can't stay in one place too long." He lurched for the door, his aching feet obviously bothering him in the winter cold.

"He doesn't stick around long, does he," Margaret said.

"You know," Beck responded. "I'm not sure if he came to talk about Christman or to get a meal. But I really wish we hadn't learned this new information."

"Relax, Beck, we may never need to deal with it."

"And if we do, are you going to confront him or will I have to?"

"You will. For now, let's drop it and get this place cleaned up so we can get to bed."

"Is that a command or an invitation?"

"It's an order, from the chief—now move it!"

The Anabaptist movement in Strasbourg grew steadily, though not without strong resistance. The city council, in response to what they had learned from their informant, wrote a statement that threatened the dozen or more small Anabaptist house churches that met in the city. Though the statement had little effect, citizens were warned not to give the Anabaptists shelter, food, or drink; they were to turn them away under pain of punishment. The council made it clear in their statement that Anabaptists should leave the city.

Margaret noticed the printers who had produced the statement. "Johann and Magdalene Knobloch at work again," she said to herself, "helping to stamp out heretics."

Margaret and Beck worked hard to print Grebel's pamphlet. The little document would help the Anabaptists, Margaret was sure, and she hoped to have it finished by early

December. She had read the council's statement against Anabaptists, but she believed that as long as Matthew and Wolfgang preached for the Reformation from their pulpits, the council wouldn't take harsh actions against the growing movement.

Grebel's pamphlet summarized the core convictions of the Anabaptists: The church should be free from state control or protection. Believers baptism is a public sign of one's intent to join the community of faith. Christians are called to a life of discipleship, of holy living, that goes beyond receiving the sacraments. And believers are called to live a life separate from the world around them, to live in the world, but not be of it.

"Beck," Margaret said at lunch almost a week after Heinrich disappeared, "I want you to find the Scripture passage where Jesus told his disciples to 'live in the world, but not be of it.'"

"How can I do that?"

"When was the last time you read the New Testament?"

"Well, I mean, I've read *from* the New Testament, Margaret."

"Try the Gospel of John," Ryff called out, rescuing the new husband.

"Sure, that's where I thought it was," Beck answered confidently.

"Balt, it's time you started reading the New Testament. When you find the text in John's Gospel, let me know. You can start tonight!"

"I can't, Margaret. Did you forget about our guild meeting? I guess I'll have to dig into the Gospel of John tomorrow night."

When Anna Weiler, the accused witch, escaped her prison in Worms, she fled to Strasbourg, the city of refuge. The drunken guard had passed out in the hallway in front of Anna's cell, so she reached for the key, opened the door, and fled to Strasbourg. This city was a place where someone like herself could find an open door and a room for protection from the authorities. They'd eventually catch up to her, but what did she really have to lose by trying to run and hide?

The informal network that operated on Anna's behalf was already in motion when Margaret and Beck went to the guild meeting Monday evening. The guild was one place where Catholics, Lutherans, and Anabaptists met and agreed not to bring up religious issues. It was an economic association of like-minded businessmen, and a few women, like Margaret.

The secret system of housing escapees in Strasbourg worked because the hosts all agreed that accusing women of being witches needed to be stopped. Indians being attacked in America were far away, holy men on pilgrimages to Jerusalem seemed to be in another world, but helping falsely accused women find refuge was a joint effort of this group of men and women in Strasbourg, regardless of their Christian beliefs.

Margaret got the news that she and Beck would keep Anna on Saturday night. In the meantime, the guild accepted Beck's request to join their ranks. Margaret had joined several years earlier, and it was a foregone conclusion that once the two married, their peers would accept him.

"The Beck Press." Margaret liked the way the name looked at the top of the official license the guild gave them. She'd hang it in her print shop. "That is," she reminded herself, "*our* print shop."

Margaret did speak up at the guild meeting about Heinrich's disappearance. "It's strange that he hasn't come to work since last Monday. If anybody knows anything about him, please talk to me."

Magdalene had other business to carry out that evening

and hadn't come to the meeting. Johann, however, made a mental note to ask his wife if she knew anything about Heinrich's disappearance. He was also curious to know if Katie had seen him in the past week.

When Anna came to stay with the Becks, Margaret observed that she was a seeker. The young woman knew that her time was short—in Strasbourg and probably on earth. She'd had a lot of time to think in prison, and in spite of what happened to her, she was ready to make a new declaration of faith.

Margaret also noticed, once Anna was settled in the Becks' apartment, that Anna was clearly pregnant. She layered her clothing in an attempt to disguise her condition, but Margaret noticed and asked Anna about it.

"I concealed it in the jail when you came to visit me in July," Anna replied. "Do you remember the man I warned you about?"

"I do."

"I was only three months along then," Anna said. "Now, I'm about seven months pregnant."

"We'll have to find a safe place for you to have your child," Margaret said. "You can't keep running in the condition you're in now."

The Becks took Anna along to Clement's barn for the Sunday-evening preaching. It got cold in the barn, but the wind was blocked, and the animals gave off some warmth to chase the shivers away. Of course, this winter Margaret had her own heater sitting next to her on the straw.

Grebel preached again, but told the group he'd be leaving for Switzerland the next day. He wanted to see his wife and children again, even at the risk of being imprisoned. When Anna knelt to receive baptism from Grebel, Margaret noticed the frightened look in her eyes. Everyone knew that the judge in Worms would really throw the book at her if he learned about the rebaptism. But Anna resolved to face the future with God's Spirit and the grace she would receive. After Anna sat back down on the straw, Margaret believed she saw a new determination in her face.

"We're printing Grebel's outlawed pamphlet, hosting a weekly Anabaptist fellowship, and now we get to keep an accused witch," Margaret thought as they entered their own room. She turned to Beck and said, "Have you ever seen the inside of a prison cell?"

"No, can't say that I have. But I'm sure if one of us ends up there, we'll have a drunken guard who'll make it easy to get a key. Look!" he cried as he lunged across the bed and blew out the candle. "I see the key now!"

23

Cold Winds

A cold wind swept through the streets of Strasbourg late Sunday night, hastening the steps of the guards. They burst into Margaret and Beck's apartment, threw open the doors, wakened everyone, and grabbed Anna.

"Come with us," they barked. "You're under arrest."

That night, the frail woman who had escaped prison in the distant city of Worms was locked again behind bars, this time in the Tower of Chains that guarded Strasbourg's western entrance. A cold wind blew into the cell and rats scurried around looking for food and a warm place to hide. Anna knelt on the floor and prayed. It was all she could do, and though she didn't know how to pray very well, her urgent cries to God gave her courage to face the storm that had blown her way.

That same night, as they had done almost a month earlier, guards knocked impatiently on Jörg's door on Stone Street and asked for Conrad Grebel. This time Grebel didn't escape, and he too landed in a cold cell, a floor beneath Anna. Though independent cities like Strasbourg, Zurich, and Worms had only distant political ties, they did exchange notes on criminals and other wanted renegades. The Strasbourg City Council had acted promptly when their sister cities informed them that Anna and Grebel were on the run.

On Monday morning, Jörg and Christman hustled down to the prison to check on Grebel and to see if there was any way to help him. By the time they got there, though, Grebel was already being loaded aboard a canal boat that would take him to Zurich.

With his painful ankles shackled in chains, Grebel stood at the front of the boat and encouraged Jörg and Christman to keep the Reformation fire alive in Strasbourg. Further, he told them that his packages were needed right away. Both men understood that Grebel meant the pamphlets that the Becks were printing.

On that cold Monday morning, the captain of the boat wasted no time pushing off and heading toward the Rhine.

"Christman," Grebel said as the guard came up to him and pushed him back, "there's sin in your life—deal with it soon."

On their way toward the Beck press, Christman mumbled to Jörg, "Sometimes he overdoes his preaching thing."

"What he said," Jörg said, "could apply to any one of us."

"Grebel's on his way to prison in Zurich," Jörg told the Becks in their shop. Christman stood behind him with arms crossed. "What can we do to help get his pamphlets ready for shipment?"

"Right now it seems that the best thing you could do for us is to figure out who's tipping the city council off about our every move," Margaret answered. "Somebody's telling Sturm who's in town and what we're doing."

Beck added, "The other thing you can do for us, Jörg, is to plan on taking the pamphlets to Zurich yourself when they're ready to be delivered. I think we can be done in a week, sooner than what I first thought."

In an attempt to lighten an otherwise serious discussion, Margaret added, "You know the guilds don't cross lines, so you can't help us work inside the print shop, but you could stand guard outside the door until we're done if you'd like."

"Yes," Christman replied, "and just advertise to everyone that the Becks are printing another questionable pamphlet. Didn't the censorship committee come after you a couple of months ago for the Mass petition you printed?"

"They sure did," Margaret answered, "and I don't want to see them again anytime soon. Remember, you helped pay for that petition, Christman, so maybe you can pay me back now by helping us get this bundle of pamphlets out of the city without being caught."

"We'll do what we can," Christman said, and with that the two men headed back to Stone Street.

Passing by the great cathedral, a wary Jörg paused, glanced up at the tall spire, and told Christman, "We've got to figure out who the informant is, before the weight of the city's power crushes our movement."

"We're all at risk," Christman said. "Just keep your ears and eyes wide open."

Johann Knobloch listened carefully when his daughter told him that she was no longer seeing Heinrich the printer. "He turned me down," she said.

"Why?" her father asked.

"Said he wanted to get out of Strasbourg and see more of the world before he settled down."

"That's reasonable. Did he say where he was going?"

"Not a clue. Why do you ask?"

"He's disappeared. Been gone for about two weeks."

When Magdalene learned about her husband's inquiry, she tucked the information away and hoped no one would probe the matter further. Meanwhile, she needed to find a suitable husband for her daughter.

Winter's cold grip had firmly settled into the city by the last week of November. Families struggled to keep their homes heated, children discovered that ponds had frozen over, and snow fell regularly on the cobblestone streets. In Strasbourg, the winters came early and lingered long.

On a cold morning in the middle of the week, Sturm confronted Lucas in his office at the relief center. Sturm had brought Matthew, Jacob Meyer, the city inspector, and Martin Bucer, the city's Lutheran leader, along with him.

Lucas didn't have long to wait before he learned why the men were there. Fingering his shiny buttons, Sturm asked, "Are you an Anabaptist?"

"Councilman Sturm," Lucas stalled for time to think, "why have you come here to question me?"

"We have reason to believe that you've joined the Anabaptists," Bucer answered. "You're aware, I'm sure, that the city council has taken action to stop these radicals from meeting in our city. Their cell meetings disrupt the progress of the Reformation in Strasbourg."

"Sturm asked whether you're an Anabaptist," Meyer said sternly. "You need to give him a clear answer."

"My friends, you know that I have worked faithfully here at the relief center with Pastor Matthew's wife," Lucas answered. "We have helped many people."

"You have done a good job here," Matthew responded, "but we are here to learn about your involvement with the Anabaptists."

Acting for the council as the city's Lutheran pastor, Matthew questioned Lucas. "Their movement is growing so fast that we must confront those whom we believe to be in their number. Are you an Anabaptist?"

"I worship regularly in the cathedral and listen to your preaching."

"Have you been baptized with water a second time?" Sturm asked.

Pausing to compose himself, Lucas answered carefully. "In

truth, yes, I have received a second baptism, but I believe myself to be a member in good standing of the cathedral church."

"Not if you have taken a second baptism," Meyer said. "That makes you an Anabaptist and is reason enough to remove you from your job here at the relief center."

"Anabaptists have been ordered out of the city," Sturm added. "You now have two options. You can recant your beliefs and renounce your false baptism, or you can leave the city immediately and give up your position here."

"May I have some time to consider these demands?" Lucas pleaded.

"No," Sturm replied. "We know you like your work, but we believe a recantation, right now, in front of these ministers, would be best for you and the city. Make your decision now."

Lucas turned and walked to the little window in his office. The view was distorted by the poor-quality glass, which really wasn't for looking through, but was there to allow light into the room. The four visitors weren't going to leave without an answer. The prospect of giving up his job, disgracing his family, and forcing them to leave the city with him made the preacher turn to the four men and agree to recant.

"I was wrong in accepting my second baptism," he answered as he stroked his little mustache. "I confess my failure in joining this radical movement. And I will give up these beliefs in order to remain a member of the Lutheran Church of Strasbourg."

"You have made a wise decision, Lucas," Sturm said. "Come to our meeting tomorrow evening and recant before the council, as you've done to us just now. We'll ask that you swear your oath of allegiance to the city again."

"And on Sunday," Matthew added, "you'll need to confess your sin before the people in the cathedral."

"In the cathedral?" Lucas asked. "Isn't my confession here and before the council enough?"

"No, it is best that you tell everyone of your errors," Bucer said.

"You won't lose your job," Sturm added. "I can see to that."

After the men left his office, Lucas stared for a long time at the dense glass window. How had his life gotten so mixed up? How had he allowed himself to get involved with the Anabaptists? And now the shame of two public confessions. How could all of this be?

As usual, when the council wanted everyone to know about an upcoming event, Sturm and other officers knocked on doors of businesses and announced the details. "There'll be a public confession from Lucas Hackfurt at the cathedral on Sunday," Sturm informed Margaret and Beck. "He got mixed up with and accepted baptism from the Anabaptists."

"How do you know this?" Margaret asked.

"We have our ways of finding out," Sturm answered. "We recommend that you attend the service."

On Sunday, Margaret and Beck sat in the back of the mammoth cathedral so they couldn't make out Lucas's expression as he sat up front with Matthew. It was painful for Margaret to watch him being raked over the coals in front of everyone he knew. But it was the only way for him to keep from being tossed out of the city for good, with his family. His wife had agreed that he must recant.

Lucas's statement wasn't long, just a simple confession of sin in accepting the heretical second baptism. When he finished reading his statement, Matthew prayed for him that he would understand the failure of his ways, that he could be restored to the church, and that God might forgive him.

When they stood for the reading of the Scripture after

Matthew finished praying, Margaret had heard enough. She headed out the back door and Beck quickly followed.

Magdalene, already finished with her Mass in a side chapel of the cathedral and talking with friends outside, noticed the Becks hurrying away.

"Where are they going?" she wondered aloud to Johann.

"Who knows," he replied. "Maybe they're looking for Heinrich, their printer. Seems the poor soul's disappeared."

"I'd say we need to keep an eye on them," Magdalene said.

During the first week of December, Seiler came back into town to help smuggle Grebel's pamphlets upstream to Switzerland. He had been successful in getting the pamphlets on baptism out of the print shop and to south Germany and Switzerland, and he was back for another round.

On Thursday evening at the discussion group, Seiler updated those gathered on the Anabaptist movement in south Germany and Switzerland. "Grebel and Blaurock are both in prison, and the congregation in Waldshut has been battered and bruised. The authorities have cracked down. The pastor at Waldshut is hiding in the Black Forest. But the harder they try, the faster the movement grows."

"When you fan a growing fire it gets hotter," Margaret said.

"How many Anabaptists are in Strasbourg?" Seiler asked.

"Nobody really knows for sure," Margaret answered. "But I'd guess several hundred people have joined or are sympathetic to our cause. And our numbers are growing. Of course, after Lucas's forced recantation we're down one."

Seiler surprised the group when he pulled a piece of paper from his jacket and showed them lyrics to a hymn some of the Anabaptists in Switzerland were singing. Zwingli had eliminated singing from his church services because of the way music had been abused in the Catholic Church. Some of the Anabaptists, influenced by Zwingli's leadership, had initially rejected singing as well.

Slowly, the Anabaptists meeting in villages and towns in the surrounding mountains and valleys of Switzerland were beginning to sing in their worship services. In prison, Anabaptists would sing to communicate with other prisoners and to help those on the outside locate their cell. Luther promoted singing and worshipful music. He and other reformers, along with Anabaptists, borrowed secular tunes that many people already knew then wrote words that could be used in worship.

The Anabaptists in Strasbourg were slow to sing in their worship times, partly out of concern that if they were heard, the authorities would be notified, and their meeting would be broken up. But the worshippers did sing that night as Seiler led them.

"Who wrote the words?" Margaret asked.

"Michael Sattler," Seiler answered. "Now that several of our leaders are imprisoned, Sattler has emerged as one of our main organizers in Switzerland."

"I remember Sattler's smooth tenor voice from our university days," Beck told the group. "He would lead us in singing the liturgy during Mass. Common people didn't join us because they didn't know the Latin, but Michael, he could sing."

"This song has caught on in Switzerland because the words invite God to walk with us and lead us, and because we can worship with the music as well," Seiler said.

"In the world, but not of it," Beck added. "As Sattler's words say, those who truly follow Christ are among the faithful few, called upon to live in the world, but yet not be a part of it. I read that recently in John's Gospel." He shot a wink toward Margaret and Ryff.

"Luther is right," Kniebs said. "We join Christ's kingdom by faith in Jesus, not by being sprinkled with water within a week after we're born. 'The just shall live by faith.' Book of Romans."

"I'm impressed with the way you're quoting Scripture," Margaret said. "Here's another Scripture that Grebel uses in the third part of his pamphlet, the section on discipleship. Let's see if anyone knows where it's found in the Gospels: 'If anyone would come after me,' Jesus said, 'he must deny himself and take up his cross and follow me. For whoever wants to save his life will lose it, but whoever loses his life for me will find it.'"

Margaret paused to let them ponder the meaning of the words. "Does anyone know where that text is found?"

Ryff looked through his German New Testament. He didn't yet have all the books of the New Testament, because Luther hadn't finished translating them when the printers went to work. The Gospels, however, had been translated. "The Gospel of Matthew," he finally answered.

"Seiler, lead that song again," Margaret said. "But read the words first so we can worship when we sing."

A cold wind whistled around the inn that night, but inside, the warm wind of God's Spirit had blown into the believers' hearts in a fresh way. Many in Europe in 1525 had experienced new life in Christ, whether Catholic, Lutheran, or Anabaptist. The Scriptures spoke clearly to whoever read or listened to them, regardless of their church identity.

"Praise to the Holy Ghost," the Anabaptist cell group sang again. "Come now Thy kingdom claim." Exactly what that last petition meant for Margaret and Beck, and the rest of the group, no one knew for sure. But somehow, Margaret believed, her print shop had a small part in the advancement of Christ's kingdom. Whatever happened next, she knew she'd print pamphlets and books to help people grow in their spiritual lives, to help Christ's church to grow, and to increase the knowledge of Scripture among her neighbors in Strasbourg and south Germany.

While Margaret resolved to promote the Reformation, Christman, who'd given up on her two months earlier, continued to chase Katie. This time, though, it appeared he would succeed.

Katie figured she didn't have much to lose by telling her mother that Christman was her new suitor. "Bring him around, then," Magdalene said.

When she did, both mother and father Knobloch responded favorably. He wasn't a printer, but he was economically independent, and he was a citizen of the city with a business future ahead of him.

"Get to know him, Catherine, and see if you really like him," was all her parents finally said.

Almost a month after Heinrich had disappeared, the owner of his apartment cleaned out his belongings and advertised the apartment with the city's middleman. No one had any idea what had happened to Heinrich.

Once, Johann Jr. came through the Cronenbourg Gate to inspect the place where they had sunk the body. "Good," he thought while crunching through the snow, "before long, there won't be anything left that could possibly surface."

On the second Sunday of December, Margaret took a plate of food to help the shivering Anna warm up in the Tower of Chains. The guard put up little resistance to her request to see the prisoner. After Anna had eaten, Margaret told her some of the news of what was taking place in the city. For no particular reason, Margaret commented, "Christman's got a new girlfriend."

Grimacing at the thought of him, Anna decided that someone needed to share her eight-month-old secret. "The child I carry is his. From when I stayed in Zieglers' barn."

Shocked, Margaret asked, "Are you sure?"

"It couldn't have been anyone else. Do you remember that I warned you about him when you came to see me in Worms?"

"I do."

"There's one more part of the story I must tell someone. Have they discovered the guard who disappeared in April?"

"How did you know anyone disappeared? Do you mean Jacob Sturm's nephew?"

"I don't know his name or who he was related to, I just know that Christman buried the man outside the barn, Margaret."

"So that's why you fled in such a hurry," Margaret said. Anna nodded in agreement.

"That's enough time," the guard grumbled as he rattled the keys on his way down the hallway. "You'll have to move along now."

24

Faith Fires

In Strasbourg along the Rhine, the flames of Reformation grew stronger with each passing day. Fanned by differences in beliefs and opinions, those who felt threatened turned the embers, those who stood in the mainstream Reformation movement felt the heat, while the radicals on the edge got scorched.

Balthasar Beck topped the city council's list when the emperor demanded, as he had in August, that Strasbourg supply him with two hundred soldiers. A newly minted citizen of Strasbourg, thirty-five years of age, and without children, Beck received orders to ship out to the eastern front immediately.

When the council posted their list of men who would go, Beck joined the group to learn of his responsibilities and options. "Strasbourg must supply the emperor with men," Sturm lectured. "You will go to Vienna for the winter, then most likely to the eastern front, where the Turks plan an invasion in the spring."

"What if we don't go?" one man shot back.

"A year in the Tower of Chains," Sturm answered firmly.

Beck laid out his options to Margaret that evening. "I have one week to get my things in order before I leave. If I choose not to fight in the emperor's army, I'll be jailed for a year. And of course, if you don't feed me real food, Margaret, I could starve on the gruel they give those prisoners."

It didn't take a long conversation between Margaret and Beck, or a discussion at the Thursday evening group, or a sermon from Clement for the new groom to make up his mind. He wouldn't fight, he wouldn't enlist, and he'd accept the consequences. "Maybe a miracle will turn up in the next week," he thought.

"We could move to another city," he suggested later to Margaret.

"I'm not going anywhere. My roots lie in this city."

"The Tower of Chains it is then."

On the day before Beck gave himself up to be a prisoner, the newlyweds took a long walk along the snowy canal. The canal never completely froze over, but there were layers of ice along the edges.

They found their little wooden bench, scraped it off, and sat down, just like they had all spring, summer, and fall. "This little bench is ours," Margaret said. "It's where our love started."

"I loved you the first time I laid eyes on you, long before we got to this bench."

"Yes, but this is where we first looked into each other's eyes, Balt, where we first kissed, where we first heard the sound of our laughter together."

The groom noticed a tear in the corner of his bride's eye. "I can't bear the thought of a year without being able to hold you close. I need your strength, Margaret. You've made me a better man, a stronger man, a complete man."

"I'll be here when you get out. And I'll be with you in spirit inside that prison."

After an embrace, they headed back to their little inn for one last night together.

The next day, when Beck told Sturm that he wouldn't fight because of his religious convictions, two guards immediately took him to the Tower of Chains and locked him in a small cell on the third floor.

The hangman locked him in with a scowl. "You and I together for a year," he chuckled. "I'll work you down to skin and bones till your kin don't even recognize you. Welcome to my little apartment building."

By the time the new prisoner had inspected the four walls, looked up at the bars in the small window, and walked the cell once, he was cold. Freezing cold. A rat scurried by. "This is my place," the little critter seemed to chirp.

Ryff's medical manual sold well and Margaret began to make a real profit from her investment. She had shipped copies to most of the cities within a five-hundred-mile radius of Strasbourg. In an age when the best medicine was primitive, Ryff's self-help guide to a longer life and better health found an eager and willing audience.

Margaret's book distributor had shipped several bundles of Ryff's books all the way to Amsterdam. Just that week, at a place a lot like the Billy Goat Inn in that distant city, several men sat around a table after they had eaten their dinner and analyzed the contents of a well-used pamphlet from which a priest was reading. The peasants' war escapee from Strasbourg who had been shipped down the Rhine in the bottom of a bundle of cloth sat at the table and told the men that he knew the writer, the pastor of the Anabaptist congregation in Waldshut, Germany.

"I picked this up at a print shop in Strasbourg," Menno Simons said. "It was a gift from a friend of mine who worked there near the cathedral—picked it up when I went to that debate on the Lord's Supper. Anyone know much about the Anabaptists?"

"Their cell groups are spreading like wildfire in south Germany and Switzerland," the war survivor replied.

"I'd like to know more about them," Simons said. "There are some pretty good ideas in this pamphlet. I wonder what the Bible says about baptism. Maybe I should read it for myself."

High in the mountains of Switzerland, hundreds of miles south of Amsterdam, Grebel tramped through the snow, visiting villages where people seemed open to discussing Anabaptist ideas. The Joders in Steffisburg, southwest of Zurich, had invited Grebel to meet with them, along with their neighbors, the Brönnimanns, and Müller's widow. The Anabaptist leader huddled near the fireplace to warm his aching feet and spoke to the group in the Joder kitchen. When he finished, he left behind the believers baptism pamphlet produced by the Beck press. Grebel moved on the next day, planting faith kernels wherever he went, hoping and believing that others would bring in a harvest later on.

Margaret's dilemma about where she'd live for the next year was soon solved. Nicholas Kniebs announced that the council planned to shut the inn down at the end of the year. "They're trying to root out gambling and prostitution centers, and those two activities often go with inns. I'm pretty sure they know that I'm allowing this place to be used for Anabaptist meetings, so you'll need to move out."

It was easy for Margaret to go back to her one-room apartment at the print shop. She wouldn't have to pay rent at the inn, and she'd be living where she worked, just like old times.

The nobleman Philip Hagen surprised Margaret at the Sunday-evening service. She was delighted to see the upper-class traveler to the Holy Land. The Anabaptist meetings at the barn had continued because they took place outside city walls, beyond the reach of the council. And everyone knew Clement and figured he was harmless.

Jörg functioned in the Anabaptist world of Strasbourg as a dashing, young, eligible evangelist. He had followed up with Hagen, made friends with him, and finally invited him to his cousin's church service by the fire and the soup pot.

Hagen's journey to the Holy Land had sparked within him an interest in spiritual things. With the Anabaptists, he found a group that reminded him of Ignatius of Loyola, the little monk who had struck out from Barcelona to help others and find his own soul. Now Hagen had found himself spiritually, and that evening Margaret watched the nobleman in amazement, so out of place among the middle- and lower-class seekers who usually came.

Earlier that day, the third Sunday of December, Margaret had listened to Matthew's sermon in the cathedral. His theme usually revolved around faith and salvation, themes Luther had written about for years. In the afternoon, Margaret took a plate of food to Beck and got to see him briefly. Only on Sundays would the guards allow family members to visit the prisoners. Though food could be delivered daily, sometimes the guards ate it before it got to the intended cell. "No wonder the hangman looks so healthy," Margaret thought.

The new prisoner sported a ragged beard. "At the rate things were going," Margaret thought, "he'll be a lot thinner by this time next year." But in his eyes she saw his courage and determination to survive.

Margaret told Beck about the sermon that morning, reviewed the Scriptures that had been read, and caught him up on community news. Grebel's pamphlets weren't quite finished, "because my partner has been tied up elsewhere," Margaret kidded. But she hoped to be finished with them that week. Seiler and Christman planned to get them out of Strasbourg and up the Rhine to Switzerland.

Margaret didn't bother Beck with her new information about Christman. He couldn't do anything about it anyway.

At this point, with Christman's increasing connection with the Knoblochs, no one would believe her story. Besides, her source of information was an accused witch. Maybe someday she'd go talk to Sturm, but not now.

The guard came and interrupted Margaret's visit. She promised Beck she'd see him again next week. After a touch of their fingers through the bars, she was gone.

Hagen moved quickly when Clement announced he would baptize anyone who desired to give witness in water to the Spirit's work in their lives. Clement always gave individuals a chance to say a few words before he baptized them, and Hagen declared his faith in Christ and told the group that he was anything but a saint. "I intend to follow Jesus's leading in my life wherever that takes me. I'm sure I'll pay a price for this decision, but I don't care. This is where God has led me, and I'll live with the consequences."

Clement was not timid about pouring water on those who wished to be baptized. The old preacher soaked Hagen, and Jörg was there to greet him when he rose to his feet. They finished that night by singing the new song that Seiler had brought with him from Switzerland. It didn't sound like the practiced choir in the cathedral that morning, nor was it polished like the Latin liturgies sung by the priests at Mass. But it moved the hearts of those who raised their voices in worship to God, who Margaret believed was leading this ragged band along.

"Christmas packages for the Brethren in Switzerland," Margaret said to Peter, her only remaining worker. "Special delivery from Strasbourg."

Christman and Seiler were to move the four big bundles out of the city. They decided to go by night. Christman, a giant compared to the tiny Seiler, assured Margaret that he had a boatman lined up to get the bundles down to the river. "Once we are out of Strasbourg, few merchants or boat owners will ask questions about the bundles."

When it got dark on Friday, Christman and Seiler grabbed the packages, one in each hand, and headed off into the night. "May these little pamphlets bring light," Margaret said to no one in particular. She believed her father would have approved of her decision to print them. These were for her people. "Let there be light," he had always said.

"I wish Beck and I could celebrate tonight," Margaret thought. Instead, by candlelight and without fanfare, Margaret picked up a pamphlet by the Dominican Las Casas and examined the Latin text. She agreed with this spiritual man in a far-off place, who believed that the Indians should not be converted by force, but rather by persuasion. If only the church in Strasbourg could operate on such terms, Margaret thought, her husband wouldn't be in prison. She wouldn't have to worship in a barn and wouldn't have to send pamphlets off in the dead of night. Perhaps, she reflected, in another age, another time. . . .

"Oh God," she prayed, "bring light to this world through the power of your Holy Spirit. Amen."

The censorship committee reacted swiftly when they discovered what the Beck press had produced. They assembled at once and ordered that Margaret appear before them immediately. An hour before lunch on Saturday, she had to give an answer for why she printed heresy.

Johann held a single Grebel pamphlet in the air and waved it at Margaret. "Anabaptist literature, blasphemy!" he raged. Turning to the council, he said, "This is propaganda of the enemy!"

As he turned to Margaret and frowned, he said, "We'll shut your press down. You can join your cowardly husband in prison, or better yet, you can discover what the bottom of the river looks like on a cold winter day."

"Calm down, Knobloch," Sturm interrupted. "The woman hasn't committed a capital offense. She has printed Anabaptist literature, to be sure, but her family has a long history of loyalty to this city and we can find a way, I'm confident, of guiding her business enterprise in the proper direction."

Margaret realized that her life was in the hands of this powerful committee. They could close her shop and throw her out of the printers' guild. That would put an end to her ability to make money and a living. "Maybe Katherine or Agnes would take me in," Margaret thought.

Fortunately, Sturm had known her father, and he was able to soften the demands of the most critical members of the committee. But the verdict the committee handed down was not so soft: Margaret would have to pay a fine of one hundred gulden, about six months' wages; the four bundles of Grebel pamphlets would be publicly burned, to show the citizens of Strasbourg the errors of Margaret's ways; and finally, every item that she printed from that day forward would be examined by the committee.

Sturm announced that the burning of the pamphlets would take place that evening at the barn. It had recently come to the attention of the city council that peasants had stored weapons there during the uprising in May. Everything illegal in the grain bins would be piled on the fire as well.

Four days before Christmas at the old wooden barn, the guards lit the fire that would burn Margaret's Anabaptist pamphlets. A crowd gathered for the warmth as well as for the spectacle of watching a citizen be disciplined by the heavy hand of the law.

All the leftover weapons in Clement's arsenal were stacked for kindling. When the flames shot up into the nighttime sky, the guards took handfuls of the pamphlets from the bundles and threw them on the fire, fistful by fistful. One by one they burned. Margaret didn't even have any left in her print shop because the officials had taken out all the Anabaptist literature.

"Beck has no idea this is going on," Margaret thought to herself.

Suddenly, Rabbi Loria pushed his way up to Margaret. "We've experienced persecution like this for centuries," he whispered to his printer friend. "May God give you strength to endure and to conquer the dark forces of evil."

"Can you rescue a copy for me?" Margaret whispered back. Without hesitation, he shuffled through the crowd and, at great risk, managed to lift two copies from the bundles without being noticed. Just as quickly, he disappeared into the crowd and into the night.

Katherine and Agnes pushed through the crowd and surrounded Margaret. "You'll always be my friend, Margaret," Katherine said with an embrace. "You're welcome in my home anytime."

"You and I can learn to be friends," Agnes whispered in Margaret's ear.

On the other side of the fire, through the flames, Margaret noticed Christman. He looked relaxed, almost pleased. Beside him she noticed Katie and Magdalene. A thought came to her: "He's the informer."

Looking in the same direction as Margaret, Agnes whispered, "He's the father of my baby."

"Christman?" Margaret gasped. When Agnes nodded, Margaret remembered Wolfgang's confession to fathering the baby, so she asked once again, "Are you sure?"

"He's the only one it could possibly have been," Agnes declared. "Wolfgang's a good man. He confessed in the church to protect me."

Margaret turned to Agnes, unable to process all that was

happening. The two women hugged and wept. "I'm pregnant too," Margaret confided. "Now what will I do?"

"What a party of crying pregnant women we make," Katherine said as she smiled through her tears.

"We're friends," Margaret sobbed, "but will our children be friends?"

None of the attending officials seemed to mind that sparks jumped to the old barn and set the dry wood ablaze. The furious flames consumed the timbers, straw, wood, and everything inside. In just a few minutes the entire structure was flattened. Only the heavy snow and wet ground prevented the fire from spreading further.

Margaret slipped over to Sturm, and for a moment they watched the fire together. He spoke without looking at her. "Your father would not have approved of the pamphlets you print."

"He would have supported his daughter tonight," Margaret declared, "and you knew him well enough to know that. Who's the informer?"

"I can't tell you."

"I can tell you about your nephew's disappearance. Are you still offering the reward money?"

"Do you have an eyewitness?"

"I do, but first tell me who the informer is."

After a long pause, Sturm slowly turned and looked across the fire at the tall betrayer. Shaken, Margaret said, "He's the one you want to ask about your nephew's disappearance. And talk to Anna Weiler, your prisoner in the tower. She was in the barn when your nephew was murdered, and she saw everything that happened."

Before Sturm walked away, he said, "What you said about your father is true. He would have supported you today. He was an honorable man."

When Margaret turned to find her friends, Sturm marched toward Christman. With Meyer and Johann to back him up, he demanded that Christman sit down with him in the Zieglers' kitchen immediately and answer some questions. A whole troop of people followed the action to the Ziegler house.

"I have an eyewitness to the murder of my nephew," Sturm told Christman across the table. "A prisoner in the tower saw everything. What can you tell me?"

Four Knoblochs crowded around the table, eager to hear what was on Sturm's mind and to stand behind Katie's man. In the packed and tiny room, everyone leaned forward to hear his reply.

Christman knew that Anna had been in the barn with him that spring day when he had killed Sturm's nephew. He also knew that she was in the prison tower. Thinking quickly, but taking his time to respond, he suggested a deal to Sturm. He was sure he could pin the blame on the accused woman instead of himself.

"It was that witch in the tower who killed your nephew, Jacob. Now, just so you won't be too angry with me for not telling you sooner, I can help you solve the mystery of what happened to Heinrich the printer. You ask him," Kenlin said coolly with a glance at the Johann Jr. standing in the doorway. "He can tell you what happened."

"Get some help," Sturm ordered Meyer. "And arrest both of these men. Don't let either one get away."

High in the Tower of Chains a guard noticed a roaring blaze in the distance to the east. After staring for a while with little interest, he casually asked Beck, "Know anyone at Robertsau? Looks like a barn or a house is on fire."

Clement squeezed Margaret with his bony arms. It was awkward, hugging the old man, but it was about the only thing that made sense in the world right then. The flames had started to die down, though the heat was still intense, and many of the people were returning to their homes.

"Margaret," Clement said, "rise above the crackling roar. "Don't let this blaze stop your work."

"I won't, Clement," she said as she wept. "I won't. But what about you?"

"Our little church can still meet here. Our church doesn't have any walls. I'll build another fire here tomorrow night for our people—a welcome one. Spread the word, and invite your friends to come.

"And Margaret," he added with shadows dancing on his wrinkled face, "the old granary's gone for good. Your little print shop is now the new arsenal for the Anabaptist peoples' movement."

"No." Margaret squeezed Clement's arm hard. Quickly she realized she had gripped him too hard, and she eased up and gazed into the glowing embers. "All those weapons stored in your barn didn't bring about the changes the people wanted. The peasants still lost."

"I'm sorry," the weary old farmer responded. He was beginning to understand the reason for Margaret's quick response. "What you're doing in the print shop *is* different from what the peasants tried to accomplish on the battlefield."

"The pamphlets and books that Beck and I will print, Clement, have the power to change our world and bring peace to this war-torn land."

"Without drawing a single sword or attacking any nobles."

"That's right, Clement. And out of these ashes a church will emerge that's based on faith and love, not power and persecution. See you tomorrow night."

With a dry handkerchief from Gertrude's apron to wipe

her face and a renewed sense of courage, Margaret turned into the darkness, spotted the cathedral spire, and trudged through the snow toward her little print shop in the Wood Market.

Alone atop their bridge over the canal, she reached into the cold night toward the prison tower and cried out, "Beck, we've got more work to do."

Epilogue

After the tumultuous events of 1525, Margaret and Balthasar Beck went on to operate a successful print shop in Strasbourg for many years. They printed numerous books and pamphlets that appear to have had a significant impact on the Reformation and the Anabaptist movement in south Germany. It is known that they had at least one daughter.

Conrad Grebel wrote a pamphlet about believers baptism, as described in this book, but for unknown reasons no copies of the pamphlet survived. After persecution for his beliefs, Grebel died of the plague in 1526.

George Blaurock was sentenced to death by drowning for his Anabaptist beliefs in 1529.

Michael Sattler became a leader of the Swiss Brethren, outlining the distinctive beliefs of the Anabaptist movement in February 1527 and dying for his convictions several months later.

Wilhelm Reublin, on the other hand, renounced the Anabaptist movement in the 1530s and died a natural death many years later.

Ulrich Zwingli led the Reformed Movement in Zurich until he died on the battlefield in 1531. Martin Luther directed the German Lutheran Reformation for many years until he died of natural causes in 1546. There is no historical evidence that Menno Simons ever visited Strasbourg or met Margaret.

Little is known historically about Christman Kenlin. It is known that he was involved with the radical reformation in Strasbourg in 1525 and that he had sympathies with the peasants and their revolt. Kenlin's intrigues in this book were created in order to serve the purposes of the novel.

Strasbourg continued to be a city of refuge for Anabaptists for several decades after 1525. Later the Anabaptists held conferences in Strasbourg to establish theology and seek ways to work together. Today several Christian denominations come from the Anabaptists, including the Mennonites, Amish, Brethren in Christ, and Hutterites. In 1984, the Mennonite World Conference was held in Strasbourg, where the main office of Mennonite World Conference is located.

The Author

Elwood Yoder grew up in the Mennonite community of Hartville, Ohio. He holds a Bachelor of Arts in Bible and a Bachelor of Science in history and social science, secondary education, from Eastern Mennonite University; a Masters in education from Temple University; and is a senior MDiv candidate at Eastern Mennonite Seminary.

Elwood is married to Joy Risser Yoder. They are the parents of three children and are active members of Zion Mennonite Church in Broadway, Virginia.

He is coauthor of *Through Fire and Water* (1996). Elwood has been teaching high-school social studies and Bible at Eastern Mennonite High School, Harrisonburg, Virginia, since 1989.